PRAISE FOR JUST AFTER SUNSET

'Nobody does it better than the master . . . A chilling cornucopia' – *Time Out*

'He has forged what may be his most accomplished work: 13 beautifully turned tales, no two of which are alike . . . Stephen King loves the power of words and is an admirer of the great English writers of classic ghost and horror stories. Their legacy is transformed in his hands' – *Daily Express*

'[A] succinct, fast-moving collection' – *New York Times*

'The reader reaps the benefits of King's mastery of the form . . . All 13 stories are wonderfully wicked and highlight what happens when, as one character says, "a trapdoor open(s) between reality and the twilight zone" and "anything is possible."' – *USA Today*

PRAISE FOR DUMA KEY

'Page-turning . . . A first class beach read' – Matt Thorne, *Independent on Sunday*

'The story is so elegant and wide ranging, and the three central characters so delicately evoked . . . the sort of fiction that comes along only rarely and only from a writer at the top of his game' – *Daily Mail*

'Fresh and frightening and highly recommended . . . King knows how to keep the pulse of suspense throbbing . . . This is a powerful piece of work' – *Observer*

'You feel as if the individual characters are actually real. Another masterpiece' – *Sun*

ABOUT THE AUTHOR

Stephen King was born in Portland, Maine, in 1947. He won a scholarship award to the University of Maine and later taught English, while his wife, Tabitha, got her degree.

It was the publication of his first novel *Carrie* and its subsequent adaptation to film that set him on his way to his present position as perhaps the bestselling author in the world.

Carrie was followed by over forty worldwide bestsellers including *It*, *The Stand*, *Misery*, *Dolores Claiborne*, *Duma Key* and *Just After Sunset*. Some of his stories have also been adapted into first-rate film including those in this collection.

Stephen King is the 2003 recipient of the National Book Foundation Medal for Distinguished Contribution to American Letters. In 2007 he was inducted as a Grand Master of the Mystery Writers of America.

He lives with his wife, novelist Tabitha King, in Bangor, Maine.

By Stephen King and published by
Hodder & Stoughton

FICTION:

Carrie
'Salem's Lot
The Shining
Night Shift
The Stand
The Dead Zone
Firestarter
Cujo
Different Seasons
Cycle of the Werewolf
Christine
The Talisman (with Peter Straub)
Pet Sematary
It
Skeleton Crew
The Eyes of the Dragon
Misery
The Tommyknockers
The Dark Half
Four Past Midnight
Needful Things
Gerald's Game
Dolores Claiborne
Nightmares and Dreamscapes
Insomnia
Rose Madder
Desperation
Bag of Bones
The Girl Who Loved Tom Gordon
Hearts in Atlantis
Dreamcatcher
Everything's Eventual
From a Buick 8
Cell
Lisey's Story
Duma Key
Just After Sunset
The Dark Tower I: The Gunslinger
The Dark Tower II: The Drawing of the Three
The Dark Tower III: The Waste Lands
The Dark Tower IV: Wizard and Glass
The Dark Tower V: Wolves of the Calla
The Dark Tower VI: Song of Susannah
The Dark Tower VII: The Dark Tower

By Stephen King as Richard Bachman

Thinner
The Running Man
The Bachman Books
The Regulators
Blaze

NON-FICTION:

Danse Macabre
On Writing (A Memoir of the Craft)

STEPHEN KING

GOES TO THE MOVIES

HODDER

Grateful acknowledgement is made for permission to reprint excerpts
from the following copyrighted material:

'Black Slacks' words and music by Joe Bennett and Jimmy Denton.
© Copyright 1957 by Duchess Music Corporation. Copyright renewed.
All Rights Administered by MCA MUSIC PUBLISHING, a Division of MCA INC.,
1755 Broadway, New York, NY 10019.

'Tallahassee Lassie' words and music by Frank C. Slay, Bob Crewe and Frederick
Piscariello. Copyright © 1958, 1959 CONLEY MUSIC INC. Copyright Renewed
1986, 1987 MPL COMMUNICATIONS, INC. All Rights Reserved.

'Twilight Time' lyrics by Buck Ram; music by Morty Nevins and Al Nevins. TRO Copyright
© 1944 (Renewed) Devon Music, Inc., New York, NY 10011-4298. All rights for the
United States of America are controlled by Devon Music, Inc. All rights for the World
outside the United States of America are controlled by MCA Duchess Music Corporation.

First published as a paperback original in
Great Britain in 2009 by Hodder & Stoughton
An Hachette UK company

7

A CIP catalogue record for this title is available from the British Library.

ISBN 978 0 340 98030 9

Typeset in Bembo by Palimpsest Book Production Limited,
Grangemouth, Stirlingshire

Printed and bound by Clays Ltd, St Ives plc

Hodder & Stoughton policy is to use papers that are natural,
renewable and recyclable products and made from wood grown
in sustainable forests. The logging and manufacturing processes
are expected to conform to the environmental regulations
of the country of origin.

Hodder & Stoughton
338 Euston Road
London NW1 3BH

www.hodder.co.uk

For Frank Darabont, who made my dreams real

CONTENTS

1408

It's a miracle that this story exists in any form at all, print *or* film. The first thousand words were scribbled longhand in the living room of a Sanibel Island rental, when heavy afternoon thunderstorms kept me and my family off the beach. It was intended as an example (for the book *On Writing*) of how my rewriting process works. I had done my haunted hotel story (*The Shining*) and ordinarily feel no urge to chew my cabbage twice.

The reason it got finished was because the main character, a cynical hack (who once coulda been a contender) churning out books debunking supposedly haunted locations, started to interest me. What, I wondered, would happen if such a fellow had to face the real thing?

Serious actors rarely take roles in modestly budgeted horror movies, but John Cusack took the part of Mike Enslin, and although I can't say for sure why (he may have said in some of his pre-opening interviews, but I never heard him address the question directly), I think the character may also have caught his imagination. He shines in the part, and does what is very nearly a one-man show.

I knew this was going to be a good movie when the producer, Bob Weinstein, sent me an advance trailer. It had a claustrophobic perfection that exactly reflected the tone of the story. I imagined a haunting that would literally drive the occupants of room 1408 to insanity by exposing them to the sort of alien sensations and mental input people only experience in fever dreams or while under the influence of LSD or mescaline. The moviemakers 'got' this, and as a result produced a rarity: a horror movie that actually horrifies. I pushed for the PG-13 rating (which the film was eventually awarded), because there's almost no blood or gore. Like one of the great old Val Lewton films, this baby works on your nerves, not your gag reflex.

One final word: the writers added a backstory that doesn't exist in the tale that follows. This is an old Hollywood trick, always dangerous and rarely successful. Here it works, although I believe it took a reshoot of the ending to make that happen.

1408

I

Mike Enslin was still in the revolving door when he saw Olin, the manager of the Hotel Dolphin, sitting in one of the overstuffed lobby chairs. Mike's heart sank. *Maybe I should have brought the lawyer along again, after all,* he thought. Well, too late now. And even if Olin had decided to throw up another roadblock or two between Mike and room 1408, that wasn't all bad; there were compensations.

Olin was crossing the room with one pudgy hand held out as Mike left the revolving door. The Dolphin was on Sixty-first Street, around the corner from Fifth Avenue, small but smart. A man and a woman dressed in evening clothes passed Mike as he reached for Olin's hand, switching his small overnight case to his left hand in order to do it. The woman was blond, dressed in black, of course, and the light, flowery smell of her perfume seemed to summarize New York. On the mezzanine level, someone was playing 'Night and Day' in the bar, as if to underline the summary.

'Mr Enslin. Good evening.'

'Mr Olin. Is there a problem?'

Olin looked pained. For a moment he glanced around the small, smart lobby, as if for help. At the concierge's stand, a man was discussing theater tickets with his wife while the concierge himself watched them with a small, patient smile. At the front desk, a man with the rumpled look one only got after long hours in Business Class was discussing his reservation with a woman in a smart black suit that could itself have doubled for evening wear. It was business as usual at the Hotel Dolphin. There was help for everyone except poor Mr Olin, who had fallen into the writer's clutches.

'Mr Olin?' Mike repeated.

'Mr Enslin . . . could I speak to you for a moment in my office?'

Well, and why not? It would help the section on room 1408, add to the ominous tone the readers of his books seemed to crave, and that wasn't all. Mike Enslin hadn't been sure until now, in spite of all the backing and filling; now he was. Olin was really afraid of room 1408, and of what might happen to Mike there tonight.

'Of course, Mr Olin.'

Olin, the good host, reached for Mike's bag. 'Allow me.'

'I'm fine with it,' Mike said. 'Nothing but a change of clothes and a toothbrush.'

'Are you sure?'

'Yes,' Mike said. 'I'm already wearing my lucky Hawaiian shirt.' He smiled. 'It's the one with the ghost repellent.'

Olin didn't smile back. He sighed instead, a little round man in a dark cutaway coat and a neatly knotted tie. 'Very good, Mr Enslin. Follow me.'

The hotel manager had seemed tentative in the lobby, almost beaten. In his oak-paneled office, with the pictures of the hotel on the walls (the Dolphin had opened in 1910 – Mike might publish without the benefit of reviews in the journals or the big-city papers, but he did his research), Olin seemed to gain assurance again. There was a Persian carpet on the floor. Two standing lamps cast a mild yellow light. A desk-lamp with a green lozenge-shaped shade stood on the desk, next to a humidor. And next to the humidor were Mike Enslin's last three books. Paperback editions, of course; there had been no hardbacks. *Mine host has been doing a little research of his own*, Mike thought.

Mike sat down in front of the desk. He expected Olin to sit behind the desk, but Olin surprised him. He took the chair beside Mike's, crossed his legs, then leaned forward over his tidy little belly to touch the humidor.

'Cigar, Mr Enslin?'

'No, thank you. I don't smoke.'

Olin's eyes shifted to the cigarette behind Mike's right ear – parked on a jaunty jut the way an old-time wisecracking reporter might have parked his next smoke just below the PRESS tag stuck in the band of his fedora. The cigarette had become so much a part of him that for a moment Mike honestly didn't know what Olin was looking at. Then he laughed, took it down, looked at it himself, and looked back at Olin.

'Haven't had a one in nine years,' he said. 'Had an older brother who died of lung cancer. I quit after he died. The cigarette behind the ear . . .' He shrugged. 'Part affectation, part superstition, I guess. Like the Hawaiian shirt. Or the cigarettes you sometimes see on people's desks or walls, mounted in a little box with a sign saying BREAK GLASS IN CASE OF EMERGENCY. Is 1408 a smoking room, Mr Olin? Just in case nuclear war breaks out?'

'As a matter of fact, it is.'

'Well,' Mike said heartily, 'that's one less worry in the watches of the night.'

Mr Olin sighed again, but this sigh didn't have the disconsolate quality of his lobby-sigh. Yes, it was the office, Mike reckoned. *Olin's* office, his special place. Even this afternoon, when Mike had come accompanied by Robertson, the lawyer, Olin had seemed less flustered once they were in here. And why not? Where else could you feel in charge, if not in your special place? Olin's office was a room with good pictures on the walls, a good rug on the floor, and good cigars in the humidor. A lot of managers had no doubt conducted a lot of business in here since 1910; in its own way it was as New York as the blond in her black off-the-shoulder dress, her smell of perfume, and her unarticulated promise of sleek New York sex in the small hours of the morning.

'You still don't think I can talk you out of this idea of yours, do you?' Olin asked.

'I know you can't,' Mike said, replacing the cigarette behind his ear. He didn't slick his hair back with Vitalis or Wildroot Cream Oil, as those colorful fedora-wearing scribblers of yore had, but he still changed the cigarette every day, just as he changed his underwear. You sweat back there behind your ears; if he examined the cigarette at the end of the day before throwing its unsmoked deadly length into the toilet, Mike could see the faint yellow-orange residue of that sweat on the thin white paper. It did not increase the temptation to light up. How he had smoked for almost twenty years – thirty butts a day, sometimes forty – was now beyond him. *Why* he had done it was an even better question.

Olin picked up the little stack of paperbacks from the blotter. 'I sincerely hope you're wrong.'

Mike ran open the zipper on the side pocket of his overnight bag. He brought out a Sony minicorder. 'Would you mind if I taped our conversation, Mr Olin?'

Olin waved a hand. Mike pushed RECORD and the little red light came on. The reels began to turn.

Olin, meanwhile, was shuffling slowly through the stack of books, reading the titles. As always when he saw his books in someone else's hands, Mike Enslin felt the oddest mix of emotions: pride, unease, amusement, defiance, and shame. He had no business feeling ashamed of them, they had kept him nicely over these last five years, and he didn't have to share any of the profits with a packager ('book-whores' was what his agent called them, perhaps partly in envy), because he had come up with the concept himself. Although after the first book had sold so well, only a moron could have missed the concept. What was there to do after *Frankenstein* but *Bride of Frankenstein*?

Still, he had gone to Iowa. He had studied with Jane Smiley. He had once been on a panel with Stanley Elkin. He had once aspired (absolutely no one in his current circle of friends and acquaintances had any least inkling of this) to be published as a Yale Younger Poet. And, when the hotel manager began speaking the titles aloud, Mike found himself wishing he hadn't challenged Olin with the recorder. Later he would listen to Olin's measured tones and imagine he heard contempt in them. He touched the cigarette behind his ear without being aware of it.

'*Ten Nights in Ten Haunted Houses*,' Olin read. '*Ten Nights in Ten Haunted Graveyards. Ten Nights in Ten Haunted Castles.*' He looked up at Mike with a faint smile at the corners of his mouth. 'Got to Scotland on that one. Not to mention the Vienna Woods. And all tax-deductible, correct? Hauntings are, after all, your business.'

'Do you have a point?'

'You're sensitive about these, aren't you?' Olin asked.

'Sensitive, yes. Vulnerable, no. If you're hoping to persuade me out of your hotel by critiquing my books—'

'No, not at all. I was curious, that's all. I sent Marcel – he's the concierge on days – out to get them two days ago, when you first appeared with your . . . request.'

'It was a demand, not a request. Still is. You heard Mr Robertson; New York State law – not to mention two federal civil rights laws – forbids you to deny me a specific room, if I request that specific room and the room is vacant. And 1408 is vacant. 1408 is *always* vacant these days.'

But Mr Olin was not to be diverted from the subject of Mike's last three books – *New York Times* best-sellers, all – just yet. He simply shuffled through them a third time. The mellow lamplight reflected off their shiny covers. There was a lot of purple on the covers. Purple sold scary books better than any other color, Mike had been told.

'I didn't get a chance to dip into these until earlier this evening,' Olin said. 'I've been quite busy. I usually am. The Dolphin is small by New York standards, but we run at ninety per cent occupancy and usually a problem comes through the front door with every guest.'

'Like me.'

Olin smiled a little. 'I'd say you're a bit of a special problem, Mr Enslin. You and your Mr Robertson and all your threats.'

Mike felt nettled all over again. He had made no threats, unless Robertson himself was a threat. And he had been forced to use the lawyer, as a man might be forced to use a crowbar on a rusty lockbox which would no longer accept the key.

The lockbox isn't yours, a voice inside told him, but the laws of the state and the country said differently. The laws said that room 1408 in the Hotel Dolphin was his if he wanted it, and as long as no one else had it first.

He became aware that Olin was watching him, still with that faint smile. As if he had been following Mike's interior dialogue almost word for word. It was an uncomfortable feeling, and Mike was finding this an unexpectedly uncomfortable meeting. It felt as if he had been on the defensive ever since he'd taken out the minicorder (which was usually intimidating) and turned it on.

'If any of this has a point, Mr Olin, I'm afraid I lost sight of it a turn or two back. And I've had a long day. If our wrangle over room 1408 is really over, I'd like to go on upstairs and—'

'I read one . . . uh, what would you call them? Essays? Tales?'

Bill-payers was what Mike called them, but he didn't intend to say that with the tape running. Not even though it was his tape.

'Story,' Olin decided. 'I read one story from each book. The one about the Rilsby house in Kansas from your *Haunted Houses* book—'

'Ah, yes. The axe murders.' The fellow who had chopped up all six members of the Eugene Rilsby family had never been caught.

'Exactly so. And the one about the night you spent camped out on the graves of the lovers in Alaska who committed suicide – the ones people keep claiming to see around Sitka – and the account of your night in Gartsby Castle. That was actually quite amusing. I was surprised.'

Mike's ear was carefully tuned to catch the undernotes of

11

contempt in even the blandest comments about his *Ten Nights* books, and he had no doubt that he sometimes heard contempt that wasn't there — few creatures on earth are so paranoid as the writer who believes, deep in his heart, that he is slumming, Mike had discovered — but he didn't believe there was any contempt here.

'Thank you,' he said. 'I guess.' He glanced down at his minicorder. Usually its little red eye seemed to be watching the other guy, daring him to say the wrong thing. This evening it seemed to be looking at Mike himself.

'Oh yes, I meant it as a compliment.' Olin tapped the books. 'I expect to finish these . . . but for the writing. It's the writing I like. I was surprised to find myself laughing at your quite unsupernatural adventures in Gartsby Castle, and I was surprised to find you as good as you are. As *subtle* as you are. I expected more hack and slash.'

Mike steeled himself for what would almost certainly come next, Olin's variation of *What's a nice girl like you doing in a place like this.* Olin the urbane hotelier, host to blond women who wore black dresses out into the night, hirer of weedy, retiring men who wore tuxes and tinkled old standards like 'Night and Day' in the hotel bar. Olin who probably read Proust on his nights off.

'But they are disturbing, too, these books. If I hadn't looked at them, I don't think I would have bothered waiting for you this evening. Once I saw that lawyer with his briefcase, I knew you meant to stay in that goddamned room, and that nothing I could say was apt to dissuade you. But the books . . .'

Mike reached out and snapped off the minicorder — that little red staring eye was starting to give him the willies. 'Do you want to know why I'm bottom-feeding? Is that it?'

12

'I assume you do it for the money,' Olin said mildly. 'And you're feeding a long way from the bottom, at least in my estimation . . . although it's interesting that you would jump so nimbly to such a conclusion.'

Mike felt warmth rising in his cheeks. No, this wasn't going the way he had expected at all; he had *never* snapped his recorder off in the middle of a conversation. But Olin wasn't what he had seemed. *I was led astray by his hands*, Mike thought. *Those pudgy little hotel manager's hands with their neat white crescents of manicured nail.*

'What concerned me – what *frightened* me – is that I found myself reading the work of an intelligent, talented man who doesn't believe *one single thing* he has written.'

That wasn't exactly true, Mike thought. He'd written perhaps two dozen stories he believed in, had actually published a few. He'd written reams of poetry he believed in during his first eighteen months in New York, when he had starved on the payroll of *The Village Voice*. But did he believe that the headless ghost of Eugene Rilsby walked his deserted Kansas farmhouse by moonlight? No. He had spent the night in that farmhouse, camped out on the dirty linoleum hills of the kitchen floor, and had seen nothing scarier than two mice trundling along the baseboard. He had spent a hot summer night in the ruins of the Transylvanian castle where Vlad Tepes supposedly still held court; the only vampires to actually show up had been a fog of European mosquitoes. During the night camped out by the grave of serial killer Jeffrey Dahmer, a white, blood-streaked figure waving a knife *had* come at him out of the two o'clock darkness, but the giggles of the apparition's friends had given him away, and Mike Enslin hadn't been terribly impressed, anyway; he knew a teenage ghost

13

waving a rubber knife when he saw one. But he had no intention of telling any of this to Olin. He couldn't afford—

Except he *could*. The minicorder (a mistake from the getgo, he now understood) was stowed away again, and this meeting was about as off-the-record as you could get. Also, he had come to admire Olin in a weird way. And when you admired a man, you wanted to tell him the truth.

'No,' he said, 'I don't believe in ghoulies and ghosties and long-leggety beasties. I think it's good there are no such things, because I don't believe there's any good Lord that can protect us from them, either. That's what I believe, but I've kept an open mind from the very start. I may never win the Pulitzer Prize for investigating The Barking Ghost in Mount Hope Cemetery, but I would have written fairly about him if he had shown up.'

Olin said something, only a single word, but too low for Mike to make it out.

'I beg pardon?'

'I said no.' Olin looked at him almost apologetically.

Mike sighed. Olin thought he was a liar. When you got to that point, the only choices were to put up your dukes or disengage totally from the discussion. 'Why don't we leave this for another day, Mr Olin? I'll just go on upstairs and brush my teeth. Perhaps I'll see Kevin O'Malley materialize behind me in the bathroom mirror.'

Mike started to get out of his chair, and Olin put out one of his pudgy, carefully manicured hands to stop him. 'I'm not calling you a liar,' he said, 'but, Mr Enslin, *you don't believe*. Ghosts rarely appear to those who don't believe in them, and when they do, they are rarely seen. Why, Eugene Rilsby could have bowled his severed head all the way down the front hall of his home, and you wouldn't have heard a thing!'

Mike stood up, then bent to grab his overnight case. 'If that's so, I won't have anything to worry about in room 1408, will I?'

'But you will,' Olin said. 'You will. Because there are no ghosts in room 1408 and never have been. There's *something* in there – I've felt it myself – but it's not a spirit presence. In an abandoned house or an old castle keep, your unbelief may serve you as protection. In room 1408, it will only render you more vulnerable. Don't do it, Mr Enslin. That's why I waited for you tonight, to ask you, *beg* you, not to do it. Of all the people on earth who don't belong in that room, the man who wrote those cheerful, exploitative true-ghost books leads the list.'

Mike heard this and didn't hear it at the same time. *And you turned off your tape recorder!* he was raving. *He embarrasses me into turning off my tape recorder and then he turns into Boris Karloff hosting The All-Star Spook Weekend! Fuck it. I'll quote him anyway. If he doesn't like it, let him sue me.*

All at once he was burning to get upstairs, not just so he could start getting his long night in a corner hotel room over with, but because he wanted to transcribe what Olin had just said while it was still fresh in his mind.

'Have a drink, Mr Enslin.'

'No, I really—'

Mr Olin reached into his coat pocket and brought out a key on a long brass paddle. The brass looked old and scratched and tarnished. Embossed on it were the numbers **1408**. 'Please,' Olin said. 'Humor me. You give me ten more minutes of your time – long enough to consume a short Scotch – and

I'll hand you this key. I would give almost anything to be able to change your mind, but I like to think I can recognize the inevitable when I see it.'

'You still use actual keys here?' Mike asked. 'That's sort of a nice touch. Antiquey.'

'The Dolphin went to a MagCard system in 1979, Mr Enslin, the year I took the job as manager. 1408 is the only room in the house that still opens with a key. There was no need to put a MagCard lock on its door, because there's never anyone inside; the room was last occupied by a paying guest in 1978.'

'You're shitting me!' Mike sat down again, and unlimbered his minicorder again. He pushed the RECORD button and said, 'House manager Olin claims 1408 not rented to a paying guest in over twenty years.'

'It is just as well that 1408 has never needed a MagCard lock on its door, because I am completely positive the device wouldn't work. Digital wristwatches don't work in room 1408. Sometimes they run backwards, sometimes they simply go out, but you can't tell time with one. Not in room 1408, you can't. The same is true of pocket calculators and cell-phones. If you're wearing a beeper, Mr Enslin, I advise you to turn it off, because once you're in room 1408, it will start beeping at will.' He paused. 'And turning it off isn't guaranteed to work, either; it may turn itself back on. The only sure cure is to pull the batteries.' He pushed the STOP button on the minicorder without examining the buttons; Mike supposed he used a similar model for dictating memos. 'Actually, Mr Enslin, the only sure cure is to stay the hell out of that room.'

'I can't do that,' Mike said, taking his minicorder back and stowing it once more, 'but I think I can take time for that drink.'

While Olin poured from the fumed-oak bar beneath an oil painting of Fifth Avenue at the turn of the century, Mike asked him how, if the room had been continuously unoccupied since 1978, Olin knew that high-tech gadgets didn't work inside.

'I didn't intend to give you the impression that no one had set foot through the door since 1978,' Olin replied. 'For one thing, there are maids in once a month to give the place a light turn. That means—'

Mike, who had been working on *Ten Haunted Hotel Rooms* for about four months at that point, said: 'I know what it means.' A light turn in an unoccupied room would include opening the windows to change the air, dusting, enough Ty-D-Bowl in the can to turn the water briefly blue, a change of the towels. Probably not the bed-linen, not on a light turn. He wondered if he should have brought his sleeping-bag.

Crossing the Persian from the bar with their drinks in his hands, Olin seemed to read Mike's thought on his face. 'The sheets were changed this very afternoon, Mr Enslin.'

'Why don't you drop that? Call me Mike.'

'I don't think I'd be comfortable with that,' Olin said, handing Mike his drink. 'Here's to you.'

'And you.' Mike lifted his glass, meaning to clink it against Olin's, but Olin pulled his back.

'No, to you, Mr Enslin. I insist. Tonight we should both drink to you. You'll need it.'

Mike sighed, clinked the rim of his glass against the rim of Olin's, and said: 'To me. You would have been right at home in a horror movie, Mr Olin. You could have played the gloomy old butler who tries to warn the young married couple away from Castle Doom.'

Olin sat down. 'It's a part I haven't had to play often, thank God. Room 1408 isn't listed on any of the websites dealing with paranormal locations or psychic hotspots—'

That'll change after my book, Mike thought, sipping his drink.

'—and there are no ghost-tours with stops at the Hotel Dolphin, although they do tour through the Sherry-Netherland, the Plaza, and the Park Lane. We have kept 1408 as quiet as possible . . . although, of course, the history has always been there for a researcher who is both lucky and tenacious.'

Mike allowed himself a small smile.

'Veronique changed the sheets,' Olin said. 'I accompanied her. You should feel flattered, Mr Enslin; it's almost like having your night's linen put on by royalty. Veronique and her sister came to the Dolphin as chambermaids in 1971 or '72. Vee, as we call her, is the Hotel Dolphin's longest-running employee, with at least six years' seniority over me. She has since risen to head housekeeper. I'd guess she hadn't changed a sheet in six years before today, but she used to do all the turns in 1408 – she and her sister – until about 1992. Veronique and Celeste were twins, and the bond between them seemed to make them . . . how shall I put it? Not *immune* to 1408, but its equal . . . at least for the short periods of time needed to give a room a light turn.'

'You're not going to tell me this Veronique's sister died in the room, are you?'

'No, not at all,' Olin said. 'She left service here around 1988, suffering from ill health. But I don't rule out the idea that 1408 may have played a part in her worsening mental and physical condition.'

'We seem to have built a rapport here, Mr Olin. I hope I don't snap it by telling you I find that ridiculous.'

Olin laughed. 'So hardheaded for a student of the airy world.'

'I owe it to my readers,' Mike said blandly.

'I suppose I simply could have left 1408 as it is anyway during most of its days and nights,' the hotel manager mused. 'Door locked, lights off, shades drawn to keep the sun from fading the carpet, coverlet pulled up, doorknob breakfast menu on the bed . . . but I can't bear to think of the air getting stuffy and old, like the air in an attic. Can't bear to think of the dust piling up until it's thick and fluffy. What does that make me, persnickety or downright obsessive?'

'It makes you a hotel manager.'

'I suppose. In any case, Vee and Cee turned that room – very quick, just in and out – until Cee retired and Vee got her first big promotion. After that, I got other maids to do it in pairs, always picking ones who got on well with each other—'

'Hoping for that bond to withstand the bogies?'

'Hoping for that bond, yes. And you can make fun of the room 1408 bogies as much as you want, Mr Enslin, but you'll feel them almost at once, of that I'm confident. Whatever there is in that room, it's not shy.

'On many occasions – all that I could manage – I went with the maids, to supervise them.' He paused, then added, almost reluctantly, 'To pull them out, I suppose, if anything really awful started to happen. Nothing ever did. There were several who had weeping fits, one who had a laughing fit –

I don't know why someone laughing out of control should be more frightening than someone sobbing, but it is — and a number who fainted. Nothing too terrible, however. I had time enough over the years to make a few primitive experiments — beepers and cell-phones and such — but nothing too terrible. Thank God.' He paused again, then added in a queer, flat tone: 'One of them went blind.'

'What?'

'She went blind. Rommie Van Gelder, that was. She was dusting the top of the television, and all at once she began to scream. I asked her what was wrong. She dropped her dustrag and put her hands over her eyes and screamed that she was blind . . . but that she could see the most awful colors. They went away almost as soon as I got her out through the door, and by the time I got her down the hallway to the elevator, her sight had begun to come back.'

'You're telling me all this just to scare me, Mr Olin, aren't you? To scare me off.'

'Indeed I am not. You know the history of the room, beginning with the suicide of its first occupant.'

Mike did. Kevin O'Malley, a sewing machine salesman, had taken his life on October 13, 1910, a leaper who had left a wife and seven children behind.

'Five men and one woman have jumped from that room's single window, Mr Enslin. Three women and one man have overdosed with pills in that room, two found in bed, two found in the bathroom, one in the tub and one sitting slumped on the toilet. A man hanged himself in the closet in 1970—'

'Henry Storkin,' Mike said. 'That one was probably accidental . . . erotic asphyxia.'

'Perhaps. There was also Randolph Hyde, who slit his

20

wrists, and then cut off his genitals for good measure while he was bleeding to death. *That* one wasn't erotic asphyxiation. The point is, Mr Enslin, that if you can't be swayed from your intention by a record of twelve suicides in sixty-eight years, I doubt if the gasps and fibrillations of a few chambermaids will stop you.'

Gasps and fibrillations, that's nice, Mike thought, and wondered if he could steal it for the book.

'Few of the pairs who have turned 1408 over the years care to go back more than a few times,' Olin said, and finished his drink in a tidy little gulp.

'Except for the French twins.'

'Vee and Cee, that's true.' Olin nodded.

Mike didn't care much about the maids and their . . . what had Olin called them? Their gasps and fibrillations. He did feel mildly rankled by Olin's enumeration of the suicides . . . as if Mike was so thick he had missed, not the *fact* of them, but their *import*. Except, really, there *was* no import. Both Abraham Lincoln and John Kennedy had vice presidents named Johnson; the names Lincoln and Kennedy had seven letters; both Lincoln and Kennedy had been elected in years ending in 60. What did all of these coincidences prove? Not a damned thing.

'The suicides will make a wonderful segment for my book,' Mike said, 'but since the tape recorder is off, I can tell you they amount to what a statistician resource of mine calls "the cluster effect".'

'Charles Dickens called it "the potato effect",' Olin said.

'I beg your pardon?'

'When Jacob Marley's ghost first speaks to Scrooge, Scrooge tells him he could be nothing but a blob of mustard or a bit of underdone potato.'

'Is that supposed to be funny?' Mike asked, a trifle coldly.

'Nothing about this strikes me as funny, Mr Enslin. Nothing at all. Listen very closely, please. Vee's sister, Celeste, died of a heart attack. At that point, she was suffering mid-stage Alzheimer's, a disease which struck her very early in life.'

'Yet her sister is fine and well, according to what you said earlier. An American success story, in fact. As you are yourself, Mr Olin, from the look of you. Yet you've been in and out of room 1408 how many times? A hundred? Two hundred?'

'For very short periods of time,' Olin said. 'It's perhaps like entering a room filled with poison gas. If one holds one's breath, one may be all right. I see you don't like that comparison. You no doubt find it overwrought, perhaps ridiculous. Yet I believe it's a good one.'

He steepled his fingers beneath his chin.

'It's also possible that some people react more quickly and more violently to whatever lives in that room, just as some people who go scuba-diving are more prone to the bends than others. Over the Dolphin's near-century of operation, the hotel staff has grown ever more aware that 1408 is a poisoned room. It has become part of the house history, Mr Enslin. No one talks about it, just as no one mentions the fact that here, as in most hotels, the fourteenth floor is actually the thirteenth . . . but they know it. If all the facts and records pertaining to that room were available, they would tell an amazing story . . . one more uncomfortable than your readers might enjoy.

'I should guess, for example, that every hotel in New York has had its suicides, but I would be willing to wager my life that only in the Dolphin have there been a dozen of them *in a single room*. And leaving Celeste Romandeau aside, what about the natural deaths in 1408? The so-called natural deaths?'

'How many have there been?' The idea of so-called natural deaths in 1408 had never occurred to him.

'Thirty,' Olin replied. 'Thirty, at least. Thirty that I know of.'

'You're lying!' The words were out of his mouth before he could call them back.

'No, Mr Enslin, I assure you I'm not. Did you really think that we keep that room empty just out of some vapid old wives' superstition or ridiculous New York tradition . . . the idea, maybe, that every fine old hotel should have at least one unquiet spirit, clanking around in the Suite of Invisible Chains?'

Mike Enslin realized that just such an idea – not articulated but there, just the same – had indeed been hanging around his new *Ten Nights* book. To hear Olin scoff at it in the irritated tones of a scientist scoffing at a *bruja*-waving native did nothing to soothe his chagrin.

'We have our superstitions and traditions in the hotel trade, but we don't let them get in the way of our business, Mr Enslin. There's an old saying in the Midwest, where I broke into the business: "There are no drafty rooms when the cattlemen are in town." If we have empties, we fill them. The only exception to that rule I have ever made – and the only talk like this I have ever had – is on account of room 1408, a room on the thirteenth floor whose very numerals add up to thirteen.'

Olin looked levelly at Mike Enslin.

'It is a room not only of suicides but of strokes and heart attacks and epileptic seizures. One man who stayed in that room – this was in 1973 – apparently drowned in a bowl of soup. You would undoubtedly call that ridiculous, but I spoke to the man who was head of hotel security at that time, and he saw the death certificate. The power of whatever inhabits the room seems to be less around midday, which is when the room-turns always occur, and yet I know of several maids who have turned that room who now suffer from heart problems, emphysema, diabetes. There was a heating problem on that floor three years ago, and Mr Neal, the head main-tenance engineer at that time, had to go into several of the rooms to check the heating units. 1408 was one of them. He seemed fine then – both in the room and later on – but he died the following afternoon of a massive cerebral hemorrhage.'

'Coincidence,' Mike said. Yet he could not deny that Olin was good. Had the man been a camp counselor, he would have scared ninety per cent of the kiddies back home after the first round of campfire ghost stories.

'Coincidence,' Olin repeated softly, not quite contemptu-ously. He held out the old-fashioned key on its old-fashioned brass paddle. 'How is your own heart, Mr Enslin? Not to mention your blood-pressure and psychological condition?'

Mike found it took an actual, conscious effort to lift his hand . . . but once he got it moving, it was fine. It rose to the key without even the minutest trembling at the finger-tips, so far as he could see.

'All fine,' he said, grasping the worn brass paddle. 'Besides, I'm wearing my lucky Hawaiian shirt.'

★　★　★

Olin insisted on accompanying Mike to the fourteenth floor in the elevator, and Mike did not demur. He was interested to see that, once they were out of the manager's office and walking down the hall which led to the elevators, the man reverted to his less consequential self; he became once again poor Mr Olin, the flunky who had fallen into the writer's clutches.

A man in a tux – Mike guessed he was either the restaurant manager or the maître d' – stopped them, offered Olin a thin sheaf of papers, and murmured to him in French. Olin murmured back, nodding, and quickly scribbled his signature on the sheets. The fellow in the bar was now playing 'Autumn in New York'. From this distance, it had an echoey sound, like music heard in a dream.

The man in the tuxedo said *'Merci bien'* and went on his way. Mike and the hotel manager went on theirs. Olin again asked if he could carry Mike's little valise, and Mike again refused. In the elevator, Mike found his eyes drawn to the neat triple row of buttons. Everything was where it should have been, there were no gaps . . . and yet, if you looked more closely, you saw that there was. The button marked **12** was followed by one marked **14**. *As if*, Mike thought, *they could make the number nonexistent by omitting it from the control-panel of an elevator.* Foolishness . . . and yet Olin was right; it was done all over the world.

As the car rose, Mike said, 'I'm curious about something. Why didn't you simply create a fictional resident for room 1408, if it scares you all as badly as you say it does? For that matter, Mr Olin, why not declare it as your own residence?'

'I suppose I was afraid I would be accused of fraud, if not by the people responsible for enforcing state and federal civil rights statutes – hotel people feel about civil rights laws as many of your readers probably feel about clanking chains in the night – then by my bosses, if they got wind of it. If I couldn't persuade you to stay out of 1408, I doubt that I would have had much more luck in convincing the Stanley Corporation's board of directors that I took a perfectly good room off the market because I was afraid that the spooks cause the occasional travelling salesman to jump out the window and splatter himself all over Sixty-first Street.'

Mike found this the most disturbing thing Olin had said yet. *Because he's not trying to convince me anymore*, he thought. *Whatever salesmanship powers he had in his office – maybe it's some vibe that comes up from the Persian rug – he loses it out here. Competency, yes, you could see that when he was signing the maître d's chits, but not salesmanship. Not personal magnetism. Not out here. But he believes it. He believes it all.*

Above the door, the illuminated **12** went out and the **14** came on. The elevator stopped. The door slid open to reveal a perfectly ordinary hotel corridor with a red-and-gold carpet (most definitely not a Persian) and electric fixtures that looked like nineteenth-century gaslights.

'Here we are,' Olin said. 'Your floor. You'll pardon me if I leave you here. 1408 is to your left, at the end of the hall. Unless I absolutely have to, I don't go any closer than this.'

Mike Enslin stepped out of the elevator on legs that seemed heavier than they should have. He turned back to Olin, a pudgy little man in a black coat and a carefully knotted wine-colored tie. Olin's manicured hands were clasped behind him now, and Mike saw that the little man's face was as pale as cream. On his high, lineless forehead, drops of perspiration stood out.

'There's a telephone in the room, of course,' Olin said.

'You could try it, if you find yourself in trouble . . . but I doubt that it will work. Not if the room doesn't want it to.'

Mike thought of a light reply, something about how that would save him a room-service charge at least, but all at once his tongue seemed as heavy as his legs. It just lay there on the floor of his mouth.

Olin brought one hand out from behind his back, and Mike saw it was trembling. 'Mr Enslin,' he said. 'Mike. Don't do this. For God's sake—'

Before he could finish, the elevator door slid shut, cutting him off. Mike stood where he was for a moment, in the perfect New York hotel silence of what no one on the staff would admit was the thirteenth floor of the Hotel Dolphin, and thought of reaching out and pushing the elevator's call-button.

Except if he did that, Olin would win. And there would be a large, gaping hole where the best chapter of his new book should have been. The readers might not know that, his editor and his agent might not know it, Robertson the lawyer might not . . . but *he* would.

Instead of pushing the call-button, he reached up and touched the cigarette behind his ear – that old, distracted gesture he no longer knew he was making – and flicked the collar of his lucky shirt. Then he started down the hallway toward 1408, swinging his overnight case by his side.

II

The most interesting artifact left in the wake of Michael Enslin's brief stay (it lasted about seventy minutes) in room 1408 was the eleven minutes of recorded tape in his minicorder, which was charred a bit but not even close to destroyed. The fascinating thing about the narration was how *little* narration there was. And how odd it became.

The minicorder had been a present from his ex-wife, with whom he had remained friendly, five years before. On his first 'case expedition' (the Rilsby farm in Kansas) he had taken it almost as an afterthought, along with five yellow legal pads and a leather case filled with sharpened pencils. By the time he reached the door of room 1408 in the Hotel Dolphin three books later, he came with a single pen and notebook, plus five fresh ninety-minute cassettes in addition to the one he had loaded into the machine before leaving his apartment.

He had discovered that narration served him better than note-taking; he was able to catch anecdotes, some of them pretty damned great, as they happened – the bats that had dive-bombed him in the supposedly haunted tower of Gartsby Castle, for instance. He had shrieked like a girl on her first trip through a carny haunted house. Friends hearing this were invariably amused.

The little tape recorder was more practical than written notes, too, especially when you were in a chilly New Brunswick graveyard and a squall of rain and wind collapsed your tent at three in the morning. You couldn't take very successful notes in such circumstances, but you *could* talk . . . which was what Mike had done, gone on talking as he struggled out of the wet, flapping canvas of his tent, never losing sight of the minicorder's comforting red eye. Over the years and the 'case expeditions', the Sony minicorder had become his friend. He had never recorded a first-hand account of a true supernatural event on the filament-thin ribbon of tape running between its reels, and that included the broken comments he made while in 1408, but it was probably not surprising that he had arrived at such feelings of affection for the gadget. Long-haul truckers come to love their Kenworths and Jimmy-Petes; writers treasure a certain pen or battered old typewriter; professional cleaning ladies are loath to give up the old Electrolux. Mike had never had to stand up to an actual ghost or psychokinetic event with only the minicorder – his version of a cross and a bunch of garlic – to protect him, but it had been there on plenty of cold, uncomfortable nights. He was hardheaded, but that didn't make him inhuman.

His problems with 1408 started even before he got into the room.

The door was crooked.

Not by a lot, but it was crooked, all right, canted just the tiniest bit to the left. It made him think first of scary movies where the director tried to indicate mental distress in one of the characters by tipping the camera on the point-of-view shots. This association was followed by another one – the way doors looked when you were on a boat and the weather was a little heavy. Back and forth they went, right and left they went, tick and tock they went, until you started to feel a bit woozy in your head and stomach. Not that he felt that way himself, not at all, but—

Yes, I do. Just a little.

And he would say so, too, if only because of Olin's insinuation that his attitude made it impossible for him to be fair in the undoubtedly subjective field of spook journalism.

He bent over (aware that the slightly woozy feeling in his stomach left as soon as he was no longer looking at that subtly off-kilter door), unzipped the pocket on his overnighter, and took out his minicorder. He pushed RECORD as he straightened up, saw the little red eye go on, and opened his mouth to say, 'The door of room 1408 offers its own unique greeting; it appears to have been set crooked, tipped slightly to the left.'

He said *The door*, and that's all. If you listen to the tape, you can hear both words clearly, *The door*, and then the click of the STOP button. Because the door *wasn't* crooked. It was perfectly straight. Mike turned, looked at the door of 1409 across the hall, then back at the door of 1408. Both doors were the same, white with gold number-plaques and gold doorknobs. Both perfectly straight.

Mike bent, picked up his overnight case with the hand holding the minicorder, moved the key in his other hand toward the lock, then stopped again.

The door was crooked again.

This time it tilted slightly to the right.

'This is ridiculous,' Mike murmured, but that woozy feeling had already started in his stomach again. It wasn't just *like* seasickness; it *was* seasickness. He had crossed to England on the *QE2* a couple of years ago, and one night had been extremely rough. What Mike remembered most clearly was lying on the bed in his stateroom, always on the verge of throwing up but never quite able to do it. And how the feeling of nauseated vertigo got worse if you looked at a doorway . . . or a table . . . or a chair . . . at how they would go back and forth . . . right and left . . . tick and tock . . .

This is Olin's fault, he thought. *Exactly what he wants. He built you up for it, buddy. He set you up for it. Man, how he'd laugh if he could see you. How—*

His thoughts broke off as he realized Olin very likely *could* see him. Mike looked back down the corridor toward the elevator, barely noticing that the slightly whoopsy feeling in his stomach left the moment he stopped staring at the door. Above and to the left of the elevators, he saw what he had expected: a closed-circuit camera. One of the house dicks might be looking at it this very moment, and Mike was willing to bet that Olin was right there with him, both of them grinning like apes. *Teach him to come in here and start throwing his weight and his lawyer around*, Olin says. *Lookit him!* the security man replies, grinning more widely than ever. *White as a ghost himself, and he hasn't even touched the key to the lock yet. You got him, boss! Got him hook, line, and sinker!*

Damned if you do, Mike thought. *I stayed in the Rilsby house, slept in the room where at least two of them were killed — and I did sleep, whether you believed it or not. I spent a night right next to Jeffrey Dahmer's grave and another two stones over from H.P. Lovecraft's; I brushed my teeth next to the tub where Sir David Smythe supposedly drowned both of his wives. I stopped being scared of campfire stories a long time ago. I'll be damned if you do!*

He looked back at the door and the door was straight. He grunted, pushed the key into the lock, and turned it. The door opened. Mike stepped in. The door did not swing slowly shut behind him as he felt for the light switch, leaving him in total darkness (besides, the lights of the apartment building next door shone through the window). He found the switch. When he flicked it, the overhead light, enclosed in a collection of dangling crystal ornaments, came on. So did the standing lamp by the desk on the far side of the room.

The window was above this desk, so someone sitting there writing could pause in his work and look out on Sixty-first

Street . . . or *jump* out on Sixty-first, if the urge so took him. Except—

Mike set down his bag just inside the door, closed the door, and pushed RECORD again. The little red light went on.

'According to Olin, six people have jumped from the window I'm looking at,' he said, 'but I won't be taking any dives from the fourteenth – excuse me, the *thirteenth* – floor of the Hotel Dolphin tonight. There's an iron or steel mesh grille over the outside. Better safe than sorry. 1408 is what you'd call a junior suite, I guess. The room I'm in has two chairs, a sofa, a writing desk, a cabinet that probably contains the TV and maybe a minibar. Carpet on the floor is un-remarkable – not a patch on Olin's, believe me. Wallpaper, ditto. It . . . wait . . .'

At this point the listener hears another click on the tape as Mike hits the STOP button again. All the scant narration on the tape has that same fragmentary quality, which is utterly unlike the other hundred and fifty or so tapes in his literary agent's possession. In addition, his voice grows steadily more distracted; it is not the voice of a man at work, but of a perplexed individual who has begun talking to himself without realizing it. The elliptical nature of the tapes and that growing verbal distraction combine to give most listeners a distinct feeling of unease. Many ask that the tape be turned off long before the end is reached. Mere words on a page cannot adequately convey a listener's growing conviction that he is hearing a man lose, if not his mind, then his hold on conven-tional reality, but even the flat words themselves suggest that *something* was happening.

What Mike had noticed at that point were the pictures

on the walls. There were three of them: a lady in twenties-style evening dress standing on a staircase, a sailing ship done in the fashion of Currier & Ives, and a still life of fruit, the latter painted with an unpleasant yellow-orange cast to the apples as well as the oranges and bananas. All three pictures were in glass frames and all three were crooked. He had been about to mention the crookedness on tape, but what was so unusual, so worthy of comment, about three off-kilter pictures? That a *door* should be crooked . . . well, that had a little of that old *Cabinet of Dr Caligari* charm. But the door *hadn't* been crooked; his eyes had tricked him for a moment, that was all.

The lady on the stairs tilted left. So did the sailing ship, which showed bell-bottomed British tars lining the rail to watch a school of flying fish. The yellowish-orange fruit – to Mike it looked like a bowl of fruit painted by the light of a suffocating equatorial sun, a Paul Bowles desert sun – tilted to the right. Although he was not ordinarily a fussy man, he circled the room, setting them straight. Looking at them crooked like that was making him feel a touch nause-ated again. He wasn't entirely surprised, either. One grew susceptible to the feeling; he had discovered that on the *QE2*. He had been told that if one persevered through that period of increased susceptibility, one usually adapted . . . 'got your sealegs,' some of the old hands still said. Mike hadn't done enough sailing to get his sealegs, nor cared to. These days he stuck with his land legs, and if straightening the three pictures in the unremarkable sitting room of 1408 would settle his midsection, good for him.

There was dust on the glass covering the pictures. He trailed his fingers across the still life and left two parallel streaks. The dust had a greasy, slippery feel. *Like silk just before it rots* was what came into his mind, but he was damned if he was going to put that on tape, either. How was *he* supposed to know what silk felt like just before it rotted? It was a drunk's thought.

When the pictures were set to rights, he stepped back and surveyed them in turn: the evening-dressed lady by the door leading into the bedroom, the ship plying one of the seven seas to the left of the writing desk, and finally the nasty (and quite badly painted) fruit by the TV cabinet. Part of him expected that they would be crooked again, or fall crooked as he looked at them – that was the way things happened in movies like *House on Haunted Hill* and in old episodes of *The Twilight Zone* – but the pictures remained perfectly straight, as he had fixed them. Not, he told himself, that he would have found anything supernatural or paranormal in a return to their former crooked state; in his experience, reversion was the nature of things – people who had given up smoking (he touched the cigarette cocked behind his ear without being aware of it) wanted to go on smoking, and pictures that had been hanging crooked since Nixon was President wanted to go on hanging crooked. *And they've been here a long time, no doubt about that*, Mike thought. *If I lifted them away from the walls, I'd see lighter patches on the wallpaper. Or bugs squirming out, the way they do when you turn over a rock.*

There was something both shocking and nasty about this idea; it came with a vivid image of blind white bugs oozing out of the pale and formerly protected wallpaper like living pus.

Mike raised the minicorder, pushed RECORD, and said: 'Olin has certainly started a train of thought in my head. Or

34

a chain of thought, which is it? He set out to give me the heebie-jeebies, and he certainly succeeded. I don't mean . . .' Didn't mean what? To be racist? Was 'heebie-jeebies' short for *Hebrew* jeebies? But that was ridiculous. That would be 'Hebrew-jeebrews', a phrase which was meaningless. It—

On the tape at this point, flat and perfectly articulated, Mike Enslin says: 'I've got to get hold of myself. Right now.' This is followed by another click as he shuts the tape off again.

He closed his eyes and took four long, measured breaths, holding each one in to a five-count before letting it out again. Nothing like this had ever happened to him – not in the supposedly haunted houses, the supposedly haunted grave-yards, or the supposedly haunted castles. This wasn't like being haunted, or what he imagined being haunted would be like; this was like being stoned on bad, cheap dope.

Olin did this. Olin hypnotized you, but you're going to break out of it. You're going to spend the goddamned night in this room, and not just because it's the best location you've ever been in – leave out Olin and you've got damned near enough for the ghost-story of the decade already – but because Olin doesn't get to win. Him and his bullshit story about how thirty people have died in here, they don't get to win. I'm the one in charge of bullshit around here, so just breathe in . . . and out. Breathe in . . . and out. In . . . and out . . .

He went on like that for nearly ninety seconds, and when he opened his eyes again, he felt normal. The pictures on the wall? Still straight. Fruit in the bowl? Still yellow-orange and uglier than ever. Desert fruit for sure. Eat one piece of that and you'd shit until it hurt.

He pushed RECORD. The red eye went on. 'I had a little

vertigo for a minute or two,' he said, crossing the room to the writing desk and the window with its protective mesh outside. 'It might have been a hangover from Olin's yarning, but I could believe I feel a genuine presence here.' He felt no such thing, of course, but once that was on tape he could write almost anything he pleased. 'The air is stale. Not musty or foul-smelling. Olin said the place gets aired every time it gets turned, but the turns are quick and . . . yeah . . . it's stale. Hey, look at this.'

There was an ashtray on the writing desk, one of those little ones made of thick glass that you used to see in hotels everywhere, and in it was a book of matches. On the front was the Hotel Dolphin. In front of the hotel stood a smiling doorman in a very old-fashioned uniform, the kind with shoulder-boards, gold frogging, and a cap that looked as if it belonged in a gay bar, perched on the head of a motorcycle ramrod wearing nothing else but a few silver body-rings. Going back and forth on Fifth Avenue in front of the hotel were cars from another era – Packards and Hudsons, Studebakers and finny Chrysler New Yorkers.

'The matchbook in the ashtray looks like it comes from about 1955,' Mike said, and slipped it into the pocket of his lucky Hawaiian shirt. 'I'm keeping it as a souvenir. Now it's time for a little fresh air.'

There is a clunk as he sets the minicorder down, presumably on the writing desk. There is a pause followed by vague sounds and a couple of effortful grunts. After these come a second pause and then a squeaking sound. 'Success!' he says. This is a little off-mike, but the follow-up is closer.

'Success!' Mike repeated, picking the minicorder up off the desk. 'The bottom half wouldn't budge . . . it's like it's nailed shut . . . but the top half came down all right. I can hear the traffic on Fifth Avenue, and all the beeping horns have a comforting quality. Someone is playing a saxophone, perhaps in front of the Plaza, which is across the street and two blocks down. It reminds me of my brother.'

Mike stopped abruptly, looking at the little red eye. It seemed to accuse him. Brother? His brother was dead, another fallen soldier in the tobacco wars. Then he relaxed. What of it? These were the spook wars, where Michael Enslin had always come off the winner. As for Donald Enslin . . .

'My brother was actually eaten by wolves one winter on the Connecticut Turnpike,' he said, then laughed and pushed STOP. There is more on the tape — a little more — but that is the final statement of any coherence . . . the final statement, that is, to which a clear meaning can be ascribed.

Mike turned on his heels and looked at the pictures. Still hanging perfectly straight, good little pictures that they were. That still life, though — what an ugly fucking thing that was!

He pushed RECORD and spoke two words — *fuming oranges* — into the minicorder. Then he turned it off again and walked across the room to the door leading into the bedroom. He paused by the evening-dressed lady and reached into the darkness, feeling for the light switch. He had just one moment to register

(*it feels like skin like old dead skin*)

something wrong with the wallpaper under his sliding palm, and then his fingers found the switch. The bedroom was flooded with yellow light from another of those ceiling fixtures buried in hanging glass baubles. The bed was a double hiding under a yellow-orange coverlet.

'Why say hiding?' Mike asked the minicorder, then pushed the STOP button again. He stepped in, fascinated by the fuming desert of the coverlet, by the tumorous bulges of the pillows beneath it. Sleep there? Not at all, sir! It would be like sleeping inside that goddam still-life, sleeping in that horrible hot Paul Bowles room you couldn't quite see, a room for lunatic expatriate Englishmen who were blind from syphilis caught while fucking their mothers, the film version starring either Laurence Harvey or Jeremy Irons, one of those actors you just naturally associated with unnatural acts—

Mike pushed RECORD, the little red eye came on, he said 'Orpheus on the Orpheum Circuit!' into the mike, then pushed STOP again. He approached the bed. The coverlet gleamed yellow-orange. The wallpaper, perhaps cream-colored by daylight, had picked up the yellow-orange glow of the coverlet. There was a little night-table to either side of the bed. On one was a telephone – black and large and equipped with a dial. The finger-holes in the dial looked like surprised white eyes. On the other table was a dish with a plum on it. Mike pushed RECORD and said: 'That isn't a real plum. That's a plastic plum.' He pushed STOP again.

On the bed itself was a doorknob menu. Mike sidled up one side of the bed, being quite careful to touch neither the bed nor the wall, and picked the menu up. He tried not to touch the coverlet, either, but the tips of his fingers brushed it and he moaned. It was soft in some terrible wrong way. Nevertheless, he picked the menu up. It was in French, and although it had been years since he had taken the language, one of the breakfast items appeared to be birds roasted in shit. *That at least* sounds *like something the French might eat*, he thought, and uttered a wild, distracted laugh.

He closed his eyes and opened them.

The menu was in Russian.

He closed his eyes and opened them.

The menu was in Italian.

Closed his eyes, opened them.

There *was* no menu. There was a picture of a screaming little woodcut boy looking back over his shoulder at the woodcut wolf which had swallowed his left leg up to the knee. The wolf's ears were laid back and he looked like a terrier with its favorite toy.

I don't see that, Mike thought, and of course he didn't. Without closing his eyes he saw neat lines of English, each line listing a different breakfast temptation. Eggs, waffles, fresh berries; no birds roasted in shit. Still—

He turned around and very slowly edged himself out of the little space between the wall and the bed, a space that now felt as narrow as a grave. His heart was beating so hard that he could feel it in his neck and wrists as well as in his chest. His eyes were throbbing in their sockets. 1408 was wrong, yes indeed, 1408 was *very* wrong. Olin had said something about poison gas, and that was what Mike felt like: someone who has been gassed or forced to smoke strong hashish laced with insect poison. Olin had done this, of course, probably with the active laughing connivance of the security people. Pumped his special poison gas up through the vents. Just because he could *see* no vents didn't mean the vents weren't there.

Mike looked around the bedroom with wide, frightened eyes. There was no plum on the endtable to the left of the bed.

No plate, either. The table was bare. He turned, started for the door leading back to the sitting room, and stopped. There was a picture on the wall. He couldn't be absolutely sure – in his present state he couldn't be absolutely sure of his own name – but he was *fairly* sure that there had been no picture there when he first came in. It was a still life. A single plum sat on a tin plate in the middle of an old plank table. The light falling across the plum and the plate was a feverish yellow-orange.

Tango-light, he thought. *The kind of light that makes the dead get up out of their graves and tango. The kind of light—*

'I have to get out of here,' he whispered, and blundered back into the sitting room. He became aware that his shoes had begun to make odd smooching sounds, as if the floor beneath them were growing soft.

The pictures on the living room wall were crooked again, and there were other changes, as well. The lady on the stairs had pulled down the top of her gown, baring her breasts. She held one in each hand. A drop of blood hung from each nipple. She was staring directly into Mike's eyes and grinning ferociously. Her teeth were filed to cannibal points. At the rail of the sailing ship, the tars had been replaced by a line of pallid men and women. The man on the far left, nearest the ship's bow, wore a brown wool suit and held a derby hat in one hand. His hair was slicked to his brow and parted in the middle. His face was shocked and vacant. Mike knew his name: Kevin O'Malley, this room's first occupant, a sewing machine salesman who had jumped from this room in October of 1910. To O'Malley's left were the others who had died here, all with that same vacant, shocked expression. It made them look related, all members of the same inbred and cataclysmically retarded family.

In the picture where the fruit had been, there was now a severed human head. Yellow-orange light swam off the sunken cheeks, the sagging lips, the upturned, glazing eyes, the cigarette parked behind the right ear.

Mike blundered toward the door, his feet smooching and now actually seeming to stick a little at each step. The door wouldn't open, of course. The chain hung unengaged, the thumbbolt stood straight up like clock hands pointing to six o'clock, but the door wouldn't open.

Breathing rapidly, Mike turned from it and waded – that was what it felt like – across the room to the writing desk. He could see the curtains beside the window he had cracked open waving desultorily, but he could feel no fresh air against his face. It was as though the room were swallowing it. He could still hear horns on Fifth, but they were now very distant. Did he still hear the saxophone? If so, the room had stolen its sweetness and melody and left only an atonal reedy drone, like the wind blowing across a hole in a dead man's neck or a pop bottle filled with severed fingers or—

Stop it, he tried to say, but he could no longer speak. His heart was hammering at a terrible pace; if it went much faster, it would explode. His minicorder, faithful companion of many 'case expeditions', was no longer in his hand. He had left it somewhere. In the bedroom? If it was in the bedroom, it was probably gone by now, swallowed by the room; when it was digested, it would be excreted into one of the pictures.

Gasping for breath like a runner nearing the end of a long race, Mike put a hand to his chest, as if to soothe his heart. What he felt in the left breast pocket of his gaudy shirt was the small square shape of the minicorder. The feel of it, so solid and known, steadied him a little – brought him back a little. He became aware that he was humming . . . and that the room seemed to be humming back at him, as if myriad mouths were concealed beneath its smoothly nasty wallpaper. He was aware that his stomach was now so nauseated that it seemed to be swinging in its own greasy hammock. He could feel the air crowding against his ears in soft, coagulating clots, and it made him think of how fudge was when it reached the soft-ball stage.

But he was back a little, enough to be positive of one thing: he had to call for help while there was still time. The thought of Olin smirking (in his deferential New York hotel manager way) and saying *I told you so* didn't bother him, and the idea that Olin had somehow induced these strange perceptions and horrible fear by chemical means had entirely left his mind. It was the *room*. It was the goddamned *room*.

He meant to jab out a hand to the old-fashioned tele-phone – the twin of the one in the bedroom – and snatch it up. Instead he watched his arm descend to the table in a kind of delirious slow motion, so like the arm of a diver he almost expected to see bubbles rising from it.

He closed his fingers around the handset and picked it up. His other hand dove, as deliberate as the first, and dialed 0. As he put the handset of the phone against his ear, he heard a series of clicks as the dial spun back to its original position. It sounded like the wheel on *Wheel of Fortune*, do you want to spin or do you want to solve the puzzle? Remember that if you try to solve the puzzle and fail, you will be put out into the snow beside the Connecticut Turnpike and the wolves will eat you.

There was no ring in his ear. Instead, a harsh voice simply began speaking. 'This is *nine! Nine!* This is *nine! Nine!* This is *ten! Ten!* We have killed your friends! Every friend is now dead! This is *six! Six!*'

Mike listened with growing horror, not at what the voice was saying but at its rasping emptiness. It was not a machine-generated voice, but it wasn't a human voice, either. It was the voice of the room. The presence pouring out of the walls and the floor, the presence speaking to him from the telephone, had nothing in common with any haunting or paranormal event he had ever read about. There was something alien here.

No, not here yet . . . but coming. It's hungry, and you're dinner.

The phone fell from his relaxing fingers and he turned around. It swung at the end of its cord the way his stomach was swinging back and forth inside him, and he could still hear that voice rasping out of the black: '*Eighteen!* This is now *eighteen!* Take cover when the siren sounds! This is *four! Four!*'

He was not aware of taking the cigarette from behind his ear and putting it in his mouth, or of fumbling the book of matches with the old-fashioned gold-frogged doorman on it out of his bright shirt's right breast pocket, not aware that, after nine years, he had finally decided to have a smoke.

Before him, the room had begun to melt.

It was sagging out of its right angles and straight lines, not into curves but into strange Moorish arcs that hurt his eyes. The glass chandelier in the center of the ceiling began to sag like a thick glob of spit. The pictures began to bend, turning into shapes like the windshields of old cars. From behind the glass of the picture by the door leading into the bedroom, the twenties woman with the bleeding nipples and grinning cannibal-teeth whirled around and ran back up the stairs, going with the jerky delirious high knee-pistoning of a vamp in a silent movie. The telephone continued to grind and spit, the voice coming from it now the voice of an electric hair-clipper that has learned how to talk: '*Five!* This is *five!* Ignore the siren! Even if you leave this room, you can never leave this room! *Eight!* This is *eight!*'

The door to the bedroom and the door to the hall had begun to collapse downward, widening in the middle and becoming doorways for beings possessed of unhallowed shapes. The light began to grow bright and hot, filling the room with that yellow-orange glow. Now he could see rips in the wallpaper, black pores that quickly grew to become mouths. The floor sank into a concave arc and now he could hear it coming, the dweller in the room behind the room, the thing in the walls, the owner of the buzzing voice. '*Six!*' the phone screamed. '*Six,* this is *six,* this is *goddam fucking SIX!*'

He looked down at the matchbook in his hand, the one he had plucked out of the bedroom ashtray. Funny old doorman, funny old cars with their big chrome grilles . . . and words running across the bottom that he hadn't seen in a long time, because now the strip of abrasive stuff was always on the back.

CLOSE COVER BEFORE STRIKING.

Without thinking about it − he no longer *could* think − Mike Enslin tore out a single match, allowing the cigarette to drop out of his mouth at the same time. He struck the match and immediately touched it to the others in the book. There was a *ffffhut!* sound, a strong whiff of burning sulfur that went into his head like a whiff of smelling salts, and a bright flare of match heads. And again, without so much as a single thought, Mike held the flaring bouquet of fire against the front of his shirt. It was a cheap thing made in Korea or Cambodia or Borneo, old now; it caught fire at once. Before the flames could blaze up in front of his eyes, rendering the room once more unstable, Mike saw it clearly, like a man who has awakened from a nightmare only to find the nightmare all around him.

His head was clear – the strong whiff of sulfur and the sudden rising heat from his shirt had done that much – but the room maintained its insanely Moorish aspect. *Moorish* was wrong, not even very close, but it was the only word that seemed even to reach toward what had happened here . . . what was still happening. He was in a melting, rotting cave full of swoops and mad tilts. The door to the bedroom had become the door to some sarcophagal inner chamber. And to his left, where the picture of the fruit had been, the wall was bulging outward toward him, splitting open in those long cracks that gaped like mouths, opening on a world from which *something* was now approaching. Mike Enslin could hear its slobbering, avid breath, and smell something alive and dangerous. It smelled a little like the lion-house in the—

Then flames scorched the undershelf of his chin, banishing thought. The heat rising from his blazing shirt put that waver back into the world, and as he began to smell the crispy aroma of his chest-hair starting to fry, Mike again bolted across the sagging rug to the hall door. An

45

insectile buzzing sound had begun to sweat out of the walls. The yellow-orange light was steadily brightening, as if a hand were turning up an invisible rheostat. But this time when he reached the door and turned the knob, the door opened. It was as if the thing behind the bulging wall had no use for a burning man; did not, perhaps, relish cooked meat.

III

A popular song from the fifties suggests that love makes the world go 'round, but coincidence would probably be a better bet. Rufus Dearborn, who was staying that night in room 1414, up near the elevators, was a salesman for the Singer Sewing Machine Company, in town from Texas to talk about moving up to an executive position. And so it happened that, ninety or so years after room 1408's first occupant jumped to his death, another sewing machine salesman saved the life of the man who had come to write about the purportedly haunted room. Or perhaps that is an exaggeration; Mike Enslin might have lived even if no one – especially a fellow on his way back from a visit to the ice machine – had been in the hallway at that moment. Having your shirt catch fire is no joke, though, and he certainly would have been burned much more severely and extensively if not for Dearborn, who thought fast and moved even faster.

Not that Dearborn ever remembered exactly what happened. He constructed a coherent enough story for the newspapers and TV cameras (he liked the idea of being a hero very much, and it certainly did no harm to his executive aspirations), and he clearly remembered seeing the man on fire lunge out into the hall, but after that everything was a blur. Thinking about it was like trying to reconstruct the things you had done during the vilest, deepest drunk of your life.

One thing he was sure of but didn't tell any of the reporters, because it made no sense: the burning man's scream seemed to grow in volume, as if he were a stereo that was being turned up. He was right there in front of Dearborn, and the *pitch* of the scream never changed, but the volume most certainly did. It was as if the man were some incredibly loud object that was just arriving here.

Dearborn ran down the hall with the full ice-bucket in his hand. The burning man – 'It was just his shirt on fire, I saw that right away,' he told the reporters – struck the door opposite the room he had come out of, rebounded, staggered, and fell to his knees. That was when Dearborn reached him. He put his foot on the burning shoulder of the screaming man's shirt and pushed him over onto the hall carpet. Then he dumped the contents of the ice-bucket onto him.

These things were blurred in his memory, but accessible. He was aware that the burning shirt seemed to be casting far too much light – a sweltering yellow-orange light that made him think of a trip he and his brother had made to Australia two years before. They had rented an all-wheel drive and had taken off across the Great Australian Desert (the few natives called it the Great Australian Bugger-All, the Dearborn brothers discovered), a hell of a trip, great, but spooky. Especially the big rock in the middle, Ayers Rock. They had reached it right around sunset and the light on its man faces was like this . . . hot and strange . . . not really what you thought of as earthlight at all . . .

He dropped beside the burning man who was now only the smoldering man, the covered-with-ice-cubes man, and rolled him over to stifle the flames reaching around to the back of the shirt. When he did, he saw the skin on the left side of the man's neck had gone a smoky, bubbly red, and the lobe of his ear on that side had melted a little, but otherwise . . . otherwise . . .

Dearborn looked up, and it seemed – this was crazy, but it seemed the door to the room the man had come out of was filled with the burning light of an Australian sundown, the hot light of an empty place where things no man had ever seen might live. It was terrible, that light (and the low buzzing, like an electric clipper that was trying desperately to speak), but it was fascinating, too. He wanted to go into it. He wanted to see what was behind it.

Perhaps Mike saved Dearborn's life, as well. He was certainly aware that Dearborn was getting up – as if Mike no longer held any interest for him – and that his face was filled with the blazing, pulsing light coming out of 1408. He remembered this better than Dearborn later did himself, but of course Rufe Dearborn had not been reduced to setting himself on fire in order to survive.

Mike grabbed the cuff of Dearborn's slacks. 'Don't go in there,' he said in a cracked, smoky voice. 'You'll never come out.'

Dearborn stopped, looking down at the reddening, blistering face of the man on the carpet.

'It's haunted,' Mike said, and as if the words had been a talisman, the door of room 1408 slammed furiously shut, cutting off the light, cutting off the terrible buzz that was almost words.

Rufus Dearborn, one of Singer Sewing Machine's finest, ran down to the elevators and pulled the fire alarm.

IV

There's an interesting picture of Mike Enslin in *Treating the Burn Victim: A Diagnostic Approach*, the sixteenth edition of which appeared about sixteen months after Mike's short stay in room 1408 of the Hotel Dolphin. The photo shows just his torso, but it's Mike, all right. One can tell by the white square on the left side of his chest. The flesh all around it is an angry red, actually blistered into second-degree burns in some places. The white square marks the left breast pocket of the shirt he was wearing that night, the lucky shirt with his minicorder in the pocket.

The minicorder itself melted around the corners, but it still works, and the tape inside it was fine. It's the things on it which are not fine. After listening to it three or four times, Mike's agent, Sam Farrell, tossed it into his wall-safe, refusing to acknowledge the gooseflesh all over his tanned, scrawny arms. In that wall-safe the tape has stayed ever since. Farrell has no urge to take it out and play it again, not for himself, not for his curious friends, some of whom would cheerfully kill to hear it; New York publishing is a small community, and word gets around.

He doesn't like Mike's voice on the tape, he doesn't like the stuff that voice is saying (*My brother was actually eaten by wolves one winter on the Connecticut Turnpike . . .* what in God's name is *that* supposed to mean?), and most of all he doesn't like the background sounds on the tape, a kind of liquid smooshing that sometimes sounds like clothes churning around in an oversudsed washer, sometimes like one of those old electric hair-clippers . . . and sometimes weirdly like a voice.

While Mike was still in the hospital, a man named Olin – the manager of the goddamned hotel, if you please – came and asked Sam Farrell if he could listen to that tape. Farrell said no, he couldn't; what Olin could do was take himself on out of the agent's office at a rapid hike and thank God all the way back to the fleabag where he worked that Mike Enslin had decided not to sue either the hotel or Olin for negligence.

'I tried to persuade him not to go in,' Olin said quietly. A man who spent most of his working days listening to tired travellers and petulant guests bitch about everything from their rooms to the magazine selection in the newsstand, he wasn't much perturbed by Farrell's rancor. 'I tried everything in my power. If anyone was negligent that night, Mr Farrell, it was your client. He believed too much in nothing. Very unwise behavior. Very *unsafe* behavior. I would guess he has changed somewhat in that regard.'

In spite of Farrell's distaste for the tape, he would like Mike to listen to it, acknowledge it, perhaps use it as a pad from which to launch a new book. There is a book in what happened to Mike, Farrell knows it – not just a chapter, a forty-page case history, but an entire book. One that might outsell all three of the *Ten Nights* books combined. And of course he doesn't believe Mike's assertion that he has finished not only with ghost-tales but with all writing. Writers say that from time to time, that's all. The occasional prima donna outburst is part of what makes writers in the first place.

As for Mike Enslin himself, he got off lucky, all things considered. And he knows it. He could have been burned much more badly than he actually was; if not for Mr Dearborn and his bucket of ice, he might have had twenty or even thirty different skin-graft procedures to suffer through instead of only four. His neck is scarred on the left side in spite of the grafts, but the doctors at the Boston Burn Institute tell him the scars will fade on their own. He also knows that the burns, painful as they were in the weeks and months after that night, were necessary. If not for the matches with CLOSE COVER BEFORE STRIKING written on the front, he would have died in 1408, and his end would have been unspeakable. To a coroner it might have looked like a stroke or a heart attack, but the actual cause of death would have been much nastier.

Much nastier.

He was also lucky in having produced three popular books on ghosts and hauntings before actually running afoul of a place that *is* haunted — this he also knows. Sam Farrell may not believe Mike's life as a writer is over, but Sam doesn't need to; Mike knows it for both of them. He cannot so much as write a postcard without feeling cold all over his skin and being nauseated deep in the pit of his belly. Sometimes just looking at a pen (or a tape recorder) will make him think: *The pictures were crooked. I tried to straighten the pictures.* He doesn't know what this means. He can't remember the pictures or anything else from room 1408, and he is glad. That is a mercy. His blood-pressure isn't so good these days (his doctor told him that burn victims often develop problems with their blood-pressure and put him on medication), his eyes trouble him (his ophthalmologist told him to start taking Ocuvites), he has consistent back problems, his prostate has gotten too large . . . but he can deal with these things. He knows he isn't the first person to escape 1408 without really escaping – Olin tried to tell him – but it isn't all bad. At least he doesn't remember. Sometimes he has nightmares, quite often, in fact (almost every goddam *night*, in fact), but he rarely remembers them when he wakes up. A sense that things are rounding off at the corners, mostly – melting the way the corners of his minicorder melted. He lives on Long Island these days, and when the weather is good he takes long walks on the beach. The closest he has ever come to articulating what he does remember about his seventy-odd (*very* odd) minutes in 1408 was on one of those walks. 'It was never human,' he told the incoming waves in a choked, halting voice. 'Ghosts . . . at least ghosts were once human. The thing in the wall, though . . . that thing . . .'

Time may improve it, he can and does hope for that. Time may fade it, as it will fade the scars on his neck. In the meantime, though, he sleeps with the lights on in his bedroom, so he will know at once where he is when he wakes up from the bad dreams. He has had all the phones taken out of the house; at some point just below the place where his conscious mind seems able to go, he is afraid of picking the phone up and hearing a buzzing, inhuman voice spit, 'This is *nine! Nine!* We have killed your friends! Every friend is now dead!'

And when the sun goes down on clear evenings, he pulls every shade and blind and drape in the house. He sits like a man in a darkroom until his watch tells him the light – even the last fading glow along the horizon – must be gone.

He can't stand the light that comes at sunset.

That yellow deepening to orange, like light in the Australian desert.

THE MANGLER

When my brother David and I were kids, our mother worked on the speed-ironer at the Stratford Laundry, in Stratford, Connecticut. She told us that the machine, which the crew called the mangler, was dangerous. I remember thinking, 'With a name like that, how could it not be?'

Mom worked herself nearly to death – there, and in other minimum-wage sweat-pits – in order to ensure her boys a college education, and my first job upon graduation was . . . in a laundry! I was the motel sheets guy – a spunky specialty, my friends – but I got to see the mangler close up every day; the feed end was less than thirty feet from my big Washex suds-o-matics. It was indeed dangerous. One of the floor foremen, Harry Cross, had hooks instead of hands to prove it. One Saturday during World War II, he fell into it while it was running. Hence the hooks, which he occasionally held under the men's room taps (left hook equaled HOT, right hook equaled COLD) and then put on the backs of the unsuspecting mangle-girls' necks. Nowadays this sort of thing is called 'sexual harassment'; Harry called it 'horsing around.' I took no stand; I just wondered how he tied his tie in the morning (sometimes I wondered about other things, too, but let's not go there).

Given my habit of imagining the worst, it's not so surprising that I would imagine a vampire mangler. And maybe not surprising the resulting story became a movie. Tobe Hooper, who directed it, is something of a genius . . . *The Texas Chain Saw Massacre* proves that beyond doubt. But when genius goes wrong, brother, watch out. The film version of *The Mangler* is energetic and colorful, but it's also a mess with Robert (Freddy Krueger) Englund stalking through it for reasons which remain unclear to me even now. I think he had one eye and a limp, but I could be wrong about that.

The movie's visuals are surreal and the sets are eye-popping, but somewhere along the way (maybe in the copious amounts of steam generated by the film's mechanical star), the story got lost. That's a shame, because Hooper did wonders with *Salem's Lot* in its first miniseries incarnation. When people talk about the stuff of mine that's frightened them onscreen, they're apt to mention Pennywise the Clown first, then Kathy Bates as Annie Wilkes, and then the floating vampire-boys in *Lot*.

There are no such indelible images in *The Mangler*, but I maintain it's still the best short story you will ever read in which a laundry machine escapes on pressing business, heh-heh-heh.

THE MANGLER

THE MANGLER

Officer Hunton got to the laundry just as the ambulance was leaving – slowly, with no siren or flashing lights. Ominous. Inside, the office was stuffed with milling, silent people, some of them weeping. The plant itself was empty; the big automatic washers at the far end had not even been shut down. It made Hunton very wary. The crowd should be at the scene of the accident, not in the office. It was the way things worked – the human animal had a built-in urge to view the remains. A very bad one, then. Hunton felt his stomach tighten as it always did when the accident was very bad. Fourteen years of cleaning human litter from highways and streets and the sidewalks at the bases of very tall buildings had not been able to erase that little hitch in the belly, as if something evil had clotted there.

A man in a white shirt saw Hunton and walked toward him reluctantly. He was a buffalo of a man with head thrust forward between shoulders, nose and cheeks vein-broken either from high blood pressure or too many conversations with the brown bottle. He was trying to frame words, but after two tries Hunton cut him off briskly:

'Are you the owner? Mr Gartley?'

'No . . . no. I'm Stanner. The foreman. God, this—'

Hunton got out his notebook. 'Please show me the scene of the accident, Mr Stanner, and tell me what happened.'

Stanner seemed to grow even more white; the blotches on his nose and cheeks stood out like birthmarks. 'D-do I have to?'

Hunton raised his eyebrows. 'I'm afraid you do. The call I got said it was serious.'

'Serious—' Stanner seemed to be battling with his gorge; for a moment his Adam's apple went up and down like a monkey on a stick. 'Mrs Frawley is dead. Jesus, I wish Bill Gartley *was* here.'

'What happened?'

Stanner said, 'You better come over here.'

He led Hunton past a row of hand presses, a shirt-folding unit, and then stopped by a laundry-marking machine. He passed a shaky hand across his forehead. 'You'll have to go over by yourself, Officer. I can't look at it again. It makes me . . . I can't. I'm sorry.'

Hunton walked around the marking machine with a mild feeling of contempt for the man. They run a loose shop, cut corners, run live steam through home-welded pipes, they work with dangerous cleaning chemicals without the proper protection, and finally, someone gets hurt. Or gets dead. Then they can't look. They can't—

Hunton saw it.

The machine was still running. No one had shut it off. The machine he later came to know intimately: the Hadley-Watson Model-6 Speed Ironer and Folder. A long and clumsy name. The people who worked here in the steam and the wet had a better name for it. The mangler.

Hunton took a long, frozen look, and then he performed

a first in his fourteen years as a law-enforcement officer: he turned around, put a convulsive hand to his mouth, and threw up.

'You didn't eat much,' Jackson said.

The women were inside, doing dishes and talking babies while John Hunton and Mark Jackson sat in lawn chairs near the aromatic barbecue. Hunton smiled slightly at the understatement. He had eaten nothing.

'There was a bad one today,' he said. 'The worst.'

'Car crash?'

'No. Industrial.'

'Messy?'

Hunton did not reply immediately, but his face made an involuntary, writhing grimace. He got a beer out of the cooler between them, opened it, and emptied half of it. 'I suppose you college profs don't know anything about industrial laundries?'

Jackson chuckled. 'This one does. I spent a summer working in one as an undergraduate.'

'Then you know the machine they call the speed ironer?'

Jackson nodded. 'Sure. They run damp flatwork through them, mostly sheets and linen. A big, long machine.'

'That's it,' Hunton said. 'A woman named Adelle Frawley got caught in it at the Blue Ribbon Laundry crosstown. It sucked her right in.'

Jackson looked suddenly ill. 'But . . . that can't happen, Johnny. There's a safety bar. If one of the women feeding the machine accidentally gets a hand under it, the bar snaps up and stops the machine. At least that's how I remember it.'

Hunton nodded. 'It's a state law. But it happened.'

Hunton closed his eyes and in the darkness he could see the Hadley-Watson speed ironer again, as it had been that afternoon. It formed a long, rectangular box in shape, thirty feet by six. At the feeder end, a moving canvas belt moved under the safety bar, up at a slight angle, and then down. The belt carried the damp-dried, wrinkled sheets in continuous cycle over and under sixteen huge revolving cylinders that made up the main body of the machine. Over eight and under eight, pressed between them like thin ham between layers of superheated bread. Steam heat in the cylinders could be adjusted up to 300 degrees for maximum drying. The pressure on the sheets that rode the moving canvas belt was set at 800 pounds per square foot to get out every wrinkle.

And Mrs Frawley, somehow, had been caught and dragged in. The steel, asbestos-jacketed pressing cylinders had been as red as barn paint, and the rising steam from the machine had carried the sickening stench of hot blood. Bits of her white blouse and blue slacks, even ripped segments of her bra and panties, had been torn free and ejected from the machine's far end thirty feet down, the bigger sections of cloth folded with grotesque and blood-stained neatness by the automatic folder. But not even that was the worst.

'It tried to fold everything,' he said to Jackson, tasting bile in his throat. 'But a person isn't a sheet, Mark. What I saw . . . what was left of her . . .' Like Stanner, the hapless foreman, he could not finish. 'They took her out in a basket,' he said softly.

Jackson whistled. 'Who's going to get it in the neck? The laundry or the state inspectors?'

'Don't know yet,' Hunton said. The malign image still hung behind his eyes, the image of the mangler wheezing and thumping and hissing, blood dripping down the green sides of the long cabinet in runnels, the burning *stink* of her . . . 'It depends on who okayed that goddamn safety bar and under what circumstances.'

'If it's the management, can they wiggle out of it?'

Hunton smiled without humor. 'The woman died, Mark. If Gartley and Stanner were cutting corners on the speed ironer's maintenance, they'll go to jail. No matter who they know on the City Council.'

'Do you think they were cutting corners?'

Hunton thought of the Blue Ribbon Laundry, badly lighted, floors wet and slippery, some of the machines incredibly ancient and creaking. 'I think it's likely,' he said quietly.

They got up to go in the house together. 'Tell me how it comes out, Johnny,' Jackson said. 'I'm interested.'

Hunton was wrong about the mangler; it was clean as a whistle.

Six state inspectors went over it before the inquest, piece by piece. The net result was absolutely nothing. The inquest verdict was death by misadventure.

Hunton, dumbfounded, cornered Roger Martin, one of the inspectors, after the hearing. Martin was a tall drink of water with glasses as thick as the bottoms of shot glasses. He fidgeted with a ball-point pen under Hunton's questions.

'Nothing? Absolutely nothing doing with the machine?'

'Nothing,' Martin said. 'Of course, the safety bar was the guts of the matter. It's in perfect working order. You heard that Mrs Gillian testify. Mrs Frawley must have pushed her hand too far. No one saw that; they were watching their own work. She started screaming. Her hand was gone already, and the machine was taking her arm. They tried to pull her out instead of shutting it down – pure panic. Another woman, Mrs Keene, said she *did* try to shut it off, but it's a fair assumption that she hit the start button rather than the stop in the confusion. By then it was too late.'

'Then the safety bar malfunctioned,' Hunton said flatly. 'Unless she put her hand over it rather than under?'

'You can't. There's a stainless-steel facing above the safety bar. And the bar itself didn't malfunction. It's circuited into the machine itself. If the safety bar goes on the blink, the machine shuts down.'

'Then how did it happen, for Christ's sake?'

'We don't know. My colleagues and I are of the opinion that the only way the speed ironer could have killed Mrs Frawley was for her to have fallen into it from above. And she had both feet on the floor when it happened. A dozen witnesses can testify to that.'

'You're describing an impossible accident,' Hunton said.

'No. Only one we don't understand.' He paused, hesitated, and then said: 'I will tell you one thing, Hunton, since you seem to have taken this case to heart. If you mention it to anyone else, I'll deny I said it. But I didn't like that machine. It seemed . . . almost to be mocking us. I've inspected over a dozen speed ironers in the last five years on a regular basis. Some of them are in such bad shape that I wouldn't have a dog unleashed around them – the state law is lamentably lax. But they were only machines for all that. But this one . . . it's a spook. I don't know why, but it is. I think if I'd found one thing, even a technicality, that was off whack, I would have ordered it shut down. Crazy, huh?'

'I felt the same way,' Hunton said.

'Let me tell you about something that happened two years ago in Milton,' the inspector said. He took off his glasses and began to polish them slowly on his vest. 'Fella had parked an old ice-box out in his backyard. The woman who called us said her dog had been caught in it and suffocated. We got the state policeman in the area to inform him it had to go to the town dump. Nice enough fella, sorry about the dog. He loaded it into his pickup and took it to the dump the next morning. That afternoon a woman in the neighbor-hood reported her son missing.'

'God,' Hunton said.

'The icebox was at the dump and the kid was in it, dead. A smart kid, according to the mother. She said he'd no more play in an empty icebox than he would take a ride with a strange man. Well, he did. We wrote it off. Case closed?'

'I guess,' Hunton said.

'No. The dump caretaker went out next day to take the door off the thing. City Ordinance No. 58 on the maintenance of public dumping places.' Martin looked at him expression-lessly. 'He found six dead birds inside. Gulls, sparrows, a robin. And he said the door closed on his arm while he was brushing them out. Gave him a hell of a jump. The mangler at the Blue Ribbon strikes me like that, Hunton. I don't like it.'

They looked at each other wordlessly in the empty inquest chamber, some six city blocks from where the Hadley-Watson Model-6 Speed Ironer and Folder sat in the busy laundry, steaming and fuming over its sheets. The case was driven out of his mind in the space of a week by the press of more prosaic police work. It was only brought back when he and his wife dropped over to Mark Jackson's house for an evening of bid whist and beer.

Jackson greeted him with: 'Have you ever wondered if that laundry machine you told me about is haunted, Johnny?'

Hunton blinked, at a loss. 'What?'

'The speed ironer at the Blue Ribbon Laundry, I guess you didn't catch the squeal this time.'

'What squeal?' Hunton asked, interested.

Jackson passed him the evening paper and pointed to an item at the bottom of page two. The story said that a steam line had let go on the large speed ironer at the Blue Ribbon Laundry, burning three of the six women working at the feeder end. The accident had occurred at 3.45 P.M. and was attributed to a rise in steam pressure from the laundry's boiler. One of the women, Mrs Annette Gillian, had been held at City Receiving Hospital with second-degree burns.

'Funny coincidence,' he said, but the memory of Inspector Martin's words in the empty inquest chamber suddenly recurred: *It's a spook . . .* And the story about the dog and the boy and the birds caught in the discarded refrigerator.

He played cards very badly that night.

Mrs Gillian was propped up in bed reading *Screen Secrets* when Hunton came into the four-bed hospital room. A large bandage blanketed one arm and the side of her neck. The room's other occupant, a young woman with a pallid face, was sleeping.

Mrs Gillian blinked at the blue uniform and then smiled tentatively. 'If it was for Mrs Cherinikov, you'll have to come back later. They just gave her medication.'

'No, it's for you, Mrs Gillian.' Her smile faded a little. 'I'm here unofficially – which means I'm curious about the accident at the laundry. John Hunton.' He held out his hand.

It was the right move. Mrs Gillian's smile became brilliant and she took his grip awkwardly with her unburnt hand. 'Anything I can tell you, Mr Hunton. God, I thought my Andy was in trouble at school again.'

'What happened?'

'We was running sheets and the ironer just blew up – or it seemed that way. I was thinking about going home an' getting off my dogs when there's this great big bang, like a bomb. Steam is everywhere and this hissing noise . . . awful.' Her smile trembled on the verge of extinction. 'It was like the ironer was breathing. Like a dragon, it was. And Alberta – that's Alberta Keene – shouted that something was exploding and everyone was running and screaming and Ginny Jason started yelling she was burnt. I started to run away and I fell down. I didn't know I got it worst until then. God forbid it was no worse than it was. That live steam is three hundred degrees.'

'The paper said a steam line let go. What does that mean?'

'The overhead pipe comes down into this kinda flexible line that feeds the machine. George – Mr Stanner – said there must have been a surge from the boiler or something. The line split wide open.'

Hunton could think of nothing else to ask. He was making ready to leave when she said reflectively:

'We never used to have these things on that machine. Only lately. The steam line breaking. That awful, awful accident with Mrs Frawley, God rest her. And little things. Like the day Essie got her dress caught in one of the drive chains. That could have been dangerous if she hadn't ripped it right out. Bolts and things fall off. Oh, Herb Diment – he's the laundry repairman – has had an awful time with it. Sheets get caught in the folder. George says that's because they're using too much bleach in the washers, but it never used to happen. Now the girls hate to work on it. Essie even says there are still little bits of Adelle Frawley caught in it and it's sacrilege or something. Like it had a curse. It's been that way ever since Sherry cut her hand on one of the clamps.'

'Sherry?' Hunton asked.

'Sherry Ouelette. Pretty little thing, just out of high school. Good worker. But clumsy sometimes. You know how young girls are.'

'She cut her hand on something?'

'Nothing strange about *that*. There are clamps to tighten down the feeder belt, see. Sherry was adjusting them so we could do a heavier load and probably dreaming about some boy. She cut her finger and bled all over everything.' Mrs Gillian looked puzzled. 'It wasn't until after that the bolts started falling off. Adelle was . . . you know . . . about a week later. As if the machine had tasted blood and found it liked it. Don't women get funny ideas sometimes, Officer Hinton?'

'Hunton,' he said absently, looking over her head and into space.

Ironically, he had met Mark Jackson in a washateria in the block that separated their houses, and it was there that the cop and the English professor still had their most interesting conversations.

Now they sat side by side in bland plastic chairs, their clothes going round and round behind the glass portholes of the coin-op washers. Jackson's paperback copy of Milton's collected works lay neglected beside him while he listened to Hunton tell Mrs Gillian's story.

When Hunton had finished, Jackson said, 'I asked you once if you thought the mangler might be haunted. I was only half joking. I'll ask you again now.'

'No,' Hunton said uneasily. 'Don't be stupid.'

Jackson watched the turning clothes reflectively. 'Haunted is a bad word. Let's say possessed. There are almost as many spells for casting demons in as there are for casting them out. Frazier's *Golden Bough* is replete with them. Druidic and Aztec lore contain others. Even older ones, back to Egypt. Almost all of them can be reduced to startlingly common denominators. The most common, of course, is the blood of a virgin.' He looked at Hunton, 'Mrs Gillian said the trouble started after this Sherry Ouelette accidentally cut herself.'

'Oh, come on,' Hunton said.

'You have to admit she sounds just the type,' Jackson said.

'I'll run right over to her house,' Hunton said with a small smile. 'I can see it. "Miss Ouelette, I'm Officer John Hunton. I'm investigating an ironer with a bad case of demon possession and would like to know if you're a virgin." Do you think I'd get a chance to say goodbye to Sandra and the kids before they carted me off to the booby hatch?'

'I'd be willing to bet you'll end up saying something just like that,' Jackson said without smiling. 'I'm serious, Johnny. That machine scares the hell out of me and I've never seen it.'

'For the sake of conversation,' Hunton said, 'what are some of the other so-called common denominators?'

Jackson shrugged. 'Hard to say without study. Most Anglo-Saxon hex formulas specify graveyard dirt or the eye of a toad. European spells often mention the hand of glory, which can be interpreted as the actual hand of a dead man or one of the hallucinogenics used in connection with the Witches' Sabbath – usually belladonna or a psilocybin derivative. There could be others.'

'And you think all those things got into the Blue Ribbon ironer? Christ, Mark, I'll bet there isn't any belladonna within a five-hundred-mile radius. Or do you think someone whacked off their Uncle Fred's hand and dropped it in the folder?'

'If seven hundred monkeys typed for seven hundred years—'

'One of them would turn out the works of Shakespeare,' Hunton finished sourly. 'Go to hell. Your turn to go across to the drugstore and get some dimes for the dryers.'

It was very funny how George Stanner lost his arm in the mangler.

Seven o'clock Monday morning the laundry was deserted except for Stanner and Herb Diment, the maintenance man. They were performing the twice-yearly function of greasing the mangler's bearings before the laundry's regular day began at seven-thirty. Diment was at the far end, greasing the four secondaries and thinking of how unpleasant this machine made him feel lately, when the mangler suddenly roared into life.

He had been holding up four of the canvas exit belts to get at the motor beneath and suddenly the belts were running in his hands, ripping the flesh off his palms, dragging him along.

He pulled free with a convulsive jerk seconds before the belts would have carried his hands into the folder.

'What the Christ, George!' he yelled. 'Shut the frigging thing *off*'

George Stanner began to scream.

It was a high, wailing, blood-maddened sound that filled the laundry, echoing off the steel faces of the washers, the grinning mouths of the steam presses, the vacant eyes of the industrial dryers. Stanner drew in a great, whooping gasp of air and screamed again: '*Oh God of Christ I'm caught I'M CAUGHT—*'

The rollers began to produce rising steam. The folder gnashed and thumped. Bearings and motors seemed to cry out with a hidden life of their own.

Diment raced to the other end of the machine.

The first roller was already going a sinister red. Diment made a moaning, gobbling noise in his throat. The mangler howled and thumped and hissed.

A deaf observer might have thought at first that Stanner was merely bent over the machine at an odd angle. Then even a deaf man would have seen the pallid, eye-bulging rictus of his face, mouth twisted open in a continuous scream. The arm was disappearing under the safety bar and beneath the first roller; the fabric of his shirt had torn away at the shoulder seam and his upper arm bulged grotesquely as the blood was pushed steadily backwards.

'Turn if off!' Stanner screamed. There was a snap as his elbow broke.

Diment thumbed the off button.

The mangler continued to hum and growl and turn.

Unbelieving, he slammed the button again and again – nothing. The skin of Stanner's arm had grown shiny and taut. Soon it would split with the pressure the roll was putting on it; and still he was conscious and screaming. Diment had a nightmare cartoon image of a man flattened by a steam-roller, leaving only a shadow.

'Fuses—' Stanner screeched. His head was being pulled down, down, as he was dragged forward.

Diment whirled and ran to the boiler room, Stanner's screams chasing him like lunatic ghosts. The mixed stench of blood and steam rose in the air.

On the left wall were three heavy gray boxes containing all the fuses for the laundry's electricity. Diment yanked them open and began to pull the long, cylindrical fuses like a crazy man, throwing them back over his shoulders. The overhead lights went out; then the air compressor; then the boiler itself, with a huge dying whine.

And still the mangler turned. Stanner's screams had been reduced to bubbly moans.

Diment's eye happened on the fire ax in its glassed-in box. He grabbed it with a small, gagging whimper and ran back. Stanner's arm was gone almost to the shoulder. Within seconds his bent and straining neck would be snapped against the safety bar.

'I can't,' Diment blubbered, holding the ax. 'Jesus, George, I can't, I can't, I—'

The machine was an abattoir now. The folder spat out pieces of shirt sleeve, scraps of flesh, a finger. Stanner gave a huge, whooping scream and Diment swung the ax up and brought it down in the laundry's shadowy lightlessness. Twice. Again.

Stanner fell away, unconscious and blue, blood jetting from the stump just below the shoulder. The mangler sucked what was left into itself . . . and shut down.

Weeping, Diment pulled his belt out of its loops and began to make a tourniquet.

★　★　★

Hunton was talking on the phone with Roger Martin, the inspector. Jackson watched him while he patiently rolled a ball back and forth for three-year-old Patty Hunton to chase.

'He pulled *all* the fuses?' Hunton was asking. 'And the off button just didn't function, huh? . . . Has the ironer been shut down? . . . Good. Great. Huh? . . . No, not official.' Hunton frowned, then looked sideways at Jackson. 'Are you still reminded of that refrigerator, Roger? . . . Yes. Me too, Goodbye.'

He hung up and looked at Jackson. 'Let's go see the girl, Mark.'

She had her own apartment (the hesitant yet proprietary way she showed them in after Hunton had flashed his buzzer made him suspect that she hadn't had it long), and she sat uncomfortably across from them in the carefully decorated, postage-stamp living room.

'I'm Officer Hunton and this is my associate, Mr Jackson. It's about the accident at the laundry.' He felt hugely uncomfortable with this dark, shyly pretty girl.

'Awful,' Sherry Ouelette murmured. 'It's the only place I've ever worked. Mr Gartley is my uncle. I liked it because it let me have this place and my own friends. But now . . . it's so *spooky*.'

'The State Board of Safety has shut the ironer down pending a full investigation,' Hunton said. 'Did you know that?'

'Sure,' She sighed restlessly. 'I don't know what I'm going to do—'

'Miss Ouelette,' Jackson interrupted, 'you had an accident with the ironer, didn't you? Cut your hand on a clamp, I believe?'

'Yes, I cut my finger.' Suddenly her face clouded. 'That was the first thing.' She looked at them woefully. 'Sometimes I feel like the girls don't like me so much any more . . . as if I were to blame.'

'I have to ask you a hard question,' Jackson said slowly. 'A question you won't like. It seems absurdly personal and off the subject, but I can only tell you it is not. Your answers won't ever be marked down in a file or record.'

She looked frightened. 'D–did I do something?'

Jackson smiled and shook his head; she melted. *Thank God for Mark*, Hunton thought.

'I'll add this, though: the answer may help you keep your nice little flat here, get your job back, and make things at the laundry the way they were before.'

'I'd answer anything to have that,' she said.

'Sherry, are you a virgin?'

She looked utterly flabbergasted, utterly shocked, as if a priest had given communion and then slapped her. Then she lifted her head, made a gesture at her neat efficiency apartment, as if asking them how they could believe it might be a place of assignation.

'I'm saving myself for my husband,' she said simply.

Hunton and Jackson looked calmly at each other, and in that tick of a second, Hunton knew that it was all true: a devil had taken over the inanimate steel and cogs and gears of the mangler and had turned it into something with its own life.

'Thank you,' Jackson said quietly.

'What now?' Hunton asked bleakly as they rode back. 'Find a priest to exorcise it?'

Jackson snorted. 'You'd go a far piece to find one that wouldn't hand you a few tracts to read while he phoned the booby hatch. It has to be our play, Johnny.'

'Can we do it?'

'Maybe. The problem is this: We know something is in the mangler. We don't know *what*.' Hunton felt cold, as if touched by a fleshless finger. 'There are a great many demons. Is the one we're dealing with in the circle of Bubastis or Pan? Baal? Or the Christian deity we call Satan? We don't know. If the demon had been deliberately cast, we would have a better chance. But this seems to be a case of random possession.'

Jackson ran his fingers through his hair. 'The blood of a virgin, yes. But that narrows it down hardly at all. We have to be sure, very sure.'

'Why?' Hunton asked bluntly. 'Why not just get a bunch of exorcism formulas together and try them out?'

Jackson's face went cold. 'This isn't cops 'n' robbers, Johnny. For Christ's sake, don't think it is. The rite of exorcism is horribly dangerous. It's like controlled nuclear fission, in a way. We could make a mistake and destroy ourselves. The demon is caught in that piece of machinery. But give it a chance and—'

'It could get out?'

'It would love to get out,' Jackson said grimly. 'And it likes to kill.'

When Jackson came over the following evening, Hunton had sent his wife and daughter to a movie. They had the living room to themselves, and for this Hunton was relieved. He could still barely believe what he had become involved in.

'I cancelled my classes,' Jackson said, 'and spent the day with some of the most god-awful books you can imagine. This afternoon I fed over thirty recipes for calling demons into the tech computer. I've got a number of common elements. Surprisingly few.'

He showed Hunton the list: blood of a virgin, graveyard dirt, hand of glory, bat's blood, night moss, horse's hoof, eye of toad.

There were others, all marked secondary.

'Horse's hoof,' Hunton said thoughtfully. 'Funny—'

'Very common. In fact—'

'Could these things – any of them – be interpreted loosely?' Hunton interrupted.

'If lichens picked at night could be substituted for night moss, for instance?'

'Yes.'

'It's very likely,' Jackson said. 'Magical formulas are often ambiguous and elastic. The black arts have always allowed plenty of room for creativity.'

'Substitute Jell-O for horse's hoof,' Hunton said. 'Very popular in bag lunches. I noticed a little container of it sitting under the ironer's sheet platform on the day the Frawley woman died. Gelatine is made from horses' hooves.'

Jackson nodded. 'Anything else?'

'Bat's blood . . . well, it's a big place. Lots of unlighted nooks and crannies. Bats seem likely, although I doubt if the management would admit to it. One could conceivably have been trapped in the mangler.'

Jackson tipped his head back and knuckled bloodshot eyes. 'It fits . . . it all fits.'

'It does?'

74

'Yes. We can safely rule out the hand of glory, I think. Certainly no one dropped a hand into the ironer *before* Mrs Frawley's death, and belladonna is definitely not indigenous to the area.'

'Graveyard dirt?'

'What do you think?'

'It would have to be a hell of a coincidence,' Hunton said. 'Nearest cemetery is Pleasant Hill, and that's five miles from the Blue Ribbon.'

'Okay,' Jackson said. 'I got the computer operator – who thought I was getting ready for Halloween – to run a positive breakdown of all the primary and secondary elements on the list. Every possible combination. I threw out some two dozen which were completely meaningless. The others fall into fairly clear-cut categories. The elements we've isolated are in one of those.'

'What is it?'

Jackson grinned. 'An easy one. The mythos centers in South America with branches in the Caribbean. Related to voodoo. The literature I've got looks on the deities as strictly bush league, compared to some of the real heavies, like Saddath or He-Who-Cannot-Be-Named. The thing in that machine is going to slink away like the neighborhood bully.'

'How do we do it?'

'Holy water and a smidgen of the Holy Eucharist ought to do it. And we can read some of the Leviticus to it. Strictly Christian white magic.'

'You're sure it's not worse?'

'Don't see how it can be,' Jackson said pensively. 'I don't mind telling you I was worried about that hand of glory. That's very black juju. Strong magic.'

75

'Holy water wouldn't stop it?'

'A demon called up in conjunction with the hand of glory could eat a stack of Bibles for breakfast. We would be in bad trouble messing with something like that at all. Better to pull the goddamn thing apart.'

'Well, are you completely sure—'

'No, but fairly sure. It all fits too well.'

'When?'

'The sooner, the better,' Jackson said. 'How do we get in? Break a window?'

Hunton smiled, reached into his pocket, and dangled a key in front of Jackson's nose.

'Where'd you get that? Gartley?'

'No,' Hunton said. 'From a state inspector named Martin.'

'He knows what we're doing?'

'I think he suspects. He told me a funny story a couple of weeks ago.'

'About the mangler?'

'No,' Hunton said. 'About a refrigerator. Come on.'

Adelle Frawley was dead; sewed together by a patient under-taker, she lay in her coffin. Yet something of her spirit perhaps remained in the machine, and if it did, it cried out. She would have known, could have warned them. She had been prone to indigestion, and for this common ailment she had taken a common stomach tablet called E-Z Gel, purchasable over the counter of any drugstore for seventy-nine cents. The side panel holds a printed warning: People with glaucoma must not take E-Z Gel, because the active ingredient causes an aggravation of that condition. Unfortunately, Adelle Frawley did not have that condition. She might have remembered the day, shortly before Sherry Ouelette cut her hand, that she had dropped a full box of E-Z Gel tablets into the mangler by accident. But she was dead, unaware that the active ingredient which soothed her heartburn was a chemical derivative of belladonna, known quaintly in some European countries as the hand of glory.

There was a sudden ghastly burping noise in the spectral silence of the Blue Ribbon Laundry – a bat fluttered madly for its hole in the insulation above the dryers where it had roosted, wrapping wings around its blind face.

It was a noise almost like a chuckle.

The mangler began to run with a sudden, lurching grind – belts hurrying through the darkness, cogs meeting and meshing and grinding, heavy pulverizing rollers rotating on and on.

It was ready for them.

When Hunton pulled into the parking lot it was shortly after midnight and the moon was hidden behind a raft of moving clouds. He jammed on the brakes and switched off the lights in the same motion; Jackson's forehead almost slammed against the padded dash.

He switched off the ignition and the steady thump–hiss-thump became louder. 'It's the mangler,' he said slowly. 'It's the mangler. Running by itself. In the middle of the night.'

They sat for a moment in silence, feeling the fear crawl up their legs.

Hunton said, 'All right. Let's do it.'

They got out and walked to the building, the sound of the mangler growing louder. As Hunton put the key into the lock of the service door, he thought that the machine *did* sound alive – as if it were breathing in great hot gasps and speaking to itself in hissing, sardonic whispers.

'All of a sudden I'm glad I'm with a cop,' Jackson said. He shifted the brown bag he held from one arm to the other. Inside was a small jelly jar filled with holy water wrapped in waxed paper, and a Gideon Bible.

They stepped inside and Hunton snapped up the light switches by the door. The fluorescents flickered into cold life. At the same instant the mangler shut off.

A membrane of steam hung over its rollers. It waited for them in its new ominous silence.

'God, it's an ugly thing,' Jackson whispered.

'Come on,' Hunton said. 'Before we lose our nerve.'

They walked over to it. The safety bar was in its down position over the belt which fed the machine.

Hunton put out a hand. 'Close enough, Mark. Give me the stuff and tell me what to do.'

'But—'

'No argument.'

Jackson handed him the bag and Hunton put it on the sheet table in front of the machine. He gave Jackson the Bible.

'I'm going to read,' Jackson said. 'When I point at you, sprinkle the holy water on the machine with your fingers. You say: In the name of the Father, and of the Son, and of the Holy Ghost, get thee from this place, thou unclean. Got it?'

'Yes.'

'The second time I point, break the wafer and repeat the incantation again.'

'How will we know if it's working?'

78

'You'll know. The thing is apt to break every window in the place getting out. If it doesn't work the first time, we keep doing it until it does.'

'I'm scared green,' Hunton said.

'As a matter of fact, so am I.'

'If we're wrong about the hand of glory—'

'We're not,' Jackson said. 'Here we go.'

He began. His voice filled the empty laundry with spectral echoes. 'Turnest not thou aside to idols, nor make molten gods for yourself. I am the Lord thy God . . .' The words fell like stones into a silence that had suddenly become filled with a creeping, tomblike cold. The mangler remained still and silent under the flourescents, and to Hunton it still seemed to grin.

'. . . and the land will vomit you out for having defiled it, as it vomited out nations before you.' Jackson looked up, his face strained, and pointed.

Hunton sprinkled holy water across the feeder belt.

There was a sudden, gnashing scream of tortured metal. Smoke rose from the canvas belts where the holy water had touched and took on writhing, red-tinged shapes. The mangler suddenly jerked into life.

'We've got it!' Jackson cried above the rising clamor. 'It's on the run!'

He began to read again, his voice rising over the sound of the machinery. He pointed to Hunton again, and Hunton sprinkled some of the host. As he did so he was suddenly swept with a bone-freezing terror, a sudden vivid feeling that it had gone wrong, that the machine had called their bluff – and was the stronger.

Jackson's voice was still rising, approaching climax.

Sparks began to jump across the arc between the main motor and the secondary; the smell of ozone filled the air, like the copper smell of hot blood. Now the main motor was smoking; the mangler was running at an insane, blurred speed; a finger touched to the central belt would have caused the whole body to be hauled in and turned to a bloody rag in the space of five seconds. The concrete beneath their feet trembled and thrummed.

A main bearing blew with a searing flash of purple light, filling the chill air with the smell of thunderstorms, and still the mangler ran, faster and faster, belts and rollers and cogs moving at a speed that made them seem to blend and merge, change, melt, transmute—

Hunton, who had been standing almost hypnotized, suddenly took a step backward. 'Get away!' he screamed over the blaring racket.

'We've almost got it!' Jackson yelled back. 'Why—'

There was a sudden indescribable ripping noise and a fissure in the concrete floor suddenly raced toward them and past, widening. Chips of ancient cement flew up in a starburst.

Jackson looked at the mangler and screamed.

It was trying to pull itself out of the concrete, like a dinosaur trying to escape a tar pit. And it wasn't precisely an ironer any more. It was still changing, melting. The 550-volt cable fell, spitting blue fire, into the rollers and was chewed away. For a moment two fireballs glared at them like lambent eyes, eyes filled with a great and cold hunger.

Another fault line tore open. The mangler leaned toward them, within an ace of being free of the concrete moorings that held it. It leered at them; the safety bar had slammed up and what Hunton saw was a gaping, hungry mouth filled with steam.

They turned to run and another fissure opened at their feet. Behind them, a great screaming roar as the thing came free. Hunton leaped over, but Jackson stumbled and fell sprawling.

Hunton turned to help and a huge, amorphous shadow fell over him, blocking the fluorescents.

It stood over Jackson, who lay on his back, staring up in a silent rictus of terror – the perfect sacrifice. Hunton had only a confused impression of something black and moving that bulked to a tremendous height above them both, something with glaring electric eyes the size of footballs, an open mouth with a moving canvas tongue.

He ran: Jackson's dying scream followed him.

When Roger Martin finally got out of bed to answer the doorbell, he was still only a third awake; but when Hunton reeled in, shock slapped him fully into the world with a rough hand.

Hunton's eyes bulged madly from his head, and his hands were claws as he scratched at the front of Martin's robe. There was a small oozing cut on his cheek and his face was splashed with dirty gray specks of powdered cement.

His hair had gone dead white.

'Help me . . . for Jesus' sake, help me. Mark is dead. Jackson is dead.'

'Slow down,' Martin said. 'Come in the living room.'

Hunton followed him, making a thick whining noise in this throat, like a dog.

Martin poured him a two-ounce knock of Jim Beam and

Hunton held the glass in both hands, downing the raw liquor in a choked gulp. The glass fell unheeded to the carpet and his hands, like wandering ghosts, sought Martin's lapels again.

'The mangler killed Mark Jackson. It . . . it . . . oh God, it might get out! We can't let it get out! We can't . . . we . . . oh—' He began to scream, a crazy, whooping sound that rose and fell in jagged cycles.

Martin tried to hand him another drink but Hunton knocked it aside. 'We have to burn it,' he said. 'Burn it before it can get out. Oh, what if it gets out? Oh Jesus, what if—' His eyes suddenly flickered, glazed, rolled up to show the whites, and he fell to the carpet in a stonelike faint.

Mrs Martin was in the doorway, clutching her robe to her throat. 'Who is he, Rog? Is he crazy? I thought—' She shuddered.

'I don't think he's crazy.' She was suddenly frightened by the sick shadow of fear on her husband's face. 'God, I hope he came quick enough.'

He turned to the telephone, picked up the receiver, froze.

There was a faint, swelling noise from the east of the house, the way that Hunton had come. A steady, grinding clatter, growing louder. The living-room window stood half open and now Martin caught a dark smell on the breeze. An odor of ozone . . . or blood.

He stood with his hand on the useless telephone as it grew louder, louder, gnashing and fuming, something in the streets that was hot and steaming. The blood stench filled the room.

His hand dropped from the telephone.

It was already out.

HEARTS IN ATLANTIS
('Low Men In Yellow Coats')

Autobiographical in setting if not in event (I also grew up in suburban Connecticut, and my mom and brother and I lived in an apartment house very similar to the one in this story), 'Low Men in Yellow Coats' is the story of a boy's awakening to the fact that adults are often fallible and sometimes cruel beyond belief. With its elements of precognition, first love, and growing friendship between the child protagonist and the mysterious old man upstairs, it almost cried out to be a movie. Would that it had been a better one, especially in light of Anthony Hopkins's excellent performance as a kind of anti-Hannibal Lecter.

But there were shoals, and the film ultimately runs aground on them. The first is the fact that 'Low Men' is only the first part of a loosely constructed novel, which still isn't really done ('The House on Benefit Street,' the story of what happened to Bobby's childhood girlfriend, Carol, remains to be written). The second is 'Low Men's' relationship to the *Dark Tower* books. Although I knew Ted Brautigan's appearance in *Hearts* would be relatively brief, I also knew he had more work to do in the final volume of the Roland Deschain saga.

Without the underlying reason for Ted's fugitive status in

the town of Harwich (which I won't mention here lest I be found guilty of committing the dreaded SPOILER), the movie's motivation first grew thin . . . and then just disappeared. Many of the individual scenes are great, and I love the *spirit* of the thing, but the story works better, and in the end it's always about what works. Don't ever let anybody tell you different.

LOW MEN
IN YELLOW COATS

1960: They had a stick sharpened at both ends.

CHAPTER ONE

A BOY AND HIS MOTHER.
BOBBY'S BIRTHDAY. THE
NEW ROOMER. OF TIME
AND STRANGERS.

Bobby Garfield's father had been one of those fellows who start losing their hair in their twenties and are completely bald by the age of forty-five or so. Randall Garfield was spared this extremity by dying of a heart attack at thirty-six. He was a real-estate agent, and breathed his last on the kitchen floor of someone else's house. The potential buyer was in the living room, trying to call an ambulance on a disconnected phone, when Bobby's dad passed away. At this time Bobby was three. He had vague memories of a man tickling him and then kissing his cheeks and his forehead. He was pretty sure that man had been his dad. SADLY MISSED, it said on Randall Garfield's gravestone, but his mom never seemed all that sad, and as for Bobby himself . . . well, how could you miss a guy you could hardly remember?

Eight years after his father's death, Bobby fell violently in love with the twenty-six-inch Schwinn in the window of the Harwich Western Auto. He hinted to his mother about the Schwinn in every way he knew, and finally pointed it out to her one night when they were walking home from the movies (the show had been *The Dark at the Top of the Stairs*, which Bobby didn't understand but liked anyway, especially the part where Dorothy McGuire flopped back in a chair and showed off her long legs). As they passed the hardware store, Bobby mentioned casually that the bike in the window would sure make a great eleventh-birthday present for some lucky kid.

'Don't even think about it,' she said. 'I can't afford a bike for your birthday. Your father didn't exactly leave us well off, you know.'

Although Randall had been dead ever since Truman was President and now Eisenhower was almost done with his eight-year cruise, *Your father didn't exactly leave us well off* was still his mother's most common response to anything Bobby suggested which might entail an expenditure of more than a dollar. Usually the comment was accompanied by a reproachful look, as if the man had run off rather than died.

No bike for his birthday. Bobby pondered this glumly on their walk home, his pleasure at the strange, muddled movie they had seen mostly gone. He didn't argue with his mother, or try to coax her – that would bring on a counterattack, and when Liz Garfield counterattacked she took no prisoners – but he brooded on the lost bike . . . and the lost father. Sometimes he almost hated his father. Sometimes all that kept him from doing so was the sense, unanchored but very strong, that his mother wanted him to. As they reached Commonwealth Park and walked along the side of it – two blocks up they would turn left onto Broad Street, where they lived – he went against his usual misgivings and asked a question about Randall Garfield.

'Didn't he leave anything, Mom? Anything at all?' A week or two before, he'd read a Nancy Drew mystery where some poor kid's inheritance had been hidden behind an old clock in an abandoned mansion. Bobby didn't really think his father had left gold coins or rare stamps stashed someplace, but if there was *something*, maybe they could sell it in Bridgeport. Possibly at one of the hockshops. Bobby didn't know exactly how hocking things worked, but he knew what the shops looked like – they had three gold balls hanging out front. And he was sure the hockshop guys would be happy to help them. Of course it was just a kid's dream, but Carol Gerber up the street had a whole set of dolls her father, who was in the Navy, had sent from overseas. If fathers *gave* things – which they did – it stood to reason that fathers sometimes *left* things.

When Bobby asked the question, they were passing one of the streetlamps which ran along this side of Commonwealth Park, and Bobby saw his mother's mouth change as it always did when he ventured a question about his late father. The change made him think of a purse she had: when you pulled on the drawstrings, the hole at the top got smaller.

'I'll tell you what he left,' she said as they started up Broad Street Hill. Bobby already wished he hadn't asked, but of course it was too late now. Once you got her started, you couldn't get her stopped, that was the thing. 'He left a life insurance policy which lapsed the year before he died. Little did I know that until he was gone and everyone – including the undertaker – wanted their little piece of what I didn't have. He also left a large stack of unpaid bills, which I have now pretty much taken care of – people have been very understanding of my situation, Mr Biderman in particular, and I'll never say they haven't been.'

All this was old stuff, as boring as it was bitter, but then she told Bobby something new. 'Your father,' she said as they approached the apartment house which stood halfway up Broad Street Hill, 'never met an inside straight he didn't like.'

'What's an inside straight, Mom?'

'Never mind. But I'll tell you one thing, Bobby-O: you don't ever want to let me catch you playing cards for money. I've had enough of that to last me a lifetime.'

Bobby wanted to enquire further, but knew better; more questions were apt to set off a tirade. It occurred to him that perhaps the movie, which had been about unhappy husbands and wives, had upset her in some way he could not, as a mere kid, understand. He would ask his friend John Sullivan about inside straights at school on Monday. Bobby thought it was poker, but wasn't completely sure.

'There are places in Bridgeport that take men's money,' she said as they neared the apartment house where they lived. 'Foolish men go to them. Foolish men make messes, and it's usually the women of the world that have to clean them up later on. Well . . .'

Bobby knew what was coming next; it was his mother's all-time favorite.

'Life isn't fair,' said Liz Garfield as she took out her housekey and prepared to unlock the door of 149 Broad Street in the town of Harwich, Connecticut. It was April of 1960, the night breathed spring perfume, and standing beside her was a skinny boy with his dead father's risky red hair. She hardly ever touched his hair; on the infrequent occasions when she caressed him, it was usually his arm or his cheek which she touched.

'Life isn't fair,' she repeated. She opened the door and they went in.

It was true that his mother had not been treated like a princess, and it was certainly too bad that her husband had expired on a linoleum floor in an empty house at the age of thirty-six, but Bobby sometimes thought that things could have been worse. There might have been two kids instead of just one, for instance. Or three. Hell, even four.

Or suppose she had to work some really hard job to support the two of them? Sully's mom worked at the Tip-Top Bakery downtown, and during the weeks when she had to light the ovens, Sully-John and his two older brothers hardly even saw her. Also Bobby had observed the women who came filing out of the Peerless Shoe Company when the three o'clock whistle blew (he himself got out of school at two-thirty), women who all seemed way too skinny or way too fat, women with pale faces and fingers stained a dreadful old-blood color, women with downcast eyes who carried their work-shoes and -pants in Total Grocery shopping bags. Last fall he'd seen men and women picking apples outside of town when he went to a church fair with Mrs Gerber and Carol and little Ian (who Carol always called Ian-the-Snot). When he asked about them Mrs Gerber said they were migrants, just like some kinds of birds – always on the move, picking whatever crops had just come ripe. Bobby's mother could have been one of those, but she wasn't.

What she *was* was Mr Donald Biderman's secretary at Home Town Real Estate, the company Bobby's dad had been working for when he had his heart attack. Bobby guessed she might first have gotten the job because Donald Biderman liked

Randall and felt sorry for her – widowed with a son barely out of diapers – but she was good at it and worked hard. Quite often she worked late. Bobby had been with his mother and Mr Biderman together on a couple of occasions – the company picnic was the one he remembered most clearly, but there had also been the time Mr Biderman had driven them to the dentist's in Bridgeport when Bobby had gotten a tooth knocked out during a recess game – and the two grownups had a way of looking at each other. Sometimes Mr Biderman called her on the phone at night, and during those conversations she called him Don. But 'Don' was old and Bobby didn't think about him much.

Bobby wasn't exactly sure what his mom did during her days (and her evenings) at the office, but he bet it beat making shoes or picking apples or lighting the Tip-Top Bakery ovens at four-thirty in the morning. Bobby bet it beat those jobs all to heck and gone. Also, when it came to his mom, if you asked about certain stuff you were asking for trouble. If you asked, for instance, how come she could afford three new dresses from Sears, one of them silk, but not three monthly payments of $11.50 on the Schwinn in the Western Auto window (it was red and silver, and just looking at it made Bobby's gut cramp with longing). Ask about stuff like that and you were asking for *real* trouble.

Bobby didn't. He simply set out to earn the price of the bike himself. It would take him until the fall, perhaps even until the winter, and that particular model might be gone from the Western Auto's window by then, but he would keep at it. You had to keep your nose to the grindstone and your shoulder to the wheel. Life wasn't easy, and life wasn't fair.

★ ★ ★

When Bobby's eleventh birthday rolled around on the last Tuesday of April, his mom gave him a small flat package wrapped in silver paper. Inside was an orange library card. An *adult* library card. Goodbye Nancy Drew, Hardy Boys, and Don Winslow of the Navy. Hello to all the rest of it, stories as full of mysterious muddled passion as *The Dark at the Top of the Stairs*. Not to mention bloody daggers in tower rooms. (There were mysteries and tower rooms in the stories about Nancy Drew and the Hardy Boys, but precious little blood and never any passion.)

'Just remember that Mrs Kelton on the desk is a friend of mine,' Mom said. She spoke in her accustomed dry tone of warning, but she was pleased by his pleasure – she could see it. 'If you try to borrow anything racy like *Peyton Place* or *Kings Row*, I'll find out.'

Bobby smiled. He knew she would.

'If it's that other one, Miss Busybody, and she asks what you're doing with an orange card, you tell her to turn it over. I've put written permission over my signature.'

'Thanks, Mom. This is swell.'

She smiled, bent, and put a quick dry swipe of the lips on his cheek, gone almost before it was there. 'I'm glad you're happy. If I get home early enough, we'll go to the Colony for fried clams and ice cream. You'll have to wait for the weekend for your cake; I don't have time to bake until then. Now put on your coat and get moving, sonnyboy. You'll be late for school.'

They went down the stairs and out onto the porch together. There was a Town Taxi at the curb. A man in a poplin jacket was leaning in the passenger window, paying the driver. Behind him was a little cluster of luggage and paper bags, the kind with handles.

'That must be the man who just rented the room on the third floor,' Liz said. Her mouth had done its shrinking trick again. She stood on the top step of the porch, appraising the man's narrow fanny, which poked toward them as he finished his business with the taxi driver. 'I don't trust people who move their things in paper bags. To me a person's things in a paper sack just looks *slutty*.'

'He has suitcases, too,' Bobby said, but he didn't need his mother to point out that the new tenant's three little cases weren't such of a much. None matched; all looked as if they had been kicked here from California by someone in a bad mood.

Bobby and his mom walked down the cement path. The Town Taxi pulled away. The man in the poplin jacket turned around. To Bobby, people fell into three broad categories: kids, grownups, and old folks. Old folks were grownups with white hair. The new tenant was of this third sort. His face was thin and tired-looking, not wrinkled (except around his faded blue eyes) but deeply lined. His white hair was baby-fine and receding from a liverspotted brow. He was tall and stooped-over in a way that made Bobby think of Boris Karloff in the Shock Theater movies they showed Friday nights at 11:30 on WPIX. Beneath the poplin jacket were cheap workingman's clothes that looked too big for him. On his feet were scuffed cordovan shoes.

'Hello, folks,' he said, and smiled with what looked like an effort. 'My name's Theodore Brautigan. I guess I'm going to live here awhile.'

He held out his hand to Bobby's mother, who touched it just briefly. 'I'm Elizabeth Garfield. This is my son, Robert. You'll have to pardon us, Mr Brattigan—'

'It's Brautigan, ma'am, but I'd be happy if you and your boy would just call me Ted.'

'Yes, well, Robert's late for school and I'm late for work. Nice to meet you, Mr Brattigan. Hurry on, Bobby. *Tempus fugit.*'

She began walking downhill toward town; Bobby began walking uphill (and at a slower pace) toward Harwich Elementary, on Asher Avenue. Three or four steps into this journey he stopped and looked back. He felt that his mom had been rude to Mr Brautigan, that she had acted stuck-up. Being stuck-up was the worst of vices in his little circle of friends. Carol loathed a stuck-up person; so did Sully-John. Mr Brautigan would probably be halfway up the walk by now, but if he wasn't, Bobby wanted to give him a smile so he'd know at least one member of the Garfield family wasn't stuck-up.

His mother had also stopped and was also looking back. Not because she wanted another look at Mr Brautigan; that idea never crossed Bobby's mind. No, it was her son she had looked back at. She'd known he was going to turn around before Bobby knew it himself, and at this he felt a sudden darkening in his normally bright nature. She sometimes said it would be a snowy day in Sarasota before Bobby could put one over on her, and he supposed she was right about that. How old did you have to be to put one over on your mother, anyway? Twenty? Thirty? Or did you maybe have to wait until *she* got old and a little chicken-soupy in the head?

Mr Brautigan hadn't started up the walk. He stood at its sidewalk end with a suitcase in each hand and the third one under his right arm (the three paper bags he had moved onto the grass of 149 Broad), more bent than ever under this weight. He was right between them, like a tollgate or something.

Liz Garfield's eyes flew past him to her son's. *Go,* they said. *Don't say a word. He's new, a man from anywhere or nowhere, and he's arrived here with half his things in shopping bags. Don't say a word, Bobby, just go.*

But he wouldn't. Perhaps because he had gotten a library card instead of a bike for his birthday. 'It was nice to meet you, Mr Brautigan,' Bobby said. 'Hope you like it here. Bye.'

'Have a good day at school, son,' Mr Brautigan said. 'Learn a lot. Your mother's right – *tempus fugit.*'

Bobby looked at his mother to see if his small rebellion might be forgiven in light of this equally small flattery, but Mom's mouth was ungiving. She turned and started down the hill without another word. Bobby went on his own way, glad he had spoken to the stranger even if his mother later made him regret it.

As he approached Carol Gerber's house, he took out the orange library card and looked at it. It wasn't a twenty-six-inch Schwinn, but it was still pretty good. Great, actually. A whole world of books to explore, and so what if it had only cost two or three rocks? Didn't they say it was the thought that counted?

Well . . . it was what his *mom* said, anyway.

He turned the card over. Written on the back in her strong hand was this message: '*To whom it may concern: This is my son's library card. He has my permission to take out three books a week from the adult section of the Harwich Public Library.*' It was signed *Elizabeth Penrose Garfield.*

Beneath her name, like a P.S., she had added this: *Robert will be responsible for his own overdue fines.*

'Birthday boy!' Carol Gerber cried, startling him, and rushed out from behind a tree where she had been lying in wait. She threw her arms around his neck and smacked him hard on the cheek. Bobby blushed, looking around to see if anyone was watching – God, it was hard enough to be friends with a girl without surprise kisses – but it was okay. The usual morning flood of students was moving schoolward along Asher Avenue at the top of the hill, but down here they were alone.

Bobby scrubbed at his cheek.

'Come on, you liked it,' she said, laughing.

'Did not,' said Bobby, although he had.

'What'd you get for your birthday?'

'A library card,' Bobby said, and showed her. 'An *adult* library card.'

'Cool!' Was that sympathy he saw in her eyes? Probably not. And so what if it was? 'Here. For you.' She gave him a Hallmark envelope with his name printed on the front. She had also stuck on some hearts and teddy bears.

Bobby opened the envelope with mild trepidation, reminding himself that he could tuck the card deep into the back pocket of his chinos if it was gushy.

It wasn't, though. Maybe a little bit on the baby side (a kid in a Stetson on a horse, HAPPY BIRTHDAY BUCKAROO in letters that were supposed to look like wood on the inside), but not gushy. *Love, Carol* was a little gushy, but of course she was a girl, what could you do?

'Thanks.'

'It's sort of a baby card, I know, but the others were even worse,' Carol said matter-of-factly. A little farther up the hill Sully-John was waiting for them, working his Bo-lo Bouncer for all it was worth, going under his right arm, going under his left arm, going behind his back. He didn't try going between his legs anymore; he'd tried it once in the school-yard and rapped himself a good one in the nuts. Sully had screamed. Bobby and a couple of other kids had laughed until they cried. Carol and three of her girlfriends had rushed over to ask what was wrong, and the boys all said nothing – Sully-John said the same, although he'd been pale and almost crying. *Boys are boogers*, Carol had said on that occasion, but Bobby didn't believe she really thought so. She wouldn't have jumped out and given him that kiss if she did, and it had been a good kiss, a smackeroo. Better than the one his mother had given him, actually.

'It's not a baby card,' he said.

'No, but it *almost* is,' she said. 'I thought about getting you a grownup card, but man, they *are* gushy.'

'I know,' Bobby said.

'Are you going to be a gushy adult, Bobby?'

'I hope not,' he said. 'Are you?'

'No. I'm going to be like my mom's friend Rionda.'

'Rionda's pretty fat,' Bobby said doubtfully.

'Yeah, but she's cool. I'm going to go for the cool without the fat.'

'There's a new guy moving into our building. The room on the third floor. My mom says it's really hot up there.'

'Yeah? What's he like?' She giggled. 'Is he ushy-gushy?'

'He's old,' Bobby said, then paused to think. 'But he had an interesting face. My mom didn't like him on sight because he had some of his stuff in shopping bags.'

Sully-John joined them. 'Happy birthday, you bastard,' he said, and clapped Bobby on the back. *Bastard* was Sully-John's current favorite word; Carol's was *cool*; Bobby was currently between favorite words, although he thought *ripshit* had a certain ring to it.

'If you swear, I won't walk with you,' Carol said.

'Okay,' Sully-John said companionably. Carol was a fluffy blonde who looked like a Bobbsey Twin after some growing up; John Sullivan was tall, black-haired, and green-eyed. A Joe Hardy kind of boy. Bobby Garfield walked between them, his momentary depression forgotten. It was his birthday and he was with his friends and life was good. He tucked Carol's birthday card into his back pocket and his new library card down deep in his front pocket, where it could not fall out or be stolen. Carol started to skip. Sully-John told her to stop.

'Why?' Carol asked. 'I *like* to skip.'

'I like to say *bastard*, but I don't if you ask me,' Sully-John replied reasonably.

Carol looked at Bobby.

'Skipping – at least without a rope – is a little on the baby side, Carol,' Bobby said apologetically, then shrugged. 'But you can if you want. We don't mind, do we, S-J?'

'Nope,' Sully-John said, and got going with the Bo-lo Bouncer again. Back to front, up to down, whap-whap-whap.

Carol didn't skip. She walked between them and pretended she was Bobby Garfield's girlfriend, that Bobby had a driver's license and a Buick and they were going to Bridgeport to see the WKBW Rock and Roll Extravaganza. She thought Bobby was extremely cool. The coolest thing about him was that he didn't know it.

Bobby got home from school at three o'clock. He could have been there sooner, but picking up returnable bottles was part of his Get-a-Bike-by-Thanksgiving campaign, and he detoured through the brushy area just off Asher Avenue looking for them. He found three Rheingolds and a Nehi. Not much, but hey, eight cents was eight cents. 'It all mounts up' was another of his mom's sayings.

Bobby washed his hands (a couple of those bottles had been pretty scurgy), got a snack out of the icebox, read a couple of old *Superman* comics, got another snack out of the icebox, then watched *American Bandstand*. He called Carol to tell her Bobby Darin was going to be on – she thought Bobby Darin was deeply cool, especially the way he snapped his fingers when he sang 'Queen of the Hop' – but she already knew. She was watching with three or four of her numbskull girlfriends; they all giggled pretty much nonstop in the background. The sound made Bobby think of birds in a petshop. On TV, Dick Clark was currently showing how much pimple-grease *just one* Stri-Dex Medicated Pad could sop up.

Mom called at four o'clock. Mr Biderman needed her to work late, she said. She was sorry, but birthday supper at the Colony was off. There was leftover beef stew in the fridge; he could have that and she would be home by eight to tuck him in. And for heaven's sake, Bobby, remember to turn off the gas-ring when you're done with the stove.

Bobby returned to the television feeling disappointed but not really surprised. On *Bandstand*, Dick was now announcing the Rate-a-Record panel. Bobby thought the guy in the middle looked as if he could use a lifetime supply of Stri-Dex pads.

He reached into his front pocket and drew out the new orange library card. His mood began to brighten again. He didn't need to sit here in front of the TV with a stack of old comic-books if he didn't want to. He could go down to the library and break in his new card – his new *adult* card. Miss Busybody would be on the desk, only her real name was Miss Harrington and Bobby thought she was beautiful. She wore perfume. He could always smell it on her skin and in her hair, faint and sweet, like a good memory. And although Sully-John would be at his trombone lesson right now, after the library Bobby could go up his house, maybe play some pass.

Also, he thought, *I can take those bottles to Spicer's – I've got a bike to earn this summer.*

All at once, life seemed very full.

Sully's mom invited Bobby to stay for supper, but he told her no thanks, I better get home. He would much have preferred Mrs Sullivan's pot roast and crispy oven potatoes to what was waiting for him back at the apartment, but he knew that one of the first things his mother would do when she got back from the office was check in the fridge and see if the Tupperware with the leftover stew inside was gone. If it wasn't, she would ask Bobby what he'd had for supper. She would be calm about this question, even offhand. If he told her he'd eaten at Sully-John's she would nod, ask him what they'd had and if there had been dessert, also if he'd thanked Mrs Sullivan; she might even sit on the couch with him and share a bowl of ice cream while they watched *Sugarfoot* on TV. Everything would be fine . . . except it wouldn't be. Eventually there would be a payback. It might not come for a day or two, even a week, but it *would* come. Bobby knew that almost without knowing he knew it. She undoubtedly *did* have to work late, but eating leftover stew by himself on his birthday was also punishment for talking to the new tenant when he wasn't supposed to. If he tried to duck that punishment, it would mount up just like money in a savings account.

When Bobby came back from Sully-John's it was quarter past six and getting dark. He had two new books to read, a Perry Mason called *The Case of the Velvet Claws* and a science-fiction novel by Clifford Simak called *Ring Around the Sun*. Both looked totally ripshit, and Miss Harrington hadn't given him a hard time at all. On the contrary: she told him he was reading above his level and to keep it up.

Walking home from S-J's, Bobby made up a story where he and Miss Harrington were on a cruise-boat that sank. They were the only two survivors, saved from drowning by finding a life preserver marked SS *LUSITANIC*. They washed up on a little island with palm trees and jungles and a volcano, and as they lay on the beach Miss Harrington was shivering and saying she was cold, so cold, couldn't he please hold her and warm her up, which he of course could and did, my pleasure, Miss Harrington, and then the natives came out of the jungle and at first they seemed friendly but it turned out they were cannibals who lived on the slopes of the volcano and killed their victims in a clearing ringed with skulls, so things looked bad but just as he and Miss Harrington were pulled toward the cooking pot the volcano started to rumble and—

'Hello, Robert.'

Bobby looked up, even more startled than he'd been when Carol Gerber raced out from behind the tree to put a birthday smackeroo on his cheek. It was the new man in the house. He was sitting on the top porch step and smoking a cigarette. He had exchanged his old scuffed shoes for a pair of old scuffed slippers and had taken off his poplin jacket – the evening was warm. He looked at home, Bobby thought.

'Oh, Mr Brautigan. Hi.'

'I didn't mean to startle you.'

'You didn't—'

'I think I did. You were a thousand miles away. And it's Ted. Please.'

'Okay.' But Bobby didn't know if he could stick to Ted. Calling a grownup (especially an *old* grownup) by his first name went against not only his mother's teaching but his own inclination.

'Was school good? You learned new things?'

'Yeah, fine.' Bobby shifted from foot to foot; swapped his new books from hand to hand.

'Would you sit with me a minute?'

'Sure, but I can't for long. Stuff to do, you know.' Supper to do, mostly – the leftover stew had grown quite attractive in his mind by now.

'Absolutely. Things to do and *tempus fugit.*'

As Bobby sat down next to Mr Brautigan – Ted – on the wide porch step, smelling the aroma of his Chesterfield, he thought he had never seen a man who looked as tired as this one. It couldn't be the moving in, could it? How worn out could you get when all you had to move in was three little suitcases and three carryhandle shopping bags? Bobby supposed there might be men coming later on with stuff in a truck, but he didn't really think so. It was just a room – a big one, but still just a single room with a kitchen on one side and everything else on the other. He and Sully-John had gone up there and looked around after old Miss Sidley had her stroke and went to live with her daughter.

'*Tempus fugit* means time flies,' Bobby said. 'Mom says it a lot. She also says time and tide wait for no man and time heals all wounds.'

'Your mother is a woman of many sayings, is she?'

'Yeah,' Bobby said, and suddenly the idea of all those sayings made him tired. 'Many sayings.'

'Ben Jonson called time the old bald cheater,' Ted Brautigan said, drawing deeply on his cigarette and then exhaling twin streams through his nose. 'And Boris Pasternak said we are time's captives, the hostages of eternity.'

Bobby looked at him in fascination, his empty belly temporarily forgotten. He loved the idea of time as an old bald cheater – it was absolutely and completely right, although he couldn't have said why . . . and didn't that very inability to say why somehow add to the coolness? It was like a thing inside an egg, or a shadow behind pebbled glass.

'Who's Ben Jonson?'

'An Englishman, dead these many years,' Mr Brautigan said. 'Self-centered and foolish about money, by all accounts; prone to flatulence as well. But—'

'What's that? Flatulence?'

Ted stuck his tongue between his lips and made a brief but very realistic farting sound. Bobby put his hands to his mouth and giggled into his cupped fingers.

'Kids think farts are funny,' Ted Brautigan said, nodding. 'Yeah. To a man my age, though, they're just part of life's increasingly strange business. Ben Jonson said a good many wise things between farts, by the way. Not so many as *Dr* Johnson – Samuel Johnson, that would be – but still a good many.'

'And Boris . . .'

'Pasternak. A Russian,' Mr Brautigan said dismissively. 'Of no account, I think. May I see your books?'

Bobby handed them over. Mr Brautigan (*Ted*, he reminded himself, *you're supposed to call him Ted*) passed the Perry Mason back after a cursory glance at the title. The Clifford Simak novel he held longer, at first squinting at the cover through the curls of cigarette smoke that rose past his eyes, then paging through it. He nodded as he did so.

'I have read this one,' he said. 'I had a lot of time to read previous to coming here.'

'Yeah?' Bobby kindled. 'Is it good?'

'One of his best,' Mr Brautigan – Ted – replied. He looked sideways at Bobby, one eye open, the other still squinted shut against the smoke. It gave him a look that was at once wise and mysterious, like a not-quite-trustworthy character in a detective movie. 'But are you sure you can read this? You can't be much more than twelve.'

'I'm eleven,' Bobby said. He was delighted that Ted thought he might be as old as twelve. 'Eleven today. I can read it. I won't be able to understand it all, but if it's a good story, I'll like it.'

'Your birthday!' Ted said, looking impressed. He took a final drag on his cigarette, then flicked it away. It hit the cement walk and fountained sparks. 'Happy birthday, dear Robert, happy birthday to you!'

'Thanks. Only I like Bobby a lot better.'

'Bobby, then. Are you going out to celebrate?'

'Nah, my mom's got to work late.'

'Would you like to come up to my little place? I don't have much, but I know how to open a can. Also, I might have a pastry—'

'Thanks, but Mom left me some stuff. I should eat that.'

'I understand.' And, wonder of wonders, he looked as if he actually did. Ted returned Bobby's copy of *Ring Around the Sun*. 'In this book,' he said, 'Mr Simak postulates the idea that there are a number of worlds like ours. Not other planets but other Earths, *parallel* Earths, in a kind of ring around the sun. A fascinating idea.'

'Yeah,' Bobby said. He knew about parallel worlds from other books. From the comics, as well.

Ted Brautigan was now looking at him in a thoughtful, speculative way.

'What?' Bobby asked, feeling suddenly self-conscious. *See something green?* his mother might have said.

For a moment he thought Ted wasn't going to answer — he seemed to have fallen into some deep and dazing train of thought. Then he gave himself a little shake and sat up straighter. 'Nothing,' he said. 'I have a little idea. Perhaps you'd like to earn some extra money? Not that I have much, but—'

'Yeah! Cripes, yeah!' *There's this bike*, he almost went on, then stopped himself. *Best keep yourself to yourself* was yet another of his mom's sayings. 'I'd do just about anything you wanted!'

Ted Brautigan looked simultaneously alarmed and amused. It seemed to open a door to a different face, somehow, and Bobby could see that, yeah, the old guy had once been a young guy. One with a little sass to him, maybe. 'That's a bad thing to tell a stranger,' he said, 'and although we've progressed to Bobby and Ted — a good start — we're still really strangers to each other.'

'Did either of those Johnson guys say anything about strangers?'

'Not that I recall, but here's something on the subject from the Bible: "For I am a stranger with thee, and a sojourner. Spare me, that I may recover strength, before I go hence . . ."' Ted trailed off for a moment. The fun had gone out of his face and he looked old again. Then his voice firmed and he finished. '". . . before I go hence, and be no more." Book of Psalms. I can't remember which one.'

'Well,' Bobby said, 'I wouldn't kill or rob anyone, don't worry, but I'd sure like to earn some money.'

'Let me think,' Ted said. 'Let me think a little.'

'Sure. But if you've got chores or something, I'm your guy. Tell you that right now.'

'Chores? Maybe. Although that's not the word I would have chosen.' Ted clasped his bony arms around his even bonier knees and gazed across the lawn at Broad Street. It was growing dark now; Bobby's favorite part of the evening had arrived. The cars that passed had their parking lights on, and from somewhere on Asher Avenue Mrs Sigsby was calling for her twins to come in and get their supper. At this time of day – and at dawn, as he stood in the bathroom, urinating into the bowl with sunshine falling through the little window and into his half-open eyes – Bobby felt like a dream in someone else's head.

'Where did you live before you came here, Mr . . . Ted?'

'A place that wasn't as nice,' he said. 'Nowhere near as nice. How long have *you* lived here, Bobby?'

'Long as I can remember. Since my dad died, when I was three.'

'And you know everyone on the street? On this block of the street, anyway?'

'Pretty much, yeah.'

'You'd know strangers. Sojourners. Faces of those unknown.'

Bobby smiled and nodded. 'Uh-huh, I think so.'

He waited to see where this would lead next – it was interesting – but apparently this was as far as it went. Ted stood up, slowly and carefully. Bobby could hear little bones creak in his back when he put his hands around there and stretched, grimacing.

'Come on,' he said. 'It's getting chilly. I'll go in with you. Your key or mine?'

Bobby smiled. 'You better start breaking in your own, don't you think?'

Ted – it was getting easier to think of him as Ted – pulled a keyring from his pocket. The only keys on it were the one which opened the big front door and the one to his room. Both were shiny and new, the color of bandit gold. Bobby's own two keys were scratched and dull. How old was Ted? he wondered again. Sixty, at least. A sixty-year-old man with only two keys in his pocket. That was weird.

Ted opened the front door and they went into the big dark foyer with its umbrella stand and its old painting of Lewis and Clark looking out across the American West. Bobby went to the door of the Garfield apartment and Ted went to the stairs. He paused there for a moment with his hand on the bannister. 'The Simak book is a great story,' he said. 'Not such great writing, though. Not bad, I don't mean to say that, but take it from me, there is better.'

Bobby waited.

'There are also books full of great writing that don't have very good stories. Read sometimes for the story, Bobby. Don't be like the book-snobs who won't do that. Read sometimes for the words – the language. Don't be like the play-it-safers that won't do *that*. But when you find a book that has both a good story and good words, treasure that book.'

'Are there many of those, do you think?' Bobby asked.

'More than the book-snobs and play-it-safers think. Many more. Perhaps I'll give you one. A belated birthday present.'

'You don't have to do that.'

'No, but perhaps I will. And do have a happy birthday.'

'Thanks. It's been a great one.' Then Bobby went into the apartment, heated up the stew (remembering to turn off the gas-ring after the stew started to bubble, also remembering to put the pan in the sink to soak), and ate supper by himself, reading *Ring Around the Sun* with the TV on for company. He hardly heard Chet Huntley and David Brinkley gabbling the evening news. Ted was right about the book; it was a corker. The words seemed okay to him, too, although he supposed he didn't have a lot of experience just yet.

I'd like to write a story like this, he thought as he finally closed the book and flopped down on the couch to watch *Sugarfoot. I wonder if I ever could?*

Maybe. Maybe so. *Someone* had to write stories, after all, just like someone had to fix the pipes when they froze or change the streetlights in Commonwealth Park when they burned out.

An hour or so later, after Bobby had picked up *Ring Around the Sun* and begun reading again, his mother came in. Her lipstick was a bit smeared at one corner of her mouth and her slip was hanging a little. Bobby thought of pointing this out to her, then remembered how much she disliked it when someone told her it was 'snowing down south.' Besides, what did it matter? Her working day was over and, as she sometimes said, there was no one here but us chickens.

She checked the fridge to make sure the leftover stew was gone, checked the stove to make sure the gas-ring was off, checked the sink to make sure the pot and the Tupperware storage container were both soaking in soapy water. Then she kissed him on the temple, just a brush in passing, and went into her bedroom to change out of her office dress and hose. She seemed distant, preoccupied. She didn't ask if he'd had a happy birthday.

Later on he showed her Carol's card. His mom glanced at it, not really seeing it, pronounced it 'cute,' and handed it back. Then she told him to wash up, brush up, and go to bed. Bobby did so, not mentioning his interesting talk with Ted. In her current mood that was apt to make her angry. The best thing was to let her be distant, let her keep to herself as long as she needed to, give her time to drift back to him. Yet he felt that sad mood settling over him again as he finished brushing his teeth and climbed into bed. Sometimes he felt almost hungry for her, and she didn't know.

He reached out of bed and closed the door, blocking off the sound of some old movie. He turned off the light. And then, just as he was starting to drift off, she came in, sat on the side of his bed, and said she was sorry she'd been so stand-offy tonight, but there had been a lot going on at the office and she was tired. Sometimes it was a madhouse, she said. She stroked a finger across his forehead and then kissed him there, making him shiver. He sat up and hugged her. She stiffened momentarily at his touch, then gave in to it. She even hugged him back briefly. He thought maybe it would now be all right to tell her about Ted. A little, anyway.

'I talked with Mr Brautigan when I came home from the library,' he said.

'Who?'

'The new man on the third floor. He asked me to call him Ted.'

'You won't – I should say nitzy! You don't know him from Adam.'

'He said giving a kid an adult library card was a great present.' Ted had said no such thing, but Bobby had lived with his mother long enough to know what worked and what didn't.

She relaxed a little. 'Did he say where he came from?'

'A place not as nice as here, I think he said.'

'Well, that doesn't tell us much, does it?' Bobby was still hugging her. He could have hugged her for another hour easily, smelling her White Rain shampoo and Aqua-Net hold-spray and the pleasant odor of tobacco on her breath, but she disengaged from him and laid him back down. 'I guess if he's going to be your friend – your *adult* friend – I'll have to get to know him a little.'

'Well—'

'Maybe I'll like him better when he doesn't have shopping bags scattered all over the lawn.' For Liz Garfield this was downright placatory, and Bobby was satisfied. The day had come to a very acceptable ending after all. 'Goodnight, birthday boy.'

'Goodnight, Mom.'

She went out and closed the door. Later that night – much later – he thought he heard her crying in her room, but perhaps that was only a dream.

CHAPTER TWO

DOUBTS ABOUT TED. BOOKS ARE LIKE PUMPS. DON'T EVEN THINK ABOUT IT. SULLY WINS A PRIZE. BOBBY GETS A JOB. SIGNS OF THE LOW MEN.

During the next few weeks, as the weather warmed toward summer, Ted was usually on the porch smoking when Liz came home from work. Sometimes he was alone and sometimes Bobby was sitting with him, talking about books. Sometimes Carol and Sully-John were there, too, the three kids playing pass on the lawn while Ted smoked and watched them throw. Sometimes other kids came by – Denny Rivers with a taped-up balsa glider to throw, soft-headed Francis Utterson, always pushing along on his scooter with one overdeveloped leg, Angela Avery and Yvonne Loving to ask Carol if she wanted to go over Yvonne's and play dolls or a game called Hospital Nurse – but mostly it was just S-J and Carol, Bobby's special friends. All the kids called Mr Brautigan Ted, but when Bobby explained why it would be better if they called him Mr Brautigan when his mom was around, Ted agreed at once.

As for his mom, she couldn't seem to get *Brautigan* to come out of her mouth. What emerged was always *Brattigan*. That might not have been on purpose, however; Bobby was starting to feel a cautious sense of relief about his mother's view of Ted. He had been afraid that she might feel about Ted as she had about Mrs Evers, his second-grade teacher. Mom had disliked Mrs Evers on sight, disliked her *deeply*, for no reason at all Bobby could see or understand, and hadn't had a good word to say about her all year long – Mrs Evers dressed like a frump, Mrs Evers dyed her hair, Mrs Evers wore too much makeup, Bobby had just better tell Mom if Mrs Evers laid so much as *one finger* on him, because she looked like the kind of woman who would like to pinch and poke. All of this following a single parent–teacher conference in which Mrs Evers had told Liz that Bobby was doing well in all his subjects. There had been four other parent–teacher conferences that year, and Bobby's mother had found reasons to duck every single one.

Liz's opinions of people hardened swiftly; when she wrote BAD under her mental picture of you, she almost always wrote in ink. If Mrs Evers had saved six kids from a burning schoolbus, Liz Garfield might well have sniffed and said they probably owed the pop-eyed old cow two weeks' worth of milk-money.

Ted made every effort to be nice without actually sucking up to her (people *did* suck up to his mother, Bobby knew; hell, sometimes he did it himself), and it worked . . . but only to a degree. On one occasion Ted and Bobby's mom had talked for almost ten minutes about how awful it was that the Dodgers had moved to the other side of the country without so much as a faretheewell, but not even both of them being Ebbets Field Dodger fans could strike a real spark between them. They were never going to be pals. Mom didn't dislike Ted Brautigan the way she had disliked Mrs Evers, but there was still something wrong. Bobby supposed he knew what it was; he had seen it in her eyes on the morning the new tenant had moved in. Liz didn't trust him.

Nor, it turned out, did Carol Gerber. 'Sometimes I wonder if he's on the run from something,' she said one evening as she and Bobby and S-J walked up the hill toward Asher Avenue.

They had been playing pass for an hour or so, talking off and on with Ted as they did, and were now heading to Moon's Roadside Happiness for ice cream cones. S-J had thirty cents and was treating. He also had his Bo-lo Bouncer, which he now took out of his back pocket. Pretty soon he had it going up and down and all around, whap-whap-whap.

'On the run? Are you kidding?' Bobby was startled by the idea. Yet Carol was sharp about people; even his mother had noticed it. *That girl's no beauty, but she doesn't miss much*, she'd said one night.

'"Stick em up, McGarrigle!"' Sully-John cried. He tucked his Bo-lo Bouncer under his arm, dropped into a crouch, and fired an invisible tommygun, yanking down the right side of his mouth so he could make the proper sound to go with it, a kind of *eh-eh-eh* from deep in his throat. '"You'll never take me alive, copper! Blast em, Muggsy! Nobody runs out on Rico! *Ah, jeez, they got me!*"' S-J clutched his chest, spun around, and fell dead on Mrs Conlan's lawn.

That lady, a grumpy old rhymes-with-witch of seventy-five or so, cried: 'Boy! *Youuu*, boy! Get off there! You'll mash my flowers!'

There wasn't a flowerbed within ten feet of where Sully-John had fallen, but he leaped up at once. 'Sorry, Mrs Conlan.'

She flapped a hand at him, dismissing his apology without a word, and watched closely as the children went on their way.

'You don't really mean it, do you?' Bobby asked Carol. 'About Ted?'

'No,' she said, 'I guess not. But . . . have you ever watched him watch the street?'

'Yeah. It's like he's looking for someone, isn't it?'

'Or looking *out* for them,' Carol replied.

Sully-John resumed Bo-lo Bouncing. Pretty soon the red rubber ball was blurring back and forth again. Sully paused only when they passed the Asher Empire, where two Brigitte Bardot movies were playing, Adults Only, Must Have Driver's License or Birth Certificate, No Exceptions. One of the pictures was new; the other was that old standby *And God Created Woman*, which kept coming back to the Empire like a bad cough. On the posters, Brigitte was dressed in nothing but a towel and a smile.

'My mom says she's trashy,' Carol said.

'If she's trash, I'd love to be the trashman,' S-J said, and wiggled his eyebrows like Groucho.

'Do *you* think she's trashy?' Bobby asked Carol.

'I'm not sure what that means, even.'

As they passed out from under the marquee (from within her glass ticket-booth beside the doors, Mrs Godlow – known to the neighborhood kids as Mrs Godzilla – watched them suspiciously), Carol looked back over her shoulder at Brigitte Bardot in her towel. Her expression was hard to read. Curiosity? Bobby couldn't tell. 'But she's pretty, isn't she?'

'Yeah, I guess.'

'And you'd have to be brave to let people look at you with nothing on but a towel. That's what I think, anyway.'

Sully-John had no interest in *la femme Brigitte* now that she was behind them. 'Where'd Ted come from, Bobby?'

'I don't know. He never talks about that.'

Sully-John nodded as if he expected just that answer, and threw his Bo-lo Bouncer back into gear. Up and down, all around, whap-whap-whap.

In May Bobby's thoughts began turning to summer vacation. There was really nothing in the world better than what Sully called 'the Big Vac.' He would spend long hours goofing with his friends, both on Broad Street and down at Sterling House on the other side of the park — they had lots of good things to do in the summer at Sterling House, including baseball and weekly trips to Patagonia Beach in West Haven — and he would also have plenty of time for himself. Time to read, of course, but what he really wanted to do with some of that time was find a part-time job. He had a little over seven rocks in a jar marked BIKE FUND, and seven rocks was a start . . . but not what you'd call a *great* start. At this rate Nixon would have been President two years before he was riding to school.

On one of these vacation's-almost-here days, Ted gave him a paperback book. 'Remember I told you that some books have both a good story and good writing?' he asked. 'This is one of that breed. A belated birthday present from a new friend. At least, I hope I am your friend.'

'You are. Thanks a lot!' In spite of the enthusiasm in his voice, Bobby took the book a little doubtfully. He was accustomed to pocket books with bright, raucous covers and sexy come-on lines ('She hit the gutter . . . AND BOUNCED LOWER!'); this one had neither. The cover was mostly white. In one corner of it was sketched – *barely* sketched – a group of boys standing in a circle. The name of the book was *Lord of the Flies*. There was no come-on line above the title, not even a discreet one like 'A story you will never forget.' All in all, it had a forbidding, un-welcoming look, suggesting that the story lying beneath the cover would be hard. Bobby had nothing in particular against hard books, as long as they were a part of one's schoolwork. His view about reading for pleasure, however, was that such stories should be easy – that the writer should do everything except move your eyes back and forth for you. If not, how much pleasure could there be in it?

He started to turn the book over. Ted gently put his hand on Bobby's, stopping him. 'Don't,' he said. 'As a personal favor to me, don't.'

Bobby looked at him, not understanding.

'Come to the book as you would come to an unexplored land. Come without a map. Explore it and draw your own map.'

'But what if I don't like it?'

Ted shrugged. 'Then don't finish it. A book is like a pump. It gives nothing unless first you give to it. You prime a pump with your own water, you work the handle with your own strength. You do this because you expect to get back more than you give . . . eventually. Do you go along with that?'

Bobby nodded.

'How long would you prime a water-pump and flail the handle if nothing came out?'

'Not too long, I guess.'

'This book is two hundred pages, give or take. You read the first ten per cent — twenty pages, that is, I know already your math isn't as good as your reading — and if you don't like it by then, if it isn't giving more than it's taking by then, put it aside.'

'I wish they'd let you do that in school,' Bobby said. He was thinking of a poem by Ralph Waldo Emerson which they were supposed to memorize. 'By the rude bridge that arched the flood,' it started. S-J called the poet Ralph Waldo Emerslop.

'School is different.' They were sitting at Ted's kitchen table, looking out over the back yard, where everything was in bloom. On Colony Street, which was the next street over, Mrs O'Hara's dog Bowser barked its endless *roop-roop-roop* into the mild spring air. Ted was smoking a Chesterfield. 'And speaking of school, don't take this book there with you. There are things in it your teacher might not want you to read. There could be a brouhaha.'

'A *what*?'

'An uproar. And if you get in trouble at school, you get in trouble at home — this I'm sure you don't need me to tell you. And your mother . . .' The hand not holding the cigarette made a little seesawing gesture which Bobby understood at once. *Your mother doesn't trust me.*

Bobby thought of Carol saying that maybe Ted was on the run from something, and remembered his mother saying Carol didn't miss much.

'What's in it that could get me in trouble?' He looked at *Lord of the Flies* with new fascination.

'Nothing to froth at the mouth about,' Ted said dryly. He

118

crushed his cigarette out in a tin ashtray, went to his little refrigerator, and took out two bottles of pop. There was no beer or wine in there, just pop and a glass bottle of cream. 'Some talk of putting a spear up a wild pig's ass, I think that's the worst. Still, there is a certain kind of grownup who can only see the trees and never the forest. Read the first twenty pages, Bobby. You'll never look back. This I promise you.'

Ted set the pop down on the table and lifted the caps with his churchkey. Then he lifted his bottle and clinked it against Bobby's. 'To your new friends on the island.'

'What island?'

Ted Brautigan smiled and shot the last cigarette out of a crumpled pack. 'You'll find out,' he said.

Bobby did find out, and it didn't take him twenty pages to also find out that *Lord of the Flies* was a hell of a book, maybe the best he'd ever read. Ten pages into it he was captivated; twenty pages and he was lost. He lived on the island with Ralph and Jack and Piggy and the littluns; he trembled at the Beast that turned out to be a rotting airplane pilot caught in his parachute; he watched first in dismay and then in horror as a bunch of harmless schoolboys descended into savagery, finally setting out to hunt down the only one of their number who had managed to remain halfway human.

He finished the book one Saturday the week before school ended for the year. When noon came and Bobby was still in his room – no friends over to play, no Saturday-morning cartoons, not even Merrie Melodies from ten to eleven – his mom looked in on him and told him to get off his bed, get his nose out of that book, and go on down to the park or something.

119

'Where's Sully?' she asked.

'Dalhouse Square. There's a school band concert.' Bobby looked at his mother in the doorway and the ordinary stuff around her with dazed, perplexed eyes. The world of the story had become so vivid to him that this real one now seemed false and drab.

'What about your girlfriend? Take her down to the park with you.'

'Carol's not my girlfriend, Mom.'

'Well, whatever she is. Goodness sakes, Bobby, I wasn't suggesting the two of you were going to run off and elope.'

'She and some other girls slept over Angie's house last night. Carol says when they sleep over they stay up and hen-party practically all night long. I bet they're still in bed, or eating breakfast for lunch.'

'Then go to the park by yourself. You're making me nervous. With the TV off on Saturday morning I keep thinking you're dead.' She came into his room and plucked the book out of his hands. Bobby watched with a kind of numb fascination as she thumbed through the pages, reading random snatches here and there. Suppose she spotted the part where the boys talked about sticking their spears up the wild pig's ass (only they were English and said 'arse,' which sounded even dirtier to Bobby)? What would she make of it? He didn't know. All his life they had lived together, it had been just the two of them for most of it, and he still couldn't predict how she'd react to any given situation.

'Is this the one Brattigan gave you?'

'Yeah.'

'As a birthday present?'

'Yeah.'

'What's it about?'

'Boys marooned on an island. Their ship gets sunk. I think it's supposed to be after World War II or something. The guy who wrote it never says for sure.'

'So it's science fiction.'

'Yeah,' Bobby said. He felt a little giddy. He thought *Lord of the Flies* was about as far from *Ring Around the Sun* as you could get, but his mom hated science fiction, and if anything would stop her potentially dangerous thumbing, that would.

She handed the book back and walked over to his window. 'Bobby?' Not looking back at him, at least not at first. She was wearing an old shirt and her Saturday pants. The bright noonlight shone through the shirt; he could see her sides and noticed for the first time how thin she was, as if she was forgetting to eat or something. 'What, Mom?'

'Has Mr Brattigan given you any other presents?'

'It's *Brautigan*, Mom.'

She frowned at her reflection in the window . . . or more likely it was his reflection she was frowning at. 'Don't correct me, Bobby-O. Has he?'

Bobby considered. A few rootbeers, sometimes a tuna sandwich or a cruller from the bakery where Sully's mom worked, but no presents. Just the book, which was one of the best presents he had ever gotten. 'Jeepers, no, why would he?'

'I don't know. But then, I don't know why a man you just met would give you a birthday present in the first place.' She sighed, folded her arms under her small sharp breasts, and went on looking out Bobby's window. 'He told me he used to work in a state job up in Hartford but now he's retired. Is that what he told you?'

'Something like that.' In fact, Ted had never told Bobby

121

anything about his working life, and asking had never crossed Bobby's mind.

'What kind of state job? What department? Health and Welfare? Transportation? Office of the Comptroller?'

Bobby shook his head. What in heck was a comptroller?

'I bet it was education,' she said meditatively. 'He talks like someone who used to be a teacher. Doesn't he?'

'Sort of, yeah.'

'Does he have hobbies?'

'I don't know.' There was reading, of course; two of the three bags which had so offended his mother were full of paperback books, most of which looked *very* hard.

The fact that Bobby knew nothing of the new man's pastimes for some reason seemed to ease her mind. She shrugged, and when she spoke again it seemed to be to herself rather than to Bobby. 'Shoot, it's only a book. And a paperback, at that.'

'He said he might have a job for me, but so far he hasn't come up with anything.'

She turned around fast. 'Any job he offers you, any chores he asks you to do, you talk to me about it first. Got that?'

'Sure, got it.' Her intensity surprised him and made him a little uneasy.

'Promise.'

'I promise.'

'*Big* promise, Bobby.'

He dutifully crossed his heart and said, 'I promise my mother in the name of God.'

That usually finished things, but this time she didn't look satisfied.

'Has he ever . . . does he ever . . .' There she stopped,

looking uncharacteristically flustered. Kids sometimes looked that way when Mrs Bramwell sent them to the blackboard to pick the nouns and verbs out of a sentence and they couldn't.

'Has he ever what, Mom?'

'Never mind!' she said crossly. 'Get out of here, Bobby, go to the park or Sterling House, I'm tired of looking at you.'

Why'd you come in, then? he thought (but of course did not say). *I wasn't bothering you, Mom. I wasn't bothering you.*

Bobby tucked *Lord of the Flies* into his back pocket and headed for the door. He turned back when he got there. She was still at the window, but now she was watching him again. He never surprised love on her face at such moments; at best he might see a kind of speculation, sometimes (but not always) affectionate.

'Hey, Mom?' He was thinking of asking for fifty cents – half a rock. With that he could buy a soda and two hotdogs at the Colony Diner. He loved the Colony's hotdogs, which came in toasted buns with potato chips and pickle slices on the side.

Her mouth did its tightening trick, and he knew this wasn't his day for hotdogs. 'Don't ask, Bobby, don't even think about it.' *Don't even think about it* – one of her all-time faves. 'I have a ton of bills this week, so get those dollar-signs out of your eyes.'

She *didn't* have a ton of bills, though, that was the thing. Not this week she didn't. Bobby had seen both the electric bill and the check for the rent in its envelope marked *Mr Monteleone* last Wednesday. And she couldn't claim he would soon need clothes because this was the end of the school-year, not the beginning. The only dough he'd asked for lately was five bucks for Sterling House – quarterly dues – and she had even been chintzy about that, although she knew it covered swimming and Wolves and Lions Baseball, plus the insurance. If it had been anyone but his mom, he would have thought of this as cheapskate behavior. He couldn't say anything about it to her, though; talking to her about money almost always turned into an argument, and disputing any part of her view on money matters, even in the most tiny particulars, was apt to send her into ranting hysterics. When she got like that she was scary.

Bobby smiled. 'It's okay, Mom.'

She smiled back and then nodded to the jar marked Bike Fund. 'Borrow a little from there, why don't you? Treat yourself. I'll never tell, and you can always put it back later.'

He held onto his smile, but only with an effort. How easily she said that, never thinking of how furious she'd be if Bobby suggested she borrow a little from the electric money, or the phone money, or what she set aside to buy her 'business clothes,' just so he could get a couple of hotdogs and maybe a pie à la mode at the Colony. If he told her breezily that he'd never tell and she could always put it back later. Yeah, sure, and get his face smacked.

By the time he got to Commonwealth Park, Bobby's resentment had faded and the word *cheapskate* had left his brain. It was a beautiful day and he had a terrific book to finish; how could you be resentful and pissed off with stuff like that going for you? He found a secluded bench and reopened *Lord of the Flies*. He had to finish it today, had to find out what happened.

The last forty pages took him an hour, and during that

time he was oblivious to everything around him. When he finally closed the book, he saw he had a lapful of little white flowers. His hair was full of them, too – he'd been sitting unaware in a storm of apple-blossoms.

He brushed them away, looking toward the playground as he did. Kids were teetertottering and swinging and batting the tetherball around its pole. Laughing, chasing each other, rolling in the grass. Could kids like that ever wind up going naked and worshipping a rotting pig's head? It was tempting to dismiss such ideas as the imaginings of a grownup who didn't like kids (there were lots who didn't, Bobby knew), but then Bobby glanced into the sandbox and saw a little boy sitting there and wailing as if his heart would break while another, bigger kid sat beside him, unconcernedly playing with the Tonka truck he had yanked out of his friend's hands.

And the book's ending – happy or not? Crazy as such a thing would have seemed a month ago, Bobby couldn't really tell. Never in his life had he read a book where he didn't know if the ending was good or bad, happy or sad. Ted would know, though. He would ask Ted.

Bobby was still on the bench fifteen minutes later when Sully came bopping into the park and saw him. 'Say there, you old bastard!' Sully exclaimed. 'I went by your house and your mom said you were down here, or maybe at Sterling House. Finally finish that book?'

'Yeah.'

'Was it good?'

'Yeah.'

S-J shook his head. 'I never met a book I really liked, but I'll take your word for it.'

125

'How was the concert?'

Sully shrugged. 'We blew til everyone went away, so I guess it was good for us, anyway. And guess who won the week at Camp Winiwinaia?' Camp Winnie was the YMCA's co-ed camp on Lake George, up in the woods north of Storrs. Each year HAC – the Harwich Activities Committee – had a drawing and gave away a week there.

Bobby felt a stab of jealousy. 'Don't tell me.'

Sully-John grinned. 'Yeah, man! Seventy names in the hat, seventy at *least*, and the one that bald old bastard Mr Coughlin pulled out was John L. Sullivan, Junior, 93 Broad Street. My mother just about weewee'd her pants.'

'When do you go?'

'Two weeks after school lets out. Mom's gonna try and get her week off from the bakery at the same time, so she can go see Gramma and Grampy in Wisconsin. She's gonna take the Big Gray Dog.' The Big Vac was summer vacation; the Big Shew was *Ed Sullivan* on Sunday night; the Big Gray Dog was, of course, a Greyhound bus. The local depot was just up the street from the Asher Empire and the Colony Diner.

'Don't you wish you could go to Wisconsin with her?' Bobby asked, feeling a perverse desire to spoil his friend's happiness at his good fortune just a little.

'Sorta, but I'd rather go to camp and shoot arrows.' He slung an arm around Bobby's shoulders. 'I only wish you could come with me, you book-reading bastard.'

That made Bobby feel mean-spirited. He looked down at *Lord of the Flies* again and knew he would be rereading it soon. Perhaps as early as August, if things got boring (by August they usually did, as hard as that was to believe in

May). Then he looked up at Sully-John, smiled, and put his arm around S-J's shoulders. 'Well, you're a lucky duck,' he said.

'Just call me Donald,' Sully-John agreed.

They sat on the bench that way for a little while, arms around each other's shoulders in those intermittent showers of apple-blossoms, watching the little kids play. Then Sully said he was going to the Saturday matinee at the Empire, and he'd better get moving if he didn't want to miss the previews.

'Why don't you come, Bobborino? *The Black Scorpion*'s playing. Monsters galore throughout the store.'

'Can't, I'm broke,' Bobby said. This was the truth (if you excluded the seven dollars in the Bike Fund jar, that was) and he didn't want to go to the movies today anyhow, even though he'd heard a kid at school say *The Black Scorpion* was really great, the scorpions poked their stingers right through people when they killed them and also mashed Mexico City flat.

What Bobby wanted to do was go back to the house and talk to Ted about *Lord of the Flies*.

'Broke,' Sully said sadly. 'That's a sad fact, Jack. I'd pay your way, but I've only got thirty-five cents myself.'

'Don't sweat it. Hey – where's your Bo-lo Bouncer?'

Sully looked sadder than ever. 'Rubber band snapped. Gone to Bolo Heaven, I guess.'

Bobby snickered. Bolo Heaven, that was a pretty funny idea. 'Gonna buy a new one?'

'I doubt it. There's a magic kit in Woolworth's that I want. Sixty different tricks, it says on the box. I wouldn't mind being a magician when I grow up, Bobby, you know it?

Travel around with a carnival or a circus, wear a black suit and a top hat. I'd pull rabbits and shit out of the hat.'

'The rabbits would probably shit *in* your hat,' Bobby said.

Sully grinned. 'But I'd be a cool bastard! Wouldn't I love to be! At anything!' He got up. 'Sure you don't want to come along? You could probably sneak in past Godzilla.'

Hundreds of kids showed up for the Saturday shows at the Empire, which usually consisted of a creature feature, eight or nine cartoons, Prevues of Coming Attractions, and the MovieTone News. Mrs Godlow went nuts trying to get them to stand in line and shut up, not understanding that on Saturday afternoon you couldn't get even basically well-behaved kids to act like they were in school. She was also obsessed by the conviction that dozens of kids over twelve were trying to enter at the under-twelve rate; Mrs G. would have demanded a birth certificate for the Saturday matinees as well as the Brigitte Bardot double features, had she been allowed. Lacking the authority to do that, she settled for barking 'WHATYEARYABORN?' to any kid over five and a half feet tall. With all that going on you could sometimes sneak past her quite easily, and there was no ticket-ripper on Saturday afternoons. But Bobby didn't want giant scorpions today; he had spent the last week with more realistic monsters, many of whom had probably looked pretty much like him.

'Nah, I think I'll just hang around,' Bobby said.

'Okay.' Sully-John scrummed a few apple-blossoms out of his black hair, then looked solemnly at Bobby. 'Call me a cool bastard, Big Bob.'

'Sully, you're one cool bastard.'

'Yes!' Sully-John leaped skyward, punching at the air and

laughing. 'Yes I am! A cool bastard today! A great big cool bastard of a magician tomorrow! Pow!'

Bobby collapsed against the back of the bench, legs outstretched, sneakers toed in, laughing hard. S-J was just so funny when he got going.

Sully started away, then turned back. 'Man, you know what? I saw a couple of weird guys when I came into the park.'

'What was weird about them?'

Sully-John shook his head, looking puzzled. 'Don't know,' he said. 'Don't really know.' Then he headed off, singing 'At the Hop'. It was one of his favorites. Bobby liked it, too. Danny and the Juniors were great.

Bobby opened the paperback Ted had given him (it was now looking exceedingly well-thumbed) and read the last couple of pages again, the part where the adults finally showed up. He began to ponder it again – happy or sad? – and Sully-John slipped from his mind. It occurred to him later that if S-J had happened to mention that the weird guys he'd seen were wearing yellow coats, some things might have been quite different later on.

'William Golding wrote an interesting thing about that book, one which I think speaks to your concern about the ending . . . want another pop, Bobby?'

Bobby shook his head and said no thanks. He didn't like rootbeer all that much; he mostly drank it out of politeness when he was with Ted. They were sitting at Ted's kitchen table again, Mrs O'Hara's dog was still barking (so far as Bobby could tell, Bowser *never* stopped barking), and Ted was still smoking Chesterfields. Bobby had peeked in at his mother when he came back from the park, saw she was napping on her bed, and then had hastened up to the third floor to ask Ted about the ending of *Lord of the Flies*.

Ted crossed to the refrigerator . . . and then stopped, standing there with his hand on the fridge door, staring off into space. Bobby would realize later that this was his first clear glimpse of something about Ted that wasn't right; that was in fact wrong and going wronger all the time.

'One feels them first in the back of one's eyes,' he said in a conversational tone. He spoke clearly; Bobby heard every word.

'Feels what?'

'One feels them first in the back of one's eyes.' Still staring into space with one hand curled around the handle of the refrigerator, and Bobby began to feel frightened. There seemed to be something in the air, something almost like pollen – it made the hairs inside his nose tingle, made the backs of his hands itch.

Then Ted opened the fridge door and bent in. 'Sure you don't want one?' he asked. 'It's good and cold.'

'No . . . no, that's okay.'

Ted came back to the table, and Bobby understood that he had either decided to ignore what had just happened, or didn't remember it. He also understood that Ted was okay now, and that was good enough for Bobby. Grownups were weird, that was all. Sometimes you just had to ignore the stuff they did.

'Tell me what he said about the ending. Mr Golding.'

'As best as I can remember, it was something like this: "The boys are rescued by the crew of a battle-cruiser, and that is very well for them, but who will rescue the crew?"'

Ted poured himself a glass of rootbeer, waited for the foam to subside, then poured a little more. 'Does that help?'

Bobby turned it over in his mind the way he would a riddle. Hell, it *was* a riddle. 'No,' he said at last. 'I still don't understand. They don't need to be rescued – the crew of the boat, I mean – because they're not on the island. Also . . .' He thought of the kids in the sandbox, one of them bawling his eyes out while the other played placidly with the stolen toy. 'The guys on the cruiser are grownups. Grownups don't need to be rescued.'

'No?'

'No.'

'Never?'

Bobby suddenly thought of his mother and how she was about money. Then he remembered the night he had awakened and thought he heard her crying. He didn't answer.

'Consider it,' Ted said. He drew deeply on his cigarette, then blew out a plume of smoke. 'Good books are for consideration after, too.'

'Okay.'

'*Lord of the Flies* wasn't much like the Hardy Boys, was it?'

Bobby had a momentary image, very clear, of Frank and Joe Hardy running through the jungle with homemade spears, chanting that they'd kill the pig and stick their spears up her arse. He burst out laughing, and as Ted joined him he knew that he was done with the Hardy Boys, Tom Swift, Rick Brant, and Bomba the Jungle Boy. *Lord of the Flies* had finished them off. He was very glad he had an adult library card.

'No,' he said, 'it sure wasn't.'

'And good books don't give up all their secrets at once. Will you remember that?'

'Yes.'

'Terrific. Now tell me – would you like to earn a dollar a week from me?'

The change of direction was so abrupt that for a moment Bobby couldn't follow it. Then he grinned and said, 'Cripes, yes!' Figures ran dizzily through his mind; Bobby was good enough at math to figure out a dollar a week added up to at least fifteen bucks by September. Put with what he already had, plus a reasonable harvest of returnable bottles and some summer lawn-mowing jobs on the street . . . jeepers, he might be riding a Schwinn by Labor Day. 'What do you want me to do?'

'We have to be careful about that. Quite careful.' Ted meditated quietly and for so long Bobby began to be afraid he was going to start talking about feeling stuff in the backs of his eyes again. But when Ted looked up there was none of that strange emptiness in his gaze. His eyes were sharp, if a little rueful. 'I would never ask a friend of mine – especially a young friend – to lie to his parents, Bobby, but in this case I'm going to ask you to join me in a little misdirection. Do you know what that is?'

'Sure.' Bobby thought about Sully and his new ambition to travel around with the circus, wearing a black suit and pulling rabbits out of his hat. 'It's what the magician does to fool you.'

'Doesn't sound very nice when you put it that way, does it?'

Bobby shook his head. No, take away the spangles and the spotlights and it didn't sound very nice at all.

132

Ted drank a little rootbeer and wiped foam from his upper lip. 'Your mother, Bobby. She doesn't quite dislike me, I don't think it would be fair to say that . . . but I think she *almost* dislikes me. Do you agree?'

'I guess. When I told her you might have a job for me, she got weird about it. Said I had to tell her about anything you wanted me to do before I could do it.'

Ted Brautigan nodded.

'I think it all comes back to you having some of your stuff in paper bags when you moved in. I know that sounds nuts, but it's all I can figure.'

He thought Ted might laugh, but he only nodded again. 'Perhaps that's all it is. In any case, Bobby, I wouldn't want you to go against your mother's wishes.'

That sounded good but Bobby Garfield didn't entirely believe it. If it was really true, there'd be no need for misdirection.

'Tell your mother that my eyes now grow tired quite easily. It's the truth.' As if to prove it, Ted raised his right hand to his eyes and massaged the corners with his thumb and forefinger. 'Tell her I'd like to hire you to read bits of the newspaper to me each day, and for this I will pay you a dollar a week – what your friend Sully calls a rock?'

Bobby nodded . . . but a buck a week for reading about how Kennedy was doing in the primaries and whether or not Floyd Patterson would win in June? With maybe *Blondie* and *Dick Tracy* thrown in for good measure? His mom or Mr Biderman down at Home Town Real Estate might believe that, but Bobby didn't.

Ted was still rubbing his eyes, his hand hovering over his narrow nose like a spider.

'What else?' Bobby asked. His voice came out sounding

strangely flat, like his mom's voice when he'd promised to pick up his room and she came in at the end of the day to find the job still undone. 'What's the real job?'

'I want you to keep your eyes open, that's all,' Ted said.

'For what?'

'Low men in yellow coats.' Ted's fingers were still working the corners of his eyes. Bobby wished he'd stop; there was something creepy about it. Did he feel something behind them, was that why he kept rubbing and kneading that way? Something that broke his attention, interfered with his normally sane and well-ordered way of thinking?

'Lo *mein?*' It was what his mother ordered on the occasions when they went out to Sing Lu's on Barnum Avenue. Lo mein in yellow coats made no sense, but it was all he could think of.

Ted laughed, a sunny, genuine laugh that made Bobby aware of just how uneasy he'd been.

'Low *men,*' Ted said. 'I use "low" in the Dickensian sense, meaning fellows who look rather stupid . . . and rather dangerous as well. The sort of men who'd shoot craps in an alley, let's say, and pass around a bottle of liquor in a paper bag during the game. The sort who lean against telephone poles and whistle at women walking by on the other side of the street while they mop the backs of their necks with handkerchiefs that are never quite clean. Men who think hats with feathers in the brims are sophisticated. Men who look like they know all the right answers to all of life's stupid questions. I'm not being terribly clear, am I? Is any of this getting through to you, is any of it ringing a bell?'

Yeah, it was. In a way it was like hearing time described as the old bald cheater: a sense that the word or phrase was

134

exactly right even though you couldn't say just why. It reminded him of how Mr Biderman always looked unshaven even when you could still smell sweet aftershave drying on his cheeks, the way you somehow knew Mr Biderman would pick his nose when he was alone in his car or check the coin return of any pay telephone he walked past without even thinking about it.

'I get you,' he said.

'Good. I'd never in a hundred lifetimes ask you to speak to such men, or even approach them. But I *would* ask you to keep an eye out, make a circuit of the block once a day – Broad Street, Commonwealth Street, Colony Street, Asher Avenue, then back here to 149 – and just see what you see.'

It was starting to fit together in Bobby's mind. On his birthday – which had also been Ted's first day at 149 – Ted had asked him if he knew everyone on the street, if he would recognize

(*sojourners faces of those unknown*)

strangers, if any strangers showed up. Not three weeks later Carol Gerber had made her comment about wondering sometimes if Ted was on the run from something.

'How many guys are there?' he asked.

'Three, five, perhaps more by now.' Ted shrugged. 'You'll know them by their long yellow coats and olive skin . . . although that darkish skin is just a disguise.'

'What . . . you mean like Man-Tan, or something?'

'I suppose, yes. If they're driving, you'll know them by their cars.'

'What makes? What models?' Bobby felt like Darren McGavin on *Mike Hammer* and warned himself not to get carried away. This wasn't TV. Still, it was exciting.

Ted was shaking his head. 'I have no idea. But you'll know just the same, because their cars will be like their yellow coats and sharp shoes and the greasy perfumed stuff they use to slick back their hair: loud and vulgar.'

'Low,' Bobby said – it was not quite a question.

'Low,' Ted repeated, and nodded emphatically. He sipped rootbeer, looked away toward the sound of the eternally barking Bowser . . . and remained that way for several moments, like a toy with a broken spring or a machine that has run out of gas. 'They sense me,' he said. 'And I sense them, as well. Ah, what a world.'

'What do they want?'

Ted turned back to him, appearing startled. It was as if he had forgotten Bobby was there . . . or had forgotten for a moment just who Bobby was. Then he smiled and reached out and put his hand over Bobby's. It was big and warm and comforting; a man's hand. At the feel of it Bobby's half-hearted reservations disappeared.

'A certain something I happen to have,' Ted said. 'Let's leave it at that.'

'They're not cops, are they? Or government guys? Or—'

'Are you asking if I'm one of the FBI's Ten Most Wanted, or a communist agent like on *I Led Three Lives*? A bad guy?'

'I know you're not a bad guy,' Bobby said, but the flush mounting into his cheeks suggested otherwise. Not that what he thought changed much. You could like or even love a bad guy; even Hitler had a mother, his own mom liked to say.

'I'm not a bad guy. Never robbed a bank or stole a military secret. I've spent too much of my life reading books and scamped on my share of fines – if there were Library Police,

I'm afraid they'd be after me – but I'm not a bad guy like the ones you see on television.'

'The men in yellow coats are, though.'

Ted nodded. 'Bad through and through. And, as I say, dangerous.'

'Have you seen them?'

'Many times, but not here. And the chances are ninety-nine in a hundred that you won't, either. All I ask is that you keep an eye out for them. Could you do that?'

'Yes.'

'Bobby? Is there a problem?'

'No.' Yet something nagged at him for a moment – not a connection, only a momentary sense of groping toward one.

'Are you sure?'

'Uh-huh.'

'All right. Now, here is the question: could you in good conscience – in *fair* conscience, at least – neglect to mention this part of your duty to your mother?'

'Yes,' Bobby said at once, although he understood doing such a thing would mark a large change in his life . . . and would be risky. He was more than a little afraid of his mom, and this fear was only partly caused by how angry she could get and how long she could bear a grudge. Mostly it grew from an unhappy sense of being loved only a little, and needing to protect what love there was. But he liked Ted . . . and he had loved the feeling of Ted's hand lying over his own, the warm roughness of the big palm, the touch of the fingers, thickened almost into knots at the joints. And this wasn't lying, not really. It was leaving out.

'You're really sure?'

If you want to learn to lie, Bobby-O, I suppose leaving things out is as good a place to start as any, an interior voice whispered. Bobby ignored it. 'Yes,' he said, 'really sure. Ted . . . are these guys just dangerous to you or to anybody?' He was thinking of his mom, but he was also thinking of himself.

'To me they could be very dangerous indeed. To other people – *most* other people – probably not. Do you want to know a funny thing?'

'Sure.'

'The majority of people don't even see them unless they're very, very close. It's almost as if they have the power to cloud men's minds, like The Shadow on that old radio program.'

'Do you mean they're . . . well . . .' He supposed *supernatural* was the word he wasn't quite able to say.

'No, no, not at all.' Waving his question away before it could be fully articulated. Lying in bed that night and sleepless for longer than usual, Bobby thought that Ted had almost been afraid for it to be spoken aloud. 'There are lots of people, quite ordinary ones, we don't see. The waitress walking home from work with her head down and her restaurant shoes in a paper bag. Old fellows out for their afternoon walks in the park. Teenage girls with their hair in rollers and their transistor radios playing Peter Tripp's countdown. But children see them. Children see them all. And Bobby, you are still a child.'

'These guys don't sound exactly easy to miss.'

'The coats, you mean. The shoes. The loud cars. But those are the very things which cause some people – many people, actually – to turn away. To erect little roadblocks between the eye and the brain. In any case, I won't have you taking chances. If you do see the men in the yellow coats, *don't approach them.* Don't speak to them even if they should speak to you. I can't think why they would, I don't believe they would even see you – just as most people don't really see them – but there are plenty of things I don't know about them. Now tell me what I just said. Repeat it back. It's important.'

'Don't approach them and don't speak to them.'

'Even if they speak to you.' Rather impatiently.

'Even if they speak to me, right. What *should* I do?'

'Come back here and tell me they're about and where you saw them. Walk until you're certain you're out of their sight, then run. Run like the wind. Run like hell was after you.'

'And what will you do?' Bobby asked, but of course he knew. Maybe he wasn't as sharp as Carol, but he wasn't a complete dodo, either. 'You'll go away, won't you?'

Ted Brautigan shrugged and finished his glass of rootbeer without meeting Bobby's eyes. 'I'll decide when that time comes. *If* it comes. If I'm lucky, the feelings I've had for the last few days – my sense of these men – will go away.'

'Has that happened before?'

'Indeed it has. Now why don't we talk of more pleasant things?'

For the next half an hour they discussed baseball, then music (Bobby was startled to discover Ted not only knew the music of Elvis Presley but actually liked some of it), then Bobby's hopes and fears concerning the seventh grade in September. All this was pleasant enough, but behind each topic Bobby sensed the lurk of the low men. The low men were here in Ted's third-floor room like peculiar shadows which cannot quite be seen.

It wasn't until Bobby was getting ready to leave that Ted raised the subject of them again. 'There are things you should look for,' he said. 'Signs that my . . . my old friends are about.'

'What are they?'

'On your travels around town, keep an eye out for lost-pet posters on walls, in shop windows, stapled to telephone poles on residential streets. "Lost, a gray tabby cat with black ears, a white bib, and a crooked tail. Call IRoquois 7-7661." "Lost, a small mongrel dog, part beagle, answers to the name of Trixie, loves children, ours want her to come home. Call IRoquois 7-0984 or bring to 77 Peabody Street." That sort of thing.'

'What are you saying? Jeepers, are you saying they kill people's *pets*? Do you think . . .'

'I think many of those animals don't exist at all,' Ted said. He sounded weary and unhappy. 'Even when there is a small, poorly reproduced photograph, I think most are pure fiction. I think such posters are a form of communication, although why the men who put them up shouldn't just go into the Colony Diner and do their communicating over pot roast and mashed potatoes I don't know.

'Where does your mother shop, Bobby?'

'Total Grocery. It's right next door to Mr Biderman's real-estate agency.'

'And do you go with her?'

'Sometimes.' When he was younger he met her there every Friday, reading a *TV Guide* from the magazine rack until she showed up, loving Friday afternoons because it was the start of the weekend, because Mom let him push the cart and he always pretended it was a racing car, because he loved *her*.

But he didn't tell Ted any of this. It was ancient history. Hell, he'd only been eight.

'Look on the bulletin board every supermarket puts up by the checkout registers,' Ted said. 'On it you'll see a number of little hand-printed notices that say things like CAR FOR SALE BY OWNER. Look for any such notices that have been thumbtacked to the board upside down. Is there another supermarket in town?'

'There's the A&P, down by the railroad overpass. My mom doesn't go there. She says the butcher's always giving her the glad-eye.'

'Can you check the bulletin board there, as well?'

'Sure.'

'Good so far, very good. Now – you know the hopscotch patterns kids are always drawing on the sidewalks?'

Bobby nodded.

'Look for ones with stars or moons or both chalked near them, usually in chalk of a different color. Look for kite tails hanging from telephone lines. Not the kites themselves, but only the tails. And . . .'

Ted paused, frowning, thinking. As he took a Chesterfield from the pack on the table and lit it, Bobby thought quite reasonably, quite clearly, and without the slightest shred of fear: *He's crazy, y'know. Crazy as a loon.*

Yes, of course, how could you doubt it? He only hoped Ted could be careful as well as crazy. Because if his mom heard Ted talking about stuff like this, she'd never let Bobby go near him again. In fact, she'd probably send for the guys with the butterfly nets . . . or ask good old Don Biderman to do it for her.

'You know the clock in the town square, Bobby?'

141

'Yeah, sure.'

'It may begin ringing wrong hours, or between hours. Also, look for reports of minor church vandalism in the paper. My friends dislike churches, but they never do anything too outrageous; they like to keep a – pardon the pun – low profile. There are other signs that they're about, but there's no need to overload you. Personally I believe the posters are the surest clue.'

' "If you see Ginger, please bring her home." '

'That's exactly r—'

'Bobby?' It was his mom's voice, followed by the ascending scuff of her Saturday sneakers. 'Bobby, are you up there?'

CHAPTER THREE

A MOTHER'S POWER. BOBBY
DOES HIS JOB.
'DOES HE TOUCH YOU?'
THE LAST DAY OF SCHOOL.

Bobby and Ted exchanged a guilty look. Both of them sat back on their respective sides of the table, as if they had been doing something crazy instead of just talking about crazy stuff.

She'll see we've been up to something, Bobby thought with dismay. *It's all over my face.*

'No,' Ted said to him. 'It is not. That is her power over you, that you believe it. It's a mother's power.'

Bobby stared at him, amazed. *Did you read my mind? Did you read my mind just then?*

Now his mom was almost to the third-floor landing and there was no time for a reply even if Ted had wanted to make one. But there was no look on his face saying he *would* have replied if there had been time, either. And Bobby at once began to doubt what he had heard.

Then his mother was in the open doorway, looking from her son to Ted and back to her son again, her eyes assessing.

143

'So here you are after all,' she said. 'My goodness, Bobby, didn't you hear me calling?'

'You were up here before I got a chance to say boo, Mom.'

She snorted. Her mouth made a small, meaningless smile – her automatic social smile. Her eyes went back and forth between the two of them, back and forth, looking for something out of place, something she didn't like, something wrong. 'I didn't hear you come in from outdoors.'

'You were asleep on your bed.'

'How are you today, Mrs Garfield?' Ted asked.

'Fine as paint.' Back and forth went her eyes. Bobby had no idea what she was looking for, but that expression of dismayed guilt must have left his face. If she had seen it, he would know already; would know that *she* knew.

'Would you like a bottle of pop?' Ted asked. 'I have rootbeer. It's not much, but it's cold.'

'That would be nice,' Liz said. 'Thanks.' She came all the way in and sat down next to Bobby at the kitchen table. She patted him absently on the leg, watching Ted as he opened his little fridge and got out the rootbeer. 'It's not hot up here yet, Mr Brattigan, but I guarantee you it will be in another month. You want to get yourself a fan.'

'There's an idea.' Ted poured rootbeer into a clean glass, then stood in front of the fridge holding the glass up to the light, waiting for the foam to go down. To Bobby he looked like a scientist in a TV commercial, one of those guys obsessed with Brand X and Brand Y and how Rolaids consumed fifty-seven times its own weight in excess stomach acid, amazing but true.

'I don't need a full glass, that will be fine,' she said a little impatiently. Ted brought the glass to her, and she raised it to him. 'Here's how.' She took a swallow and grimaced as if it had been rye instead of rootbeer. Then she watched over the top of the glass as Ted sat down, tapped the ash from his smoke, and tucked the stub of the cigarette back into the corner of his mouth.

'You two have gotten thicker than thieves,' she remarked. 'Sitting here at the kitchen table, drinking rootbeer – cozy, thinks I! What've you been talking about today?'

'The book Mr Brautigan gave me,' Bobby said. His voice sounded natural and calm, a voice with no secrets behind it. '*Lord of the Flies*. I couldn't figure out if the ending was happy or sad, so I thought I'd ask him.'

'Oh? And what did he say?'

'That it was both. Then he told me to consider it.'

Liz laughed without a great deal of humor. 'I read mysteries, Mr Brattigan, and save my consideration for real life. But of course I'm not retired.'

'No,' Ted said. 'You are obviously in the very prime of life.'

She gave him her *flattery-will-get-you-nowhere* look. Bobby knew it well.

'I also offered Bobby a small job,' Ted told her. 'He has agreed to take it . . . with your permission, of course.'

Her brow furrowed at the mention of a job, smoothed at the mention of permission. She reached out and briefly touched Bobby's red hair, a gesture so unusual that Bobby's eyes widened a little. Her eyes never left Ted's face as she did it. Not only did she not trust the man, Bobby realized, she was likely *never* going to trust him. 'What sort of job did you have in mind?'

'He wants me to—'

'Hush,' she said, and still her eyes peered over the top of her glass, never leaving Ted.

'I'd like him to read me the paper, perhaps in the afternoons,' Ted said, then explained how his eyes weren't what they used to be and how he had worse problems every day with the finer print. But he liked to keep up with the news – these were very interesting times, didn't Mrs Garfield think so? – and he liked to keep up with the columns, as well, Stewart Alsop and Walter Winchell and such. Winchell was a gossip, of course, but an *interesting* gossip, didn't Mrs Garfield agree?

Bobby listened, increasingly tense even though he could tell from his mother's face and posture – even from the way she sipped her rootbeer – that she believed what Ted was telling her. That part of it was all right, but what if Ted went blank again? Went blank and started babbling about low men in yellow coats or the tails of kites hanging from telephone wires, all the time gazing off into space?

But nothing like that happened. Ted finished by saying he also liked to know how the Dodgers were doing – Maury Wills, especially – even though they had gone to L.A. He said this with the air of one who is determined to tell the truth even if the truth is a bit shameful. Bobby thought it was a nice touch.

'I suppose that would be fine,' his mother said (almost grudgingly, Bobby thought). 'In fact it sounds like a plum. I wish *I* could have a plum job like that.'

'I'll bet you're excellent at your job, Mrs Garfield.'

She flashed him her dry flattery-won't-work-with-me expression again. 'You'll have to pay him extra to do the crossword for you,' she said, getting up, and although Bobby didn't understand the remark, he was astonished by the cruelty he sensed in it, embedded like a piece of glass in a marsh-mallow. It was as if she wanted to make fun of Ted's failing eyesight and his intellect at the same time; as if she wanted to hurt him for being nice to her son. Bobby was still ashamed at deceiving her and frightened that she would find out, but now he was also glad . . . almost viciously glad. She deserved it. 'He's good at the crossword, my Bobby.'

Ted smiled. 'I'm sure he is.'

'Come on downstairs, Bob. It's time to give Mr Brattigan a rest.'

'But—'

'I think I *would* like to lie down awhile, Bobby. I've a little bit of a headache. I'm glad you liked *Lord of the Flies*. You can start your job tomorrow, if you like, with the feature section of the Sunday paper. I warn you it's apt to be a trial by fire.'

'Okay.'

Mom had reached the little landing outside of Ted's door. Bobby was behind her. Now she turned back and looked at Ted over Bobby's head. 'Why not outside on the porch?' she asked. 'The fresh air will be nice for both of you. Better than this stuffy room. And I'll be able to hear, too, if I'm in the living room.'

Bobby thought some message was passing between them. Not via telepathy, exactly . . . only it *was* telepathy, in a way. The humdrum sort adults practiced.

'A fine idea,' Ted said. 'The front porch would be lovely. Good afternoon, Bobby. Good afternoon, Mrs Garfield.'

Bobby came very close to saying *Seeya, Ted* and substituted 'See you, Mr Brautigan' at the last moment. He moved toward the stairs, smiling vaguely, with the sweaty feeling of someone who has just avoided a nasty accident.

His mother lingered. 'How long have you been retired, Mr Brattigan? Or do you mind me asking?'

Bobby had almost decided she wasn't mispronouncing Ted's name deliberately; now he swung the other way. She was. Of course she was.

'Three years.' He crushed his cigarette out in the brimming tin ashtray and immediately lit another.

'Which would make you . . . sixty-eight?'

'Sixty-six, actually.' His voice continued mild and open, but Bobby had an idea he didn't much care for these questions. 'I was granted retirement with full benefits two years early. Medical reasons.'

Don't ask him what's wrong with him, Mom, Bobby moaned inside his own head. *Don't you dare.*

She didn't. She asked what he'd done in Hartford instead.

'Accounting. I was in the Office of the Comptroller.'

'Bobby and I guessed something to do with education. Accounting! That sounds very responsible.'

Ted smiled. Bobby thought there was something awful about it. 'In twenty years I wore out three adding machines. If that is responsibility, Mrs Garfield, why yes – I was responsible. Apeneck Sweeney spreads his knees; the typist puts a record on the gramophone with an automatic hand.'

'I don't follow you.'

'It's my way of saying that it was a lot of years in a job that never seemed to mean much.'

'It might have meant a good deal if you'd had a child to feed, shelter, and raise.' She looked at him with her chin slightly tilted, the look that meant if Ted wanted to discuss this, she was ready. That she would go to the mat with him on the subject if that was his pleasure.

148

Ted, Bobby was relieved to find, didn't want to go to the mat or anywhere near it. 'I expect you're right, Mrs Garfield. Entirely.'

She gave him a moment more of the lifted chin, asking if he was sure, giving him time to change his mind. When Ted said nothing else, she smiled. It was her victory smile. Bobby loved her, but suddenly he was tired of her as well. Tired of knowing her looks, her sayings, and the adamant cast of her mind.

'Thank you for the rootbeer, Mr Brattigan. It was very tasty.' And with that she led her son downstairs. When they got to the second-floor landing she dropped his hand and went the rest of the way ahead of him.

Bobby thought they would discuss his new job further over supper, but they didn't. His mom seemed far away from him, her eyes distant. He had to ask her twice for a second slice of meatloaf and when later that evening the telephone rang, she jumped up from the couch where they had been watching TV to get it. She jumped for it the way Ricky Nelson did when it rang on the *Ozzie and Harriet* show. She listened, said something, then came back to the couch and sat down.

'Who was it?' Bobby asked.

'Wrong number,' Liz said.

In that year of his life Bobby Garfield still waited for sleep with a child's welcoming confidence: on his back, heels spread to the corners of the bed, hands tucked into the cool under the pillow so his elbows stuck up. On the night after Ted spoke to him about the low men in their yellow coats (*and don't forget their cars*, he thought, *their big cars with the fancy paintjobs*), Bobby lay in this position with the sheet pushed down to his waist. Moonlight fell on his narrow child's chest, squared in four by the shadows of the window muntins.

If he had thought about it (he hadn't), he would have expected Ted's low men to become more real once he was alone in the dark, with only the tick of his wind-up Big Ben and the murmur of the late TV news from the other room to keep him company. That was the way it had always been with him – it was easy to laugh at Frankenstein on Shock Theater, to go fake-swoony and cry 'Ohhh, *Frankie!*' when the monster showed up, especially if Sully-John was there for a sleepover. But in the dark, after S-J had started to snore (or worse, if Bobby was alone), Dr Frankenstein's creature seemed a lot more . . . not real, exactly, but . . . *possible.*

That sense of possibility did not gather around Ted's low men. If anything, the idea that people would communicate with each other via lost-pet posters seemed even crazier in the dark. But not a dangerous crazy. Bobby didn't think Ted was really, deeply crazy, anyhow; just a bit too smart for his own good, especially since he had so few things with which to occupy his time. Ted was a little . . . well . . . cripes, a little *what?* Bobby couldn't express it. If the word *eccentric* had occurred to him he would have seized it with pleasure and relief.

But . . . it seemed like he read my mind. What about that?

Oh, he was wrong, that was all, mistaken about what he thought he'd heard. Or maybe Ted *had* read his mind, read it with that essentially uninteresting adult ESP, peeling guilt off his face like a wet decal off a piece of glass. God knew his mother could always do that . . . at least until today.

But—

But nothing. Ted was a nice guy who knew a lot about books, but he was no mind-reader. No more than Sully-John Sullivan was a magician, or ever would be.

'It's all misdirection,' Bobby murmured. He slipped his hands out from under his pillow, crossed them at the wrists, wagged them. The shadow of a dove flew across the moonlight on his chest.

Bobby smiled, closed his eyes, and went to sleep.

The next morning he sat on the front porch and read several pieces aloud from the Harwich Sunday *Journal*. Ted perched on the porch glider, listening quietly and smoking Chesterfields. Behind him and to his left, the curtains flapped in and out of the open windows of the Garfield front room. Bobby imagined his mom sitting in the chair where the light was best, sewing basket beside her, listening and hemming skirts (hemlines were going down again, she'd told him a week or two before; take them up one year, pick out the stitches the following spring and lower them again, all because a bunch of poofers in New York and London said to, and why she bothered she didn't know). Bobby had no idea if she really was there or not, the open windows and blowing curtains meant nothing by themselves, but he imagined it all the same. When he was a little older it would occur to him that he had *always* imagined her there – outside doors, in that part of the bleachers where the shadows were too thick to see properly, in the dark at the top of the stairs, he had always imagined she was there.

The sports pieces he read were interesting (Maury Wills was stealing up a storm), the feature articles less so, the opinion columns boring and long and incomprehensible, full of phrases like 'fiscal responsibility' and 'economic indicators of a recessionary nature.' Even so, Bobby didn't mind reading them. He was doing a job, after all, earning dough, and a lot of jobs were boring at least some of the time. 'You have to work for your Wheaties,' his mother sometimes said after Mr Biderman had kept her late. Bobby was proud just to be able to get a phrase like 'economic indicators of a recessionary nature' to come off his tongue. Besides, the other job – the hidden job – arose from Ted's crazy idea that some men were out to get him, and Bobby would have felt weird taking money just for doing that one; would have felt like he was tricking Ted somehow even though it had been Ted's idea in the first place.

That was still part of his job, though, crazy or not, and he began doing it that Sunday afternoon. Bobby walked around the block while his mom was napping, looking for either low men in yellow coats or signs of them. He saw a number of interesting things – over on Colony Street a woman arguing with her husband about something, the two of them standing nose-to-nose like Gorgeous George and Haystacks Calhoun before the start of a rassling match; a little kid on Asher Avenue bashing caps with a smoke-blackened rock; liplocked teenagers outside of Spicer's Variety Store on the corner of Commonwealth and Broad; a panel truck with the interesting slogan YUMMY FOR THE TUMMY written on the side – but he saw no yellow coats or lost-pet announcements on phone poles; not a single kite tail hung from a single telephone wire.

He stopped in at Spicer's for a penny gumball and gleeped the bulletin board, which was dominated by photos of this year's Miss Rheingold candidates. He saw two cards offering cars for sale by owner, but neither was upside down. There was another one that said MUST SELL MY BACKYARD POOL, GOOD SHAPE, YOUR KIDS WILL LOVE IT, and that one was crooked, but Bobby didn't guess crooked counted.

On Asher Avenue he saw a whale of a Buick parked at a hydrant, but it was bottle-green, and Bobby didn't think it qualified as loud and vulgar in spite of the portholes up the sides of the hood and the grille, which looked like the sneery mouth of a chrome catfish.

On Monday he continued looking for low men on his way to and from school. He saw nothing . . . but Carol Gerber, who was walking with him and S-J, saw him looking. His mother was right, Carol was really sharp.

'Are the commie agents after the plans?' she asked.

'Huh?'

'You keep staring everywhere. Even behind you.'

For a moment Bobby considered telling them what Ted had hired him to do, then decided it would be a bad idea. It might have been a good one if he believed there was really something to look for – three pairs of eyes instead of one, Carol's sharp little peepers included – but he didn't. Carol and Sully-John knew that he had a job reading Ted the paper every day, and that was all right. It was enough. If he told them about the low men, it would feel like making fun, somehow. A betrayal.

'Commie agents?' Sully asked, whirling around. 'Yeah, I see em, I see em!' He drew down his mouth and made the *eh-eh-eh* noise again (it was his favorite). Then he staggered, dropped his invisible tommygun, clutched his chest. 'They got me! I'm hit bad! Go on without me! Give my love to Rose!'

'I'll give it to my aunt's fat fanny,' Carol said, and elbowed him.

'I'm looking for guys from St Gabe's, that's all,' Bobby said.

This was plausible; boys from St Gabriel the Steadfast Upper and Secondary were always harassing the Harwich Elementary kids as the Elementary kids walked to school – buzzing them on their bikes, shouting that the boys were sissies, that the girls 'put out' . . . which Bobby was pretty sure meant tongue-kissing and letting boys touch their titties.

'Nah, those dinkberries don't come along until later,' Sully-John said. 'Right now they're all still home puttin on their crosses and combin their hair back like Bobby Rydell.'

'Don't swear,' Carol said, and elbowed him again.

Sully-John looked wounded. 'Who swore? I didn't swear.'

'Yes you did.'

'I did not, Carol.'

'Did.'

'No sir, did not.'

'*Yes* sir, did too, you said dinkberries.'

'That's not a swear! Dinkberries are *berries*!' S-J looked at Bobby for help, but Bobby was looking up at Asher Avenue, where a Cadillac was cruising slowly by. It was big, and he supposed it was a little flashy, but wasn't any Cadillac? This one was painted a conservative light brown and didn't look low to him. Besides, the person at the wheel was a woman.

'Yeah? Show me a picture of a dinkberry in the encyclopedia and maybe I'll believe you.'

'I ought to poke you,' Sully said amiably. 'Show you who's boss. Me Tarzan, you Jane.'

'Me Carol, you Jughead. Here.' Carol thrust three books

– arithmetic, *Adventures in Spelling*, and *The Little House on the Prairie* – into S-J's hands. 'Carry my books cause you swore.'

Sully-John looked more wounded than ever. 'Why should I have to carry your stupid books even if I *did* swear, which I didn't?'

'It's pennants,' Carol said.

'What the heck is pennants?'

'Making up for something you do wrong. If you swear or tell a lie, you have to do pennants. One of the St Gabe's boys told me. Willie, his name is.'

'You shouldn't hang around with them,' Bobby said. 'They can be mean.' He knew this from personal experience. Just after Christmas vacation ended, three St Gabe's boys had chased him down Broad Street, threatening to beat him up because he had 'looked at them wrong.' They would have done it, too, Bobby thought, if the one in the lead hadn't slipped in the slush and gone to his knees. The others had tripped over him, allowing Bobby just time enough to nip in through the big front door of 149 and turn the lock. The St Gabe's boys had hung around outside for a little while, then had gone away after promising Bobby that they would 'see him later.'

'They're not all hoods, some of them are okay,' Carol said. She looked at Sully-John, who was carrying her books, and hid a smile with one hand. You could get S-J to do anything if you talked fast and sounded sure of yourself. It would have been nicer to have Bobby carry her books, but it wouldn't have been any good unless he asked her. Someday he might; she was an optimist. In the meantime it was nice to be walking here between them in the morning sunshine. She

155

stole a glance at Bobby, who was looking down at a hopscotch grid drawn on the sidewalk. He was so cute, and he didn't even know it. Somehow that was the cutest thing of all.

The last week of school passed as it always did, with a maddening, half-crippled slowness. On those early June days Bobby thought the smell of the paste in the library was almost strong enough to gag a maggot, and geography seemed to last ten thousand years. Who cared how much tin there was in Paraguay?

At recess Carol talked about how she was going to her aunt Cora and uncle Ray's farm in Pennsylvania for a week in July; S-J went on and on about the week of camp he'd won and how he was going to shoot arrows at targets and go out in a canoe every day he was there. Bobby, in turn, told them about the great Maury Wills, who might set a record for base-stealing that would never be broken in their lifetime.

His mom was increasingly preoccupied, jumping each time the telephone rang and then running for it, staying up past the late news (and sometimes, Bobby suspected, until the Nite-Owl Movie was over), and only picking at her meals. Sometimes she would have long, intense conversations on the phone with her back turned and her voice lowered (as if Bobby wanted to eavesdrop on her conversations, anyway). Sometimes she'd go to the telephone, start to dial it, then drop it back in its cradle and return to the couch.

On one of these occasions Bobby asked her if she had forgotten what number she wanted to call. 'Seems like I've forgotten a lot of things,' she muttered, and then 'Mind your beeswax, Bobby-O.'

He might have noticed more and worried even more than he did – she was getting thin and had picked up the cigarette habit again after almost stopping for two years – if he hadn't had lots of stuff to occupy his own mind and time. The best thing was the adult library card, which seemed like a better gift, a more *inspired* gift, each time he used it. Bobby felt there were a billion science-fiction novels alone in the adult section that he wanted to read. Take Isaac Asimov, for instance. Under the name of Paul French, Mr Asimov wrote science-fiction novels for kids about a space pilot named Lucky Starr, and they were pretty good. Under his own name he had written other novels, even better ones. At least three of them were about robots. Bobby loved robots, Robby the Robot in *Forbidden Planet* was one of the all-time great movie characters, in his opinion, totally ripshit, and Mr Asimov's were almost as good. Bobby thought he would be spending a lot of time with them in the summer ahead. (Sully called this great writer Isaac Ass-Move, but of course Sully was almost totally ignorant about books.)

Going to school he looked for the men in the yellow coats, or signs of them; going to the library after school he did the same. Because school and library were in opposite directions, Bobby felt he was covering a pretty good part of Harwich. He never expected to actually see any low men, of course. After supper, in the long light of evening, he would read the paper to Ted, either on the porch or in Ted's kitchen. Ted had followed Liz Garfield's advice and gotten a fan, and Bobby's mom no longer seemed concerned that Bobby should read to 'Mr Brattigan' out on the porch. Some of this was her growing preoccupation with her own adult matters, Bobby felt, but perhaps she was also coming to trust Ted a little more. Not that trust was the same as liking. Not that it had come easily, either.

One night while they were on the couch watching *Wyatt Earp*, his mom turned to Bobby almost fiercely and said, 'Does he ever touch you?'

Bobby understood what she was asking, but not why she was so wound up. 'Well, sure,' he said. 'He claps me on the back sometimes, and once when I was reading the paper to him and screwed up some really long word three times in a row he gave me a Dutch rub, but he doesn't roughhouse or anything. I don't think he's strong enough for stuff like that. Why?'

'Never mind,' she said. 'He's fine, I guess. Got his head in the clouds, no question about it, but he doesn't seem like a . . .' She trailed off, watching the smoke from her Kool cigarette rise in the living-room air. It went up from the coal in a pale gray ribbon and then disappeared, making Bobby think of the way the characters in Mr Simak's *Ring Around the Sun* followed the spiraling top into other worlds.

At last she turned to him again and said, 'If he ever touches you in a way you don't like, you come and tell me. Right away. You hear?'

'Sure, Mom.' There was something in her look that made him remember once when he'd asked her how a woman knew she was going to have a baby. *She bleeds every month*, his mom had said. *If there's no blood, she knows it's because the blood is going into a baby*. Bobby had wanted to ask where this blood came out when there was no baby being made (he remembered a nosebleed his mom had had once, but no other instances of maternal bleeding). The look on her face, however, had made him drop the subject. She wore the same look now.

Actually there *had* been other touches: Ted might run one of his big hands across Bobby's crewcut, kind of patting the bristles; he would sometimes gently catch Bobby's nose between his knuckles and intone *Sound it out!* if Bobby mispronounced a word; if they spoke at the same moment he would hook one of his little fingers around one of Bobby's little fingers and say *Good luck, good will, good fortune, not ill.* Soon Bobby was saying it with him, their little fingers locked, their voices as matter-of-fact as people saying pass the peas or how you doing.

Only once did Bobby feel uncomfortable when Ted touched him. Bobby had just finished the last newspaper piece Ted wanted to hear – some columnist blabbing on about how there was nothing wrong with Cuba that good old American free enterprise couldn't fix. Dusk was beginning to streak the sky. Back on Colony Street, Mrs O'Hara's dog Bowser barked on and on, *roop-roop-roop*, the sound lost and somehow dreamy, seeming more like something remembered than something happening at that moment.

'Well,' Bobby said, folding the paper and getting up, 'I think I'll take a walk around the block and see what I see.' He didn't want to come right out and say it, but he wanted Ted to know he was still looking for the low men in the yellow coats.

Ted also got up and approached him. Bobby was saddened to see the fear on Ted's face. He didn't want Ted to believe in the low men too much, didn't want Ted to be too crazy. 'Be back before dark, Bobby. I'd never forgive myself if something happened to you.'

'I'll be careful. And I'll be back years before dark.'

Ted dropped to one knee (he was too old to just hunker, Bobby guessed) and took hold of Bobby's shoulders. He drew Bobby forward until their brows were almost bumping. Bobby could smell cigarettes on Ted's breath and ointment on his skin – he rubbed his joints with Musterole because they ached. These days they ached even in warm weather, he said.

Being this close to Ted wasn't scary, but it was sort of awful, just the same. You could see that even if Ted wasn't totally old now, he soon would be. He'd probably be sick, too. His eyes were watery. The corners of his mouth were trembling a little. It was too bad he had to be all alone up here on the third floor, Bobby thought. If he'd had a wife or something, he might never have gotten this bee in his bonnet about the low men. Of course, if he'd had a wife, Bobby might never have read *Lord of the Flies*. A selfish way to think, but he couldn't help it.

'No sign of them, Bobby?'

Bobby shook his head.

'And you feel nothing? Nothing here?' He took his right hand from Bobby's left shoulder and tapped his own temple, where two blue veins nested, pulsing slightly. Bobby shook his head. 'Or here?' Ted pulled down the corner of his right eye. Bobby shook his head again. 'Or here?' Ted touched his stomach. Bobby shook his head a third time.

'Okay,' Ted said, and smiled. He slipped his left hand up to the back of Bobby's neck. His right hand joined it. He looked solemnly into Bobby's eyes and Bobby looked solemnly back. 'You'd tell me if you did, wouldn't you? You wouldn't try to . . . oh, I don't know . . . to spare my feelings?'

'No,' Bobby said. He liked Ted's hands on the back of his

neck and didn't like them at the same time. It was where a guy in a movie might put his hands just before he kissed the girl. 'No, I'd tell, that's my job.'

Ted nodded. He slowly unlaced his hands and let them drop. He got to his feet, using the table for support and grimacing when one knee popped loudly. 'Yes, you'd tell me, you're a good kid. Go on, take your walk. But stay on the sidewalk, Bobby, and be home before dark. You have to be careful these days.'

'I'll be careful.' He started down the stairs.

'And if you see them—'

'I'll run.'

'Yeah.' In the fading light, Ted's face was grim. 'Like hell was after you.'

So there had been touching, and perhaps his mother's fears had been justified in a way – perhaps there had been too much touching and some of the wrong sort. Not wrong in whatever way she thought, maybe, but still wrong. Still dangerous.

On the Wednesday before school let out for the summer, Bobby saw a red strip of cloth hanging from somebody's TV antenna over on Colony Street. He couldn't tell for sure, but it looked remarkably like a kite tail. Bobby's feet stopped dead. At the same time his heart accelerated until it was hammering the way it did when he raced Sully-John home from school.

It's a coincidence even if it is *a kite tail*, he told himself. *Just a lousy coincidence. You know that, don't you?*

Maybe. Maybe he knew. He had almost come to believe it, anyway, when school let out for the summer on Friday.

161

Bobby walked home by himself that day; Sully-John had volunteered to stay and help put books away in the store-room and Carol was going over Tina Lebel's for Tina's birthday party. Just before crossing Asher Avenue and starting down Broad Street Hill, he saw a hopscotch grid drawn on the sidewalk in purple chalk. It looked like this:

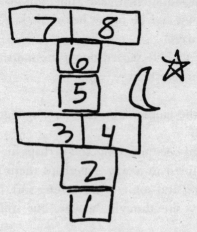

'Oh Christ no,' Bobby whispered. 'You gotta be kidding.'

He dropped to one knee like a cavalry scout in a western movie, oblivious of the kids passing by him on their way home – some walking, some on bikes, a couple on roller skates, buck-toothed Francis Utterson on his rusty red scooter, honking laughter at the sky as he paddled along. They were almost as oblivious of him; the Big Vac had just started, and most were dazed by all the possibilities.

'Oh no, oh no, I don't believe it, you *gotta* be kidding.' He reached out toward the star and the crescent moon – they were drawn in yellow chalk, not purple – almost touched them, then drew his hand back. A piece of red ribbon caught

162

on a TV antenna didn't have to mean anything. When you added this, though, could it still be coincidence? Bobby didn't know. He was only eleven and there were a bazillion things he didn't know. But he was afraid . . . afraid that . . .

He got to his feet and looked around, half-expecting to see a whole line of long, overbright cars coming down Asher Avenue, rolling slow the way cars did when they were following a hearse to the graveyard, with their headlights on in the middle of the day. Half-expecting to see men in yellow coats standing beneath the marquee of the Asher Empire or out in front of Sukey's Tavern, smoking Camels and watching him.

No cars. No men. Just kids heading home from school. The first ones from St Gabe's, conspicuous in their green uniform pants and skirts, were visible among them.

Bobby turned around and backtracked for three blocks up Asher Avenue, too worried about what he'd seen chalked on the sidewalk to concern himself about bad-tempered St Gabe's boys. There was nothing on the Avenue telephone poles but a few posters advertising Bingo Nite at the St Gabriel Parish Hall and one on the corner of Asher and Tacoma announcing a rock-and-roll show in Hartford starring Clyde McPhatter and Dwayne Eddy, the Man with the Twangy Guitar.

By the time he got to Asher Avenue News, which was almost all the way back to school, Bobby was starting to hope he had overreacted. Still, he went in to look at their bulletin board, then all the way down Broad Street to Spicer's Variety, where he bought another gumball and checked that bulletin board as well. Nothing suspicious on either one. In Spicer's the card advertising the backyard pool was gone, but so what? The guy had probably sold it. Why else had he put the card up in the first place, for God's sake?

Bobby left and stood on the corner, chewing his gumball and trying to make up his mind what to do next.

Adulthood is accretive by nature, a thing which arrives in ragged stages and uneven overlaps. Bobby Garfield made the first adult decision of his life on the day he finished the sixth grade, concluding it would be wrong to tell Ted about the stuff he had seen . . . at least for the time being.

His assumption that the low men didn't exist had been shaken, but Bobby wasn't ready to give it up. Not on the evidence he had so far. Ted would be upset if Bobby told him what he had seen, maybe upset enough to toss his stuff back into his suitcases (plus those carryhandle bags folded up behind his little fridge) and just take off. If there really were bad guys after him, flight would make sense, but Bobby didn't want to lose the only adult friend he'd ever had if there weren't. So he decided to wait and see what, if anything, happened next.

That night Bobby Garfield experienced another aspect of adulthood: he lay awake until well after his Big Ben alarm clock said it was two in the morning, looking up at the ceiling and wondering if he had done the right thing.

CHAPTER FOUR

TED GOES BLANK. BOBBY GOES TO THE BEACH. MCQUOWN. THE WINKLE.

The day after school ended, Carol Gerber's mom crammed her Ford Estate Wagon with kids and took them to Savin Rock, a seaside amusement park twenty miles from Harwich. Anita Gerber had done this three years running, which made it an ancient tradition to Bobby, S-J, Carol, Carol's little brother, and Carol's girlfriends, Yvonne, Angie, and Tina. Neither Sully-John nor Bobby would have gone anywhere with three girls on his own, but since they were together it was okay. Besides, the lure of Savin Rock was too strong to resist. It would still be too cold to do much more than wade in the ocean, but they could goof on the beach and all the rides would be open – the midway, too. The year before, Sully-John had knocked down three pyramids of wooden milk-bottles with just three baseballs, winning his mother a large pink teddy bear which still held pride of place on top of the Sullivan TV. Today S-J wanted to win it a mate.

For Bobby, just getting away from Harwich for a little while was an attraction. He had seen nothing suspicious since the star and the moon scribbled next to the hopscotch grid, but Ted gave him a bad scare while Bobby was reading him the Saturday newspaper, and hard on the heels of that came an ugly argument with his mother.

The thing with Ted happened while Bobby was reading an opinion piece scoffing at the idea that Mickey Mantle would ever break Babe Ruth's home-run record. He didn't have the stamina or the dedication, the columnist insisted. '"Above all, the character of this man is wrong,"' Bobby read. '"The so-called Mick is more interested in night-clubbing than—"'

Ted had blanked out again. Bobby knew this, felt it somehow, even before he looked up from the newspaper. Ted was staring emptily out his window toward Colony Street and the hoarse, monotonous barking of Mrs O'Hara's dog. It was the second time he'd done it this morning, but the first lapse had lasted only a few seconds (Ted bent into the open refrigerator, eyes wide in the frosty light, not moving . . . then giving a jerk, a little shake, and reaching for the orange juice). This time he was totally gone. Wigsville, man, as Kookie might have said on 77 *Sunset Strip*. Bobby rattled the newspaper to see if he could wake him up that way. Nothing.

'Ted? Are you all r—'With sudden dawning horror, Bobby realized something was wrong with the pupils of Ted's eyes. They were growing and shrinking in his face as Bobby watched. It was as if Ted were plunging rapidly in and out of some abysmally black place . . . and yet all he was doing was sitting there in the sunshine.

'Ted?'

A cigarette was burning in the ashtray, except it was now

nothing but stub and ash. Looking at it, Bobby realized Ted must have been out for almost the entire article on Mantle. And that thing his eyes were doing, the pupils swelling and contracting, swelling and contracting . . .

He's having an epilepsy attack or something. God, don't they sometimes swallow their tongues when that happens?

Ted's tongue looked to be where it belonged, but his eyes . . . his *eyes*—

'Ted! Ted, wake up!'

Bobby was around to Ted's side of the table before he was even aware he was moving. He grabbed Ted by the shoulders and shook him. It was like shaking a piece of wood carved to look like a man. Under his cotton pullover shirt Ted's shoulders were hard and scrawny and unyielding.

'Wake up! *Wake up!*'

'They draw west now.' Ted continued to look out the window with his strange moving eyes. 'That's good. But they may be back. They . . .'

Bobby stood with his hands on Ted's shoulders, frightened and awestruck. Ted's pupils expanded and contracted like a heartbeat you could see. 'Ted, what's wrong?'

'I must be very still. I must be a hare in the bush. They may pass by. There will be water if God wills it, and they may pass by. All things serve . . .'

'Serve what?' Almost whispering now. 'Serve what, Ted?'

'All things serve the Beam,' Ted said, and suddenly his hands closed over Bobby's. They were very cold, those hands, and for a moment Bobby felt nightmarish, fainting terror. It was like being gripped by a corpse that could only move its hands and the pupils of its dead eyes.

167

Then Ted was looking at him, and although his eyes were frightened, they were almost normal again. Not dead at all.

'Bobby?'

Bobby pulled his hands free and put them around Ted's neck. He hugged him, and as he did Bobby heard a bell tolling in his head – this was very brief but very clear. He could even hear the pitch of the bell shift, the way the pitch of a train-whistle did if the train was moving fast. It was as if something inside his head were passing at high speed. He heard a rattle of hooves on some hard surface. Wood? No, metal. He smelled dust, dry and thundery in his nose. At the same moment the backs of his eyes began to itch.

'Shhh!' Ted's breath in his ear was as dry as the smell of that dust, and somehow intimate. His hands were on Bobby's back, cupping his shoulderblades and holding him still. 'Not a word! Not a thought. Except . . . baseball! Yes, baseball, if you like!'

Bobby thought of Maury Wills getting his lead off first, a walking lead, measuring three steps . . . then four . . . Wills bent over at the waist, hands dangling, heels raised slightly off the dirt, he can go either way, it depends on what the pitcher does . . . and when the pitcher goes to the plate Wills heads for second in an explosion of speed and dust and—

Gone. Everything was gone. No bell ringing in his head, no sound of hooves, no smell of dust. No itching behind his eyes, either. Had that itching really ever been there? Or had he just made it up because Ted's eyes were scaring him?

'Bobby,' Ted said, again directly into Bobby's ear. The movement of Ted's lips against his skin made him shiver. Then: 'Good God, what am I doing?'

He pushed Bobby away, gently but firmly. His face looked

dismayed and a little too pale, but his eyes were back to normal, his pupils holding steady. For the moment that was all Bobby cared about. He felt strange, though – muzzy in the head, as if he'd just woken up from a heavy nap. At the same time the world looked amazingly brilliant, every line and shape perfectly defined.

'Shazam,' Bobby said, and laughed shakily. 'What just happened?'

'Nothing to concern you.' Ted reached for his cigarette and seemed surprised to see only a tiny smoldering scrap left in the groove where he had set it. He brushed it into the ashtray with his knuckle. 'I went off again, didn't I?'

'Yeah, *way* off. I was scared. I thought you were having an epilepsy fit or something. Your eyes—'

'It's not epilepsy,' Ted said. 'And it's not dangerous. But if it happens again, it would be best if you didn't touch me.'

'Why?'

Ted lit a fresh cigarette. 'Just because. Will you promise?'

'Okay. What's the Beam?'

Ted gazed at him sharply. 'I spoke of the Beam?'

'You said "All things serve the Beam." I think that was it.'

'Perhaps sometime I'll tell you, but not today. Today you're going to the beach, aren't you?'

Bobby jumped, startled. He looked at Ted's clock and saw it was almost nine o'clock. 'Yeah,' he said. 'Maybe I ought to start getting ready. I could finish reading you the paper when I get back.'

'Yes, good. A fine idea. I have some letters to write.'

No you don't, you just want to get rid of me before I ask any other questions you don't want to answer.

But if that was what Ted was doing it was all right. As Liz Garfield so often said, Bobby had his own fish to fry. Still, as he reached the door to Ted's room, the thought of the red scrap of cloth hanging from the TV aerial and the crescent moon and the star next to the hopscotch grid made him turn reluctantly back.

'Ted, there's something—'

'The low men, yes, I know.' Ted smiled. 'For now don't trouble yourself about them, Bobby. For now all is well. They aren't moving this way or even looking this way.'

'They draw west,' Bobby said.

Ted looked at him through a scurf of rising cigarette smoke, his blue eyes steady. 'Yes,' he said, 'and with luck they'll *stay* west. Seattle would be fine with me. Have a good time at the seaside, Bobby.'

'But I saw—'

'Perhaps you saw only shadows. In any case, this isn't the time to talk. Just remember what I said – if I should go blank like that again, just sit and wait for it to pass. If I should reach for you, stand back. If I should get up, tell me to sit down. In that state I will do as you say. It's like being hypnotized.'

'Why do you—'

'No more questions, Bobby. Please.'

'You're okay? Really okay?'

'In the pink. Now go. Enjoy your day.'

Bobby hurried downstairs, again struck by how sharp everything seemed to be: the brilliance of the light slanting through the window on the second-floor landing, a ladybug crawling around the lip of an empty milk-bottle outside the door of the Proskys' apartment, a sweet high humming in his ears that was like the voice of the day – the first Saturday of summer vacation.

Back in the apartment, Bobby grabbed his toy cars and trucks from various stashes under his bed and at the back of his closet. A couple of these – a Matchbox Ford and a blue metal dumptruck Mr Biderman had sent home with his mom a few days after Bobby's birthday – were pretty cool, but he had nothing to rival Sully's gasoline tanker or yellow Tonka bulldozer. The 'dozer was especially good to play with in the sand. Bobby was looking forward to at least an hour's serious roadbuilding while the waves broke nearby and his skin pinkened in the bright coastal sunshine. It occurred to him that he hadn't gathered up his trucks like this since some-time last winter, when he and S-J had spent a happy post-blizzard Saturday afternoon making a road-system in the fresh snow down Commonwealth Park. He was old now, eleven, almost too old for stuff like this. There was something sad about that idea, but he didn't have to be sad right now, not if he didn't want to. His toy-truck days might be fast approaching their end, but that end wouldn't be today. Nope, not today.

His mother packed him a lunch for the trip, but she wouldn't give him any money when he asked – not even a nickel for one of the private changing-stalls which lined the ocean side of the midway. And almost before Bobby realized it was happening, they were having what he most dreaded: an argument about money.

'Fifty cents'd be enough,' Bobby said. He heard the baby-whine in his voice, hated it, couldn't stop it. 'Just half a rock. Come on, Mom, what do you say? Be a sport.'

She lit a Kool, striking the match so hard it made a snapping sound, and looked at him through the smoke with her eyes narrowed. 'You're earning your own money now, Bob. Most people pay three cents for the paper and you get paid for reading it. A dollar a week! My God! When I was a girl—'

'Mom, that money's for my bike! You know that.'

She had turned to the mirror, frowning and fussing at the shoulders of her blouse – Mr Biderman had asked her to come in for a few hours even though it was Saturday. Now she turned back, cigarette still clamped between her lips, and bent her frown on him.

'You're still asking me to buy you that bike, aren't you? *Still.* I told you I couldn't afford it but you're still asking.'

'No, I'm not! I'm not either!' Bobby's eyes were wide with anger and hurt. 'Just a lousy half a rock for the—'

'Half a buck here, two bits there – it all adds up, you know. What you want is for me to buy you that bike by handing you the money for everything else. Then you don't have to give up any of the *other* things you want.'

'That's not fair!'

He knew what she would say before she said it, even had time to think that he had walked right into that one. '*Life's* not fair, Bobby-O.' Turning back to the mirror for one final pluck at the ghost of a slip-strap hovering beneath the right shoulder of her blouse.

'A nickel for the changing-room?' Bobby asked. 'Couldn't you at least—'

'Yes, probably, oh, I imagine,' she said, clipping off each word. She usually put rouge on her cheeks before going to work, but not all the color on her face this morning came out of a powderbox, and Bobby, angry as he was, knew he'd better be careful. If he lost his temper the way she was capable of losing hers, he'd be here in the hot empty apartment all day, forbidden to so much as step out into the hall.

His mother snatched her purse off the table by the end of the couch, butted out her cigarette hard enough to split the filter, then turned and looked at him. 'If I said to you, "Gee, we can't eat this week because I saw a pair of shoes at Hunsicker's that I just had to have," what would you think?'

I'd think you were a liar, Bobby thought. *And I'd say if you're so broke, Mom, what about the Sears catalogue on the top shelf of your closet? The one with the dollar bills and the five-dollar bills — even a ten or two — taped to the underwear pages in the middle? What about the blue pitcher in the kitchen dish cabinet, the one tucked all the way in the back corner behind the gravy boat with the crack in it, the blue pitcher where you put your spare quarters, where you've been putting them ever since my father died? And when the pitcher's full you roll the quarters and take them to the bank and get bills, and the bills go into the catalogue, don't they? The bills get taped to the underwear pages of the wishbook.*

But he said none of this, only looked down at his sneakers with his eyes burning.

'I have to make choices,' she said. 'And if you're old enough to work, sonnyboy of mine, you'll have to make them, too. Do you think I like telling you no?'

Not exactly, Bobby thought, looking at his sneakers and biting at his lip, which wanted to loosen up and start letting out a bunch of blubbery baby-sounds. *Not exactly, but I don't think you really mind it, either.*

'If we were the Gotrocks, I'd give you five dollars to spend at the beach — hell, ten! You wouldn't have to borrow from

173

your bike-jar if you wanted to take your little girlfriend on the Loop-the-Loop—'

She's not my girlfriend! Bobby screamed at his mother inside his head. SHE IS NOT MY LITTLE GIRLFRIEND!

'—or the Indian Railroad. But of course if we were the Gotrocks, you wouldn't need to save for a bike in the first place, would you?' Her voice rising, rising. Whatever had been troubling her over the last few months threatening to come rushing out, foaming like sodapop and biting like acid. 'I don't know if you ever noticed this, but your father didn't exactly leave us well off, and I'm doing the best I can. I feed you, I put clothes on your back, I paid for you to go to Sterling House this summer and play baseball while I push paper in that hot office. You got invited to go to the beach with the other kids, I'm very happy for you, but how you finance your day off is your business. If you want to ride the rides, take some of the money you've got in that jar and ride them. If you don't, just play on the beach or stay home. Makes no difference to me. I just want you to stop whining. I hate it when you whine. It's like . . .' She stopped, sighed, opened her purse, took out her cigarettes. 'I hate it when you whine,' she repeated.

It's like your father. That was what she had stopped herself from saying.

'So what's the story, morning-glory?' she asked. 'Are you finished?'

Bobby stood silent, cheeks burning, eyes burning, looking down at his sneakers and focusing all his will on not blubbering. At this point a single choked sob might be enough to get him grounded for the day; she was really mad, only looking for a reason to do it. And blubbering wasn't the only danger. He wanted to scream at her that he'd rather be like his father than like her, a skinflinty old cheapskate like her, not good for even a lousy nickel, and so what if the late not-so-great Randall Garfield hadn't left them well off? Why did she always make it sound like that was *his* fault? Who had married him?

'You sure, Bobby-O? No more smartass comebacks?' The most dangerous sound of all had come into her voice – a kind of brittle brightness. It sounded like good humor if you didn't know her.

Bobby looked at his sneakers and said nothing. Kept all the blubbering and all the angry words locked in his throat and said nothing. Silence spun out between them. He could smell her cigarette and all of last night's cigarettes behind this one, and those smoked on all the other nights when she didn't so much look at the TV as through it, waiting for the phone to ring.

'All right, I guess we've got ourselves straight,' she said after giving him fifteen seconds or so to open his mouth and stick his big fat foot in it. 'Have a nice day, Bobby.' She went out without kissing him.

Bobby went to the open window (tears were running down his face now, but he hardly noticed them), drew aside the curtain, and watched her head toward Commonwealth, high heels tapping. He took a couple of big, watery breaths and then went into the kitchen. He looked across it at the cupboard where the blue pitcher hid behind the gravy boat. He could take some money out of it, she didn't keep any exact count of how much was in there and she'd never miss three or four quarters, but he wouldn't. Spending it would be joyless. He wasn't sure how he knew that, but he did; had known it even at nine, when he first discovered the pitcher of change hidden there. So, with feelings of regret rather than righteousness, he went into his bedroom and looked at the Bike Fund jar instead.

It occurred to him that she was right – he *could* take a little of his saved dough to spend at Savin Rock. It might take him an extra month to accumulate the price of the Schwinn, but at least spending this money would feel all right. And there was something else, as well. If he refused to take any money out of the jar, to do anything but hoard it and save it, he'd be like *her*.

That decided the matter. Bobby fished five dimes out of the Bike Fund, put them in his pocket, put a Kleenex on top of them to keep them from bouncing out if he ran some-where, then finished collecting his stuff for the beach. Soon he was whistling, and Ted came downstairs to see what he was up to.

'Are you off, Captain Garfield?'

Bobby nodded. 'Savin Rock's a pretty cool place. Rides and stuff, you know?'

'Indeed I do. Have a good time, Bobby, and don't fall out of anything.'

Bobby started for the door, then looked back at Ted, who was standing on the bottom step of the stairs in his slippers. 'Why don't you come out and sit on the porch?' Bobby asked. 'It's gonna be hot in the house, I bet.'

Ted smiled. 'Perhaps. But I think I'll stay in.'

'You okay?'

'Fine, Bobby. I'm fine.'

As he crossed to the Gerbers' side of Broad Street, Bobby realized he felt sorry for Ted, hiding up in his hot room for no reason. And it *had* to be for no reason, didn't it? Sure it did. Even if there were low men out there, cruising around someplace (*in the west*, he thought, *they draw west*), what could they want of an old retired guy like Ted Brautigan?

At first the quarrel with his mother weighed him down a little (Mrs Gerber's pudgy, pretty friend Rionda Hewson accused him of being 'in a brown study,' whatever that was, then began tickling him up the sides and in the armpits until Bobby laughed in self-defense), but after they had been on the beach a little while he began to feel better, more himself.

Although it was still early in the season, Savin Rock was full speed ahead – the merry-go-round turning, the Wild Mouse roaring, the little kids screaming, tinny rock and roll pouring from the speakers outside the funhouse, the barkers hollering from their booths. Sully-John didn't get the teddy bear he wanted, knocking over only two of the last three milk-bottles (Rionda claimed some of them had special weights in the bottom to keep them from going over unless you whacked them just right), but the guy in the baseball-toss booth awarded him a pretty neat prize anyway – a goofy-looking anteater covered with yellow plush. S-J impulsively gave it to Carol's mom. Anita laughed and hugged him and told him he was the best kid in the world, if he was fifteen years older she'd commit bigamy and marry him. Sully-John blushed until he was purple.

Bobby tried the ringtoss and missed with all three throws. At the Shooting Gallery he had better luck, breaking two plates and winning a small stuffed bear. He gave it to Ian-the-Snot, who had actually been good for a change – hadn't thrown any tantrums, wet his pants, or tried to sock either

Sully or Bobby in the nuts. Ian hugged the bear and looked at Bobby as if Bobby were God.

'It's great and he loves it,' Anita said, 'but don't you want to take it home to your mother?'

'Nah – she's not much on stuff like that. I'd like to win her a bottle of perfume, though.'

He and Sully-John dared each other to go on the Wild Mouse and finally went together, howling deliriously as their car plunged into each dip, simultaneously sure they were going to live forever and die immediately. They went on the Tilt-a-Whirl and the Krazy Kups. Down to his last fifteen cents, Bobby found himself on the Ferris wheel with Carol. Their car stopped at the top, rocking slightly, making him feel funny in his stomach. To his left the Atlantic stepped shoreward in a series of white-topped waves. The beach was just as white, the ocean an impossible shade of deep blue. Sunlight ran across it like silk. Below them was the midway. Rising up from the speakers came the sound of Freddy Cannon: she comes from Tallahassee, she's got a hi-fi chassis.

'Everything down there looks so little,' Carol said. Her voice was also little – uncharacteristically so.

'Don't be scared, we're safe as can be. The Ferris wheel would be a kiddie-ride if it didn't go so high.'

Carol was in many ways the oldest of the three of them – tough and sure of herself, as on the day she had made S-J carry her books for swearing – but now her face had almost become a baby's face again: round, a little bit pale, dominated by a pair of alarmed blue eyes. Without thinking Bobby leaned over, put his mouth on hers, and kissed her. When he drew back, her eyes were wider than ever.

'Safe as can be,' he said, and grinned.

'Do it again!' It was her first real kiss, she had gotten it at Savin Rock on the first Saturday of summer vacation, and she hadn't been paying attention. That was what she was thinking, that was why she wanted him to do it again.

'I better not,' Bobby said. Although . . . up here who was there to see and call him a sissy?

'I dare you, and don't say dares go first.'

'Will you tell?'

'No, swear to God. Go on, hurry up! Before we go down!'

So he kissed her again. Her lips were smooth and closed, hot with the sun. Then the wheel began to move and he stopped. For just a moment Carol laid her head against his chest. 'Thank you, Bobby,' she said. 'That was nice as could be.'

'I thought so, too.'

They drew apart from each other a little, and when their car stopped and the tattooed attendant swung the safety bar up, Bobby got out and ran without looking back at her to where S-J was standing. Yet he knew already that kissing Carol at the top of the Ferris wheel was going to be the best part of the day. It was his first real kiss, too, and Bobby never forgot the feel of her lips pressing on his − dry and smooth and warmed by the sun. It was the kiss by which all the others of his life would be judged and found wanting.

Around three o'clock, Mrs Gerber told them to start gathering their things; it was time to go home. Carol gave a token 'Aw, Mom,' and then started picking stuff up. Her girlfriends helped; even Ian helped a little (refusing even as he fetched and carried to let go of the sand-matted bear). Bobby had half-expected Carol to tag after him for the rest of the day, and he had been sure she'd tell her girlfriends about kissing on the Ferris wheel (he would know she had when he saw them in a little knot, giggling with their hands over their mouths, looking at him with their merry knowing eyes), but she had done neither. Several times he had caught her looking at him, though, and several times he had caught himself sneaking glances at her. He kept remembering her eyes up there. How big and worried they had been. And he had kissed her, just like that. Bingo.

Bobby and Sully toted most of the beachbags. 'Good mules! Giddyap!' Rionda cried, laughing, as they mounted the steps between the beach and the boardwalk. She was lobster red under the cold-cream she had smeared over her face and shoulders, and she moaned to Anita Gerber that she wouldn't sleep a wink that night, that if the sunburn didn't keep her awake, the midway food would.

'Well, you didn't have to eat four wieners and two dough-boys,' Mrs Gerber said, sounding more irritated than Bobby had ever heard her – she was tired, he reckoned. He felt a little dazed by the sun himself. His back prickled with sunburn and he had sand in his socks. The beachbags with which he was festooned swung and bounced against each other.

'But amusement park food's so *gooood*,' Rionda protested in a sad voice. Bobby laughed. He couldn't help it.

They walked slowly along the midway toward the dirt parking lot, paying no attention to the rides now. The barkers looked at them, then looked past them for fresh blood. Folks loaded down and trudging back to the parking lot were, by and large, lost causes.

At the very end of the midway, on the left, was a skinny

man wearing baggy blue Bermuda shorts, a strap-style undershirt, and a bowler hat. The bowler was old and faded, but cocked at a rakish angle. Also, there was a plastic sunflower stuck in the brim. He was a funny guy, and the girls finally got their chance to put their hands over their mouths and giggle.

He looked at them with the air of a man who has been giggled at by experts and smiled back. This made Carol and her friends giggle harder. The man in the bowler hat, still smiling, spread his hands above the makeshift table behind which he was standing – a slab of fiberboard on two bright orange sawhorses. On the fiberboard were three redbacked Bicycle cards. He turned them over with quick, graceful gestures. His fingers were long and perfectly white, Bobby saw – not a bit of sun-color on them.

The card in the middle was the queen of hearts. The man in the bowler picked it up, showed it to them, walked it dextrously back and forth between his fingers. 'Find the lady in red, *cherchez la femme rouge*, that's what it's all about and all you have to do,' he said. 'It's easy as can beezy, easy-Japaneezy, easy as knitting kitten-britches.' He beckoned Yvonne Loving. 'Come on over here, dollface, and show em how it's done.'

Yvonne, still giggling and blushing to the roots of her black hair, shrank back against Rionda and murmured that she had no more money for games, it was all spent.

'Not a problem,' the man in the bowler hat said. 'It's just a demonstration, dollface – I want your mom and her pretty friend to see how easy it is.'

'Neither one's my mom,' Yvonne said, but she stepped forward.

'We really ought to get going if we're going to beat the traffic, Evvie,' Mrs Gerber said.

'No, wait a minute, this is fun,' Rionda said. 'It's three-card monte. Looks easy, just like he says, but if you're not careful you start chasing and go home dead broke.'

The man in the bowler gave her a reproachful look, then a broad and engaging grin. It was the grin of a low man, Bobby thought suddenly. Not one of those Ted was afraid of, but a low man, just the same.

'It's obvious to me,' said the man in the bowler, 'that at some point in your past you have been the victim of a scoundrel. Although how anyone could be cruel enough to mistreat such a beautiful classy dame is beyond my ability to comprehend.'

The beautiful classy dame — five-five or so, two hundred pounds or so, shoulders and face slathered with Pond's — laughed happily. 'Stow the guff and show the child how it works. And are you really telling me this is legal?'

The man behind the table tossed his head back and also laughed. 'At the ends of the midway everything's legal until they catch you and throw you out . . . as I think you probably know. Now . . . what's your name, dollface?'

'Yvonne,' she said in a voice Bobby could barely hear. Beside him, Sully-John was watching with great interest. 'Sometimes folks call me Evvie.'

'Okay, Evvie, look right here, pretty baby. What do you see? Tell me their names — I know you can, a smart kid like you — and point when you tell. Don't be afraid to touch, either. There's nothing crooked here.'

'This one on the end is the jack . . . this one on the other end is the king . . . and this is the queen. She's in the middle.'

'That's it, dollface. In the cards as in life, there is so often a woman between two men. That's their power, and in another five or six years you'll find it out for yourself.' His voice had fallen into a low, almost hypnotic chanting. 'Now watch closely and never take your eyes from the cards.' He turned them over so their backs showed. 'Now, dollface, where's the queen?'

Yvonne Loving pointed at the red back in the middle.

'Is she right?' the man in the bowler asked the little party gathered around his table.

'So far,' Rionda said, and laughed so hard her uncorseted belly jiggled under her sundress.

Smiling at her laughter, the low man in the bowler hat flicked one corner of the middle card, showing the red queen. 'One hundred per cent keerect, sweetheart, so far so good. Now watch! Watch close! It's a race between your eye and my hand! Which will win? That's the question of the day!'

He began to scramble the three cards rapidly about on his plank table, chanting as he did so.

'Up and down, all around, in and out, all about, to and fro, watch em go, now they're back, they're side by side, so tell me, dollface, where's she hide?'

As Yvonne studied the three cards, which were indeed once more lined up side by side, Sully leaned close to Bobby's ear and said, 'You don't even have to watch him mix them around. The queen's got a bent corner. Do you see it?'

Bobby nodded, and thought *Good girl* when Yvonne pointed hesitantly to the card on the far left – the one with the bent corner. The man in the bowler turned it over and revealed the queen of hearts.

'Good job!' he said. 'You've a sharp eye, dollface, a sharp eye indeed.'

'Thank you,' Yvonne said, blushing and looking almost as happy as Carol had looked when Bobby kissed her.

'If you'd bet me a dime on that go, I'd be giving you back twenty cents right now,' the man in the bowler hat said. 'Why, you ask? Because it's Saturday, and I call Saturday Twoferday! Now would one of you ladies like to risk a dime in a race between your young eyes and my tired old hands? You can tell your husbands – lucky fellas they are to have you, too, may I say – that Mr Herb McQuown, the Monte Man at Savin Rock, paid for your day's parking. Or what about a quarter? Point out the queen of hearts and I give you back fifty cents.'

'Half a rock, yeah!' Sully-John said. 'I got a quarter, Mister, and you're on.'

'Johnny, it's gambling,' Carol's mother said doubtfully. 'I don't really think I should allow—'

'Go on, let the kid learn a lesson,' Rionda said. 'Besides, the guy may let him win. Suck the rest of us in.' She made no effort to lower her voice, but the man in the bowler – Mr McQuown – only looked at her and smiled. Then he returned his attention to S-J.

'Let's see your money, kid – come on, pony up.'

Sully-John handed over his quarter. McQuown raised it into the afternoon sunlight for a moment, one eye closed.

'Yeh, looks like a good 'un to me,' he said, and planked it down on the board to the left of the three-card lineup. He looked in both directions – for cops, maybe – then tipped the cynically smiling Rionda a wink before turning his attention back to Sully-John. 'What's your name, fella?'

'John Sullivan.'

McQuown widened his eyes and tipped his bowler to

the other side of his head, making the plastic sunflower nod and bend comically. 'A name of note! You know what I refer to?'

'Sure. Someday maybe I'll be a fighter, too,' S-J said. He hooked a left and then a right at the air over McQuown's makeshift table. 'Pow, pow!'

'Pow-pow indeed,' said McQuown. 'And how's your eyes, Master Sullivan?'

'Pretty good.'

'Then get them ready, because the race is on! Yes it is! Your eyes against my hands! Up and down, all around, where'd she go, I don't know.' The cards, which had moved much faster this time, slowed to a stop.

Sully started to point, then drew his hand back, frowning. Now there were *two* cards with little folds in the corner. Sully looked up at McQuown, whose arms were folded across his dingy undershirt. McQuown was smiling. 'Take your time, son,' he said. 'The morning was whizbang, but it's been a slow afternoon.'

Men who think hats with feathers in the brims are sophisticated, Bobby remembered Ted saying. *The sort of men who'd shoot craps in an alley and pass around a bottle of liquor in a paper bag during the game.* McQuown had a funny plastic flower in his hat instead of a feather, and there was no bottle in evidence . . . but there was one in his pocket. A little one. Bobby was sure of it. And toward the end of the day, as business wound down and totally sharp hand–eye coordination became less of a priority to him, McQuown would take more and more frequent nips from it.

Sully pointed to the card on the far right. *No, S-J*, Bobby thought, and when McQuown turned that card up, it was the king of spades. McQuown turned up the card on the far left and showed the jack of clubs. The queen was back in the middle. 'Sorry, son, a little slow that time, it ain't no crime. Want to try again now that you're warmed up?'

'Gee, I . . . that was the last of my dough.' Sully-John looked crestfallen.

'Just as well for you, kid,' Rionda said. 'He'd take you for everything you own and leave you standing here in your shortie-shorts.' The girls giggled wildly at this; S-J blushed. Rionda took no notice of either. 'I worked at Revere Beach for quite awhile when I lived in Mass,' she said. 'Let me show you kids how this works. Want to go for a buck, pal? Or is that too sweet for you?'

'In your presence everything would be sweet,' McQuown said sentimentally, and snatched her dollar the moment it was out of her purse. He held it up to the light, examined it with a cold eye, then set it down to the left of the cards. 'Looks like a good 'un,' he said. 'Let's play, darling. What's your name?'

'Pudd'ntane,' Rionda said. 'Ask me again and I'll tell you the same.'

'Ree, don't you think—' Anita Gerber began.

'I told you, I'm wise to the gaff,' Rionda said. 'Run em, my pal.'

'Without delay,' McQuown agreed, and his hands blurred the three red-backed cards into motion (up and down, all around, to and fro, watch them go), finally settling them in a line of three again. And this time, Bobby observed with amazement, all three cards had those slightly bent corners.

Rionda's little smile had gone. She looked from the short row of cards to McQuown, then down at the cards again, and then at her dollar bill, lying off to one side and fluttering slightly in the little seabreeze that had come up. Finally she looked back at McQuown. 'You suckered me, pally,' she said. 'Didn't you?'

'No,' McQuown said. 'I *raced* you. Now . . . what do you say?'

'I think I say that was a real good dollar that didn't make no trouble and I'm sorry to see it go,' Rionda replied, and pointed to the middle card.

McQuown turned it over, revealed the king, and made Rionda's dollar disappear into his pocket. This time the queen was on the far left. McQuown, a dollar and a quarter richer, smiled at the folks from Harwich. The plastic flower tucked into the brim of his hat nodded to and fro in the salt-smelling air. 'Who's next?' he asked. 'Who wants to race his eye against my hand?'

'I think we're all raced out,' Mrs Gerber said. She gave the man behind the table a thin smile, then put one hand on her daughter's shoulder and the other on her sleepy-eyed son's, turning them away.

'Mrs Gerber?' Bobby asked. For just a moment he considered how his mother, once married to a man who had never met an inside straight he didn't like, would feel if she could see her son standing here at Mr McQuown's slap-dash table with that risky Randy Garfield red hair gleaming in the sun. The thought made him smile a little. Bobby knew what an inside straight was now; flushes and full houses, too. He had made inquiries. 'May I try?'

'Oh, Bobby, I really think we've had enough, don't you?'

Bobby reached under the Kleenex he had stuffed into his pocket and brought out his last three nickels. 'All I have is this,' he said, showing first Mrs Gerber and then Mr McQuown. 'Is it enough?'

'Son,' McQuown said, 'I have played this game for pennies and enjoyed it.'

Mrs Gerber looked at Rionda.

'Ah, hell,' Rionda said, and pinched Bobby's cheek. 'It's the price of a haircut, for Christ's sake. Let him lose it and then we'll go home.'

'All right, Bobby,' Mrs Gerber said, and sighed. 'If you have to.'

'Put those nickels down here, Bob, where we can all look at em,' said McQuown. 'They look like good 'uns to me, yes indeed. Are you ready?'

'I think so.'

'Then here we go. Two boys and a girl go into hiding together. The boys are worthless. Find the girl and double your money.'

The pale dextrous fingers turned the three cards over. McQuown spieled and the cards blurred. Bobby watched them move about the table but made no real effort to track the queen. That wasn't necessary.

'Now they go, now they slow, now they rest, here's the test.' The three red-backed cards were in a line again. 'Tell me, Bobby, where's she hide?'

'There,' Bobby said, and pointed to the far left.

Sully groaned. 'It's the *middle* card, you jerk. This time I never took my eye off it.'

McQuown took no notice of Sully. He was looking at Bobby. Bobby looked back at him. After a moment McQuown reached out and turned over the card Bobby had pointed at. It was the queen of hearts.

'What the *heck*?' Sully cried.

Carol clapped excitedly and jumped up and down. Rionda Hewson squealed and smacked him on the back. 'You took im to school that time, Bobby! Attaboy!'

McQuown gave Bobby a peculiar, thoughtful smile, then reached into his pocket and brought out a fistful of change. 'Not bad, son. First time I've been beat all day. That I didn't *let* myself get beat, that is.' He picked out a quarter and a nickel and put them down beside Bobby's fifteen cents. 'Like to let it ride?' He saw Bobby didn't understand. 'Like to go again?'

'May I?' Bobby asked Anita Gerber.

'Wouldn't you rather quit while you're ahead?' she asked, but her eyes were sparkling and she seemed to have forgotten all about beating the traffic home.

'I *am* going to quit while I'm ahead,' he told her.

McQuown laughed. 'A boasty boy! Won't be able to grow a single chin-whisker for another five years, but he's a boasty boy already. Well then, Boasty Bobby, what do you think? Are we on for the game?'

'Sure,' Bobby said. If Carol or Sully-John had accused him of boasting, he would have protested strongly – all his heroes, from John Wayne to Lucky Starr of the Space Patrol, were modest fellows, the kind to say 'Shucks' after saving a world or a wagon train. But he felt no need to defend himself to Mr McQuown, who was a low man in blue shorts and maybe a card-cheater as well. Boasting had been the furthest thing from Bobby's mind. He didn't think this was much like his dad's inside straights, either. Inside straights were all hope and guesswork – 'fool's poker,' according to Charlie Yearman, the Harwich Elementary janitor, who had been happy to tell

Bobby everything about the game that S-J and Denny Rivers hadn't known – but there was no guesswork about this.

Mr McQuown looked at him a moment longer; Bobby's calm confidence seemed to trouble him. Then he reached up, adjusted the slant of his bowler, stretched out his arms, and wiggled his fingers like Bugs Bunny before he played the piano at Carnegie Hall in one of the Merrie Melodies. 'Get on your mark, boasty boy. I'm giving you the whole business this time, from the soup to the nuts.'

The cards blurred into a kind of pink film. From behind him Bobby heard Sully-John mutter 'Holy crow!' Carol's friend Tina said 'That's too *fast*' in an amusing tone of prim disapproval. Bobby again watched the cards move, but only because he felt it was expected of him. Mr McQuown didn't bother with any patter this time, which was sort of a relief.

The cards settled. McQuown looked at Bobby with his eyebrows raised. There was a little smile on his mouth, but he was breathing fast and there were beads of sweat on his upper lip.

Bobby pointed immediately to the card on the right. 'That's her.'

'How do you know that?' Mr McQuown asked, his smile fading. 'How the hell do you know that?'

'I just do,' Bobby said.

Instead of flipping the card, McQuown turned his head slightly and looked down the midway. The smile had been replaced by a petulant expression – downturned lips and a crease between his eyes. Even the plastic sunflower in his hat seemed displeased, its to-and-fro bob now sulky instead of jaunty. 'No one beats that shuffle,' he said. 'No one has *ever* beaten that shuffle.'

Rionda reached over Bobby's shoulder and flipped the card he had pointed at. It was the queen of hearts. This time all the kids clapped. The sound made the crease between Mr McQuown's eyes deepen.

'The way I figure, you owe old Boasty Bobby here ninety cents,' Rionda said. 'Are you gonna pay?'

'Suppose I don't?' Mr McQuown asked, turning his frown on Rionda. 'What are you going to do, tubbo? Call a cop?'

'Maybe we ought to just go,' Anita Gerber said, sounding nervous.

'Call a cop? Not me,' Rionda said, ignoring Anita. She never took her eyes off McQuown. 'A lousy ninety cents out of your pocket and you look like Baby Huey with a load in his pants. Jesus wept!'

Except, Bobby knew, it wasn't the money. Mr McQuown had lost a lot more than this on occasion. Sometimes when he lost it was a 'hustle'; sometimes it was an 'out.' What he was steamed about now was the *shuffle*. McQuown hadn't liked a kid beating his shuffle.

'What I'll do,' Rionda continued, 'is tell anybody on the midway who wants to know that you're a cheapskate. Ninety-Cent McQuown, I'll call you. Think that'll help your business?'

'I'd like to give *you* the business,' Mr McQuown growled, but he reached into his pocket, brought out another dip of change – a bigger one this time – and quickly counted out Bobby's winnings. 'There,' he said. 'Ninety cents. Go buy yourself a martini.'

'I really just guessed, you know,' Bobby said as he swept the coins into his hand and then shoved them into his pocket, where they hung like a weight. The argument that morning with his mother now seemed exquisitely stupid. He was going home with more money than he had come with, and it meant nothing. Nothing. 'I'm a good guesser.'

Mr McQuown relaxed. He wouldn't have hurt them in any case – he might be a low man but he wasn't the kind who hurt people; he'd never subject those clever long-fingered hands to the indignity of forming a fist – but Bobby didn't want to leave him unhappy. He wanted what Mr McQuown himself would have called 'an out.'

'Yeah,' McQuown said. 'A good guesser is what you are. Like to try a third guess, Bobby? Riches await.'

'We really have to be going,' Mrs Gerber said hastily.

'And if I tried again I'd lose,' Bobby said. 'Thank you, Mr McQuown. It was a good game.'

'Yeah, yeah. Get lost, kid.' Mr McQuown was like all the other midway barkers now, looking farther down the line. Looking for fresh blood.

Going home, Carol and her girlfriends kept looking at him with awe; Sully-John with a kind of puzzled respect. It made Bobby feel uncomfortable. At one point Rionda turned around and regarded him closely. 'You didn't just guess,' she said.

Bobby looked at her cautiously, withholding comment.

'You had a winkle.'

'What's a winkle?'

'My dad wasn't much of a betting man, but every now and then he'd get a hunch about a number. He called it a winkle. *Then* he'd bet. Once he won fifty dollars. Bought us groceries for a whole month. That's what happened to you, isn't it?'

'I guess so,' Bobby said. 'Maybe I had a winkle.'

When he got home, his mom was sitting on the porch glider with her legs folded under her. She had changed into her Saturday pants and was looking moodily out at the street. She waved briefly to Carol's mom as she drove away; watched as Anita turned into her own driveway and Bobby trudged up the walk. He knew what his mom was thinking: Mrs Gerber's husband was in the Navy, but at least she *had* a husband. Also, Anita Gerber had an Estate Wagon. Liz had shank's mare, the bus if she had to go a little farther, or a taxi if she needed to go into Bridgeport.

But Bobby didn't think she was angry at him anymore, and that was good.

'Did you have a nice time at Savin, Bobby?'

'Super time,' he said, and thought: *What is it, Mom? You don't care what kind of time I had at the beach. What's really on your mind?* But he couldn't tell.

'Good. Listen, kiddo . . . I'm sorry we got into an argument this morning. I *hate* working on Saturdays.' This last came out almost in a spit.

'It's okay, Mom.'

She touched his cheek and shook her head. 'That fair skin of yours! You'll never tan, Bobby-O. Not you. Come on in and I'll put some Baby Oil on that sunburn.'

He followed her inside, took off his shirt, and stood in front of her as she sat on the couch and smeared the fragrant Baby Oil on his back and arms and neck – even on his cheeks. It felt good, and he thought again how much he loved her, how much he loved to be touched by her. He wondered what she would think if she knew he had kissed Carol on the Ferris wheel. Would she smile? Bobby didn't think she would smile. And if she knew about McQuown and the cards—

'I haven't seen your pal from upstairs,' she said, recapping the Baby Oil bottle. 'I know he's up there because I can hear the Yankees game on his radio, but wouldn't you think he'd go out on the porch where it's cool?'

'I guess he doesn't feel like it,' Bobby said. 'Mom, are you okay?'

She looked at him, startled. 'Fine, Bobby.' She smiled and Bobby smiled back. It took an effort, because he didn't think his mom was fine at all. In fact he was pretty sure she wasn't.

He just had a winkle.

That night Bobby lay on his back with his heels spread to the corners of the bed, eyes open and looking up at the ceiling. His window was open, too, the curtains drifting back and forth in a breath of a breeze, and from some other open window came the sound of The Platters: 'Here, in the after-glow of day, We keep our rendezvous, beneath the blue.' Farther away was the drone of an airplane, the honk of a horn.

Rionda's dad had called it a winkle, and once he'd hit the daily number for fifty dollars. Bobby had agreed with her – *a winkle, sure, I had a winkle* – but he couldn't have picked a lottery number to save his soul. The thing was . . .

The thing was Mr McQuown knew where the queen ended up every time, and so I knew.

Once Bobby realized that, other things fell into place.

Obvious stuff, really, but he'd been having fun, and . . . well
. . . you didn't question what you knew, did you? You might
question a winkle – a feeling that came to you right out of
the blue – but you didn't question *knowing*.

Except how did he *know* his mother was taping money
into the underwear pages of the Sears catalogue on the
top shelf of her closet? How did he even know the catalogue was up there? She'd never told him about it. She'd
never told him about the blue pitcher where she put her
quarters, either, but of course he had known about that
for years, he wasn't blind even though he had an idea she
sometimes thought he was. But the catalogue? The quarters
rolled and changed into bills, the bills then taped into the
catalogue? There was no way he could know about a thing
like that, but as he lay here in his bed, listening while
'Earth Angel' replaced 'Twilight Time,' he knew that the
catalogue was there. He knew because *she* knew, and it had
crossed the front part of her mind. And on the Ferris wheel
he had known Carol wanted him to kiss her again because
it had been her first real kiss from a boy and she hadn't
been paying enough attention; it had been over before she
was completely aware it was happening. But knowing that
wasn't knowing the future.

'No, it's just reading minds,' he whispered, and then
shivered all over as if his sunburn had turned to ice.

Watch out, Bobby-O – if you don't watch out you'll wind up
as nuts as Ted with his low men.

Far off, in the town square, the clock began bonging the
hour of ten. Bobby turned his head and looked at the alarm
clock on his desk. Big Ben claimed it was only nine-fifty-
two.

All right, so the clock downtown is a little fast or mine is a little slow. Big deal, McNeal. Go to sleep.

He didn't think he could do that for at least awhile, but it had been quite a day — arguments with mothers, money won from three-card monte dealers, kisses at the top of the Ferris wheel — and he began to drift in a pleasant fashion.

Maybe she is my girlfriend, Bobby thought. *Maybe she's my girlfriend after all.*

With the last premature bong of the town square clock still fading in the air, Bobby fell asleep.

CHAPTER FIVE

BOBBY READS THE PAPER. BROWN, WITH A WHITE BIB. A BIG CHANCE FOR LIZ. CAMP BROAD STREET. AN UNEASY WEEK. OFF TO PROVIDENCE.

On Monday, after his mom had gone to work, Bobby went upstairs to read Ted the paper (although his eyes were actually good enough to do it himself, Ted said he had come to enjoy the sound of Bobby's voice and the luxury of being read to while he shaved). Ted stood in his little bathroom with the door open, scraping foam from his face, while Bobby tried him on various headlines from the various sections.

'VIET SKIRMISHES INTENSIFY?'

'Before breakfast? Thanks but no thanks.'

'CARTS CORRALLED, LOCAL MAN ARRESTED?'

'First paragraph, Bobby.'

'"When police showed up at his Pond Lane residence late yesterday, John T. Anderson of Harwich told them all about his hobby, which he claims is collecting supermarket shopping carts. 'He was very interesting on the subject,' said Officer Kirby Malloy of the Harwich P.D., 'but we weren't entirely satisfied that he'd come by some of the carts in his collection honestly.' Turns out Malloy was 'right with Eversharp.' Of the more than fifty shopping carts in Mr Anderson's back yard, at least twenty had been stolen from the Harwich A&P and Total Grocery. There were even a few carts from the IGA market in Stansbury.'"'

'Enough,' Ted said, rinsing his razor under hot water and then raising the blade to his lathered neck. 'Galumphing small-town humor in response to pathetic acts of compulsive larceny.'

'I don't understand you.'

'Mr Anderson sounds like a man suffering from a neurosis – a mental problem, in other words. Do you think mental problems are funny?'

'Gee, no. I feel bad for people with loose screws.'

'I'm glad to hear you say so. I've known people whose screws were not just loose but entirely missing. A good many such people, in fact. They are often pathetic, sometimes awe-inspiring, and occasionally terrifying, but they are not funny. CARTS CORRALLED, indeed. What else is there?'

'STARLET KILLED IN EUROPEAN ROAD ACCIDENT?'

'Ugh, no.'

'YANKEES ACQUIRE INFIELDER IN TRADE WITH SENATORS?'

'Nothing the Yankees do with the Senators interests me.'

'ALBINI RELISHES UNDERDOG ROLE?'

'Yes, please read that.'

Ted listened closely as he painstakingly shaved his throat. Bobby himself found the story less than riveting – it wasn't about Floyd Patterson or Ingemar Johansson, after all (Sully called the Swedish heavyweight 'Ingie-Baby') – but he read it carefully, nevertheless. The twelve-rounder between Tommy 'Hurricane' Haywood and Eddie Albini was scheduled for Madison Square Garden on Wednesday night of the following week. Both fighters had good records, but age was considered an important, perhaps telling factor: Haywood, twenty-three to Eddie Albini's thirty-six, and a heavy favorite. The winner might get a shot at the heavyweight title in the fall, probably around the time Richard Nixon won the Presidency (Bobby's mom said that was sure to happen, and a good thing – never mind that Kennedy was a Catholic, he was just too young, and apt to be a hothead).

In the article Albini said he could understand why he was the underdog – he was getting up in years a little and some folks thought he was past it because he'd lost by a TKO to Sugar Boy Masters in his last fight. And sure, he knew that Haywood outreached him and was supposed to be mighty savvy for a younger fellow. But he'd been training hard, Albini said, skipping a lot of rope and sparring with a guy who moved and jabbed like Haywood. The article was full of words like *game* and *determined*; Albini was described as being 'full of grit.' Bobby could tell the writer thought Albini was going to get the stuffing knocked out of him and felt sorry for him. Hurricane Haywood hadn't been available to talk to the reporter, but his manager, a fellow named I. Kleindienst (Ted told Bobby how to pronounce the name), said it was likely to be Eddie Albini's last fight. 'He had his day, but his day is over,' I. Kleindienst said. 'If Eddie goes six, I'm going to send my boy to bed without his supper.'

'Irving Kleindienst's a *ka-mai*,' Ted said.

'A what?'

'A fool.' Ted was looking out the window toward the

sound of Mrs O'Hara's dog. Not totally blank the way he sometimes went blank, but distant.

'You know him?' Bobby asked.

'No, no,' Ted said. He seemed first startled by the idea, then amused. 'Know *of* him.'

'It sounds to me like this guy Albini's gonna get creamed.'

'You never know. That's what makes it interesting.'

'What do you mean?'

'Nothing. Go to the comics, Bobby. I want Flash Gordon. And be sure to tell me what Dale Arden's wearing.'

'Why?'

'Because I think she's a real hotsy-totsy,' Ted said, and Bobby burst out laughing. He couldn't help it. Sometimes Ted was a real card.

A day later, on his way back from Sterling House, where he had just filled out the rest of his forms for summer baseball, Bobby came upon a carefully printed poster thumbtacked to an elm in Commonwealth Park.

PLEASE HELP US FIND PHIL!
PHIL is our WELSH CORGI!
PHIL is 7 YRS. OLD!
PHIL is BROWN, with a WHITE BIB!
His EYES are BRIGHT & INTELLIGENT!
The TIPS OF HIS EARS are BLACK!
Will bring you a BALL if you say HURRY UP PHIL!
CALL HOusitonic 5–8337!
(OR)
BRING to 745 Highgate Avenue!
Home of THE SAGAMORE FAMILY!

There was no picture of Phil.

Bobby stood looking at the poster for a fair length of time. Part of him wanted to run home and tell Ted – not only about this but about the star and crescent moon he'd seen chalked beside the hopscotch grid. Another part pointed out that there was all sorts of stuff posted in the park – he could see a sign advertising a concert in the town square posted on another elm right across from where he was standing – and he would be *nuts* to get Ted going about this. These two thoughts contended with each other until they felt like two sticks rubbing together and his brain in danger of catching on fire.

I won't think about it, he told himself, stepping back from the poster. And when a voice from deep within his mind – a dangerously *adult* voice – protested that he was being *paid* to think about stuff like this, to *tell* about stuff like this, Bobby told the voice to just shut up. And the voice did.

When he got home, his mother was sitting on the porch glider again, this time mending the sleeve of a housedress. She looked up and Bobby saw the puffy skin beneath her eyes, the reddened lids. She had a Kleenex folded into one hand.

'Mom—?'

What's wrong? was how the thought finished . . . but finishing it would be unwise. Would likely cause trouble. Bobby had had no recurrence of his brilliant insights on the day of the trip to Savin Rock, but he *knew* her – the way she looked at him when she was upset, the way the hand with the Kleenex in it tensed, almost becoming a fist, the way she drew in breath and sat up straighter, ready to give you a fight if you wanted to go against her.

'What?' she asked him. 'Got something on your mind besides your hair?'

'No,' he said. His voice sounded awkward and oddly shy to his own ears. 'I was at Sterling House. The lists are up for baseball. I'm a Wolf again this summer.'

She nodded and relaxed a little. 'I'm sure you'll make the Lions next year.' She moved her sewing basket from the glider to the porch floor, then patted the empty place. 'Sit down here beside me a minute, Bobby. I've got something to tell you.'

Bobby sat with a feeling of trepidation – she'd been crying, after all, and she sounded quite grave – but it turned out not to be a big deal, at least as far as he could see.

'Mr Biderman – Don – has invited me to go with him and Mr Cushman and Mr Dean to a seminar in Providence. It's a big chance for me.'

'What's a seminar?'

'A sort of conference – people get together to learn about a subject and discuss it. This one is Real Estate in the Sixties. I was very surprised that Don would invite me. Bill Cushman and Curtis Dean, of course I knew *they'd* be going, they're agents. But for Don to ask *me* . . .' She trailed off for a moment, then turned to Bobby and smiled. He thought it was a genuine smile, but it went oddly with her reddened lids. 'I've wanted to become an agent myself for the longest time, and now this, right out of the blue . . . it's a big chance for me, Bobby, and it could mean a big change for us.'

Bobby knew his mom wanted to sell real estate. She had books on the subject and read a little out of them almost every night, often underlining parts. But if it was such a big chance, why had it made her cry?

'Well, that's good,' he said. 'The ginchiest. I hope you learn a lot. When is it?'

'Next week. The four of us leave early Tuesday morning and get back Thursday night around eight o'clock. All the meetings are at the Warwick Hotel, and that's where we'll be staying — Don's booked the rooms. I haven't stayed in a hotel room for twelve years, I guess. I'm a little nervous.'

Did nervous make you cry? Bobby wondered. Maybe so, if you were a grownup — especially a *female* grownup.

'I want you to ask S-J if you can stay with him Tuesday and Wednesday night. I'm sure Mrs Sullivan—'

Bobby shook his head. 'That won't work.'

'Whyever *not*?' Liz bent a fierce look at him. 'Mrs Sullivan hasn't ever minded you staying over before. You haven't gotten into her bad books somehow, have you?'

'No, Mom. It's just that S-J won a week at Camp Winnie.' The sound of all those *W*'s coming out of his mouth made him feel like smiling, but he held it in. His mother was still looking at him in that fierce way . . . and wasn't there a kind of panic in that look? Panic or something like it?

'What's Camp Winnie? What are you talking about?'

Bobby explained about S-J winning the free week at Camp Winiwinaia and how Mrs Sullivan was going to visit her parents in Wisconsin at the same time — plans which had now been finalized, Big Gray Dog and all.

'Damn it, that's just my luck,' his mom said. She almost never swore, said that cursing and what she called 'dirty talk' was the language of the ignorant. Now she made a fist and struck the arm of the glider. '*God* damn it!'

She sat for a moment, thinking. Bobby thought, as well. His only other close friend on the street was Carol, and he doubted his mom would call Anita Gerber and ask if he could stay over there. Carol was a girl, and somehow that made a difference when it came to sleepovers. One of his mother's friends? The thing was she didn't really *have* any . . . except for Don Biderman (and maybe the other two that were going to the seminar in Providence). Plenty of acquaintances, people she said hi to if they were walking back from the supermarket or going to a Friday-night movie downtown, but no one she could call up and ask to keep her eleven-year-old son for a couple of nights; no relatives, either, at least none that Bobby knew of.

Like people travelling on converging roads, Bobby and his mother gradually drew toward the same point. Bobby got there first, if only by a second or two.

'What about Ted?' he asked, then almost clapped his hand over his mouth. It actually rose out of his lap a little.

His mother watched the hand settle back with a return of her old cynical half-smile, the one she wore when dispensing sayings like *You have to eat a peck of dirt before you die* and *Two men looked out through prison bars, one saw the mud and one saw the stars* and of course that all-time favorite, *Life's not fair.*

'You think I don't know you call him Ted when the two of you are together?' she asked. 'You must think I've been taking stupid-pills, Bobby-O.' She sat and looked out at the street. A Chrysler New Yorker slid slowly past – finny, fenderskirted, and highlighted with chrome. Bobby watched it go by. The man behind the wheel was elderly and white-haired and wearing a blue jacket. Bobby thought he was probably all right. Old but not low.

'Maybe it'd work,' Liz said at last. She spoke musingly, more to herself than to her son. 'Let's go talk to Brautigan and see.'

Following her up the stairs to the third floor, Bobby wondered how long she had known how to say Ted's name correctly. A week? A month?

From the start, Dumbo, he thought. *From the very first day.*

Bobby's initial idea was that Ted could stay in his own room on the third floor while Bobby stayed in the apartment on the first floor; they'd both keep their doors open, and if either of them needed anything, they could call.

'I don't believe the Kilgallens or the Proskys would enjoy you yelling up to Mr Brautigan at three o'clock in the morning that you'd had a nightmare,' Liz said tartly. The Kilgallens and the Proskys had the two small second-floor apartments; Liz and Bobby were friendly with neither of them.

'I won't have any nightmares,' Bobby said, deeply humiliated to be treated like a little kid. 'I mean *jeepers.*'

'Keep it to yourself,' his mom said. They were sitting at Ted's kitchen table, the two adults smoking, Bobby with a rootbeer in front of him.

'It's just not the right idea,' Ted told him. 'You're a good kid, Bobby, responsible and level-headed, but eleven's too young to be on your own, I think.'

Bobby found it easier to be called too young by his friend than by his mother. Also he had to admit that it might be spooky to wake up in one of those little hours after midnight and go to the bathroom knowing he was the only person in the apartment. He could do it, he had no doubt he could do it, but yeah, it would be spooky.

'What about the couch?' he asked. 'It pulls out and makes a bed, doesn't it?' They had never used it that way, but Bobby

205

was sure she'd told him once that it did. He was right, and it solved the problem. She probably hadn't wanted Bobby in her bed (let alone 'Brattigan'), and she *really* hadn't wanted Bobby up here in this hot third-floor room – that he was sure of. He figured she'd been looking so hard for a solution that she'd looked right past the obvious one.

So it was decided that Ted would spend Tuesday and Wednesday nights of the following week on the pull-out couch in the Garfields' living room. Bobby was excited by the prospect: he would have two days on his own – three, counting Thursday – and there would be someone with him at night, when things could get spooky. Not a babysitter, either, but a grownup friend. It wasn't the same as Sully-John going to Camp Winnie for a week, but in a way it was. *Camp Broad Street*, Bobby thought, and almost laughed out loud.

'We'll have fun,' Ted said. 'I'll make my famous beans-and-franks casserole.' He reached over and ruffled Bobby's crewcut.

'If you're going to have beans and franks, it might be wise to bring *that* down,' his mom said, and pointed the fingers holding her cigarette at Ted's fan.

Ted and Bobby laughed. Liz Garfield smiled her cynical half-smile, finished her cigarette, and put it out in Ted's ashtray. When she did, Bobby again noticed the puffiness of her eyelids.

As Bobby and his mother went back down the stairs, Bobby remembered the poster he had seen in the park – the missing Corgi who would bring you a BALL if you said HURRY UP PHIL. He should tell Ted about the poster. He should tell Ted about everything. But if he did that and Ted left 149, who would stay with him next week? What would happen to Camp Broad Street, two fellows eating Ted's famous beans-and-franks casserole for supper (maybe in front of the TV, which his mom rarely allowed) and then staying up as late as they wanted?

Bobby made a promise to himself: he would tell Ted everything next Friday, after his mother was back from her conference or seminar or whatever it was. He would make a complete report and Ted could do whatever he needed to do. He might even stick around.

With this decision Bobby's mind cleared amazingly, and when he saw an upside-down FOR SALE card on the Total Grocery bulletin board two days later – it was for a washer-dryer set – he was able to put it out of his thoughts almost immediately.

That was nevertheless an uneasy week for Bobby Garfield, very uneasy indeed. He saw two more lost-pet posters, one downtown and one out on Asher Avenue, half a mile beyond the Asher Empire (the block he lived on was no longer enough; he found himself going farther and farther afield in his daily scouting trips). And Ted began to have those weird blank periods with greater frequency. They lasted longer when they came, too. Sometimes he spoke when he was in that distant state of mind, and not always in English. When he did speak in English, what he said did not always make sense. Most of the time Bobby thought Ted was one of the sanest, smartest, *neatest* guys he had ever met. When he went away, though, it was scary. At least his mom didn't know. Bobby didn't think she'd be too cool on the idea of leaving him with a guy who sometimes flipped out and started talking nonsense in English or gibberish in some other language.

After one of these lapses, when Ted did nothing for almost a minute and a half but stare blankly off into space, making no response to Bobby's increasingly agitated questions, it occurred to Bobby that perhaps Ted wasn't in his own head at all but in some other world – that he had left Earth as surely as those people in *Ring Around the Sun* who discovered they could follow the spirals on a child's top to just about anywhere.

Ted had been holding a Chesterfield between his fingers when he went blank; the ash grew long and eventually dropped off onto the table. When the coal grew unnervingly close to Ted's bunchy knuckles, Bobby pulled it gently free and was putting it out in the overflowing ashtray when Ted finally came back.

'Smoking?' he asked with a frown. 'Hell, Bobby, you're too young to smoke.'

'I was just putting it out for you. I thought . . .' Bobby shrugged, suddenly shy.

Ted looked at the first two fingers of his right hand, where there was a permanent yellow nicotine stain. He laughed – a short bark with absolutely no humor in it. 'Thought I was going to burn myself, did you?'

Bobby nodded. 'What do you think about when you go off like that? Where do you go?'

'That's hard to explain,' Ted replied, and then asked Bobby to read him his horoscope.

Thinking about Ted's trances was distracting. Not talking about the things Ted was paying him to look for was even more distracting. As a result, Bobby – ordinarily a pretty good hitter – struck out four times in an afternoon game for the Wolves at Sterling House. He also lost four straight

Battleship games to Sully at S-J's house on Friday, when it rained.

'What the heck's wrong with you?' Sully asked. 'That's the third time you called out squares you already called out before. Also, I have to practically holler in your ear before you answer me. What's up?'

'Nothing.' That was what he said. *Everything.* That was what he felt.

Carol also asked Bobby a couple of times that week if he was okay; Mrs Gerber asked if he was 'off his feed'; Yvonne Loving wanted to know if he had mono, and then giggled until she seemed in danger of exploding.

The only person who didn't notice Bobby's odd behavior was his mom. Liz Garfield was increasingly preoccupied with her trip to Providence, talking on the phone in the evenings with Mr Biderman or one of the other two who were going (Bill Cushman was one of them; Bobby couldn't exactly remember the name of the other guy), laying clothes out on her bed until the spread was almost covered, then shaking her head over them angrily and returning them to the closet, making an appointment to get her hair done and then calling the lady back and asking if she could add a manicure. Bobby wasn't even sure what a manicure was. He had to ask Ted.

She seemed excited by her preparations, but there was also a kind of grimness to her. She was like a soldier about to storm an enemy beach, or a paratrooper who would soon be jumping out of a plane and landing behind enemy lines. One of her evening telephone conversations seemed to be a whispered argument – Bobby had an idea it was with Mr Biderman, but he wasn't sure. On Saturday, Bobby came into her bedroom and saw her looking at two new dresses – *dressy* dresses, one with thin little shoulder straps and one with no straps at all, just a top like a bathing suit. The boxes they had come in lay tumbled on the floor with tissue paper foaming out of them. His mom was standing over the dresses, looking down at them with an expression Bobby had never seen before: big eyes, drawn-together brows, taut white cheeks which flared with spots of rouge. One hand was at her mouth, and he could hear bonelike clittering sounds as she bit at her nails. A Kool smoldered in an ashtray on the bureau, apparently forgotten. Her big eyes shuttled back and forth between the two dresses.

'Mom?' Bobby asked, and she jumped – literally jumped into the air. Then she whirled on him, her mouth drawn down in a grimace.

'Jesus *Christ*!' she almost snarled. 'Don't you *knock*?'

'I'm sorry,' he said, and began to back out of the room. His mother had never said anything about knocking before. 'Mom, are you all right?'

'Fine!' She spied the cigarette, grabbed it, smoked furiously. She exhaled with such force that Bobby almost expected to see smoke come from her ears as well as her nose and mouth. 'I'd be finer if I could find a cocktail dress that didn't make me look like Elsie the Cow. Once I was a size six, do you know that? Before I married your father I was a size six. Now look at me! Elsie the Cow! Moby-damn-*Dick*!'

'Mom, you're not big. In fact just lately you look—'

'Get out, Bobby. Please let Mother alone. I have a headache.'

That night he heard her crying again. The following day he saw her carefully packing one of the dresses into her luggage – the one with the thin straps. The other went back into its store-box: GOWNS BY LUCIE OF BRIDGEPORT was written across the front in elegant maroon script.

On Monday night, Liz invited Ted Brautigan down to have dinner with them. Bobby loved his mother's meatloaf and usually asked for seconds, but on this occasion he had to work hard to stuff down a single piece. He was terrified that Ted would trance out and his mother would pitch a fit over it.

His fear proved groundless. Ted spoke pleasantly of his childhood in New Jersey and, when Bobby's mom asked him, of his job in Hartford. To Bobby he seemed less comfortable talking about accounting than he did reminiscing about sleighing as a kid, but his mom didn't appear to notice. Ted *did* ask for a second slice of meatloaf.

When the meal was over and the table cleared, Liz gave Ted a list of telephone numbers, including those of Dr Gordon, the Sterling House Summer Rec office, and the Warwick Hotel. 'If there are any problems, I want to hear from you. Okay?'

Ted nodded. 'Okay.'

'Bobby? No big worries?' She put her hand briefly on his forehead, the way she used to do when he complained of feeling feverish.

'Nope. We'll have a blast. Won't we, Mr Brautigan?'

'Oh, call him Ted,' Liz almost snapped. 'If he's going to be sleeping in our living room, I guess I better call him Ted, too. May I?'

'Indeed you may. Let it be Ted from this moment on.'

He smiled. Bobby thought it was a sweet smile, open and friendly. He didn't understand how anyone could resist it. But his mother could and did. Even now, while she was returning Ted's smile, he saw the hand with the Kleenex in it tightening and loosening in its old familiar gesture of anxious displeasure. One of her absolute favorite sayings now came to Bobby's mind: *I'd trust him* (or her) *as far as I could sling a piano.*

'And from now on I'm Liz.' She held out a hand across the table and they shook like people meeting for the first time . . . except Bobby knew his mother's mind was already made up on the subject of Ted Brautigan. If her back hadn't been against the wall, she never would have trusted Bobby with him. Not in a million years.

She opened her purse and took out a plain white envelope. 'There's ten dollars in here,' she said, handing the envelope to Ted. 'You boys will want to eat out at least one night, I expect – Bobby likes the Colony Diner, if that's all right with you – and you may want to take in a movie, as well. I don't know what else there might be, but it's best to have a little cushion, don't you think?'

'Always better safe than sorry,' Ted agreed, tucking the envelope carefully into the front pocket of his slacks, 'but I don't expect we'll go through anything like ten dollars in three days. Will we, Bobby?'

'Gee, no, I don't see how we could.'

'Waste not, want not,' Liz said – it was another of her favorites, right up there with *the fool and his money soon parted.* She plucked a cigarette out of the pack on the table beside the sofa and lit it with a hand which was not quite steady. 'You boys will be fine. Probably have a better time than I will.'

Looking at her ragged, bitten fingernails, Bobby thought, *That's for sure.*

His mom and the others were going to Providence in Mr Biderman's car, and the next morning at seven o'clock Liz and Bobby Garfield stood on the porch, waiting for it to show up. The air had that early hazy hush that meant the hot days of summer had arrived. From Asher Avenue came the hoot and rumble of heavy going-to-work traffic, but down here on Broad there was only the occasional passing car or delivery truck. Bobby could hear the *hisha-hisha* of lawn-sprinklers, and, from the other side of the block, the endless *roop-roop-roop* of Bowser. Bowser sounded the same whether it was June or January; to Bobby Garfield, Bowser seemed as changeless as God.

'You don't have to wait out here with me, you know,' Liz said. She was wearing a light coat and smoking a cigarette. She had on a little more makeup than usual, but Bobby thought he could still detect shadows under her eyes – she had passed another restless night.

'I don't mind.'

'I hope it's all right, leaving you with him.'

'I wish you wouldn't worry. Ted's a good guy, Mom.'

She made a little hmphing noise.

There was a twinkle of chrome from the bottom of the hill as Mr Biderman's Mercury (not vulgar, exactly, but a boat of a car all the same) turned onto their street from Commonwealth and came up the hill toward 149.

'There he is, there he is,' his mom said, sounding nervous and excited. She bent down. 'Give me a little smooch, Bobby. I don't want to kiss you and smear my lipstick.'

Bobby put his hand on her arm and lightly kissed her cheek. He smelled her hair, the perfume she was wearing, her face-powder. He would never kiss her with that same unshadowed love again.

She gave him a vague little smile, not looking at him,

213

looking instead at Mr Biderman's boat of a Merc, which swerved gracefully across the street and pulled up at the curb in front of the house. She reached for her two suitcases (two seemed a lot for two days, Bobby thought, although he supposed the fancy dress took up a good deal of space in one of them), but he already had them by the handles.

'Those are too heavy, Bobby – you'll trip on the steps.'

'No,' he said. 'I won't.'

She gave him a distracted look, then waved to Mr Biderman and went toward the car, high heels clacking. Bobby followed, trying not to grimace at the weight of the suitcases . . . what had she put in them, clothes or bricks?

He got them down to the sidewalk without having to stop and rest, at least. Mr Biderman was out of the car by then, first putting a casual kiss on his mother's cheek, then shaking out the key that opened the trunk.

'Howya doin, Sport, howza boy?' Mr Biderman always called Bobby Sport. 'Lug em around back and I'll slide em in. Women always hafta bring the farm, don't they? Well, you know the old saying – can't live with em, can't shoot em outside the state of Montana.' He bared his teeth in a grin that made Bobby think of Jack in *Lord of the Flies*. 'Want me to take one?'

'I've got em,' Bobby said. He trudged grimly in Mr Biderman's wake, shoulders aching, the back of his neck hot and starting to sweat.

Mr Biderman opened the trunk, plucked the suitcases from Bobby's hands, and slid them in with the rest of the luggage. Behind them, his mom was looking in the back window and talking with the other two men who were going. She laughed at something one of them said. To Bobby the laugh sounded about as real as a wooden leg.

Mr Biderman closed the trunk and looked down at Bobby. He was a narrow man with a wide face. His cheeks were always flushed. You could see his pink scalp in the tracks left by the teeth of his comb. He wore little round glasses with gold rims. To Bobby his smile looked as real as his mother's laugh had sounded.

'Gonna play some baseball this summer, Sport?' Don Biderman bent his knees a little and cocked an imaginary bat. Bobby thought he looked like a dope.

'Yes, sir. I'm on the Wolves at Sterling House. I was hoping to make the Lions, but . . .'

'Good. Good.' Mr Biderman made a big deal of looking at his watch – the wide gold Twist-O-Flex band was dazzling in the early sunshine – and then patted Bobby's cheek. Bobby had to make a conscious effort not to cringe from his touch. 'Say, we gotta get this wagon-train rolling! Shake her easy, Sport. Thanks for the loan of your mother.'

He turned away and escorted Liz around the Mercury to the passenger side. He did this with a hand pressed to her back. Bobby liked that even less than watching the guy smooch her cheek. He glanced at the well-padded, business-suited men in the rear seat – Dean was the other guy's name, he remembered – just in time to see them elbowing each other. Both were grinning.

Something's wrong here, Bobby thought, and as Mr Biderman opened the passenger door for his mother, as she murmured her thanks and slid in, gathering her dress a little so it wouldn't wrinkle, he had an urge to tell her not to go, Rhode Island was too far away, *Bridgeport* would be too far away, she needed to stay home.

He said nothing, though, only stood on the curb as Mr

Biderman closed her door and walked back around to the driver's side. He opened that door, paused, and then did his stupid little batter-up pantomime again. This time he added an asinine fanny-wiggle. *What a nimrod*, Bobby thought.

'Don't do anything I wouldn't do, Sport,' he said.

'But if you do, name it after me,' Cushman called from the back seat. Bobby didn't know exactly what that meant but it must have been funny because Dean laughed and Mr Biderman tipped him one of those just-between-us-guys winks.

His mother was leaning in his direction. 'You be a good boy, Bobby,' she said. 'I'll be back around eight on Thursday night – no later than ten. You're sure you're fine with that?'

No, I'm not fine with it at all. Don't go off with them, Mom, don't go off with Mr Biderman and those two grinning dopes sitting behind you. Those two nimrods. Please don't.

'Sure he is,' Mr Biderman said. 'He's a sport. Ain't you, Sport?'

'Bobby?' she asked, not looking at Mr Biderman. 'Are you all set?'

'Yeah,' he said. 'I'm a sport.'

Mr Biderman bellowed ferocious laughter – *Kill the pig, cut his throat*, Bobby thought – and dropped the Mercury into gear. 'Providence or bust!' he cried, and the car rolled away from the curb, swerving across to the other side of Broad Street and heading up toward Asher. Bobby stood on the sidewalk, waving as the Merc passed Carol's house and Sully-John's. He felt as if he had a bone in his heart. If this was some sort of premonition – a winkle – he never wanted to have another one.

A hand fell on his shoulder. He looked around and saw

Ted standing there in his bathrobe and slippers, smoking a cigarette. His hair, which had yet to make its morning acquaintance with the brush, stood up around his ears in comical sprays of white.

'So that was the boss,' he said. 'Mr . . . Bidermeyer, is it?'

'Bider*man*.'

'And how do you like him, Bobby?'

Speaking with a low, bitter clarity, Bobby said, 'I trust him about as far as I could sling a piano.'

CHAPTER SIX

A DIRTY OLD MAN. TED'S CASSEROLE. A BAD DREAM. *VILLAGE OF THE DAMNED.* DOWN THERE.

An hour or so after seeing his mother off, Bobby went down to Field B behind Sterling House. There were no real games until afternoon, nothing but three-flies-six-grounders or rolly-bat, but even rolly-bat was better than nothing. On Field A, to the north, the little kids were futzing away at a game that vaguely resembled baseball; on Field C, to the south, some high-school kids were playing what was almost the real thing.

Shortly after the town square clock had bonged noon and the boys broke to go in search of the hotdog wagon, Bill Pratt asked, 'Who's that weird guy over there?'

He was pointing to a bench in the shade, and although Ted was wearing a trenchcoat, an old fedora hat, and dark glasses, Bobby recognized him at once. He guessed S-J would've, too, if S-J hadn't been at Camp Winnie. Bobby almost raised one hand in a wave, then didn't, because Ted was in disguise. Still, he'd come out to watch his downstairs friend play ball. Even though it wasn't a real game, Bobby felt an absurdly large lump rise in his throat. His mom had only come to watch him once in the two years he'd been playing – last August, when his team had been in the Tri-Town Championships – and even then she'd left in the fourth inning, before Bobby connected for what proved to be the game-winning triple. *Somebody has to work around here, Bobby-O*, she would have replied had he dared reproach her for that. *Your father didn't exactly leave us well off, you know.* It was true, of course – she had to work and Ted was retired. Except Ted had to stay clear of the low men in the yellow coats, and that was a full-time job. The fact that they didn't exist wasn't the point. Ted *believed* they did . . . but had come out to see him play just the same.

'Probably some dirty old man wanting to put a suckjob on one of the little kids,' Harry Shaw said. Harry was small and tough, a boy going through life with his chin stuck out a mile. Being with Bill and Harry suddenly made Bobby homesick for Sully-John, who had left on the Camp Winnie bus Monday morning (at the brain-numbing hour of five A.M.). S-J didn't have much of a temper and he was kind. Sometimes Bobby thought that was the best thing about Sully – he was kind.

From Field C there came the hefty crack of a bat – an authoritative full-contact sound which none of the Field B boys could yet produce. It was followed by savage roars of approval that made Bill, Harry, and Bobby look a little nervously in that direction.

'St Gabe's boys,' Bill said. 'They think they own Field C.'

'Cruddy Catlicks,' Harry said. 'Catlicks are sissies – I could take any one of them.'

'How about fifteen or twenty?' Bill asked, and Harry was silent. Up ahead, glittering like a mirror, was the hotdog

219

wagon. Bobby touched the buck in his pocket. Ted had given it to him out of the envelope his mother had left, then had put the envelope itself behind the toaster, telling Bobby to take what he needed when he needed it. Bobby was almost exalted by this level of trust.

'Look on the bright side,' Bill said. 'Maybe those St Gabe's boys will beat up the dirty old man.'

When they got to the wagon, Bobby bought only one hotdog instead of the two he had been planning on. His appetite seemed to have shrunk. When they got back to Field B, where the Wolves' coaches had now appeared with the equipment cart, the bench Ted had been sitting on was empty.

'Come on, come on!' Coach Terrell called, clapping his hands. 'Who wants to play some baseball here?'

That night Ted cooked his famous casserole in the Garfields' oven. It meant more hotdogs, but in the summer of 1960 Bobby Garfield could have eaten hotdogs three times a day and had another at bedtime.

He read stuff to Ted out of the newspaper while Ted put their dinner together. Ted only wanted to hear a couple of paragraphs about the impending Patterson–Johansson rematch, the one everybody was calling the fight of the century, but he wanted to hear every word of the article about tomorrow night's Albini–Haywood tilt at The Garden in New York. Bobby thought this moderately weird, but he was too happy to even comment on it, let alone complain.

He couldn't remember ever having spent an evening without his mother, and he missed her, yet he was also relieved to have her gone for a little while. There had been a queer sort of tension running through the apartment for weeks now, maybe even for months. It was like an electrical hum so constant that you got used to it and didn't realize how much a part of your life it had become until it was gone. That thought brought another of his mother's sayings to mind.

'What are you thinking?' Ted asked as Bobby came over to get the plates.

'That a change is as good as a rest,' Bobby replied. 'It's something my mom says. I hope she's having as good a time as I am.'

'So do I, Bobby,' Ted said. He bent, opened the oven, checked their dinner. 'So do I.'

The casserole was terrific, with canned B&M beans – the only kind Bobby really liked – and exotic spicy hotdogs not from the supermarket but from the butcher just off the town square. (Bobby assumed Ted had bought these while wearing his 'disguise.') All this came in a horseradish sauce that zinged in your mouth and then made you feel sort of sweaty in the face. Ted had two helpings; Bobby had three, washing them down with glass after glass of grape Kool-Aid.

Ted blanked out once during the meal, first saying that he could feel *them* in the backs of his eyeballs, then lapsing either into some foreign language or outright gibberish, but the incident was brief and didn't cut into Bobby's appetite in the slightest. The blank-outs were part of Ted, that was all, like his scuffling walk and the nicotine stains between the first two fingers of his right hand.

They cleaned up together, Ted stowing the leftover casserole in the fridge and washing the dishes, Bobby drying and putting things away because he knew where everything went.

'Interested in taking a ride to Bridgeport with me tomorrow?'

Ted asked as they worked. 'We could go to the movies – the early matinee – and then I have to do an errand.'

'Gosh, yeah!' Bobby said. 'What do you want to see?'

'I'm open to suggestions, but I was thinking perhaps *Village of the Damned*, a British film. It's based on a very fine science-fiction novel by John Wyndham. Would that suit?'

At first Bobby was so excited he couldn't speak. He had seen the ads for *Village of the Damned* in the newspaper – all those spooky-looking kids with the glowing eyes – but hadn't thought he would ever actually get to *see* it. It sure wasn't the sort of Saturday-matinee movie that would ever play at Harwich on the Square or the Asher Empire. Matinees in those theaters consisted mostly of big-bug monster shows, westerns, or Audie Murphy war movies. And although his mother usually took him if she went to an evening show, she didn't like science fiction (Liz liked moody love stories like *The Dark at the Top of the Stairs*). Also the theaters in Bridgeport weren't like the antiquey old Harwich or the somehow businesslike Empire, with its plain, undecorated marquee. The theaters in Bridgeport were like fairy castles – they had huge screens (swag upon swag of velvety curtains covered them between shows), ceilings where tiny lights twinkled in galactic profusion, brilliant electric wall-sconces . . . and *two* balconies.

'Bobby?'

'You bet!' he said at last, thinking he probably wouldn't sleep tonight. 'I'd love it. But aren't you afraid of . . . you know . . .'

'We'll take a taxi instead of the bus. I can phone for another taxi to take us back home later. We'll be fine. I think they're moving away now, anyway. I don't sense them so clearly.'

Yet Ted glanced away when he said this, and to Bobby he looked like a man trying to tell himself a story he can't quite believe. If the increasing frequency of his blank-outs meant anything, Bobby thought, he had good reason to look that way.

Stop it, the low men don't exist, they're no more real than Flash Gordon and Dale Arden. The things he asked you to look for are just . . . just things. Remember that, Bobby-O: just ordinary things.

With dinner cleared away, the two of them sat down to watch *Bronco*, with Ty Hardin. Not among the best of the so-called 'adult westerns' (*Cheyenne* and *Maverick* were the best), but not bad, either. Halfway through the show, Bobby let out a moderately loud fart. Ted's casserole had begun its work. He snuck a sideways glance to make sure Ted wasn't holding his nose and grimacing. Nope, just watching the television, seemingly absorbed.

When a commercial came on (some actress selling refrigerators), Ted asked if Bobby would like a glass of rootbeer. Bobby said okay. 'I thought I might help myself to one of the Alka-Seltzers I saw in the bathroom, Bobby. I may have eaten a bit too much.'

As he got up, Ted let out a long, sonorous fart that sounded like a trombone. Bobby put his hands to his mouth and giggled. Ted gave him a rueful smile and left the room. Bobby's giggling forced out more farts, a little tooting stream of them, and when Ted came back with a fizzy glass of Alka-Seltzer in one hand and a foamy glass of Hires rootbeer in the other, Bobby was laughing so hard that tears streamed down his cheeks and hung off his jawline like raindrops.

'This should help fix us up,' Ted said, and when he bent to hand Bobby his rootbeer, a loud honk came from behind him. 'Goose just flew out of my ass,' he added matter-of-factly, and Bobby laughed so hard that he could no longer sit in his chair. He slithered out of it and lay in a boneless heap on the floor.

'I'll be right back,' Ted told him. 'There's something else we need.'

He left open the door between the apartment and the foyer, so Bobby could hear him going up the stairs. By the time Ted got to the third floor, Bobby had managed to crawl into his chair again. He didn't think he'd ever laughed so hard in his life. He drank some of his rootbeer, then farted again. 'Goose just flew . . . flew out . . .' But he couldn't finish. He flopped back in his chair and howled, shaking his head from side to side.

The stairs creaked as Ted came back down. When he re-entered the apartment he had his fan, with the electric cord looped neatly around the base, under one arm. 'Your mother was right about this,' he said. When he bent to plug it in, another goose flew out of his ass.

'She usually is,' Bobby said, and that struck them both as funny. They sat in the living room with the fan rotating back and forth, stirring the increasingly fragrant air. Bobby thought if he didn't stop laughing soon his head would pop.

When *Bronco* was over (by then Bobby had lost all track of the story), he helped Ted pull out the couch. The bed which had been hiding inside it didn't look all that great, but Liz had made it up with some spare sheets and blankets and Ted said it would be fine. Bobby brushed his teeth, then looked out from the door of his bedroom at Ted, who was sitting on the end of the sofa-bed and watching the news.

'Goodnight,' Bobby said.

Ted looked over to him, and for a moment Bobby thought Ted would get up, cross the room, give him a hug and maybe a kiss. Instead of that, he sketched a funny, awkward little salute. 'Sleep well, Bobby.'

'Thanks.'

Bobby closed his bedroom door, turned off the light, got into bed, and spread his heels to the corners of the mattress. As he looked up into the dark he remembered the morning Ted had taken hold of his shoulders, then laced his bunchy old hands together behind his neck. Their faces that day had been almost as close as his and Carol's had been on the Ferris wheel just before they kissed. The day he had argued with his mother. The day he had known about the money taped in the catalogue. Also the day he had won ninety cents from Mr McQuown. *Go buy yourself a martini*, Mr McQuown had said.

Had it come from Ted? Had the winkle come from Ted touching him?

'Yeah,' Bobby whispered in the dark. 'Yeah, I think it probably did.'

What if he touches me again that way?

Bobby was still considering this idea when he fell asleep.

He dreamed that people were chasing his mother through the jungle – Jack and Piggy, the littluns, and Don Biderman, Cushman, and Dean. His mother was wearing her new dress from Gowns by Lucie, the black one with the thin straps, only it had been torn in places by thorns and branches. Her stockings were in tatters. They looked like strips of dead skin hanging off her legs. Her eyes were deep sweat-holes gleaming with terror. The boys chasing her were naked.

225

Biderman and the other two were wearing their business suits. All of them had alternating streaks of red and white paint on their faces; all were brandishing spears and shouting *Kill the pig, slit her throat! Kill the pig, drink her blood! Kill the pig, strew her guts!*

He woke in the gray light of dawn, shivering, and got up to use the bathroom. By the time he went back to bed he could no longer remember precisely what he had dreamed. He slept for another two hours, and woke up to the good smells of bacon and eggs. Bright summer sunshine was slanting in his bedroom window and Ted was making breakfast.

Village of the Damned was the last and greatest movie of Bobby Garfield's childhood; it was the first and greatest movie of what came after childhood – a dark period when he was often bad and always confused, a Bobby Garfield he felt he didn't really know. The cop who arrested him for the first time had blond hair, and what came to Bobby's mind as the cop led him away from the mom-n-pop store Bobby had broken into (by then he and his mother were living in a suburb north of Boston) were all those blond kids in *Village of the Damned*. The cop could have been one of them all grown up.

The movie was playing at the Criterion, the very avatar of those Bridgeport dream-palaces Bobby had been thinking about the night before. It was in black and white, but the contrasts were sharp, not all fuzzy like on the Zenith back in the apartment, and the images were *enormous*. So were the sounds, especially the shivery theremin music that played when the Midwich children really started to use their power.

Bobby was enthralled by the story, understanding even

before the first five minutes were over that it was a *real* story, the way *Lord of the Flies* had been a real story. The people seemed like real people, which made the make-believe parts scarier. He guessed that Sully-John would have been bored with it, except for the ending. S-J liked to see giant scorpions crushing Mexico City or Rodan stomping Tokyo; beyond that his interest in what he called 'creature features' was limited. But Sully wasn't here, and for the first time since he'd left, Bobby was glad.

They were in time for the one o'clock matinee, and the theater was almost deserted. Ted (wearing his fedora and with his dark glasses folded into the breast pocket of his shirt) bought a big bag of popcorn, a box of Dots, a Coke for Bobby, and a rootbeer (of course!) for himself. Every now and then he would pass Bobby the popcorn or the candy and Bobby would take some, but he was hardly aware that he was eating, let alone of *what* he was eating.

The movie began with everyone in the British village of Midwich falling asleep (a man who was driving a tractor at the time of the event was killed; so was a woman who fell face-first onto a lighted stove burner). The military was notified, and they sent a reconnaissance plane to take a look. The pilot fell asleep as soon as he was over Midwich airspace; the plane crashed. A soldier with a rope around his middle walked ten or twelve paces into the village, then swooned into a deep sleep. When he was dragged back, he awakened as soon as he was hauled over the 'sleep-line' that had been painted across the highway.

Everyone in Midwich woke up eventually, and everything seemed to be all right . . . until, a few weeks later, the women in town discovered they were pregnant. Old women, young women, even girls Carol Gerber's age, all pregnant, and the children they gave birth to were those spooky kids from the poster, the ones with the blond hair and the glowing eyes.

Although the movie never said, Bobby figured the Children of the Damned must have been caused by some sort of outer-space phenomenon, like the pod-people in *Invasion of the Body Snatchers*. In any case, they grew up faster than normal kids, they were super-smart, they could make people do what they wanted . . . and they were ruthless. When one father tried to discipline his particular Child of the Damned, all the kids clubbed together and directed their thoughts at the offending grownup (their eyes glowing, that theremin music so pulsing and strange that Bobby's arms broke out in goosebumps as he drank his Coke) until the guy put a shotgun to his head and killed himself (that part wasn't shown, and Bobby was glad).

The hero was George Sanders. His wife gave birth to one of the blond children. S-J would have scoffed at George, called him a 'queer bastard' or a 'golden oldie,' but Bobby found him a welcome change from heroes like Randolph Scott, Richard Carlson, and the inevitable Audie Murphy. George was really sort of ripshit, in a weird English way. In the words of Denny Rivers, old George knew how to lay chilly. He wore special cool ties and combed his hair back tight to his skull. He didn't look as though he could beat up a bunch of saloon baddies or anything, but he was the only guy from Midwich the Children of the Damned would have anything to do with; in fact they drafted him to be their teacher. Bobby couldn't imagine Randolph Scott or Audie Murphy teaching a bunch of super-smart kids from outer space *anything*.

In the end, George Sanders was also the one who got rid of them. He had discovered he could keep the Children from reading his mind – for a little while, anyway – if he imagined a brick wall in his head, with all his most secret thoughts behind it. And after everyone had decided the Children must go (you could teach them math, but not why it was bad to punish someone by making him drive over a cliff), Sanders put a time-bomb into his brief-case and took it into the schoolroom. That was the only place where the Children – Bobby understood in some vague way that they were only supernatural versions of Jack Merridew and his hunters in *Lord of the Flies* – were all together.

They sensed that Sanders was hiding something from them. In the movie's final excruciating sequence, you could see bricks flying out of the wall Sanders had constructed in his head, flying faster and faster as the Children of the Damned pried into him, trying to find out what he was concealing. At last they uncovered the image of the bomb in the brief-case – eight or nine sticks of dynamite wired up to an alarm clock. You saw their creepy golden eyes widen with under-standing, but they didn't have time to do anything. The bomb exploded. Bobby was shocked that the hero died – Randolph Scott never died in the Saturday-matinee movies at the Empire, neither did Audie Murphy or Richard Carlson – but he understood that George Sanders had given his life For the Greater Good of All. He thought he understood something else, as well: Ted's blank-outs.

While Ted and Bobby had been visiting Midwich, the day in southern Connecticut had turned hot and glaring. Bobby didn't like the world much after a really good movie in any case; for a little while it felt like an unfair joke, full of people with dull eyes, small plans, and facial blemishes. He sometimes thought if the world had a *plot* it would be so much better.

'Brautigan and Garfield hit the bricks!' Ted exclaimed as they stepped from beneath the marquee (a banner reading COME IN IT'S KOOL INSIDE hung from the marquee's front). 'What did you think? Did you enjoy it?'

'It was great,' Bobby said. 'Fantabulous. Thanks for taking me. It was practically the best movie I ever saw. How about when he had the dynamite? Did you think he'd be able to fool them?'

'Well . . . I'd read the book, remember. Will *you* read it, do you think?'

'Yes!' Bobby felt, in fact, a sudden urge to bolt back to Harwich, running the whole distance down the Connecticut Pike and Asher Avenue in the hot sunshine so he could borrow *The Midwich Cuckoos* with his new adult library card at once. 'Did he write any other science-fiction stories?'

'John Wyndham? Oh yes, quite a few. And will no doubt write more. One nice thing about science-fiction and mystery writers is that they rarely dither five years between books. That is the prerogative of serious writers who drink whiskey and have affairs.'

'Are the others as good as the one we just saw?'

'*The Day of the Triffids* is as good. *The Kraken Wakes* is even better.'

'What's a kraken?'

They had reached a streetcorner and were waiting for the light to change. Ted made a spooky, big-eyed face and bent down toward Bobby with his hands on his knees.

'It's a *monstah*,' he said, doing a pretty good Boris Karloff imitation.

They walked on, talking first about the movie and then about whether or not there really might be life in outer space, and then on to the special cool ties George Sanders had worn in the movie (Ted told him that kind of tie was called an ascot). When Bobby next took notice of their surroundings they had come to a part of Bridgeport he had never been in before – when he came to the city with his mom, they stuck to downtown, where the big stores were. The stores here were small and crammed together. None sold what the big department stores did: clothes and appliances and shoes and toys. Bobby saw signs for locksmiths, check-cashing services, used books. ROD'S GUNS, read one sign. WO FAT NOODLE CO., read another. FOTO FINISHING, read a third. Next to WO FAT was a shop selling SPECIAL SOUVENIRS. There was something weirdly like the Savin Rock midway about this street, so much so that Bobby almost expected to see the Monte Man standing on a street-corner with his makeshift table and his lobsterback playing cards.

Bobby tried to peer through the SPECIAL SOUVENIRS window when they passed, but it was covered by a big bamboo blind. He'd never heard of a store covering their show window during business hours. 'Who'd want a special souvenir of Bridgeport, do you think?'

'Well, I don't think they really sell souvenirs,' Ted said. 'I'd guess they sell items of a sexual nature, few of them strictly legal.'

Bobby had questions about that – a billion or so – but felt it best to be quiet. Outside a pawnshop with three golden balls hanging over the door he paused to look at a dozen straight-razors which had been laid out on velvet with their blades partly open. They'd been arranged in a circle and the result was strange and (to Bobby) beautiful: looking at them was like looking at something removed from a deadly piece of machinery. The razors' handles were much more exotic than the handle of the one Ted used, too. One looked like ivory, another like ruby etched with thin gold lines, a third like crystal.

'If you bought one of those you'd be shaving in style, wouldn't you?' Bobby asked.

He thought Ted would smile, but he didn't. 'When people buy razors like that, they don't shave with them, Bobby.'

'What do you mean?'

Ted wouldn't tell him, but he did buy him a sandwich called a gyro in a Greek delicatessen. It came in a folded-over piece of homemade bread and was oozing a dubious white sauce which to Bobby looked quite a lot like pimple-pus. He forced himself to try it because Ted said they were good. It turned out to be the best sandwich he'd ever eaten, as meaty as a hotdog or a hamburger from the Colony Diner but with an exotic taste that no hamburger or hotdog had ever had. And it was great to be eating on the sidewalk, strolling along with his friend, looking and being looked at.

'What do they call this part of town?' Bobby asked. 'Does it have a name?'

'These days, who knows?' Ted said, and shrugged. 'They used to call it Greektown. Then the Italians came, the Puerto Ricans, and now the Negroes. There's a novelist named David Goodis — the kind the college teachers never read, a genius of the drugstore paperback displays — who calls it "down there." He says every city has a neighborhood like this one, where you can buy sex or marijuana or a parrot that talks dirty, where the men sit talking on stoops like those men across the street, where the women always seem to be yelling for their kids to come in unless they want a whipping, and where the wine always comes in a paper sack.' Ted pointed into the gutter, where the neck of a Thunderbird bottle did indeed poke out of a brown bag. 'It's just down there, that's what David Goodis says, the place where you don't have any use for your last name and you can buy almost anything if you have cash in your pocket.'

Down there, Bobby thought, watching a trio of olive-skinned teenagers in gang jackets watch them as they passed. *This is the land of straight-razors and special souvenirs.*

The Criterion and Muncie's Department Store had never seemed so far away. And Broad Street? That and all of Harwich could have been in another solar system.

At last they came to a place called The Corner Pocket, Pool and Billiards, Automatic Games, Rheingold on Tap. There was also one of those banners reading COME IN IT'S KOOL INSIDE. As Bobby and Ted passed beneath it, a young man in a strappy tee-shirt and a chocolate-colored stingy-brim like the kind Frank Sinatra wore came out the door. He had a long, thin case in one hand. *That's his pool-cue*, Bobby thought with fright and amazement. *He's got his pool-cue in that case like it was a guitar or something.*

'Who a hip cat, Daddy-O?' he asked Bobby, then grinned. Bobby grinned back. The kid with the pool-cue case made a gun with his finger and pointed at Bobby. Bobby made a gun with his own finger and pointed it back. The kid nodded as if to say *Yeah, okay, you hip, we both hip* and crossed the street, snapping the fingers of his free hand and bopping to the music in his head.

Ted looked up the street in one direction, then down in the other. Ahead of them, three Negro children were capering in the spray of a partly opened hydrant. Back the way they had come, two young men — one white, the other maybe Puerto Rican — were taking the hubcaps off an old Ford, working with the rapid seriousness of doctors performing an operation. Ted looked at them, sighed, then looked at Bobby. 'The Pocket's no place for a kid, even in the middle of the day, but I'm not going to leave you out on the street. Come on.' He took Bobby by the hand and led him inside.

CHAPTER SEVEN

IN THE POCKET. THE SHIRT RIGHT OFF HIS BACK. OUTSIDE THE WILLIAM PENN. THE FRENCH SEX-KITTEN.

What struck Bobby first was the smell of beer. It was impacted, as if folks had been drinking in here since the days when the pyramids were still in the planning stages. Next was the sound of a TV, not turned to *Bandstand* but to one of the late-afternoon soap operas ('Oh John, oh Marsha' shows was what his mother called them), and the click of pool-balls. Only after these things had registered did his eyes chip in their own input, because they'd needed to adjust. The place was very dim.

And it was long, Bobby saw. To their right was an archway, and beyond it a room that appeared almost endless. Most of the pool-tables were covered, but a few stood in brilliant islands of light where men strolled languidly about, pausing every now and then to bend and shoot. Other men, hardly visible, sat in high seats along the wall, watching. One was getting his shoes shined. He looked about a thousand.

Straight ahead was a big room filled with Gottlieb pinball machines: a billion red and orange lights stuttered stomach-ache colors off a large sign which read IF YOU TILT THE SAME MACHINE TWICE YOU WILL BE ASKED TO LEAVE. A young man wearing another stingybrim hat – apparently the approved headgear for the bad motorscooters residing down there – was bent over Frontier Patrol, working the flippers frantically. A cigarette hung off his lower lip, the smoke rising past his face and the whorls of his combed-back hair. He was wearing a jacket tied around his waist and turned inside-out.

To the left of the lobby was a bar. It was from here that the sound of the TV and the smell of beer was coming. Three men sat there, each surrounded by empty stools, hunched over pilsener glasses. They didn't look like the happy beer-drinkers you saw in the ads; to Bobby they looked the loneliest people on earth. He wondered why they didn't at least huddle up and talk a little.

Closer by them was a desk. A fat man came rolling through the door behind it, and for a moment Bobby could hear the low sound of a radio playing. The fat man had a cigar in his mouth and was wearing a shirt covered with palm trees. He was snapping his fingers like the cool cat with the pool-cue case, and under his breath he was singing like this: 'Choo-choo-*chow*, choo-choo-ka-chow-chow, choo-choo-*chow-chow*!' Bobby recognized the tune: 'Tequila,' by The Champs.

'Who you, buddy?' the fat man asked Ted. 'I don't know you. And he can't be in here, anyway. Can'tcha read?' He jerked a fat thumb with a dirty nail at another sign, this one posted on the desk: B-21 OR B-GONE!

'You don't know me, but I think you know Jimmy Girardi,'

Ted said politely. 'He told me you were the man to see . . . if you're Len Files, that is.'

'I'm Len,' the man said. All at once he seemed considerably warmer. He held out a hand so white and pudgy that it looked like the gloves Mickey and Donald and Goofy wore in the cartoons. 'You know Jimmy Gee, huh? Goddam Jimmy Gee! Why, his grampa's back there getting a shine. He gets 'is boats shined a lot these days.' Len Files tipped Ted a wink. Ted smiled and shook the guy's hand.

'That your kid?' Len Files asked, bending over his desk to get a closer look at Bobby. Bobby could smell Sen-Sen mints and cigars on his breath, sweat on his body. The collar of his shirt was speckled with dandruff.

'He's a friend,' Ted said, and Bobby thought he might actually explode with happiness. 'I didn't want to leave him on the street.'

'Yeah, unless you're willing to have to pay to get im back,' Len Files agreed. 'You remind me of somebody, kid. Now why is that?'

Bobby shook his head, a little frightened to think he looked like anybody Len Files might know.

The fat man barely paid attention to Bobby's head-shake. He had straightened and was looking at Ted again. 'I can't be having kids in here, Mr . . . ?'

'Ted Brautigan.' He offered his hand. Len Files shook it.

'You know how it is, Ted. People in a business like mine, the cops keep tabs.'

'Of course. But he'll stand right here – won't you, Bobby?'

'Sure,' Bobby said.

'And our business won't take long. But it's a good little bit of business, Mr Files—'

'Len.'

Len, of course, Bobby thought. Just Len. Because in here was down there.

'As I say, Len, this is a good piece of business I want to do. I think you'll agree.'

'If you know Jimmy Gee, you know I don't do the nickels and dimes,' Len said. 'I leave the nickels and dimes to the niggers. What are we talking here? Patterson–Johansson?'

'Albini–Haywood. At The Garden tomorrow night?'

Len's eyes widened. Then his fat and unshaven cheeks spread in a smile. 'Man oh man oh Manischevitz. We need to explore this.'

'We certainly do.'

Len Files came out from around the desk, took Ted by the arm, and started to lead him toward the poolroom. Then he stopped and swung back. 'Is it Bobby when you're home and got your feet up, pal?'

'Yes, sir.' *Yes sir, Bobby Garfield*, he would have said anywhere else . . . but this was down there and he thought just plain Bobby would suffice.

'Well, Bobby, I know those pinball machines prolly look good to ya, and you prolly got a quarter or two in your pocket, but do what Adam dint and resist the temptation. Can you do that?'

'Yes, sir.'

'I won't be long,' Ted told him, and then allowed Len Files to lead him through the arch and into the poolroom. They walked past the men in the high chairs, and Ted stopped to speak to the one getting his shoes shined. Next to Jimmy Gee's grandfather, Ted Brautigan looked young. The old man peered up and Ted said something; the two men laughed into each other's faces. Jimmy Gee's grand-father had a good strong laugh for an old fellow. Ted reached out both hands and patted his sallow cheeks with gentle affection. That made Jimmy Gee's grandfather laugh again. Then Ted let Len draw him into a curtained alcove past the other men in the other chairs.

Bobby stood by the desk as if rooted, but Len hadn't said anything about not looking around, and so he did – in all directions. The walls were covered with beer signs and calendars that showed girls with most of their clothes off. One was climbing over a fence in the country. Another was getting out of a Packard with most of her skirt in her lap and her garters showing. Behind the desk were more signs, most expressing some negative concept (IF YOU DON'T LIKE OUR TOWN LOOK FOR A TIMETABLE, DON'T SEND A BOY TO DO A MAN'S JOB, THERE'S NO SUCH THING AS A FREE LUNCH, NO CHECKS ACCEPTED, NO CREDIT, CRYING TOWELS ARE NOT PROVIDED BY THE MANAGEMENT) and a big red button marked **POLICE CALL**. Suspended from the ceiling on a loop of dusty wire were Cellophane packages, some marked GINSENG ORIENTAL LOVE ROOT and others SPANISH DELITE. Bobby wondered if they were vitamins of some kind. Why would they sell vitamins in a place like this?

The young guy in the roomful of automatic games whapped the side of Frontier Patrol, stepped back, gave the machine the finger. Then he strolled into the lobby area adjusting his hat. Bobby made his finger into a gun and pointed it at him. The young man looked surprised, then grinned and pointed back as he headed for the door. He loosened the tied arms of his jacket as he went.

'Can't wear no club jacket in here,' he said, noting Bobby's wide-eyed curiosity. 'Can't even show your fuckin colors. Rules of the house.'

'Oh.'

The young guy smiled and raised his hand. Traced in blue ink on the back was a devil's pitchfork. 'But I got the sign, little brother. See it?'

'Heck, yeah.' A tattoo. Bobby was faint with envy. The kid saw it; his smile widened into a grin full of white teeth.

'Fuckin Diablos, *'mano*. Best club. Fuckin Diablos rule the streets. All others are pussy.'

'The streets down here.'

'Fuckin right down here, where else is there? Rock on, baby brother. I like you. You got a good look on you. Fuckin crewcut sucks, though.' The door opened, there was a gasp of hot air and streetlife noise, and the guy was gone.

A little wicker basket on the desk caught Bobby's eye. He tilted it so he could see in. It was full of keyrings with plastic fobs – red and blue and green. Bobby picked one out so he could read the gold printing: THE CORNER POCKET BILLIARDS, POOL, AUTO. GAMES. KENMORE 8–2127.

'Go on, kid, take it.'

Bobby was so startled he almost knocked the basket of keyrings to the floor. The woman had come through the same door as Len Files, and she was even bigger – almost as big as the circus fat lady – but she was as light on her feet as a ballerina; Bobby looked up and she was just there, looming over him. She was Len's sister, had to be.

'I'm sorry,' Bobby muttered, returning the keyring he'd picked up and pushing the basket back from the edge of the desk with little pats of his fingers. He might have succeeded in pushing it right over the far side if the fat woman hadn't stopped it with one hand. She was smiling and didn't look a bit mad, which to Bobby was a tremendous relief.

'Really, I'm not being sarcastic, you should take one.' She held out one of the keyrings. It had a green fob. 'They're just cheap little things, but they're free. We give em away for the advertising. Like matches, you know, although I wouldn't give a pack of matches to a kid. Don't smoke, do you?'

'No, ma'am.'

'That's making a good start. Stay away from the booze, too. Here. Take. Don't turn down for free in this world, kid, there isn't much of it going around.'

Bobby took the keyring with the green fob. 'Thank you, ma'am. It's neat.' He put the keyring in his pocket, knowing he would have to get rid of it – if his mother found such an item, she wouldn't be happy. She'd have twenty questions, as Sully would say. Maybe even thirty.

'What's your name?'

'Bobby.'

He waited to see if she would ask for his last name and was secretly delighted when she didn't. 'I'm Alanna.' She held out a hand crusted with rings. They twinkled like the pinball lights. 'You here with your dad?'

'With my *friend*,' Bobby said. 'I think he's making a bet on the Haywood–Albini prizefight.'

Alanna looked alarmed and amused at the same time. She leaned forward with one finger to her red lips. She made a *Shhh* sound at Bobby, and blew out a strong liquory smell with it.

'Don't say "bet" in here,' she cautioned him. 'This is a billiard parlor. Always remember that and you'll always be fine.'

'Okay.'

'You're a handsome little devil, Bobby. And you look . . .' She paused. 'Do I know your father, maybe? Is that possible?'

Bobby shook his head, but doubtfully — he had reminded Len of someone, too. 'My dad's dead. He died a long time ago.' He always added this so people wouldn't get all gushy.

'What was his name?' But before he could say, Alanna Files said it herself — it came out of her painted mouth like a magic word. 'Was it Randy? Randy Garrett, Randy Greer, something like that?'

For a moment Bobby was so flabbergasted he couldn't speak. It felt as if all the breath had been sucked out of his lungs. 'Randall Garfield. But how . . .'

She laughed, delighted. Her bosom heaved. 'Well, mostly your *hair*. But also the freckles . . . and this here ski-jump . . .' She bent forward and Bobby could see the tops of smooth white breasts that looked as big as waterbarrels. She skidded one finger lightly down his nose.

'He came in here to play pool?'

'Nah. Said he wasn't much of a stick. He'd drink a beer. Also sometimes . . .' She made a quick gesture then — dealing from an invisible deck. It made Bobby think of McQuown.

'Yeah,' Bobby said. 'He never met an inside straight he didn't like, that's what I heard.'

'I don't know about that, but he was a nice guy. He could come in here on a Monday night, when the place is always like a grave, and in half an hour or so he'd have everybody laughing. He'd play that song by Jo Stafford, I can't remember the name, and make Lennie turn up the jukebox. A real sweetie, kid, that's mostly why I remember him; a sweetie with red hair is a rare commodity. He wouldn't buy a drunk a drink, he had a thing about that, but otherwise he'd give you the shirt right off his back. All you had to do was ask.'

'But he lost a lot of money, I guess,' Bobby said. He couldn't believe he was having this conversation – that he had met someone who had known his father. Yet he supposed a lot of finding out happened like this, completely by accident. You were just going along, minding your own business, and all at once the past sideswiped you.

'Randy?' She looked surprised. 'Nah. He'd come in for a drink maybe three times a week – you know, if he happened to be in the neighborhood. He was in real estate or insurance or selling or some one of those—'

'Real estate,' Bobby said. 'It was real estate.'

'—and there was an office down here he'd visit. For the industrial properties, I guess, if it was real estate. You sure it wasn't medical supplies?'

'No, real estate.'

'Funny how your memory works,' she said. 'Some things stay clear, but mostly time goes by and green turns blue. All of the suit-n-tie businesses are gone down here now, anyway.' She shook her head sadly.

Bobby wasn't interested in how the neighborhood had gone to blazes. 'But when he *did* play, he lost. He was always trying to fill inside straights and stuff.'

'Did your mother tell you that?'

Bobby was silent.

Alanna shrugged. Interesting things happened all up and down her front when she did. 'Well, that's between you and her . . . and hey, maybe your dad threw his dough around in other places. All I know is that in here he'd just sit in once or twice a month with guys he knew, play until maybe midnight, then go home. If he left a big winner or a big loser, I'd probably remember. I don't, so he probably broke even most nights he played. Which, by the way, makes him a pretty good poker-player. Better than most back there.' She rolled her eyes in the direction Ted and her brother had gone.

Bobby looked at her with growing confusion. *Your father didn't exactly leave us well off*, his mother liked to say. There was the lapsed life insurance policy, the stack of unpaid bills; *Little did I know*, his mother had said just this spring, and Bobby was beginning to think that fit him, as well: *Little did I know.*

'He was such a good-looking guy, your dad,' Alanna said, 'Bob Hope nose and all. I'd guess you got that to look forward to – you favor him. Got a girlfriend?'

'Yes, ma'am.'

Were the unpaid bills a fiction? Was that possible? Had the life insurance policy actually been cashed and socked away, maybe in a bank account instead of between the pages of the Sears catalogue? It was a horrible thought, somehow. Bobby couldn't imagine why his mother would want him to think his dad was

(*a low man, a low man with red hair*)

a bad guy if he really wasn't, but there was something about the idea that felt . . . true. She could get mad, that was the thing about his mother. She could get *so* mad. And then she might say anything. It was possible that his father – who his mother had never once in Bobby's memory called 'Randy' – had given too many people too many shirts right off his back, and consequently made Liz Garfield mad. Liz Garfield didn't give away shirts, not off her back or from anywhere else. You had to save your shirts in this world, because life wasn't fair.

'What's her name?'

'Liz.' He felt dazed, the way he'd felt coming out of the dark theater into the bright light.

'Like Liz Taylor.' Alanna looked pleased. 'That's a nice name for a girlfriend.'

Bobby laughed, a little embarrassed. 'No, my *mother's* Liz. My girlfriend's name is Carol.'

'She pretty?'

'A real hosty-tosty,' he said, grinning and wiggling one hand from side to side. He was delighted when Alanna roared with laughter. She reached over the desk, the flesh of her upper arm hanging like some fantastic wad of dough, and pinched his cheek. It hurt a little but he liked it.

'Cute kid! Can I tell you something?'

'Sure, what?'

'Just because a man likes to play a little cards, that doesn't make him Attila the Hun. You know that, don't you?'

Bobby nodded hesitantly, then more firmly.

'Your ma's your ma, I don't say nothing against anybody's ma because I loved my own, but not everybody's ma approves of cards or pool or . . . places like this. It's a point of view, but that's all it is. Get the picture?'

'Yes,' Bobby said. He did. He got the picture. He felt very strange, like laughing and crying at the same time. *My dad was here*, he thought. This seemed, at least for the time being, much more important than any lies his mother might have told about him. *My dad was here, he might have stood right where I'm standing now.* 'I'm glad I look like him,' he blurted.

Alanna nodded, smiling. 'You coming in here like that, just walking in off the street. What are the odds?'

'I don't know. But thanks for telling me about him. Thanks a lot.'

'He'd play that Jo Stafford song all night, if you'd let him,' Alanna said. 'Now don't you go wandering off.'

'No, ma'am.'

'No, *Alanna*.'

Bobby grinned. '*Alanna*.'

She blew him a kiss as his mother sometimes did, and laughed when Bobby pretended to catch it. Then she went back through the door. Bobby could see what looked like a living room beyond it. There was a big cross on one wall.

He reached into his pocket, hooked a finger through the keyring (it was, he thought, a special souvenir of his visit down there), and imagined himself riding down Broad Street on the Schwinn from the Western Auto. He was heading for the park. He was wearing a chocolate-colored stingybrim hat cocked back on his head. His hair was long and combed in a duck's ass – no more crewcut, later for you, Jack. Tied around his waist was a jacket with his colors on it; riding the back of his hand was a blue tattoo, stamped deep and forever. Outside Field B Carol would be waiting for him. She'd be watching him ride up, she'd be thinking *Oh you crazy boy* as he swung the Schwinn around in a tight circle, spraying gravel toward (but not on) her white sneakers. Crazy, yes. A bad motorscooter and a mean go-getter.

Len Files and Ted were coming back now, both of them looking happy. Len, in fact, looked like the cat that ate the canary (as Bobby's mother often said). Ted paused to pass another, briefer, word with the old guy, who nodded and smiled. When Ted and Len got back to the lobby area, Ted started toward the telephone booth just inside the door. Len took his arm and steered him toward the desk instead.

As Ted stepped behind it, Len ruffled Bobby's hair. 'I know who you look like,' he said. 'It come to me while I was in the back room. Your dad was—'

'Garfield. Randy Garfield.' Bobby looked up at Len, who so resembled his sister, and thought how odd and sort of wonderful it was to be linked that way to your own blood kin. Linked so closely people who didn't even know you could sometimes pick you out of a crowd. 'Did you like him, Mr Files?'

'Who, Randy? Sure, he was a helluva gizmo.' But Len Files seemed a little vague. He hadn't noticed Bobby's father in the same way his sister had, Bobby decided; Len probably wouldn't remember about the Jo Stafford song or how Randy Garfield would give you the shirt right off his back. He wouldn't give a drunk a drink, though; he wouldn't do that. 'Your pal's all right, too,' Len went on, more enthusiastic now. 'I like the high class and the high class likes me, but I don't get real shooters like him in here often.' He turned to Ted, who was hunting nearsightedly through the phonebook. 'Try Circle Taxi. KEnmore 6–7400.'

'Thanks,' Ted said.

'Don't mention it.' Len brushed past Ted and went through the door behind the desk. Bobby caught another brief glimpse of the living room and the big cross. When the door shut, Ted looked over at Bobby and said: 'You bet five hundred bucks on a prizefight and you don't have to use the pay phone like the rest of the shmucks. Such a deal, huh?'

Bobby felt as if all the wind had been sucked out of him. 'You bet *five hundred dollars* on Hurricane Haywood?'

Ted shook a Chesterfield out of his pack, put it in his mouth, lit it around a grin. 'Good God, no,' he said. 'On Albini.'

After he called the cab, Ted took Bobby over to the bar and ordered them both rootbeers. *He doesn't know I don't really like rootbeer*, Bobby thought. It seemed another piece in the puzzle, somehow – the puzzle of Ted. Len served them himself, saying nothing about how Bobby shouldn't be sitting at the bar, he was a nice kid but just stinking the place up with his under-twenty-oneness; apparently a free phone call wasn't all you got when you bet five hundred dollars on a prizefight. And not even the excitement of the bet could long distract Bobby from a certain dull certainty which stole much of his pleasure in hearing that his father hadn't been such a bad guy, after all. The bet had been made to earn some runout money. Ted was leaving.

The taxi was a Checker with a huge back seat. The driver was deeply involved in the Yankees game on the radio, to the point where he sometimes talked back to the announcers.

'Files and his sister knew your father, didn't they?' It wasn't really a question.

'Yeah. Alanna especially. She thought he was a real nice guy.' Bobby paused. 'But that's not what my mother thinks.'

'I imagine your mother saw a side of him Alanna Files never did,' Ted replied. 'More than one. People are like diamonds in that way, Bobby. They have many sides.'

'But Mom said . . .' It was too complicated. She'd never exactly said *anything*, really, only sort of suggested stuff. He didn't know how to tell Ted that his mother had sides, too, and some of them made it hard to believe those things she never quite came out and said. And when you got right down to it, how much did he really want to know? His father was dead, after all. His mother wasn't, and he had to live with her . . . and he had to love her. He had no one else to love, not even Ted. Because—

'When you going?' Bobby asked in a low voice.

'After your mother gets back.' Ted sighed, glanced out the window, then looked down at his hands, which were folded on one crossed knee. He didn't look at Bobby, not yet. 'Probably Friday morning. I can't collect my money until tomorrow night. I got four to one on Albini; that's two grand. My good pal Lennie will have to phone New York to make the cover.'

They crossed a canal bridge, and down there was back there. Now they were in the part of the city Bobby had travelled with his mother. The men on the street wore coats and ties. The women wore hose instead of bobbysocks. None of them looked like Alanna Files, and Bobby didn't think many of them would smell of liquor if they went 'Shhh,' either. Not at four o'clock in the afternoon.

'I know why you didn't bet on Patterson–Johansson,' Bobby said. 'It's because you don't know who'll win.'

'I *think* Patterson will this time,' Ted said, 'because this time he's prepared for Johansson. I might flutter two dollars on Floyd Patterson, but five hundred? To bet five hundred you must either know or be crazy.'

'The Albini–Haywood fight is fixed, isn't it?'

Ted nodded. 'I knew when you read that Kleindienst was involved, and I guessed that Albini was supposed to win.'

'You've made other bets on boxing matches where Mr Kleindienst was a manager.'

Ted said nothing for a moment, only looked out the window. On the radio, someone hit a comebacker to Whitey Ford. Ford fielded the ball and threw to Moose Skowron at first. Now there were two down in the top of the eighth. At last Ted said, 'It *could* have been Haywood. It wasn't likely, but it could have been. Then . . . did you see the old man back there? The one in the shoeshine chair?'

'Sure, you patted him on the cheeks.'

'That's Arthur Girardi. Files lets him hang around because he used to be connected. That's what Files thinks – *used* to be. Now he's just some old fellow who comes in to get his shoes shined at ten and then forgets and comes in to get them shined again at three. Files thinks he's just an old fellow who don't know from nothing, as they say. Girardi lets him think whatever he wants to think. If Files said the moon was green cheese, Girardi wouldn't say boo. Old Gee, he comes in for the air conditioning. And he's still connected.'

'Connected to Jimmy Gee.'

'To all sorts of guys.'

'Mr Files didn't know the fight was fixed?'

'No, not for sure. I thought he would.'

'But old Gee knew. And he knew which one's supposed to take the dive.'

'Yes. That was my luck. Hurricane Haywood goes down in the eighth round. Then, next year when the odds are better, the Hurricane gets his payday.'

'Would you have bet if Mr Girardi hadn't been there?'

'No,' Ted replied immediately.

'Then what would you have done for money? When you go away?'

Ted looked depressed at those words – *When you go away.*

He made as if to put an arm around Bobby's shoulders, then stopped himself.

'There's always someone who knows something,' he said.

They were on Asher Avenue now, still in Bridgeport but only a mile or so from the Harwich town line. Knowing what would happen, Bobby reached for Ted's big, nicotine-stained hand.

Ted swivelled his knees toward the door, taking his hands with them. 'Better not.'

Bobby didn't need to ask why. People put up signs that said WET PAINT DO NOT TOUCH because if you put your hand on something newly painted, the stuff would get on your skin. You could wash it off, or it would wear off by itself in time, but for awhile it would be there.

'Where will you go?'

'I don't know.'

'I feel bad,' Bobby said. He could feel tears prickling at the corners of his eyes. 'If something happens to you, it's my fault. I saw things, the things you told me to look out for, but I didn't say anything. I didn't want you to go. So I told myself you were crazy – not about everything, just about the low men you thought were chasing you – and I didn't say anything. You gave me a job and I muffed it.'

Ted's arm rose again. He lowered it and settled for giving Bobby a quick pat on the leg instead. At Yankee Stadium Tony Kubek had just doubled home two runs. The crowd was going wild.

'But I knew,' Ted said mildly.

Bobby stared at him. 'What? I don't get you.'

'I felt them getting closer. That's why my trances have grown so frequent. Yet I lied to myself, just as you did. For the same reasons, too. Do you think I want to leave you now, Bobby? When your mother is so confused and unhappy? In all honesty I don't care so much for her sake, we don't get along, from the first second we laid eyes on each other we didn't get along, but she is your mother, and—'

'What's wrong with her?' Bobby asked. He remembered to keep his voice low, but he took Ted's arm and shook it. 'Tell me! You know, I know you do! Is it Mr Biderman? Is it something about Mr Biderman?'

Ted looked out the window, brow furrowed, lips drawn down tightly. At last he sighed, pulled out his cigarettes, and lit one. 'Bobby,' he said, 'Mr Biderman is not a nice man. Your mother knows it, but she also knows that sometimes we have to go along with people who are not nice. Go along to get along, she thinks, and she has done this. She's done things over the last year that she's not proud of, but she has been careful. In some ways she has needed to be as careful as I have, and whether I like her or not, I admire her for that.'

'What did she do? What did he make her do?' Something cold moved in Bobby's chest. 'Why did Mr Biderman take her to Providence?'

'For the real-estate conference.'

'Is that all? Is that *all*?'

'I don't know. *She* didn't know. Or perhaps she has covered over what she knows and what she fears with what she hopes. I can't say. Sometimes I can – sometimes I know things very directly and clearly. The first moment I saw you I knew that you wanted a bicycle, that getting one was very important to you, and you meant to earn the money for one this summer if you could. I admired your determination.'

'You touched me on purpose, didn't you?'

'Yes indeed. The first time, anyway. I did it to know you
a little. But friends don't spy; true friendship is about privacy,
too. Besides, when I touch, I pass on a kind of – well, a kind
of window. I think you know that. The second time I touched
you . . . really touching, holding on, you know what I mean
. . . that was a mistake, but not such an awful one; for a little
while you knew more than you should, but it wore off, didn't
it? If I'd gone on, though . . . touching and touching, the
way people do when they're close . . . there'd come a point
where things would change. Where it wouldn't wear off.' He
raised his mostly smoked cigarette and looked at it distaste-
fully. 'The way you smoke one too many of these and you're
hooked for life.'

'Is my mother all right now?' Bobby asked, knowing that
Ted couldn't tell him that; Ted's gift, whatever it was, didn't
stretch that far.

'I don't know. I—'

Ted suddenly stiffened. He was looking out the window
at something up ahead. He smashed his cigarette into the
armrest ashtray, doing it hard enough to send sparks scat-
tering across the back of his hand. He didn't seem to feel
them. 'Christ,' he said. 'Oh Christ, Bobby, we're in for it.'

Bobby leaned across his lap to look out the window,
thinking in the back of his mind about what Ted had just
been saying – *touching and touching, the way people do when
they're close* – even as he peered up Asher Avenue.

Ahead was a three-way intersection, Asher Avenue,
Bridgeport Avenue, and the Connecticut Pike all coming
together at a place known as Puritan Square. Trolley-tracks
gleamed in the afternoon sun; delivery trucks honked impatiently as they waited their turns to dart through the crush.

A sweating policeman with a whistle in his mouth and white gloves on his hands was directing traffic. Off to the left was the William Penn Grille, a famous restaurant which was supposed to have the best steaks in Connecticut (Mr Biderman had taken the whole office staff there after the agency sold the Waverley Estate, and Bobby's mom had come home with about a dozen William Penn Grille books of matches). Its main claim to fame, his mom had once told Bobby, was that the bar was over the Harwich town line, but the restaurant proper was in Bridgeport.

Parked in front, on the very edge of Puritan Square, was a DeSoto automobile of a purple Bobby had never seen before – had never even *suspected*. The color was so bright it hurt his eyes to look at it. It hurt his whole *head*.

Their cars will be like their yellow coats and sharp shoes and the greasy perfumed stuff they use to slick back their hair: loud and vulgar.

The purple car was loaded with swoops and darts of chrome. It had fenderskirts. The hood ornament was huge; Chief DeSoto's head glittered in the hazy light like a fake jewel. The tires were fat whitewalls and the hubcaps were spinners. There was a whip antenna on the back. From its tip there hung a raccoon tail.

'The low men,' Bobby whispered. There was really no question. It was a DeSoto, but at the same time it was like no car he had ever seen in his life, something as alien as an asteroid. As they drew closer to the clogged three-way intersection, Bobby saw the upholstery was a metallic dragonfly-green – the color nearly howled in contrast to the car's purple skin. There was white fur around the steering wheel. 'Holy crow, it's them!'

'You have to take your mind away,' Ted said. He grabbed Bobby by the shoulders (up front the Yankees blared on and on, the driver paying his two fares in the back seat no attention whatsoever, thank God for that much, at least) and shook him once, hard, before letting him go. 'You have to take your mind *away*, do you understand?'

He did. George Sanders had built a brick wall behind which to hide his thoughts and plans from the Children. Bobby had used Maury Wills once before, but he didn't think baseball was going to cut it this time. What would?

Bobby could see the Asher Empire's marquee jutting out over the sidewalk, three or four blocks beyond Puritan Square, and suddenly he could hear the sound of Sully-John's Bo-lo Bouncer: whap-whap-whap. *If she's trash*, S-J had said, *I'd love to be the trashman*.

The poster they'd seen that day filled Bobby's mind: Brigitte Bardot (*the French sex-kitten* was what the papers called her) dressed only in a towel and a smile. She looked a little like the woman getting out of the car on one of the calendars back at The Corner Pocket, the one with most of her skirt in her lap and her garters showing. Brigitte Bardot was prettier, though. And she was *real*. She was too old for the likes of Bobby Garfield, of course.

(*I'm so young and you're so old*, Paul Anka singing from a thousand transistor radios, *this my darling I've been told*) but she was still beautiful, and a cat could look at a queen, his mother always said that, too: a cat could look at a queen. Bobby saw her more and more clearly as he settled back against the seat, his eyes taking on that drifty, far-off look Ted's eyes got when he had one of his blank-outs; Bobby saw her shower-damp puff of blond hair, the slope of her breasts into the towel, her long thighs, her painted toenails standing over the words Adults Only, Must Have Driver's License or Birth Certificate. He could smell her soap – something light and flowery. He could smell

(*Nuit en Paris*)

her perfume and he could hear her radio in the next room. It was Freddy Cannon, that bebop summertime avatar of Savin Rock: 'She's dancin to the drag, the cha-cha rag-a-mop, she's stompin to the shag, *rocks* the bunny hop . . .'

He was aware – faintly, far away, in another world farther up along the swirls of the spinning top – that the cab in which they were riding had come to a stop right next to the William Penn Grille, right next to that purple bruise of a DeSoto. Bobby could almost hear the car in his head; if it had had a voice it would have screamed *Shoot me, I'm too purple! Shoot me, I'm too purple!* And not far beyond it he could sense *them*. They were in the restaurant, having an early steak. Both of them ate it the same way, bloody-rare. Before they left they might put up a lost-pet poster in the telephone lounge or leave a hand-printed CAR FOR SALE BY OWNER card; upside-down, of course. They were in there, low men in yellow coats and white shoes drinking martinis between bites of nearly raw steer, and if they turned their minds out this way . . .

Steam was drifting out of the shower. B.B. raised herself on her bare painted toes and opened her towel, turning it into brief wings before letting it fall. And Bobby saw it wasn't Brigitte Bardot at all. It was Carol Gerber. *You'd have to be brave to let people look at you with nothing on but a towel,* she had said, and now she had let even the towel fall away. He was seeing her as she would look eight or ten years from now.

Bobby looked at her, helpless to look away, helpless in love, lost in the smells of her soap and her perfume, the sound of her radio (Freddy Cannon had given way to The Platters – *heavenly shades of night are falling*), the sight of her small painted toenails. His heart spun as a top did, with its lines rising and disappearing into other worlds. Other worlds than this.

The taxi began creeping forward. The four-door purple horror parked next to the restaurant (parked in a loading zone, Bobby saw, but what did *they* care?) began to slide to the rear. The cab jolted to a stop again and the driver cursed mildly as a trolley rushed clang-a-lang through Puritan Square. The low DeSoto was behind them now, but reflections from its chrome filled the cab with erratic dancing minnows of light. And suddenly Bobby felt a savage itching attack the backs of his eyeballs. This was followed by a fall of twisting black threads across his field of vision. He was able to hold onto Carol, but he now seemed to be looking at her through a field of interference.

They sense us . . . or they sense something. Please God, get us out of here. Please get us out.

The cabbie saw a hole in the traffic and squirted through it. A moment later they were rolling up Asher Avenue at a good pace. That itching sensation behind Bobby's eyes began to recede. The black threads across his field of interior vision cleared away, and when they did he saw that the naked girl wasn't Carol at all (not anymore, at least), not even Brigitte Bardot, but only the calendar-girl from The Corner Pocket, stripped mother-naked by Bobby's imagination. The music from her radio was gone. The smells of soap and perfume were gone. The life had gone out of her; she was just a . . . a . . .

'She's just a picture painted on a brick wall,' Bobby said. He sat up.

'Say what, kid?' the driver asked, and snapped off the radio. The game was over. Mel Allen was selling cigarettes.

'Nothing,' Bobby said.

'Guess youse dozed off, huh? Slow traffic, hot day . . . they'll do it every time, just like Hatlo says. Looks like your pal's still out.'

'No,' Ted said, straightening. 'The doctor is in.' He stretched his back and winced when it crackled. 'I did doze a little, though.' He glanced out the back window, but the William Penn Grille was out of sight now. 'The Yankees won, I suppose?'

'Gahdam Injuns, they roont em,' the cabbie said, and laughed. 'Don't see how youse could sleep with the Yankees playing.'

They turned onto Broad Street; two minutes later the cab pulled up in front of 149. Bobby looked at it as if expecting to see a different color paint or perhaps an added wing. He felt like he'd been gone ten years. In a way he supposed he had been – hadn't he seen Carol Gerber all grown up?

I'm going to marry her, Bobby decided as he got out of the cab. Over on Colony Street, Mrs O'Hara's dog barked on and on, as if denying this and all human aspirations: *roop-roop, roop-roop-roop.*

Ted bent down to the driver's-side window with his wallet in his hand. He plucked out two singles, considered, then added a third. 'Keep the change.'

'You're a gent,' the cabbie said.

'He's a *shooter,*' Bobby corrected, and grinned as the cab pulled away.

'Let's get inside,' Ted said. 'It's not safe for me to be out here.'

They went up the porch steps and Bobby used his key to open the door to the foyer. He kept thinking about that weird itching behind his eyes, and the black threads. The threads had been particularly horrible, as if he'd been on the verge of going blind. 'Did they see us, Ted? Or sense us, or whatever they do?'

'You know they did . . . but I don't think they knew how close we were.' As they went into the Garfield apartment, Ted took off his sunglasses and tucked them into his shirt pocket. 'You must have covered up well. Whooo! Hot in here!'

'What makes you think they didn't know we were close?'

Ted paused in the act of opening a window, giving Bobby a level look back over his shoulder. 'If they'd known, that purple car would have been right behind us when we pulled up here.'

'It wasn't a car,' Bobby said, beginning to open windows himself. It didn't help much; the air that came in, lifting the curtains in listless little flaps, felt almost as hot as the air which had been trapped inside the apartment all day. 'I don't know what it was, but it only *looked* like a car. And what I felt of *them*—' Even in the heat, Bobby shivered.

Ted got his fan, crossed to the window by Liz's shelf of knickknacks, and set it on the sill. 'They camouflage themselves as best they can, but we still feel them. Even people who don't know what they are often feel them. A little of what's under the camouflage seeps through, and what's underneath is ugly. I hope you never know how ugly.'

Bobby hoped so, too. 'Where do they come from, Ted?'

'A dark place.'

Ted knelt, plugged in his fan, flipped it on. The air it pulled into the room was a little cooler, but not so cool as The Corner Pocket had been, or the Criterion.

'Is it in another world, like in *Ring Around the Sun*? It is, isn't it?'

Ted was still on his knees by the electrical plug. He looked as if he were praying. To Bobby he also looked exhausted – done almost to death. How could he run from the low men? He didn't look as if he could make it as far as Spicer's Variety Store without stumbling.

'Yes,' he said at last. 'They come from another world. Another where and another when. That's all I can tell you. It's not safe for you to know more.'

But Bobby had to ask one other question. 'Did you come from one of those other worlds?'

Ted looked at him solemnly. 'I came from Teaneck.'

Bobby gaped at him for a moment, then began to laugh. Ted, still kneeling by the fan, joined him.

'What did you think of in the cab, Bobby?' Ted asked when they were finally able to stop. 'Where did you go when the trouble started?' He paused. 'What did you see?'

Bobby thought of Carol at twenty with her toenails painted pink, Carol standing naked with the towel at her feet and steam rising around her. Adults Only. Must Have Driver's License. No Exceptions.

'I can't tell,' he said at last. 'Because . . . well . . .'

'Because some things are private. I understand.' Ted got to his feet. Bobby stepped forward to help him but Ted waved him away. 'Perhaps you'd like to go out and play for a little while,' he said. 'Later on – around six, shall we say? – I'll put on my dark glasses again and we'll go around the block, have a bite of dinner at the Colony Diner.'

'But no beans.'

The corners of Ted's mouth twitched in the ghost of a smile. 'Absolutely no beans, beans *verboten*. At ten o'clock I'll call my friend Len and see how the fight went. Eh?'

'The low men . . . will they be looking for me now, too?'

'I'd never let you step out the door if I thought that,' Ted replied, looking surprised. 'You're fine, and I'm going to make sure you *stay* fine. Go on now. Play some catch or ring-a-levio or whatever it is you like. I have some things to do. Only be back by six so I don't worry.'

'Okay.'

Bobby went into his room and dumped the four quarters he'd taken to Bridgeport back into the Bike Fund jar. He looked around his room, seeing things with new eyes: the cowboy bedspread, the picture of his mother on one wall and the signed photo – obtained by saving cereal boxtops – of Clayton Moore in his mask on another, his roller skates (one with a broken strap) in the corner, his desk against the wall. The room looked smaller now – not so much a place to come to as a place to leave. He realized he was growing into his orange library card, and some bitter voice inside cried out against it. Cried no, no, no.

CHAPTER EIGHT

BOBBY MAKES A CONFESSION. THE GERBER BABY AND THE MALTEX BABY. RIONDA. TED MAKES A CALL. CRY OF THE HUNTERS.

In Commonwealth Park the little kids were playing ticky-ball. Field B was empty; on Field C a few teenagers in orange St Gabriel's tee-shirts were playing scrub. Carol Gerber was sitting on a bench with her jump-rope in her lap, watching them. She saw Bobby coming and began to smile. Then the smile went away.

'Bobby, what's wrong with you?'

Bobby hadn't been precisely aware that *anything* was wrong with him until Carol said that, but the look of concern on her face brought everything home and undid him. It was the reality of the low men and the fright of the close call they'd had on their way back from Bridge-port; it was his concern over his mother; mostly it was Ted. He knew perfectly well why Ted had shooed him out of the house, and what Ted was doing right now: filling his little suitcases and those carryhandle paper bags. His friend was going away.

Bobby began to cry. He didn't want to go all ushy-gushy in front of a girl, particularly *this* girl, but he couldn't help it.

Carol looked stunned for a moment – scared. Then she got off the bench, came to him, and put her arms around him. 'That's all right,' she said. 'That's all right, Bobby, don't cry, everything's all right.'

Almost blinded by tears and crying harder than ever – it was as if there were a violent summer storm going on in his head – Bobby let her lead him into a copse of trees where they would be hidden from the baseball fields and the main paths. She sat down on the grass, still holding him, brushing one hand through the sweaty bristles of his crewcut. For a little while she said nothing at all, and Bobby was incapable of speaking; he could only sob until his throat ached and his eyeballs throbbed in their sockets.

At last the intervals between sobs became longer. He sat up and wiped his face with his arm, horrified and ashamed of what he felt: not just tears but snot and spit as well. He must have covered her with mung.

Carol didn't seem to care. She touched his wet face. Bobby pulled back from her fingers, uttering another sob, and looked down at the grass. His eyesight, freshly washed by his tears, seemed almost preternaturally keen; he could see every blade and dandelion.

'It's all right,' she said, but Bobby was still too ashamed to look at her.

They sat quietly for a little while and then Carol said, 'Bobby, I'll be your girlfriend, if you want.'

'You *are* my girlfriend,' Bobby said.

'Then tell me what's wrong.'

And Bobby heard himself telling her everything, starting with the day Ted had moved in and how his mother had taken an instant dislike to him. He told her about the first of Ted's blank-outs, about the low men, about the signs of the low men. When he got to that part, Carol touched him on the arm.

'What?' he asked. 'You don't believe me?' His throat still had that achey too-full feeling it got after a crying fit, but he was getting better. If she didn't believe him, he wouldn't be mad at her. Wouldn't blame her a bit, in fact. It was just an enormous relief to get it off his chest. 'That's okay. I know how crazy it must—'

'I've seen those funny hopscotches all over town,' she said. 'So has Yvonne and Angie. We talked about them. They have little stars and moons drawn next to them. Sometimes comets, too.'

He gaped at her. 'Are you kidding?'

'No. Girls always look at hopscotches, I don't know why. Close your mouth before a bug flies in.'

He closed his mouth.

Carol nodded, satisfied, then took his hand in hers and laced her fingers through his. Bobby was amazed at what a perfect fit all those fingers made. 'Now tell me the rest.'

He did, finishing with the amazing day he'd just put in: the movie, the trip to The Corner Pocket, how Alanna had recognized his father in him, the close call on the way home. He tried to explain how the purple DeSoto hadn't seemed like a real car at all, that it only looked like a car. The closest he could come was to say it had felt *alive* somehow, like an evil version of the ostrich Dr Dolittle sometimes rode in that series of talking-animal books they'd all gone crazy for in the second grade. The only thing Bobby didn't confess was where he'd hidden his thoughts when the cab passed the William Penn Grille and the backs of his eyes began to itch.

He struggled, then blurted the worst as a coda: he was afraid that his mother going to Providence with Mr Biderman and those other men had been a mistake. A *bad* mistake.

'Do you think Mr Biderman's sweet on her?' Carol asked. By then they were walking back to the bench where she had left her jump-rope. Bobby picked it up and handed it to her. They began walking out of the park and toward Broad Street.

'Yeah, maybe,' Bobby said glumly. 'Or at least . . .' And here was part of what he was afraid of, although it had no name or real shape; it was like something ominous covered with a piece of canvas. 'At least *she* thinks he is.'

'Is he going to ask her to marry him? If he did he'd be your stepdad.'

'God!' Bobby hadn't considered the idea of having Don Biderman as a stepfather, and he wished with all his might that Carol hadn't brought such a thing up. It was an awful thought.

'If she loves him you just better get used to the idea.' Carol spoke in an older-woman, worldly-wise fashion that Bobby could have done without; he guessed she had already spent too much time this summer watching the oh John, oh Marsha shows on TV with her mom. And in a weird way he wouldn't have cared if his mom loved Mr Biderman and that was all. It would be wretched, certainly, because Mr Biderman was a creep, but it would have been understandable. More was going on, though. His mother's miserliness about money – her *cheapskatiness* – was a part of it, and so was whatever had made her start smoking again and caused her to cry in the night sometimes. The difference between his mother's Randall Garfield, the untrustworthy man who left the unpaid bills, and Alanna's *Randy* Garfield, the nice guy who liked the jukebox turned up loud . . . even that might be a part of it. (Had there really been unpaid bills? Had there really been a lapsed insurance policy? Why would his mother lie about such things?) This was stuff he couldn't talk about to Carol. It wasn't reticence; it was that he didn't know *how*.

They started up the hill. Bobby took one end of her rope and they walked side by side, dragging it between them on the sidewalk. Suddenly Bobby stopped and pointed. 'Look.'

There was a yellow length of kite tail hanging from one of the electrical wires crossing the street farther up. It dangled in a curve that looked sort of like a question mark.

'Yeah, I see it,' Carol said, sounding subdued. They began to walk again. 'He should go today, Bobby.'

'He can't. The fight's tonight. If Albini wins Ted's got to get his dough at the billiard parlor tomorrow night. I think he needs it pretty bad.'

'Sure he does,' Carol said. 'You only have to look at his clothes to see he's almost broke. What he bet was probably the last money he had.'

His clothes — that's something only a girl would notice, Bobby thought, and opened his mouth to tell her so. Before he could, someone behind them said, 'Oh looka this. It's the Gerber Baby and the Maltex Baby. Howya doin, babies?'

They looked around. Biking slowly up the hill toward them were three St Gabe's boys in orange shirts. Piled in their bike-baskets was an assortment of baseball gear. One of the boys, a pimply galoot with a silver cross dangling from his neck on a chain, had a baseball bat in a homemade sling on his back. *Thinks he's Robin Hood,* Bobby thought, but he was scared. They were big boys, high-school boys, *parochial school* boys, and if they decided they wanted to put him in the hospital, then to the hospital he would go. *Low boys in orange shirts,* he thought.

'Hi, Willie,' Carol said to one of them – not the galoot with the bat slung on his back. She sounded calm, even cheery, but Bobby could hear fright fluttering underneath like a bird's wing. 'I watched you play. You made a good catch.'

The one she spoke to had an ugly, half-formed face below a mass of combed-back auburn hair and above a man's body. The Huffy bike beneath him was ridiculously small. Bobby thought he looked like a troll in a fairy-tale. 'What's it to you, Gerber Baby?' he asked.

The three St Gabe's boys pulled up even with them. Then two of them – the one with the dangling cross and the one Carol had called Willie – came a little farther, standing around the forks of their bikes now, walking them. With mounting dismay Bobby realized he and Carol had been surrounded. He could smell a mixture of sweat and Vitalis coming from the boys in the orange shirts.

'Who are you, Maltex Baby?' the third St Gabe's boy asked Bobby. He leaned over the handlebars of his bike for a better look. 'Are you Garfield? You are, ain'tcha? Billy Donahue's still lookin for you from that time last winter. He wants to knock your teeth out. Maybe I ought to knock one or two of em out right here, give im a head start.'

Bobby felt a wretched crawling sensation begin in his stomach – something like snakes in a basket. *I won't cry again,* he told himself. *Whatever happens I won't cry again even if they send me to the hospital. And I'll try to protect her.*

Protect her from big kids like this? It was a joke.

'Why are you being so mean, Willie?' Carol asked. She spoke solely to the boy with the auburn hair. 'You're not mean when you're by yourself. Why do you have to be mean now?'

Willie flushed. That, coupled with his dark red hair — much darker than Bobby's — made him look on fire from the neck up. Bobby guessed he didn't like his friends knowing he could act like a human being when they weren't around.

'Shut up, Gerber Baby!' he snarled. 'Why don't you just shut up and kiss your boyfriend while he's still got all his teeth?'

The third boy was wearing a motorcycle belt cinched on the side and ancient Snap-Jack shoes covered with dirt from the baseball field. He was behind Carol. Now he moved in closer, still walking his bike, and grabbed her ponytail with both hands. He pulled it.

'*Ow!*' Carol almost screamed. She sounded surprised as well as hurt. She pulled away so hard that she almost fell down. Bobby caught her and Willie — who could be nice when he wasn't with his pals, according to Carol — laughed.

'Why'd you do that?' Bobby yelled at the boy in the motorcycle belt, and as the words came out of his mouth it was as if he had heard them a thousand times before. All of this was like a ritual, the stuff that got said before the *real* yanks and pushes began and the fists began to fly. He thought of *Lord of the Flies* again — Ralph running from Jack and the others. At least on Golding's island there had been jungle. He and Carol had nowhere to run.

He says 'Because I felt like it.' That's what comes next.

But before the boy with the side-cinched belt could say

it, Robin Hood with the homemade bat-sling on his back said it for him. 'Because he felt like it. Whatcha gonna do about it, Maltex Baby?' He suddenly flicked out one hand, snake-quick, and slapped Bobby across the face. Willie laughed again.

Carol started toward him. 'Willie, please don't—'

Robin Hood reached out, grabbed the front of Carol's shirt, and squeezed. 'Got any titties yet? Nah, not much. You ain't nothing but a Gerber Baby.' He pushed her. Bobby, his head still ringing from the slap, caught her and for the second time kept her from falling down.

'Let's beat this queer up,' the kid in the motorcycle belt said. 'I hate his face.'

They moved in, the wheels of their bikes squeaking solemnly. Then Willie let his drop on its side like a dead pony and reached for Bobby. Bobby raised his fists in a feeble imitation of Floyd Patterson.

'Say, boys, what's going on?' someone asked from behind them.

Willie had drawn one of his own fists back. Still holding it cocked, he looked over his shoulder. So did Robin Hood and the boy with the motorcycle belt. Parked at the curb was an old blue Studebaker with rusty rocker panels and a magnetic Jesus on the dashboard. Standing in front of it, looking extremely busty in the chest and extremely wide in the hip, was Anita Gerber's friend Rionda. Summer clothes were never going to be her friends (even at eleven Bobby understood this), but at that moment she looked like a goddess in pedal pushers.

'Rionda!' Carol yelled – not crying, but almost. She pushed past Willie and the boy in the motorcycle belt. Neither made

269

any effort to stop her. All three of the St Gabe's boys were staring at Rionda. Bobby found himself looking at Willie's cocked fist. Sometimes Bobby woke up in the morning with his peter just as hard as a rock, standing straight up like a moon rocket or something. As he went into the bathroom to pee, it would soften and wilt. Willie's cocked arm was wilting like that now, the fist at the end of it relaxing back into fingers, and the comparison made Bobby want to smile. He resisted the urge. If they saw him smiling now, they could do nothing. Later, however . . . on another day . . .

Rionda put her arms around Carol and hugged the girl to her large bosom. She surveyed the boys in the orange shirts and *she* was smiling. Smiling and making no effort to hide it.

'Willie Shearman, isn't it?'

The formerly cocked-back arm dropped to Willie's side. Muttering, he bent to pick up his bike.

'Richie O'Meara?'

The boy in the motorcycle belt looked at the toes of his dusty Snap-Jacks and also muttered something. His cheeks burned with color.

'*One* of the O'Meara boys, anyway, there's so damned many of you now I can't keep track.' Her eyes shifted to Robin Hood. 'And who are you, big boy? Are you a Dedham? You look a little bit like a Dedham.'

Robin Hood looked at his hands. He wore a class ring on one of his fingers and now he began to twist it.

Rionda still had an arm around Carol's shoulders. Carol had one of her own arms as far around Rionda's waist as she could manage. She walked with Rionda, not looking at the boys, as Rionda stepped up from the street onto the little strip of grass between the curb and the sidewalk. She was still looking at Robin Hood. 'You better answer me when I talk to you, sonny. Won't be hard to find your mother if I want to try. All I have to do is ask Father Fitzgerald.'

'Harry Doolin, that's me,' the boy said at last. He was twirling his class ring faster than ever.

'Well, but I was close, wasn't I?' Rionda asked pleasantly, taking another two or three steps forward. They put her on the sidewalk. Carol, afraid to be so close to the boys, tried to hold her back, but Rionda would have none of it. 'Dedhams and Doolins, all married together. Right back to County Cork, tra-la-tra-lee.'

Not Robin Hood but a kid named Harry Doolin with a stupid homemade bat-sling strapped to his back. Not Marlon Brando from *The Wild One* but a kid named Richie O'Meara, who wouldn't have a Harley to go with his motorcycle belt for another five years . . . if ever. And Willie Shearman, who didn't dare to be nice to a girl when he was with his friends. All it took to shrink them back to their proper size was one overweight woman in pedal pushers and a shell top, who had ridden to the rescue not on a white stallion but in a 1954 Studebaker. The thought should have comforted Bobby but it didn't. He found himself thinking of what William Golding had said, that the boys on the island were rescued by the crew of a battle-cruiser and good for them . . . but who would rescue the crew?

That was stupid, no one ever looked less in need of rescuing than Rionda Hewson did at that moment, but the words still haunted Bobby. What if there *were* no grownups? Suppose the whole idea of grownups was an illusion? What if their money was really just playground marbles, their business deals no more than baseball-card trades, their wars only games of guns in the park? What if they were all still snotty-nosed kids inside their suits and dresses? Christ, that couldn't be, could it? It was too horrible to think about.

Rionda was still looking at the St Gabe's boys with her hard and rather dangerous smile. 'You three fellas wouldn't've been picking on kids younger and smaller than yourselves, would you? One of them a girl like your own little sisters?'

They were silent, not even muttering now. They only shuffled their feet.

'I'm sure you weren't, because that would be a cowardly thing to do, now wouldn't it?'

Again she gave them a chance to reply and plenty of time to hear their own silence.

'Willie? Richie? Harry? You weren't picking on them, were you?'

'Course not,' Harry said. Bobby thought that if he spun that ring of his much faster, his finger would probably catch fire.

'If I thought a thing like that,' Rionda said, still smiling her dangerous smile, 'I'd have to go talk to Father Fitzgerald, wouldn't I? And the Father, he'd probably feel he had to talk to your folks, and *your* fathers'd probably feel obliged to warm your asses for you . . . and you'd deserve it, boys, wouldn't you? For picking on the weak and small.'

Continued silence from the three boys, all now astride their ridiculously undersized bikes again.

'Did they pick on you, Bobby?' Rionda asked.

'No,' Bobby said at once.

Rionda put a finger under Carol's chin and turned her face up. 'Did they pick on *you*, lovey?'

'No, Rionda.'

Rionda smiled down at her, and although there were tears standing in Carol's eyes, she smiled back.

'Well, boys, I guess you're off the hook,' Rionda said. 'They say you haven't done nothing that'll cause you a single extra uncomfy minute in the confessional. I'd say that you owe them a vote of thanks, don't you?'

Mutter-mutter-mutter from the St Gabe's boys. *Please let it go at that*, Bobby pleaded silently. *Don't make them actually thank us. Don't rub their noses in it.*

Perhaps Rionda heard his thought (Bobby now had good reason to believe such things were possible). 'Well,' she said, 'maybe we can skip that part. Get along home, boys. And Harry, when you see Moira Dedham, tell her Rionda says she still goes to the Bingo over in Bridgeport every week, if she ever wants a ride.'

'I will, sure,' Harry said. He mounted his bike and rode away up the hill, eyes still on the sidewalk. Had there been pedestrians coming the other way, he would likely have run them over. His two friends followed him, standing on their pedals to catch up.

Rionda watched them go, her smile slowly fading. 'Shanty Irish,' she said at last, 'just trouble waiting to happen. Bah, good riddance to em. Carol, are you really all right?'

Carol said she really was.

'Bobby?'

'Sure, I'm fine.' It was taking him all the discipline he could manage not to start shaking right in front of her like a bowl of cranberry jelly, but if Carol could keep from falling apart, he guessed he could.

'Get in the car,' Rionda said to Carol. 'I'll give you a lift up to your house. You move along yourself, Bobby – scoot across the street and go inside. Those boys will have forgotten all about you and my Carol-girl by tomorrow, but tonight it might be smart for both of you to stay inside.'

'Okay,' Bobby said, knowing they wouldn't have forgotten by tomorrow, nor by the end of the week, nor by the end of the summer. He and Carol were going to have to watch out for Harry and his friends for a long time. 'Bye, Carol.'

'Bye.'

Bobby trotted across Broad Street. On the other side he stood watching Rionda's old car go up to the apartment house where the Gerbers lived. When Carol got out she looked back down the hill and waved. Bobby waved back, then walked up the porch steps of 149 and went inside.

Ted was sitting in the living room, smoking a cigarette and reading *Life* magazine. Anita Ekberg was on the cover. Bobby had no doubt that Ted's suitcases and the paper bags were packed, but there was no sign of them; he must have left them upstairs in his room. Bobby was glad. He didn't want to look at them. It was bad enough just knowing they were there.

'What did you do?' Ted asked.

'Not much,' Bobby said. 'I think I'll lie down on my bed and read until supper.'

He went into his room. Stacked on the floor by his bed were three books from the adult section of the Harwich Public Library – *Cosmic Engineers*, by Clifford D. Simak; *The Roman Hat Mystery*, by Ellery Queen; and *The Inheritors*, by William Golding. Bobby chose *The Inheritors* and lay down with his head at the foot of his bed and his stocking feet on his pillow. There were cave people on the book's cover, but they were drawn in a way that was almost abstract – you'd never see cave people like that on the cover of a kid's book. Having an adult library card was very neat . . . but somehow not as neat as it had seemed at first.

Hawaiian Eye was on at nine o'clock, and Bobby ordinarily would have been mesmerized (his mother claimed that shows like *Hawaiian Eye* and *The Untouchables* were too violent for children and ordinarily would not let him watch them), but tonight his mind kept wandering from the story. Less than sixty miles from here Eddie Albini and Hurricane Haywood would be mixing it up; the Gillette Blue Blades Girl, dressed in a blue bathing suit and blue high heels, would be parading around the ring before the start of every round and holding up a sign with a blue number on it. 1 . . . 2 . . . 3 . . . 4 . . .

By nine-thirty Bobby couldn't have picked out the private eye on the TV show, let alone guessed who had murdered the blond socialite. *Hurricane Haywood goes down in the eighth round*, Ted had told him; Old Gee knew it. But what if something went wrong? He didn't want Ted to go, but if he had to, Bobby couldn't bear the thought of him going with an empty wallet. Surely that couldn't happen, though . . . or could it? Bobby had seen a TV show where a fighter was supposed to take a dive and then changed his mind. What if that happened tonight? Taking a dive was bad, it was cheating – no shit, Sherlock, what was your first clue? – but if Hurricane Haywood *didn't* cheat, Ted would be in a lot of trouble; 'hurtin for certain' was how Sully-John would have put it.

Nine-thirty according to the sunburst clock on the living-room wall. If Bobby's math was right, the crucial eighth round was now underway.

'How do you like *The Inheritors*?'

Bobby was so deep into his own thoughts that Ted's voice made him jump. On TV, Keenan Wynn was standing in front of a bulldozer and saying he'd walk a mile for a Camel.

'It's a lot harder than *Lord of the Flies*,' he said. 'It seems like there are these two little families of cave people wandering around, and one family is smarter. But the other family, the dumb family, they're the heroes. I almost gave up, but now it's getting more interesting. I guess I'll stick with it.'

'The family you meet first, the one with the little girl, they're Neanderthals. The second family – only that one's really a tribe, Golding and his tribes – are Cro-Magnons. The Cro-Magnons are the inheritors. What happens between the two groups satisfies the definition of tragedy: events tending toward an unhappy outcome which cannot be avoided.'

Ted went on, talking about plays by Shakespeare and poems by Poe and novels by a guy named Theodore Dreiser. Ordinarily Bobby would have been interested, but tonight his mind kept going to Madison Square Garden. He could see the ring, lit as savagely as the few working pool-tables in The Corner Pocket had been. He could hear the crowd screaming as Haywood poured it on, smacking the surprised Eddie Albini with lefts and rights. Haywood wasn't going to tank the fight; like the boxer in the TV show, he was going to show the other guy a serious world of hurt instead. Bobby could smell sweat and hear the heavy biff and baff of gloves on flesh. Eddie Albini's eyes came up double zeros

. . . his knees buckled . . . the crowd was on its feet, screaming . . .

'—the idea of fate as a force which can't be escaped seems to start with the Greeks. There was a playwright named Euripides who—'

'Call,' Bobby said, and although he'd never had a cigarette in his life (by 1964 he would be smoking over a carton a week), his voice sounded as harsh as Ted's did late at night, after a day's worth of Chesterfields.

'Beg your pardon, Bobby?'

'Call Mr Files and see about the fight.' Bobby looked at the sunburst clock. Nine-forty-nine. 'If it only went eight, it'll be over now.'

'I agree that the fight is over, but if I call Files so soon he may suspect I knew something,' Ted said. 'Not from the radio, either – this one isn't on the radio, as we both know. It's better to wait. Safer. Let him believe I am a man of inspired hunches. I'll call at ten, as if I expected the result to be a decision instead of a knockout. And in the meantime, Bobby, don't worry. I tell you it's a stroll on the boardwalk.'

Bobby gave up trying to follow *Hawaiian Eye* at all; he just sat on the couch and listened to the actors quack. A man shouted at a fat Hawaiian cop. A woman in a white bathing suit ran into the surf. One car chased another while drums throbbed on the soundtrack. The hands on the sunburst clock crawled, struggling toward the ten and the twelve like climbers negotiating the last few hundred feet of Mount Everest. The man who'd murdered the socialite was killed himself as he ran around in a pineapple field and *Hawaiian Eye* finally ended.

Bobby didn't wait for the previews of next week's show; he snapped off the TV and said, 'Call, okay? *Please* call.'

'In a moment,' Ted said. 'I think I went one rootbeer over my limit. My holding-tanks seem to have shrunk with age.'

He shuffled into the bathroom. There was an interminable pause, and then the sound of pee splashing into the bowl. 'Aaah!' Ted said. There was considerable satisfaction in his voice.

Bobby could no longer sit. He got up and began pacing around the living room. He was sure that Tommy 'Hurricane' Haywood was right now being photographed in his corner at the Garden, bruised but beaming as the flashbulbs splashed white light over his face. The Gillette Blue Blades Girl would be there with him, her arm around his shoulders, his hand around her waist as Eddie Albini slumped forgotten in his own corner, dazed eyes puffed almost shut, still not completely conscious from the pounding he had taken.

By the time Ted returned, Bobby was in despair. He *knew* that Albini had lost the fight and his friend had lost his five hundred dollars. Would Ted stay when he found out he was broke? He might . . . but if he did and the low men came . . .

Bobby watched, fists clenching and unclenching, as Ted picked up the telephone and dialed.

'Relax, Bobby,' Ted told him. 'It's going to be okay.'

But Bobby couldn't relax. His guts felt full of wires. Ted held the phone to his ear without saying anything for what seemed like forever.

'Why don't they *answer*?' Bobby whispered fiercely.

'It's only rung twice, Bobby. Why don't you – hello? This is Mr Brautigan calling. Ted Brautigan? Yes, ma'am, from this afternoon.' Incredibly, Ted tipped Bobby a wink. How could he be so cool? Bobby didn't think he himself would have been capable of holding the phone up to his ear if he'd been in Ted's position, let alone winking. 'Yes, ma'am, he is.' Ted turned to Bobby and said, without covering the mouthpiece of the phone, 'Alanna wants to know how is your girlfriend.'

Bobby tried to speak and could only wheeze.

'Bobby says she's fine,' Ted told Alanna, 'pretty as a summer day. May I speak to Len? Yes, I can wait. But please tell me about the fight.' There was a pause which seemed to go on forever. Ted was expressionless now. And this time when he turned to Bobby he covered the mouthpiece. 'She says Albini got knocked around pretty good in the first five, held his own in six and seven, then threw a right hook out of nowhere and put Haywood on the canvas in the eighth. Lights out for the Hurricane. What a surprise, eh?'

'Yes,' Bobby said. His lips felt numb. It was true, all of it. By this time Friday night Ted would be gone. With two thousand rocks in your pocket you could do a lot of running from a lot of low men; with two thousand rocks in your pocket you could ride the Big Gray Dog from sea to shining sea.

Bobby went into the bathroom and squirted Ipana on his toothbrush. His terror that Ted had bet on the wrong fighter was gone, but the sadness of approaching loss was still there, and still growing. He never would have guessed that something that hadn't even happened could hurt so much. *A week from now I won't remember what was so neat about him. A year from now I'll hardly remember him at all.*

Was that true? God, was that true?

No, Bobby thought. *No way. I won't let it be.*

In the other room Ted was conversing with Len Files. It seemed to be a friendly enough palaver, going just as Ted had expected it would . . . and yes, here was Ted saying he'd just played a hunch, a good strong one, the kind you had to bet if you wanted to think of yourself as a sport. Sure, nine-thirty tomorrow night would be fine for the payout, assuming his friend's mother was back by eight; if she was a little late, Len would see him around ten or ten-thirty. Did that suit? More laughter from Ted, so it seemed that it suited fat Lennie Files right down to the ground.

Bobby put his toothbrush back in the glass on the shelf below the mirror, then reached into his pants pocket. There was something in there his fingers didn't recognize, not a part of the usual pocket-litter. He pulled out the keyring with the green fob, his special souvenir of a part of Bridgeport his mother knew nothing about. The part that was down there. THE CORNER POCKET, BILLIARDS, POOL, AUTO. GAMES. KENMORE 8-2127.

He probably should have hidden it already (or gotten rid of it entirely), and suddenly an idea came to him. Nothing could have really cheered Bobby Garfield up that night, but this at least came close: he would give the keyring to Carol Gerber, after cautioning her never to tell his mom where she'd gotten it. He knew that Carol had at least two keys she could put on it – her apartment key and the key to the diary Rionda had given her for her birthday. (Carol was three months older than Bobby, but she never lorded it over him on this account.) Giving her the keyring would be a little like asking her to go steady. He wouldn't have to get all gushy and embarrass himself by saying so, either; Carol would know. It was part of what made her cool.

Bobby laid the keyring on the shelf next to the toothglass, then went into his bedroom to put on his pj's. When he came out, Ted was sitting on the couch, smoking a cigarette and looking at him.

'Bobby, are you all right?'

'I guess so. I guess I have to be, don't I?'

Ted nodded. 'I guess we both have to be.'

'Will I ever see you again?' Bobby asked, pleading in his mind for Ted not to sound like the Lone Ranger, not to start talking any of that corny *we'll meet again pard* stuff . . . because it wasn't *stuff*, that word was too kind. Shit was what it was. He didn't think Ted had ever lied to him, and he didn't want him to start now that they were near the end.

'I don't know.' Ted studied the coal of his cigarette, and when he looked up, Bobby saw that his eyes were swimming with tears. 'I don't think so.'

Those tears undid Bobby. He ran across the room, wanting to hug Ted, *needing* to hug him. He stopped when Ted lifted his arms and crossed them over the chest of his baggy old man's shirt, his expression a kind of horrified surprise.

Bobby stood where he was, his arms still held out to hug. Slowly he lowered them. No hugging, no touching. It was the rule, but the rule was mean. The rule was wrong.

'Will you write?' he asked.

'I will send you postcards,' Ted replied after a moment's thought. 'Not directly to you, though – that might be dangerous for both of us. What shall I do? Any ideas?'

'Send them to Carol,' Bobby said. He didn't even stop to think.

'When did you tell her about the low men, Bobby?' There was no reproach in Ted's voice. Why would there be? He was going, wasn't he? For all the difference it made, the guy who did the story on the shopping-cart thief could write it up for the paper: CRAZY OLD MAN RUNS FROM INVADING ALIENS. People would read it to each other over their coffee and breakfast cereal and laugh. What had Ted called it that day? Galumphing small-town humor, hadn't that been it? But if it was so funny, why did it hurt? Why did it hurt so much?

'Today,' he said in a small voice. 'I saw her in the park and everything just kind of . . . came out.'

'That can happen,' Ted said gravely. 'I know it well; sometimes the dam just bursts. And perhaps it's for the best. You'll tell her I may want to get in touch with you through her?'

'Yeah.'

Ted tapped a finger against his lips, thinking. Then he nodded. 'At the top, the cards I send will say *Dear C.* Instead of *Dear Carol.* At the bottom I'll sign *A Friend.* That way you'll both know who writes. Okay?'

'Yeah,' Bobby said. 'Cool.' It wasn't cool, none of this was cool, but it would do.

He suddenly lifted his hand, kissed the fingers, and blew across them. Ted, sitting on the couch, smiled, caught the kiss, and put it on his lined cheek. 'You better go to bed now, Bobby. It's been a big day and it's late.'

Bobby went to bed.

At first he thought it was the same dream as before – Biderman, Cushman, and Dean chasing his mom through the jungle of William Golding's island. Then Bobby realized the trees and vines were part of the wallpaper, and that the path under his mother's flying feet was brown carpet. Not a jungle but a hotel corridor. This was his mind's version of the Warwick Hotel.

Mr Biderman and the other two nimrods were still chasing her, though. And now so were the boys from St Gabe's – Willie and Richie and Harry Doolin. All of them were wearing those streaks of red and white paint on their faces. And all of them were wearing bright yellow doublets upon which was drawn a brilliant red eye:

Other than the doublets they were naked. Their privates flopped and bobbed in bushy nests of pubic hair. All save Harry Doolin brandished spears; he had his baseball bat. It had been sharpened to a point on both ends.

'Kill the bitch!' Cushman yelled.

'Drink her blood!' Don Biderman cried, and threw his spear at Liz Garfield just as she darted around a corner. The spear stuck, quivering, into one of the jungle-painted walls.

'Stick it up her dirty cunt!' cried Willie – Willie who could be nice when he wasn't with his friends. The red eye on his chest stared. Below it, his penis also seemed to stare.

Run, Mom! Bobby tried to scream, but no words came out. He had no mouth, no body. He was here and yet he wasn't. He flew beside his mother like her own shadow. He heard her gasping for breath, saw her trembling, terrified mouth and her torn stockings. Her fancy dress was also torn. One of her breasts was scratched and bleeding. One of her eyes was almost closed. She looked as if she had gone a few rounds with Eddie Albini or Hurricane Haywood . . . maybe both at the same time.

'Gonna split you open!' Richie hollered.

'Eat you alive!' agreed Curtis Dean (and at top volume). 'Drink your blood, strew your guts!'

His mom looked back at them and her feet (she had lost her shoes somewhere) stuttered against each other. *Don't do that, Mom*, Bobby moaned. *For cripe's sake don't do that.*

As if she had heard him, Liz faced forward again and tried to run faster. She passed a poster on the wall:

PLEASE HELP US FIND OUR PET PIG!
LIZ is our MASCOT!
LIZ IS 34 YRS. OLD!
She is a BAD-TEMPERED SOW but WE LOVE HER!
Will do what you want if you say 'I PROMISE'
(OR)
'THERE'S MONEY IN IT'!
CALL HOusitonic 5–8337
(OR)
BRING to THE WILLIAM PENN GRILLE!
Ask for THE LOW MEN IN THE YELLOW COATS!
Motto: 'WE EAT IT **RARE**!'

His mom saw the poster, too, and this time when her ankles banged together she *did* fall.

Get up, Mom! Bobby screamed, but she didn't – perhaps couldn't. She crawled along the brown carpet instead, looking over her shoulder as she went, her hair hanging across her cheeks and forehead in sweaty clumps. The back of her dress had been torn away, and Bobby could see her bare bum – her underpants were gone. Worse, the backs of her thighs were splashed with blood. What had they done to her? Dear God, what had they done to his mother?

Don Biderman came around the corner *ahead* of her – he had found a shortcut and cut her off. The others were right behind him. Now Mr Biderman's prick was standing straight up the way Bobby's sometimes did in the morning before he got out of bed and went to the bathroom. Only Mr Biderman's prick was *huge*, it looked like a kraken, a triffid, a *monstah*, and Bobby thought he understood the blood on his mother's legs. He didn't want to but he thought he did.

Leave her alone! he tried to scream at Mr Biderman. *Leave her alone, haven't you done enough?*

The scarlet eye on Mr Biderman's yellow doublet suddenly opened wider . . . and slithered to one side. Bobby was invisible, his body one world farther down the spinning top from this one . . . but the red eye saw him. The red eye saw *everything*.

'Kill the pig, drink her blood,' Mr Biderman said in a thick, almost unrecognizable voice, and started forward.

'Kill the pig, drink her blood,' Bill Cushman and Curtis Dean chimed in.

'Kill the pig, strew her guts, eat her flesh,' chanted Willie and Richie, falling in behind the nimrods. Like those of the men, their pricks had turned into spears.

'Eat her, drink her, strew her, *screw* her,' Harry chimed in. *Get up, Mom! Run! Don't let them!*

She tried. But even as she struggled from her knees to her feet, Biderman leaped at her. The others followed, closing in, and as their hands began to tear the tatters of her clothes from her body Bobby thought: *I want to get out of here, I want to go back down the top to my own world, make it stop and spin it the other way so I can go back down to my own room in my own world . . .*

Except it wasn't a top, and even as the images of the dream began to break up and go dark, Bobby knew it. It wasn't a top but a tower, a still spindle upon which all of existence moved and spun. Then it was gone and for a little while there was a merciful nothingness. When he opened his eyes, his bedroom was full of sunshine – summer sunshine on a Thursday morning in the last June of the Eisenhower Presidency.

CHAPTER NINE
UGLY THURSDAY.

One thing you could say about Ted Brautigan: he knew how to cook. The breakfast he slid in front of Bobby − lightly scrambled eggs, toast, crisp bacon − was a lot better than anything his mother ever made for breakfast (her specialty was huge, tasteless pancakes which the two of them drowned in Aunt Jemima's syrup), and as good as anything you could get at the Colony Diner or the Harwich. The only problem was that Bobby didn't feel like eating. He couldn't remember the details of his dream, but he knew it had been a nightmare, and that he must have cried at some point while it was going on − when he woke up, his pillow had been damp. Yet the dream wasn't the only reason he felt flat and depressed this morning; dreams, after all, weren't real. Ted's going away would be real. And would be forever.

'Are you leaving right from The Corner Pocket?' Bobby asked as Ted sat down across from him with his own plate of eggs and bacon. 'You are, aren't you?'

'Yes, that will be safest.' He began to eat, but slowly and with no apparent enjoyment. So he was feeling bad, too. Bobby was glad. 'I'll say to your mother that my brother in Illinois is ill. That's all she needs to know.'

'Are you going to take the Big Gray Dog?'

Ted smiled briefly. 'Probably the train. I'm quite the wealthy man, remember.'

'Which train?'

'It's better if you don't know the details, Bobby. What you don't know you can't tell. Or be made to tell.'

Bobby considered this briefly, then asked, 'You'll remember the postcards?'

Ted picked up a piece of bacon, then put it down again. 'Postcards, plenty of postcards. I promise. Now don't let's talk about it anymore.'

'What should we talk about, then?'

Ted thought about it, then smiled. His smile was sweet and open; when he smiled, Bobby could see what he must have looked like when he was twenty, and strong.

'Books, of course,' Ted said. 'We'll talk about books.'

It was going to be a crushingly hot day, that was clear by nine o'clock. Bobby helped with the dishes, drying and putting away, and then they sat in the living room, where Ted's fan did its best to circulate the already tired air, and they talked about books . . . or rather *Ted* talked about books. And this morning, without the distraction of the Albini–Haywood fight, Bobby listened hungrily. He didn't understand all of what Ted was saying, but he understood enough to realize that books made their own world, and that the Harwich Public Library wasn't it. The library was nothing but the doorway to that world.

Ted talked of William Golding and what he called 'dystopian fantasy,' went on to H. G. Wells's *The Time Machine*, suggesting a link between the Morlocks and the

Eloi and Jack and Ralph on Golding's island; he talked about what he called 'literature's only excuses,' which he said were exploring the questions of innocence and experience, good and evil. Near the end of this impromptu lecture he mentioned a novel called *The Exorcist*, which dealt with both these questions ('in the popular context'), and then stopped abruptly. He shook his head as if to clear it.

'What's wrong?' Bobby took a sip of his rootbeer. He still didn't like it much but it was the only soft drink in the fridge. Besides, it was cold.

'What am I thinking?' Ted passed a hand over his brow, as if he'd suddenly developed a headache. 'That one hasn't been written yet.'

'What do you mean?'

'Nothing. I'm rambling. Why don't you go out for awhile? Stretch your legs? I might lie down for a bit. I didn't sleep very well last night.'

'Okay.' Bobby guessed a little fresh air – even if it was *hot* fresh air – might do him good. And while it was interesting to listen to Ted talk, he had started to feel as if the apartment walls were closing in on him. It was knowing Ted was going, Bobby supposed. Now there was a sad little rhyme for you: knowing he was going.

For a moment, as he went back into his room to get his baseball glove, the keyring from The Corner Pocket crossed his mind – he was going to give it to Carol so she'd know they were going steady. Then he remembered Harry Doolin, Richie O'Meara, and Willie Shearman. They were out there someplace, sure they were, and if they caught him by himself they'd probably beat the crap out of him. For the first time in two or three days, Bobby found himself wishing for Sully.

Sully was a little kid like him, but he was tough. Doolin and his friends might beat him up, but Sully-John would make them pay for the privilege. S-J was at camp, though, and that was that.

Bobby never considered staying in – he couldn't hide all summer from the likes of Willie Shearman, that would be buggy – but as he went outside he reminded himself that he had to be careful, had to be on the lookout for them. As long as he saw them coming, there would be no problem.

With the St Gabe's boys on his mind, Bobby left 149 with no further thought of the keyfob, his special souvenir of down there. It lay on the bathroom shelf next to the toothglass, right where he had left it the night before.

He tramped all over Harwich, it seemed – from Broad Street to Commonwealth Park (no St Gabe's boys on Field C today; the American Legion team was there, taking batting practice and shagging flies in the hot sun), from the park to the town square, from the town square to the railway station. As he stood in the little newsstand kiosk beneath the railway over-pass, looking at paperbacks (Mr Burton, who ran the place, would let you look for awhile as long as you didn't handle what he called 'the moichandise'), the town whistle went off, startling them both.

'Mothera God, what's up widdat?' Mr Burton asked indig-nantly. He had spilled packs of gum all over the floor and now stooped to pick them up, his gray change-apron hanging down. 'It ain't but quarter past eleven!'

'It's early, all right,' Bobby agreed, and left the newsstand soon after. Browsing had lost its charms for him. He walked out to River Avenue, stopping at the Tip-Top Bakery to buy half a loaf of day-old bread (two cents) and to ask Georgie Sullivan how S-J was.

'He's fine,' S-J's oldest brother said. 'We got a postcard on Tuesday says he misses the fambly and wantsa come home. We get one Wednesday says he's learning how to dive. The one this morning says he's having the time of his life, he wantsa stay forever.' He laughed, a big Irish boy of twenty with big Irish arms and shoulders. 'He may wanta stay forever, but Ma'd miss im like hell if he stayed up there. You gonna feed the ducks with some of that?'

'Yeah, like always.'

'Don't let em nibble your fingers. Those damned river ducks carry diseases. They—'

In the town square the Municipal Building clock began to chime noon, although it was still only quarter of.

'What's going on today?' Georgie asked. 'First the whistle blows early, now the damned town clock's off-course.'

'Maybe it's the heat,' Bobby said.

Georgie looked at him doubtfully. 'Well . . . it's as good an explanation as any.'

Yeah, Bobby thought, going out. *And quite a bit safer than some.*

Bobby went down to River Avenue, munching his bread as he walked. By the time he found a bench near the Housatonic River, most of the half-loaf had disappeared down his own throat. Ducks came waddling eagerly out of the reeds and Bobby began to scatter the remaining bread for them, amused as always by the greedy way they ran for the chunks and the way they threw their heads back to eat them.

After awhile he began to grow drowsy. He looked out

over the river, at the nets of reflected light shimmering on its surface, and grew drowsier still. He had slept the previous night but his sleep hadn't been restful. Now he dozed off with his hands full of breadcrumbs. The ducks finished with what was on the grass and then drew closer to him, quacking in low, ruminative tones. The clock in the town square bonged the hour of two at twelve-twenty, causing people downtown to shake their heads and ask each other what the world was coming to. Bobby's doze deepened by degrees, and when a shadow fell over him, he didn't see or sense it.

'Hey. Kid.'

The voice was quiet and intense. Bobby sat up with a gasp and a jerk, his hands opening and spilling out the remaining bread. Those snakes began to crawl around in his belly again. It wasn't Willie Shearman or Richie O'Meara or Harry Doolin – even coming out of a doze he knew that – but Bobby almost wished it had been one of them. Even all three. A beating wasn't the worst thing that could happen to you. No, not the worst. Cripes, why did he have to go and fall *asleep*?

'Kid.'

The ducks were stepping on Bobby's feet, squabbling over the unexpected windfall. Their wings were fluttering against his ankles and his shins, but the feeling was far away, far away. He could see the shadow of a man's head on the grass ahead of him. The man was standing behind him.

'Kid.'

Slowly and creakily, Bobby turned. The man's coat would be yellow and somewhere on it would be an eye, a staring red eye.

But the man who stood there was wearing a tan summer

suit, the jacket pooched out by a little stomach that was starting to grow into a big stomach, and Bobby knew at once it wasn't one of *them* after all. There was no itching behind his eyes, no black threads across his field of vision . . . but the major thing was that this wasn't some *creature* just pretending to be a person; it *was* a person.

'What?' Bobby asked, his voice low and muzzy. He still couldn't believe he'd gone to sleep like that, blanked out like that. 'What do you want?'

'I'll give you two bucks to let me blow you,' the man in the tan suit said. He reached into the pocket of his jacket and brought out his wallet. 'We can go behind that tree over there. No one'll see us. And you'll like it.'

'No,' Bobby said, getting up. He wasn't completely sure what the man in the tan suit was talking about, but he had a pretty good idea. The ducks scattered backward, but the bread was too tempting to resist and they returned, pecking and dancing around Bobby's sneakers. 'I have to go home now. My mother—'

The man came closer, still holding out his wallet. It was as if he'd decided to give the whole thing to Bobby, never mind the two lousy dollars. 'You don't have to do it to me, I'll just do it to you. Come on, what do you say? I'll make it three dollars.' The man's voice was trembling now, jigging and jagging up and down the scale, at one moment seeming to laugh, at the next almost to weep. 'You can go to the movies for a month on three dollars.'

'No, really, I—'

'You'll like it, all my boys like it.' He reached out for Bobby and suddenly Bobby thought of Ted taking hold of his shoulders, Ted putting his hands behind his neck, Ted

293

pulling him closer until they were almost close enough to kiss. That wasn't like this . . . and yet it was. Somehow it was.

Without thinking about what he was doing, Bobby bent and grabbed one of the ducks. He lifted it in a surprised squawking flurry of beak and wings and paddling feet, had just a glimpse of one black bead of an eye, and then threw it at the man in the tan suit. The man yelled and put his hands up to shield his face, dropping his wallet.

Bobby ran.

He was passing through the square, headed back home, when he saw a poster on a telephone pole outside the candy store. He walked over to it and read it with silent horror. He couldn't remember his dream of the night before, but something like this had been in it. He was positive.

HAVE YOU SEEN BRAUTIGAN!
He is an OLD MONGREL but WE LOVE HIM!
BRAUTIGAN has WHITE FUR and BLUE EYES!
He is FRIENDLY!
Will EAT SCRAPS FROM YOUR HAND!
We will pay A VERY LARGE REWARD
($ $ $ $)
IF YOU HAVE SEEN BRAUTIGAN!
CALL HOusitonic 5–8337!
(OR)
BRING BRAUTIGAN to 745 Highgate Avenue!
Home of the SAGAMORE FAMILY!

This isn't a good day, Bobby thought, watching his hand reach out and pull the poster off the telephone pole. Beyond it, hanging from a bulb on the marquee of the Harwich Theater, he saw a dangling blue kite tail. *This isn't a good day at all. I never should have gone out of the apartment. In fact, I should have stayed in bed.*

HOusitonic 5–8337, just like on the poster about Phil the Welsh Corgi . . . except if there was a HOusitonic exchange in Harwich, Bobby had never heard of it. Some of the numbers were on the HArwich exchange. Others were COmmon-wealth. But HOusitonic? No. Not here, not in Bridgeport, either.

He crumpled the poster up and threw it in the KEEP OUR TOWN CLEAN N GREEN basket on the corner, but on the other side of the street he found another just like it. Farther along he found a third pasted to a corner mailbox. He tore these down, as well. The low men were either closing in or desperate. Maybe both. Ted couldn't go out at all today – Bobby would have to tell him that. And he'd have to be ready to run. He'd tell him that, too.

Bobby cut through the park, almost running himself in his hurry to get home, and he barely heard the small, gasping cry which came from his left as he passed the baseball fields: 'Bobby . . .'

He stopped and looked toward the grove of trees where Carol had taken him the day before when he started to bawl. And when the gasping cry came again, he realized it was *her.*

'Bobby if it's you please help me . . .'

He turned off the cement path and ducked into the copse of trees. What he saw there made him drop his base-ball glove on the ground. It was an Alvin Dark model, that glove, and later it was gone. Someone came along and just kifed it, he supposed, and so what? As that day wore on, his lousy baseball glove was the very least of his concerns.

Carol sat beneath the same elm tree where she had comforted him. Her knees were drawn up to her chest. Her face was ashy gray. Black shock-circles ringed her eyes, giving her a raccoony look. A thread of blood trickled from one of her nostrils. Her left arm lay across her midriff, pulling her shirt tight against the beginning nubs of what would be breasts in another year or two. She held the elbow of that arm cupped in her right hand.

She was wearing shorts and a smock-type blouse with long sleeves – the kind of thing you just slipped on over your head. Later, Bobby would lay much of the blame for what happened on that stupid shirt of hers. She must have worn it to protect against sunburn; it was the only reason he could think of to wear long sleeves on such a murderously hot day. Had she picked it out herself or had Mrs Gerber forced her into it? And did it matter? *Yes*, Bobby would think when there was time to think. *It mattered, you're damned right it mattered.*

But for now the blouse with its long sleeves was peripheral. The only thing he noticed in that first instant was Carol's upper left arm. It seemed to have not one shoulder but two.

'Bobby,' she said, looking at him, with shining dazed eyes. 'They hurt me.'

She was in shock, of course. He was in shock himself by then, running on instinct. He tried to pick her up and she screamed in pain – dear God, what a sound.

'I'll run and get help,' he said, lowering her back. 'You just sit there and try not to move.'

She was shaking her head – carefully, so as not to joggle

her arm. Her blue eyes were nearly black with pain and terror. 'No, Bobby, no, don't leave me here, what if they come back? What if they come back and hurt me worse?' Parts of what happened on that long hot Thursday were lost to him, lost in the shockwave, but that part always stood clear: Carol looking up at him and saying *What if they come back and hurt me worse?*

'But . . . Carol . . .'

'I can walk. If you help me, I can walk.'

Bobby put a tentative arm around her waist, hoping she wouldn't scream again. That had been bad.

Carol got slowly to her feet, using the trunk of the tree to support her back. Her left arm moved a little as she rose. That grotesque double shoulder bulged and flexed. She moaned but didn't scream, thank God.

'You better stop,' Bobby said.

'No, I want to get out of here. Help me. Oh God, it hurts.'

Once she was all the way up it seemed a little better. They made their way out of the grove with the slow side-by-side solemnity of a couple about to be married. Beyond the shade of the trees the day seemed even hotter than before and blindingly bright. Bobby looked around and saw no one. Somewhere, deeper in the park, a bunch of little kids (probably Sparrows or Robins from Sterling House) were singing a song, but the area around the baseball fields was utterly deserted: no kids, no mothers wheeling baby carriages, no sign of Officer Raymer, the local cop who would sometimes buy you an ice cream or a bag of peanuts if he was in a good mood. Everyone was inside, hiding from the heat.

Still moving slowly, Bobby with his arm around Carol's waist, they walked along the path which came out on the

STEPHEN KING

corner of Commonwealth and Broad. Broad Street Hill was as deserted as the park; the paving shimmered like the air over an incinerator. There wasn't a single pedestrian or moving car in sight.

They stepped onto the sidewalk and Bobby was about to ask if she could make it across the street when Carol said in a high, whispery voice: 'Oh Bobby I'm fainting.'

He looked at her in alarm and saw her eyes roll up to glistening whites. She swayed back and forth like a tree which has been cut almost all the way through. Bobby bent, moving without thinking, catching her around the thighs and the back as her knees unlocked. He had been standing to her right and was able to do this without hurting her left arm any more than it already had been hurt; also, even in her faint Carol kept her right hand cupped over her left elbow, holding the arm mostly steady.

Carol Gerber was Bobby's height, perhaps even a little taller, and close to his weight. He should have been incapable of even staggering up Broad Street with her in his arms, but people in shock are capable of amazing bursts of strength. Bobby carried her, and not at a stagger; under that burning June sun he ran. No one stopped him, no one asked him what was wrong with the little girl, no one offered to help. He could hear cars on Asher Avenue, but this part of the world seemed eerily like Midwich, where everyone had gone to sleep at once.

Taking Carol to her mother never crossed his mind. The Gerber apartment was farther up the hill, but that wasn't the reason. Ted was all Bobby could think of. He had to take her to Ted. Ted would know what to do.

His preternatural strength began to give out as he climbed

298

the steps to the front porch of his building. He staggered, and Carol's grotesque double shoulder bumped against the railing. She stiffened in his arms and cried out, her half-lidded eyes opening wide.

'Almost there,' he told her in a panting whisper that didn't sound much like his own voice. 'Almost there, I'm sorry I bumped you but we're almost—'

The door opened and Ted came out. He was wearing gray suit pants and a strap-style undershirt. Suspenders hung down to his knees in swinging loops. He looked surprised and concerned but not frightened.

Bobby managed the last porch step and then swayed backward. For one terrible moment he thought he was going to go crashing down, maybe splitting his skull on the cement walk. Then Ted grabbed him and steadied him.

'Give her to me,' he said.

'Get over on her other side first,' Bobby panted. His arms were twanging like guitar strings and his shoulders seemed to be on fire. 'That's the bad side.'

Ted came around and stood next to Bobby. Carol was looking up at them, her sandy-blond hair hanging down over Bobby's wrist. 'They hurt me,' she whispered to Ted. 'Willie . . . I asked him to make them stop but he wouldn't.'

'Don't talk,' Ted said. 'You're going to be all right.'

He took her from Bobby as gently as he could, but they couldn't help joggling her left arm a little. The double shoulder moved under the white smock. Carol moaned, then began to cry. Fresh blood trickled from her right nostril, one brilliant red drop against her skin. Bobby had a momentary flash from his dream of the night before: the eye. The red eye.

'Hold the door for me, Bobby.'

Bobby held it wide. Ted carried Carol through the foyer and into the Garfield apartment. At that same moment Liz Garfield was descending the iron steps leading from the Harwich stop of the New York, New Haven & Hartford Railroad to Main Street, where there was a taxi stand. She moved with the slow deliberation of a chronic invalid. A suitcase dangled from each hand. Mr Burton, proprietor of the newsstand kiosk, happened to be standing in his doorway and having a smoke. He watched Liz reach the bottom of the steps, turn back the veil of her little hat, and gingerly dab at her face with a bit of handkerchief. She winced at each touch. She was wearing makeup, a lot, but the makeup didn't help. The makeup only drew attention to what had happened to her. The veil was better, even though it only covered the upper part of her face, and now she lowered it again. She approached the first of three idling taxis, and the driver got out to help her with her bags.

Burton wondered who had given her the business. He hoped whoever it had been was currently getting his head massaged by big cops with hard hickories. A person who would do something like that to a woman deserved no better. A person who would do something like that to a woman had no business running around loose. That was Burton's opinion.

Bobby thought Ted would put Carol on the couch, but he didn't. There was one straight-backed chair in the living room and that was where he sat, holding her on his lap. He held her the way the Grant's department store Santa Claus held the little kids who came up to him as he sat on his throne.

'Where else are you hurt? Besides the shoulder?'

'They hit me in the stomach. And on my side.'

'Which side?'

'The right one.'

Ted gently pulled her blouse up on that side. Bobby hissed in air over his lower lip when he saw the bruise which lay diagonally across her ribcage. He recognized the baseball-bat shape of it at once. He knew whose bat it had been: Harry Doolin's, the pimply galoot who saw himself as Robin Hood in whatever stunted landscape passed for his imagination. He and Richie O'Meara and Willie Shearman had come upon her in the park and Harry had worked her over with his ball-bat while Richie and Willie held her. All three of them laughing and calling her the Gerber Baby. Maybe it had started as a joke and gotten out of hand. Wasn't that pretty much what had happened in *Lord of the Flies*? Things had just gotten a little out of hand?

Ted touched Carol's waist; his bunchy fingers spread and then slowly slid up her side. He did this with his head cocked, as if he were listening rather than touching. Maybe he was. Carol gasped when he reached the bruise.

'Hurt?' Ted asked.

'A little. Not as bad as my sh-shoulder. They broke my arm, didn't they?'

'No, I don't think so,' Ted replied.

'I heard it pop. So did they. That's when they ran.'

'I'm sure you did hear it. Yes indeed.'

Tears were running down her cheeks and her face was still ashy, but Carol seemed calmer now. Ted held her blouse up against her armpit and looked at the bruise. *He knows what that shape is just as well as I do*, Bobby thought.

'How many were there, Carol?'

Three, Bobby thought.

'Th-three.'

'Three boys?'

She nodded.

'Three boys against one little girl. They must have been afraid of you. They must have thought you were a lion. Are you a lion, Carol?'

'I wish I was,' Carol said. She tried to smile. 'I wish I could have roared and made them go away. They h-h-*hurt* me.'

'I know they did. I know.' His hand slid down her side and cupped the bat-bruise on her ribcage. 'Breathe in.'

The bruise swelled against Ted's hand; Bobby could see its purple shape between his nicotine-stained fingers. 'Does *that* hurt?'

She shook her head.

'Not to breathe?'

'No.'

'And not when your ribs go against my hand?'

'No. Only sore. What hurts is . . .' She glanced quickly at the terrible shape of her double shoulder, then away.

'I know. Poor Carol. Poor darling. We'll get to that. Where else did they hit you? In the stomach, you said?'

'Yes.'

Ted pulled her blouse up in front. There was another bruise, but this one didn't look so deep or so angry. He prodded gently with his fingers, first above her bellybutton and then below it. She said there was no pain like in her shoulder, that her belly was only sore like her ribs were sore.

'They didn't hit you in your back?'

'N-no.'

302

'In your head or your neck?'

'Huh-uh, just my side and my stomach and then they hit me in the shoulder and there was that pop and they heard it and they ran. I used to think Willie Shearman was nice.' She gave Ted a woeful look.

'Turn your head for me, Carol . . . good . . . now the other way. It doesn't hurt when you turn it?'

'No.'

'And you're sure they never hit your head.'

'No. I mean yes, I'm sure.'

'Lucky girl.'

Bobby wondered how in the hell Ted could think Carol was *lucky*. Her left arm didn't look just broken to him; it looked half torn off. He suddenly thought of a roast-chicken Sunday dinner, and the sound the drumstick made when you pulled it loose. His stomach knotted. For a moment he thought he was going to vomit up his breakfast and the day-old bread which had been his only lunch.

No, he told himself. *Not now, you can't. Ted's got enough problems without adding you to the list.*

'Bobby?' Ted's voice was clear and sharp. He sounded like a guy with more solutions than problems, and what a relief that was. 'Are you all right?'

'Yeah.' And he thought it was true. His stomach was starting to settle.

'Good. You did well to get her up here. Can you do well a little longer?'

'Yeah.'

'I need a pair of scissors. Can you find one?'

Bobby went into his mother's bedroom, opened the top drawer of her dresser, and got out her wicker sewing basket.

Inside was a medium-sized pair of shears. He hurried back into the living room with them and showed them to Ted. 'Are these all right?'

'Fine,' he said, taking them. Then, to Carol: 'I'm going to spoil your blouse, Carol. I'm sorry, but I have to look at your shoulder now and I don't want to hurt you any more than I can help.'

'That's okay,' she said, and again tried to smile. Bobby was a little in awe of her bravery; if *his* shoulder had looked like that, he probably would have been blatting like a sheep caught in a barbed-wire fence.

'You can wear one of Bobby's shirts home. Can't she, Bobby?'

'Sure, I don't mind a few cooties.'

'Fun-*nee*,' Carol said.

Working carefully, Ted cut the smock up the back and then up the front. With that done he pulled the two pieces off like the shell of an egg. He was very careful on the left side, but Carol uttered a hoarse scream when Ted's fingers brushed her shoulder. Bobby jumped and his heart, which had been slowing down, began to race again.

'I'm sorry,' Ted murmured. 'Oh my. Look at this.'

Carol's shoulder was ugly, but not as bad as Bobby had feared – perhaps few things were once you were looking right at them. The second shoulder was higher than the normal one, and the skin there was stretched so tight that Bobby didn't understand why it didn't just split open. It had gone a peculiar lilac color, as well.

'How bad is it?' Carol asked. She was looking in the other direction, across the room. Her small face had the pinched, starved look of a UNICEF child. So far as Bobby knew she never looked at her hurt shoulder after that single quick peek. 'I'll be in a cast all summer, won't I?'

'I don't think you're going to be in a cast at all.'

Carol looked up into Ted's face wonderingly.

'It's not broken, child, only dislocated. Someone hit you on the shoulder—'

'Harry Doolin—'

'—and hard enough to knock the top of the bone in your upper left arm out of its socket. I can put it back in, I think. Can you stand one or two moments of quite bad pain if you know things may be all right again afterward?'

'Yes,' she said at once. 'Fix it, Mr Brautigan. Please fix it.'

Bobby looked at him a little doubtfully. 'Can you really do that?'

'Yes. Give me your belt.'

'*Huh?*'

'Your belt. Give it to me.'

Bobby slipped his belt – a fairly new one he'd gotten for Christmas – out of its loops and handed it to Ted, who took it without ever shifting his eyes from Carol's. 'What's your last name, honey?'

'Gerber. They called me the Gerber Baby, but I'm not a baby.'

'I'm sure you're not. And this is where you prove it.' He got up, settled her in the chair, then knelt before her like a guy in some old movie getting ready to propose. He folded Bobby's belt over twice in his big hands, then poked it at her good hand until she let go of her elbow and closed her fingers over the loops. 'Good. Now put it in your mouth.'

'Put Bobby's *belt* in my *mouth*?'

Ted's gaze never left her. He began stroking her unhurt

305

arm from the elbow to the wrist. His fingers trailed down her forearm . . . stopped . . . rose and went back to her elbow . . . trailed down her forearm again. *It's like he's hypnotizing her*, Bobby thought, but there was really no 'like' about it; Ted *was* hypnotizing her. His pupils had begun to do that weird thing again, growing and shrinking . . . growing and shrinking . . . growing and shrinking. Their movement and the movement of his fingers were exactly in rhythm. Carol stared into his face, her lips parted.

'Ted . . . your *eyes* . . .'

'Yes, yes.' He sounded impatient, not very interested in what his eyes were doing. 'Pain rises, Carol, did you know that?'

'No . . .'

Her eyes on his. His fingers on her arm, going down and rising. Going down . . . and rising. His pupils like a slow heart-beat. Bobby could see Carol relaxing in the chair. She was still holding the belt, and when Ted stopped his finger-stroking long enough to touch the back of her hand, she lifted it toward her face with no protest.

'Oh yes,' he said, 'pain rises from its source to the brain. When I put your shoulder back in its socket, there will be a lot of pain – but you'll catch most of it in your mouth as it rises toward your brain. You will bite it with your teeth and hold it against Bobby's belt so that only a little of it can get into your head, which is where things hurt the most. Do you understand me, Carol?'

'Yes . . .' Her voice had grown distant. She looked very small sitting there in the straight-backed chair, wearing only her shorts and her sneakers. The pupils of Ted's eyes, Bobby noticed, had grown steady again.

'Put the belt in your mouth.'

She put it between her lips.

'Bite when it hurts.'

'When it hurts.'

'Catch the pain.'

'I'll catch it.'

Ted gave a final stroke of his big forefinger from her elbow to her wrist, then looked at Bobby. 'Wish me luck,' he said.

'Luck,' Bobby replied fervently.

Distant, dreaming, Carol Gerber said: 'Bobby threw a duck at a man.'

'Did he?' Ted asked. Very, very gently he closed his left hand around Carol's left wrist.

'Bobby thought the man was a low man.'

Ted glanced at Bobby.

'Not that kind of low man,' Bobby said. 'Just . . . oh, never mind.'

'All the same,' Ted said, 'they are very close. The town clock, the town whistle—'

'I heard,' Bobby said grimly.

'I'm not going to wait until your mother comes back tonight − I don't dare. I'll spend the day in a movie or a park or somewhere else. If all else fails there are flophouses in Bridgeport. Carol, are you ready?'

'Ready.'

'When the pain rises, what will you do?'

'Catch it. Bite it into Bobby's belt.'

'Good girl. Ten seconds and you are going to feel a lot better.'

Ted drew in a deep breath. Then he reached out with his

right hand until it hovered just above the lilac-colored bulge in Carol's shoulder. 'Here comes the pain, darling. Be brave.'

It wasn't ten seconds; not even five. To Bobby it seemed to happen in an instant. The heel of Ted's right hand pressed directly against that knob rising out of Carol's stretched flesh. At the same time he pulled sharply on her wrist. Carol's jaws flexed as she clamped down on Bobby's belt. Bobby heard a brief creaking sound, like the one his neck sometimes made when it was stiff and he turned his head. And then the bulge in Carol's arm was gone.

'Bingo!' Ted cried. 'Looks good! Carol?'

She opened her mouth. Bobby's belt fell out of it and onto her lap. Bobby saw a line of tiny points embedded in the leather; she had bitten nearly all the way through.

'It doesn't hurt anymore,' she said wonderingly. She ran her right hand up to where the skin was now turning a darker purple, touched the bruise, winced.

'That'll be sore for a week or so,' Ted warned her. 'And you mustn't throw or lift with that arm for at least two weeks. If you do, it may pop out again.'

'I'll be careful.' Now Carol could look at her arm. She kept touching the bruise with light, testing fingers.

'How much of the pain did you catch?' Ted asked her, and although his face was still grave, Bobby thought he could hear a little smile in his voice.

'Most of it,' she said. 'It hardly hurt at all.' As soon as these words were out, however, she slumped back in the chair. Her eyes were open but unfocused. Carol had fainted for the second time.

★   ★   ★

Ted told Bobby to wet a cloth and bring it to him. 'Cold water,' he said. 'Wring it out, but not too much.'

Bobby ran into the bathroom, got a facecloth from the shelf by the tub, and wet it in cold water. The bottom half of the bathroom window was frosted glass, but if he had looked out the top half he would have seen his mother's taxi pulling up out front. Bobby didn't look; he was concentrating on his chore. He never thought of the green keyfob, either, although it was lying on the shelf right in front of his eyes.

When Bobby came back into the living room, Ted was sitting in the straight-backed chair with Carol in his lap again. Bobby noticed how tanned her arms had already become compared to the rest of her skin, which was a pure, smooth white (except for where the bruises stood out). *She looks like she's wearing nylon stockings on her arms*, he thought, a little amused. Her eyes had begun to clear and they tracked Bobby when he moved toward her, but Carol still didn't look exactly great — her hair was mussed, her face was all sweaty, and there was that drying trickle of blood between her nostril and the corner of her mouth.

Ted took the cloth and began to wipe her cheeks and forehead with it. Bobby knelt by the arm of the chair. Carol sat up a little, raising her face gratefully against the cool and the wet. Ted wiped away the blood under her nose, then put the facecloth aside on the endtable. He brushed Carol's sweaty hair off her brow. When some of it flopped back, he moved his hand to brush it away again.

Before he could, the door to the porch banged open. Footfalls crossed the foyer. The hand on Carol's damp forehead froze. Bobby's eyes met Ted's and a single thought flowed between them, strong telepathy consisting of a single word: *Them.*

'*No,*' Carol said, '*not* them, Bobby, it's your m—'

The apartment door opened and Liz stood there with her key in one hand and her hat — the one with the veil on it — in the other. Behind her and beyond the foyer the door to all the hot outside world stood open. Side by side on the porch welcome mat were her two suitcases, where the cab driver had put them.

'Bobby, how many times have I told you to lock this damn—'

She got that far, then stopped. In later years Bobby would replay that moment again and again, seeing more and more of what his mother had seen when she came back from her disastrous trip to Providence: her son kneeling by the chair where the old man she had never liked or really trusted sat with the little girl in his lap. The little girl looked dazed. Her hair was in sweaty clumps. Her blouse had been torn off — it lay in pieces on the floor — and even with her own eyes puffed mostly shut, Liz would have seen Carol's bruises: one on the shoulder, one on the ribs, one on the stomach.

And Carol and Bobby and Ted Brautigan saw her with that same amazed stop-time clarity: the two black eyes (Liz's right eye was really nothing but a glitter deep in a puffball of discolored flesh); the lower lip which was swelled and split in two places and still wearing flecks of dried blood like old ugly lipstick; the nose which lay askew and had grown a misbegotten hook, making it almost into a caricature Witch Hazel nose.

Silence, a moment's considering silence on a hot summer afternoon. Somewhere a car backfired. Somewhere a kid shouted '*Come on, you guys!*' And from behind them on Colony

Street came the sound Bobby would identify most strongly with his childhood in general and that Thursday in particular: Mrs O'Hara's Bowser barking his way ever deeper into the twentieth century: *roop-roop, roop-roop-roop*.

Jack got her, Bobby thought. *Jack Merridew and his nimrod friends*.

'Oh jeez, what happened?' he asked her, breaking the silence. He didn't want to know; he had to know. He ran to her, starting to cry out of fright but also out of grief: her face, her poor face. She didn't look like his mom at all. She looked like some old woman who belonged not on shady Broad Street but down there, where people drank wine out of bottles in paper sacks and had no last names. 'What did he do? What did that bastard do to you?'

She paid no attention, seemed not to hear him at all. She laid hold of him, though; laid hold of his shoulders hard enough for him to feel her fingers sinking into his flesh, hard enough to hurt. She laid hold and then set him aside without a single look. 'Let her go, you filthy man,' she said in a low and rusty voice. 'Let her go right now.'

'Mrs Garfield, please don't misunderstand.' Ted lifted Carol off his lap — careful even now to keep his hand well away from her hurt shoulder — and then stood up himself. He shook out the legs of his pants, a fussy little gesture that was all Ted. 'She was hurt, you see. Bobby found her—'

'*BASTARD!*' Liz screamed. To her right was a table with a vase on it. She grabbed the vase and threw it at him. Ted ducked, but too slowly to avoid it completely; the bottom of the vase struck the top of his head, skipped like a stone on a pond, hit the wall and shattered.

311

Carol screamed.

'Mom, no!' Bobby shouted. 'He didn't do anything bad! He didn't do anything bad!'

Liz took no notice. 'How dare you touch her? Have you been touching my son the same way? You have, haven't you? You don't care which flavor they are, just as long as they're *young!*'

Ted took a step toward her. The empty loops of his suspenders swung back and forth beside his legs. Bobby could see blooms of blood in the scant hair on top of his head where the vase had clipped him.

'Mrs Garfield, I assure you—'

'*Assure this, you dirty bastard!*' With the vase gone there was nothing left on the table and so she picked up the table itself and threw it. It struck Ted in the chest and drove him backward; would have floored him if not for the straight-backed chair. Ted flopped into it, looking at her with wide, incredulous eyes. His mouth was trembling.

'Was he helping you?' Liz asked. Her face was dead white. The bruises on it stood out like birthmarks. '*Did you teach my son to help?*'

'Mom, he didn't hurt her!' Bobby shouted. He grabbed her around the waist. 'He didn't hurt her, he—'

She picked him up like the vase, like the table, and he would think later she had been as strong as he had been, carrying Carol up the hill from the park. She threw him across the room. Bobby struck the wall. His head snapped back and connected with the sunburst clock, knocking it to the floor and stopping it forever. Black dots flocked across his vision, making him think briefly and confusedly

(*coming closing in now the posters have his name on them*)

312

of the low men. Then he slid to the floor. He tried to stop himself but his knees wouldn't lock.

Liz looked at him, seemingly without much interest, then back at Ted, who sat in the straight-backed chair with the table in his lap and the legs poking at his face. Blood was dripping down one of his cheeks now, and his hair was more red than white. He tried to speak and what came out instead was a dry and flailing old man's cigarette cough.

'Filthy man. Filthy, filthy man. For two cents I'd pull your pants down and yank that filthy thing right off you.' She turned and looked at her huddled son again, and the expression Bobby now saw in the one eye he could really see – the contempt, the accusation – made him cry harder. She didn't say *You too*, but he saw it in her eye. Then she turned back to Ted.

'Know what? You're going to jail.' She pointed a finger at him, and even through his tears Bobby saw the nail that had been on it when she left in Mr Biderman's Merc was gone; there was a bloody-ragged weal where it had been. Her voice was mushy, seeming to spread out somehow as it crossed her oversized lower lip. 'I'm going to call the police now. If you're wise you'll sit still while I do it. Just keep your mouth shut and sit still.' Her voice was rising, rising. Her hands, scratched and swelled at the knuckles as well as broken at the nails, curled into fists which she shook at him. 'If you run I'll chase you and carve you up with my longest butcher knife. See if I don't. I'll do it right on the street for everyone to see, and I'll start with the part of you that seems to give you . . . you *boys* . . . so much trouble. So sit still, *Brattigan*. If you want to live long enough to go to jail, don't you move.'

The phone was on the table by the couch. She went to

it. Ted sat with the table in his lap and blood flowing down his cheek. Bobby huddled next to the fallen clock, the one his mother had gotten with trading stamps. Drifting in the window on the breeze of Ted's fan came Bowser's cry: *roop-roop-roop*.

'You don't know what happened here, Mrs Garfield. What happened to you was terrible and you have all my sympathy . . . but what happened to you is not what happened to Carol.'

'Shut up.' She wasn't listening, didn't even look in his direction.

Carol ran to Liz, reached out for her, then stopped. Her eyes grew large in her pale face. Her mouth dropped open. 'They pulled your dress off?' It was half a whisper, half a moan. Liz stopped dialing and turned slowly to look at her. 'Why did they pull your dress off?'

Liz seemed to think about how to answer. She seemed to think hard. 'Shut up,' she said at last. 'Just shut up, okay?'

'Why did they chase you? Who's hitting?' Carol's voice had become uneven. 'Who's *hitting*?'

'*Shut up!*' Liz dropped the telephone and put her hands to her ears. Bobby looked at her with growing horror.

Carol turned to him. Fresh tears were rolling down her cheeks. There was knowing in her eyes – *knowing*. The kind, Bobby thought, that he had felt while Mr McQuown had been trying to fool him.

'They chased her,' Carol said. 'When she tried to leave they chased her and made her come back.'

Bobby knew. They had chased her down a hotel corridor. He had seen it. He couldn't remember where, but he had.

'*Make them stop doing it! Make me stop seeing it!*' Carol

314

screamed. '*She's hitting them but she can't get away! She's hitting them but she can't get away!*'

Ted tipped the table out of his lap and struggled to his feet. His eyes were blazing. 'Hug her, Carol! Hug her tight! That will make it stop!'

Carol threw her good arm around Bobby's mother. Liz staggered backward a step, almost falling when one of her shoes hooked the leg of the sofa. She stayed up but the telephone tumbled to the rug beside one of Bobby's outstretched sneakers, burring harshly.

For a moment things stayed that way – it was as if they were playing Statues and 'it' had just yelled *Freeze!* It was Carol who moved first, releasing Liz Garfield's waist and stepping back. Her sweaty hair hung in her eyes. Ted went toward her and reached out to put a hand on her shoulder.

'Don't touch her,' Liz said, but she spoke mechanically, without force. Whatever had flashed inside her at the sight of the child on Ted Brautigan's lap had faded a little, at least temporarily. She looked exhausted.

Nonetheless, Ted dropped his hand. 'You're right,' he said.

Liz took a deep breath, held it, let it out. She looked at Bobby, then away. Bobby wished with all his heart that she would put her hand out to him, help him a little, help him get up, just that, but she turned to Carol instead. Bobby got to his feet on his own.

'What happened here?' Liz asked Carol.

Although she was still crying and her words kept hitching as she struggled for breath, Carol told Bobby's mom about how the three big boys had found her in the park, and how at first it had seemed like just another one of their jokes, a bit meaner than most but still just a joke. Then Harry had really started hitting her while the others held her. The popping sound in her shoulder scared them and they ran away. She told Liz how Bobby had found her five or ten minutes later – she didn't know how long because the pain had been so bad – and carried her up here. And how Ted had fixed her arm, after giving her Bobby's belt to catch the pain with. She bent, picked up the belt, and showed Liz the tiny tooth-marks in it with a mixture of pride and embarrassment. 'I didn't catch all of it, but I caught a lot.'

Liz only glanced at the belt before turning to Ted. 'Why'd you tear her top off, chief?'

'It's *not* torn!' Bobby cried. He was suddenly furious with her. 'He *cut* it off so he could look at her shoulder and fix it without hurting her! I brought him the scissors, for cripe's sake! Why are you so stupid, Mom? Why can't you see—'

She swung without turning, catching Bobby completely by surprise. The back of her open hand connected with the side of his face; her forefinger actually poked into his eyes, sending a zag of pain deep into his head. His tears stopped as if the pump controlling them had suddenly shorted out.

'Don't you call me stupid, Bobby-O,' she said. 'Not on your ever-loving tintype.'

Carol was looking fearfully at the hook-nosed witch who had come back in a taxi wearing Mrs Garfield's clothes. Mrs Garfield who had run and who had fought when she couldn't run anymore. But in the end they had taken what they wanted from her.

'You shouldn't hit Bobby,' Carol said. 'He's not like those men.'

'Is he your boyfriend?' She laughed. 'Yeah? Good for you! But I'll let you in on a secret, sweetheart – he's just like his daddy and your daddy and all the rest of them. Go in the bathroom. I'll clean you up and find something for you to wear. *Christ*, what a mess!'

Carol looked at her a moment longer, then turned and went into the bathroom. Her bare back looked small and vulnerable. And white. So white in contrast to her brown arms.

'Carol!' Ted called after her. 'Is it better now?' Bobby didn't think he was talking about her arm. Not this time.

'Yes,' she said without turning. 'But I can still hear her, far away. She's screaming.'

'Who's screaming?' Liz asked. Carol didn't answer her. She went into the bathroom and closed the door. Liz looked at it for a moment, as if to make sure Carol wasn't going to pop back out again, then turned to Ted. 'Who's screaming?'

Ted only looked at her warily, as if expecting another ICBM attack at any moment.

Liz began to smile. It was a smile Bobby knew: her I'm-losing-my-temper smile. Was it possible she had any left to lose? With her black eyes, broken nose, and swollen lip, the smile made her look horrid: not his mother but some lunatic.

'Quite the Good Samaritan, aren't you? How many feels did you cop while you were fixing her up? She hasn't got much, but I bet you checked what you could, didn't you? Never miss an opportunity, right? Come on and fess up to your mamma.'

Bobby looked at her with growing despair. Carol had told her everything – all of the truth – *and it made no difference.* No difference! God!

'There is a dangerous adult in this room,' Ted said, 'but it isn't me.'

She looked first uncomprehending, then incredulous, then furious. 'How dare you? *How dare you?*'

'*He didn't do anything!*' Bobby screamed. '*Didn't you hear what Carol said? Didn't you—*'

'Shut your mouth,' she said, not looking at him. She looked only at Ted. 'The cops are going to be very interested in you, I think. Don called Hartford on Friday, before . . . before. I asked him to. He has friends there. You never worked for the State of Connecticut, not in the office of the Comptroller, not anywhere else. You were in jail, weren't you?'

'In a way I suppose I was,' Ted said. He seemed calmer now in spite of the blood flowing down the side of his face. He took the cigarettes out of his shirt pocket, looked at them, put them back. 'But not the kind you're thinking of.'

And not in this world, Bobby thought.

'What was it for?' she asked. 'Making little girls feel better in the first degree?'

'I have something valuable,' Ted said. He reached up and tapped his temple. The finger he tapped with came away dotted with blood. 'There are others like me. And there are people whose job it is to catch us, keep us, and use us for . . . well, use us, leave it at that. I and two others escaped. One was caught, one was killed. Only I remain free. If, that is . . .' He looked around. '. . . you call this freedom.'

'You're crazy. Crazy old Brattigan, nuttier than a holiday fruitcake. I'm calling the police. Let them decide if they want to put you back in the jail you broke out of or in Danbury Asylum.' She bent, reached for the spilled phone.

'No, Mom!' Bobby said, and reached for her. 'Don't—'

'*Bobby, no!*' Ted said sharply.

318

Bobby pulled back, looking first at his mom as she scooped up the phone, then at Ted.

'Not as she is now,' Ted told him. 'As she is now, she can't stop biting.'

Liz Garfield gave Ted a brilliant, almost unspeakable smile – *Good try, you bastard* – and took the receiver off the cradle.

'What's happening?' Carol cried from the bathroom. 'Can I come out now?'

'Not yet, darling,' Ted called back. 'A little longer.'

Liz poked the telephone's cutoff buttons up and down. She stopped, listened, seemed satisfied. She began to dial. 'We're going to find out who you are,' she said. She spoke in a strange, confiding tone. 'That should be pretty interesting. And what you've done. That might be even more interesting.'

'If you call the police, they'll also find out who *you* are and what *you've* done,' Ted said.

She stopped dialing and looked at him. It was a cunning sideways stare Bobby had never seen before. 'What in God's name are you talking about?'

'A foolish woman who should have chosen better. A foolish woman who had seen enough of her boss to know better – who had overheard him and his cronies often enough to know better, to know that any "seminar" they attended mostly had to do with booze and sex-parties. Maybe a little reefer, as well. A foolish woman who let her greed overwhelm her good sense—'

'What do you know about being alone?' she cried. '*I have a son to raise!*' She looked at Bobby, as if remembering the son she had to raise for the first time in a little while.

'How much of this do you want him to hear?' Ted asked.

'You don't know anything. You can't.'

'I know *everything*. The question is, how much do you want Bobby to know? How much do you want your neighbors to know? If the police come and take me, they'll know what I know, that I promise you.' He paused. His pupils remained steady but his eyes seemed to grow. 'I know *everything*. Believe me – don't put it to the test.'

'Why would you hurt me that way?'

'Given a choice I wouldn't. You have been hurt enough, by yourself as well as by others. Let me leave, that's all I'm asking you to do. I was leaving anyway. Let me leave. I did nothing but try to help.'

'Oh yes,' she said, and laughed. '*Help*. Her sitting on you practically naked. *Help.*'

'I would help *you* if I—'

'Oh yeah, and I know how.' She laughed again.

Bobby started to speak and saw Ted's eyes warning him not to. Behind the bathroom door, water was now running into the sink. Liz lowered her head, thinking. At last she raised it again.

'All right,' she said, 'here's what I'm going to do. I'll help Bobby's little *girlfriend* get cleaned up. I'll give her an aspirin and find something for her to wear home. While I'm doing those things, I'll ask her a few questions. If the answers are the right answers, you can go. Good riddance to bad rubbish.'

'Mom—'

Liz held up a hand like a traffic cop, silencing him. She was staring at Ted, who was looking back at her.

'I'll walk her home, I'll watch her go through her front door. What she decides to tell her mother is between the two of them. My job is to see her home safe, that's all. When

320

it's done I'll walk down to the park and sit in the shade for a little while. I had a rough night last night.' She drew in breath and let it out in a dry and rueful sigh. 'Very rough. So I'll go to the park and sit in the shade and think about what comes next. How I'm going to keep him and me out of the poorhouse.

'If I find you still here when I get back from the park, sweetheart, I *will* call the police . . . and don't you put *that* to the test. Say whatever you want. None of it's going to matter much to anyone if I say I walked into my apartment a few hours sooner than you expected and found you with your hand inside an eleven-year-old girl's shorts.'

Bobby stared at his mother in silent shock. She didn't see the stare; she was still looking at Ted, her swollen eyes fixed on him intently.

'If, on the other hand, I come back and you're gone, bag and baggage, I won't have to call anyone or say anything. *Tout finis.*'

I'll go with you! Bobby thought at Ted. *I don't care about the low men. I'd rather have a thousand low men in yellow coats looking for me — a* million — *than have to live with* her *anymore. I hate her!*

'Well?' Liz asked.

'It's a deal. I'll be gone in an hour. Probably less.'

'No!' Bobby cried. When he'd awakened this morning he had been resigned to Ted's going — sad but resigned. Now it hurt all over again. Worse than before, even. 'No!'

'Be quiet,' his mother said, still not looking at him.

'It's the only way, Bobby. You know that.' Ted looked up at Liz. 'Take care of Carol. I'll talk to Bobby.'

'You're in no position to give orders,' Liz said, but she

went. As she crossed to the bathroom, Bobby saw she was limping. A heel had broken off one of her shoes, but he didn't think that was the only reason she couldn't walk right. She knocked briefly on the bathroom door and then, without waiting for a response, slipped inside.

Bobby ran across the room, but when he tried to put his arms around Ted, the old man took his hands, squeezed them once briefly, then put them against Bobby's chest and let go.

'Take me with you,' Bobby said fiercely. 'I'll help you look for them. Two sets of eyes are better than one. Take me with you!'

'I can't do that, but you can come with me as far as the kitchen, Bobby. Carol isn't the only one who needs to do some cleaning up.'

Ted rose from the chair and swayed on his feet for a moment. Bobby reached out to steady him and Ted once more pushed his hand gently but firmly away. It hurt. Not as much as his mother's failure to help him up (or even look at him) after she had thrown him against the wall, but enough.

He walked with Ted to the kitchen, not touching him but close enough to grab him if he fell. Ted didn't fall. He looked at the hazy reflection of himself in the window over the sink, sighed, then turned on the water. He wet the dish-cloth and began to wipe the blood off his cheek, checking his window-reflection every now and then for reference.

'Your mother needs you more now than she ever has before,' he said. 'She needs someone she can trust.'

'She doesn't trust me. I don't think she even likes me.'

Ted's mouth tightened, and Bobby understood he had struck upon some truth Ted had seen in his mother's mind.

Bobby knew she didn't like him, he *knew* that, so why were the tears threatening again?

Ted reached out for him, seemed to remember that was a bad idea, and went back to work with the dishcloth instead. 'All right,' he said. 'Perhaps she *doesn't* like you. If that's true, it isn't because of anything you did. It's because of what you *are.*'

'A boy,' he said bitterly. 'A fucking *boy.*'

'And your father's son, don't forget that. But Bobby . . . whether she likes you or not, she loves you. Such a greeting-card that sounds, I know, but it's true. She loves you and she needs you. You're what she has. She's badly hurt right now—'

'Getting hurt was her own fault!' he burst out. 'She knew something was wrong! You said so yourself! She's known for weeks! *Months!* But she wouldn't leave that job! She knew and she still went with them to Providence! *She went with them anyway!*'

'A lion-tamer knows, but he still goes into the cage. He goes in because that's where his paycheck is.'

'She's got money,' Bobby almost spat.

'Not enough, apparently.'

'She'll never have enough,' Bobby said, and knew it was the truth as soon as it was out of his mouth.

'She loves you.'

'I don't care! I don't love her!'

'But you do. You will. You must. It is *ka.*'

'*Ka?* What's that?'

'Destiny.' Ted had gotten most of the blood out of his hair. He turned off the water and made one final check of his ghost-image in the window. Beyond it lay all of that hot summer, younger than Ted Brautigan would ever be again.

Younger than Bobby would ever be again, for that matter. '*Ka* is destiny. Do you care for me, Bobby?'

'You know I do,' Bobby said, beginning to cry again. Lately crying was all he seemed to do. His eyes ached from it. 'Lots and lots.'

'Then try to be your mother's friend. For my sake if not your own. Stay with her and help this hurt of hers to heal. And every now and then I'll send you a postcard.'

They were walking back into the living room again. Bobby was starting to feel a little bit better, but he wished Ted could have put his arm around him. He wished that more than anything.

The bathroom door opened. Carol came out first, looking down at her own feet with uncharacteristic shyness. Her hair had been wetted, combed back, and rubber-banded into a ponytail. She was wearing one of Bobby's mother's old blouses; it was so big it came almost down to her knees, like a dress. You couldn't see her red shorts at all.

'Go out on the porch and wait,' Liz said.

'Okay.'

'You won't go walking home without me, will you?'

'No!' Carol said, and her downcast face filled with alarm.

'Good. Stand right by my suitcases.'

Carol started out to the foyer, then turned back. 'Thanks for fixing my arm, Ted. I hope you don't get in trouble for it. I didn't want—'

'Go out on the damned *porch*,' Liz snapped.

'—anyone to get in trouble,' Carol finished in a tiny voice, almost the whisper of a mouse in a cartoon. Then she went out, Liz's blouse flapping around her in a way that would have been comical on another day. Liz turned to Bobby and when he got a good look at her, his heart sank. Her fury had been refreshed. A bright red flush had spread over her bruised face and down her neck.

Oh cripes, what now? Bobby thought. Then she held up the green keyfob, and he knew.

'Where did you get this, Bobby-O?'

'I . . . it . . .' But he could think of nothing to say: no fib, no outright lie, not even the truth. Suddenly Bobby felt very tired. The only thing in the world he wanted to do was creep into his bedroom and hide under the covers of his bed and go to sleep.

'I gave it to him,' Ted said mildly. 'Yesterday.'

'You took my son to a bookie joint in Bridgeport? A *poker-parlor* in Bridgeport?'

It doesn't say bookie joint on the keyfob, Bobby thought. *It doesn't say poker-parlor, either . . . because those things are against the law. She knows what goes on there because my father went there. And like father like son. That's what they say, like father like son.*

'I took him to a movie,' Ted said. '*Village of the Damned*, at the Criterion. While he was watching, I went to The Corner Pocket to do an errand.'

'What sort of errand?'

'I placed a bet on a prizefight.' For a moment Bobby's heart sank even lower and he thought, *What's wrong with you? Why didn't you lie? If you knew how she felt about stuff like that—*

But he *did* know. Of course he did.

'A bet on a prizefight.' She nodded. 'Uh-huh. You left my son alone in a Bridgeport movie theater so you could go make a bet on a prizefight.' She laughed wildly. 'Oh well, I suppose I should be grateful, shouldn't I? You brought him such a nice souvenir. If he decides to ever make a bet himself, or lose his money playing poker like his father did, he'll know where to go.'

'I left him for two hours in a movie theater,' Ted said. 'You left him with me. He seems to have survived both, hasn't he?'

Liz looked for a moment as if she had been slapped, then for a moment as if she would cry. Then her face smoothed out and became expressionless. She curled her fist around the green keyfob and slipped it into her dress pocket. Bobby knew he would never see it again. He didn't mind. He didn't *want* to see it again.

'Bobby, go in your room,' she said.

'No.'

'*Bobby, go in your room!*'

'No! I won't!'

Standing in a bar of sunlight on the welcome mat by Liz Garfield's suitcases, floating in Liz Garfield's old blouse, Carol began to cry at the sound of the raised voices.

'Go in your room, Bobby,' Ted said quietly. 'I have enjoyed meeting you and knowing you.'

'*Knowing* you,' Bobby's mom said in an angry, insinuating voice, but Bobby didn't understand her and Ted took no notice of her.

'Go in your room,' he repeated.

'Will you be all right? You know what I mean.'

'Yes.' Ted smiled, kissed his fingers, and blew the kiss toward Bobby. Bobby caught it and made a fist around it, holding it tight. 'I'm going to be just fine.'

Bobby walked slowly toward his bedroom door, his head down and his eyes on the toes of his sneakers. He was almost there when he thought *I can't do this, I can't let him go like this.*

He ran to Ted, threw his arms around him, and covered his face with kisses – forehead, cheeks, chin, lips, the thin and silky lids of his eyes. 'Ted, I love you!'

Ted gave up and hugged him tight. Bobby could smell a ghost of the lather he shaved with, and the stronger aroma of his Chesterfield cigarettes. They were smells he would carry with him a long time, as he would the memories of Ted's big hands touching him, stroking his back, cupping the curve of his skull. 'Bobby, I love you too,' he said.

'Oh for *Christ's sake!*' Liz nearly screamed. Bobby turned toward her and what he saw was Don Biderman pushing her into a corner. Somewhere the Benny Goodman Orchestra was playing 'One O'Clock Jump' on a hi-fi turned all the way up. Mr Biderman had his hand out as if to slap. Mr Biderman was asking her if she wanted a little more, was that the way she liked it, she could have a little more if that was the way she liked it. Bobby could almost taste her horrified understanding.

'You really *didn't* know, did you?' he said. 'At least not all of it, all they wanted. They thought you did, but you didn't.'

'Go in your room right now or I'm calling the police and telling them to send a squad-car,' his mother said. 'I'm not joking, Bobby-O.'

'I know you're not,' Bobby said. He went into his bedroom and closed the door. He thought at first he was all right and then he thought that he was going to throw up, or faint, or do both. He walked across to his bed on tottery, unstable legs. He only meant to sit on it but he lay back on it cross-wise instead, as if all the muscles had gone out of his stomach and back. He tried to lift his feet up but his legs only lay there, the muscles gone from them, too. He had a sudden image of Sully-John in his bathing suit, climbing the ladder of a swimming float, running to the end of the board, diving off. He wished he was with S-J now. Anywhere but here. Anywhere but here. Anywhere at all but here.

When Bobby woke up, the light in his room had grown dim and when he looked at the floor he could barely see the shadow of the tree outside his window. He had been out – asleep or unconscious – for three hours, maybe four. He was covered with sweat and his legs were numb; he had never pulled them up onto the bed.

Now he tried, and the burst of pins and needles which resulted almost made him scream. He slid onto the floor instead, and the pins and needles ran up his thighs to his crotch. He sat with his knees up around his ears, his back throbbing, his legs buzzing, his head cottony. Something terrible had happened, but at first he couldn't remember what. As he sat there propped against the bed, looking across at Clayton Moore in his Lone Ranger mask, it began to come back. Carol's arm dislocated, his mother beaten up and half-crazy as well, shaking that green keyfob in his face, furious with him. And Ted . . .

Ted would be gone by now, and that was probably for the best, but how it hurt to think of.

He got to his feet and walked twice around the room. The second time he stopped at the window and looked out, rubbing his hands together at the back of his neck, which was stiff and sweaty. A little way down the street the Sigsby twins, Dina and Dianne, were jumping rope, but the other kids had gone in, either for supper or for the night. A car slid by, showing its parking lights. It was even later than he had at first thought; heavenly shades of night were falling.

He made another circuit of his room, working the tingles out of his legs, feeling like a prisoner pacing his cell. The door had no lock on it — no more than his mom's did — but he felt like a jailbird just the same. He was afraid to go out. She hadn't called him for supper, and although he was hungry — a little, anyway — he was afraid to go out. He was afraid of how he might find her . . . or of not finding her at all. Suppose she had decided she'd finally had enough of Bobby-O, stupid lying little Bobby-O, his father's son? Even if she was here, and seemingly back to normal . . . was there even such a thing as normal? People had terrible things behind their faces sometimes. He knew that now.

When he reached the closed door of his room, he stopped. There was a scrap of paper lying there. He bent and picked it up. There was still plenty of light and he could read it easily.

Dear Bobby—

By the time you read this, I'll be gone . . . but I'll take you with me in my thoughts. Please love your mother and remember that she loves you. She was afraid and hurt and ashamed this afternoon, and when we see people that way, we see them at their worst. I have left you something in my room. I will remember my promise.

All my love,

Ted

The postcards, that's what he promised. To send me postcards.

Feeling better, Bobby folded up the note Ted had slipped into his room before leaving and opened his bedroom door.

The living room was empty, but it had been set to rights. It looked almost okay if you didn't know there was supposed to be a sunburst clock on the wall beside the TV; now there was just the little screw where it had hung, jutting out and holding nothing.

Bobby realized he could hear his mother snoring in her room. She always snored, but this was a heavy snore, like an old person or a drunk snoring in a movie. *That's because they hurt her,* Bobby thought, and for a moment he thought of

(*Howya doin Sport howza boy*)

Mr Biderman and the two nimrods elbowing each other in the back seat and grinning. *Kill the pig, cut her throat,* Bobby thought. He didn't want to think it but he did.

He tiptoed across the living room as quietly as Jack in the giant's castle, opened the door to the foyer, and went out. He tiptoed up the first flight of stairs (walking on the bannister side, because he'd read in one of the Hardy Boys mysteries that if you walked that way the stairs didn't creak so much), and ran up the second.

Ted's door stood open; the room beyond it was almost empty. The few things of his own he'd put up – a picture of a man fishing at sunset, a picture of Mary Magdalene washing Jesus' feet, a calendar – were gone. The ashtray on the table was empty, but sitting beside it was one of Ted's carryhandle bags. Inside it were four paperback books: *Animal Farm*, *The Night of the Hunter*, *Treasure Island*, and *Of Mice and Men*. Written on the side of the paper bag in Ted's shaky but completely legible handwriting was: *Read the Steinbeck first.*

'Guys like us,' George says when he tells Lennie the story Lennie always wants to hear. Who are guys like us? Who were they to Steinbeck? Who are they to you? Ask yourself this.

Bobby took the paperbacks but left the bag — he was afraid that if his mom saw one of Ted's carryhandle bags she would go crazy all over again. He looked in the refrigerator and saw nothing but a bottle of French's mustard and a box of baking soda. He closed the fridge again and looked around. It was as if no one had ever lived here at all. Except—

He went to the ashtray, held it to his nose, and breathed in deeply. The smell of Chesterfields was strong, and it brought Ted back completely, Ted sitting here at his table and talking about *Lord of the Flies*, Ted standing at his bathroom mirror, shaving with that scary razor of his, listening through the open door as Bobby read him opinion pieces Bobby himself didn't understand.

Ted leaving one final question on the side of a paper bag: Guys like us. Who are guys like us?

Bobby breathed in again, sucking up little flakes of ash and fighting back the urge to sneeze, holding the smell in, fixing it in his memory as best he could, closing his eyes, and in through the window came the endless ineluctable cry of Bowser, now calling down the dark like a dream: *roop-roop-roop, roop-roop-roop.*

He put the ashtray down again. The urge to sneeze had passed. *I'm going to smoke Chesterfields*, he decided. *I'm going to smoke them all my life.*

He went back downstairs, holding the paperbacks in front of him and walking on the outside of the staircase again as he went from the second floor to the foyer. He slipped into the apartment, tiptoed across the living room (his mother

331

was still snoring, louder than ever), and into his bedroom. He put the books under his bed – *deep* under. If his mom found them he would say Mr Burton had given them to him. That was a lie, but if he told the truth she'd take the books away. Besides, lying no longer seemed so bad. Lying might become a necessity. In time it might even become a pleasure.

What next? The rumble in his stomach decided him. A couple of peanut butter and jelly sandwiches were next.

He started for the kitchen, tiptoeing past his mother's partly open bedroom door without even thinking about it, then paused. She was shifting around on her bed. Her snores had become ragged and she was talking in her sleep. It was a low, moaning talk Bobby couldn't make out, but he realized he didn't *have* to make it out. He could hear her anyway. And he could see stuff. Her thoughts? Her dreams? Whatever it was, it was awful.

He managed three more steps toward the kitchen, then caught a glimpse of something so terrible his breath froze in his throat like ice: HAVE YOU SEEN BRAUTIGAN! He is an OLD MONGREL but WE LOVE HIM!

'No,' he whispered. 'Oh Mom, no.'

He didn't want to go in there where she was, but his feet turned in that direction anyway. He went with them like a hostage. He watched his hand reach out, the fingers spread, and push her bedroom door open all the way.

Her bed was still made. She lay on top of the coverlet in her dress, one leg drawn up so her knee almost touched her chest. He could see the top of her stocking and her garter, and that made him think of the lady in the calendar picture at The Corner Pocket, the one getting out of the car with most of her skirt in her lap . . . except the lady getting out of the Packard hadn't had ugly bruises above the top of her stocking.

Liz's face was flushed where it wasn't bruised; her hair was matted with sweat; her cheeks were smeary with tears and gooey with makeup. A board creaked under Bobby's foot as he stepped into the room. She cried out and he froze, sure her eyes would open.

Instead of awakening she rolled away from him toward the wall. Here, in her room, the jumble of thoughts and images coming out of her was no clearer but ranker and more pungent, like sweat pouring off a sick person. Running through everything was the sound of Benny Goodman playing 'One O'Clock Jump' and the taste of blood running down the back of her throat.

Have you seen Brautigan, Bobby thought. *He is an old mongrel but we love him. Have you seen . . .*

She had pulled her shades before lying down and the room was very dark. He took another step, then stopped again by the table with the mirror where she sometimes sat to do her makeup. Her purse was there. Bobby thought of Ted hugging him – the hug Bobby had wanted, needed, so badly. Ted stroking his back, cupping the curve of his skull. *When I touch, I pass on a kind of window,* Ted had told him while they were coming back from Bridgeport in the cab. And now, standing by his mother's makeup table with his fists clenched, Bobby looked tentatively through that window into his mother's mind.

He caught a glimpse of her coming home on the train, huddling by herself, looking into ten thousand back yards between Providence and Harwich so as few people as possible would see her face; he saw her spying the bright green keyfob on the shelf by the toothglass as Carol slipped into her old blouse; saw her walking Carol home, asking her questions the whole way, one after another, firing them like bullets out of a machine-gun. Carol, too shaken and worn out to dissemble, had answered them all. Bobby saw his mother walking – *limping* – down to Commonwealth Park, heard her thinking *If only some good could be salvaged from this nightmare, if only some good*, anything *good*—

He saw her sit on a bench in the shade and then get up after awhile, walking toward Spicer's for a headache powder and a Nehi to wash it down with before going back home. And then, just before leaving the park, Bobby saw her spy something tacked to a tree. These somethings were tacked up all over town; she might have passed a couple on her way to the park, so lost in thought she never noticed.

Once again Bobby felt like a passenger in his own body, no more than that. He watched his hand reach out, saw two fingers (the ones that would bear the yellow smudges of the heavy smoker in another few years) make a scissoring motion and catch what was protruding from the mouth of her purse. Bobby pulled the paper free, unfolded it, and read the first two lines in the faint light from the bedroom doorway:

HAVE YOU SEEN BRAUTIGAN!
He is an OLD MONGREL but WE LOVE HIM!

His eyes skipped halfway down to the lines that had no doubt riveted his mother and driven every other thought from her head:

We will pay A VERY LARGE REWARD
($ $ $ $)

Here was the something good she had been wishing for, hoping for, praying for; here was A VERY LARGE REWARD.

And had she hesitated? Had the thought 'Wait a minute, my kid loves that old bastard-ball!' even crossed her mind? Nah.

You *couldn't* hesitate. Because life was full of Don Bidermans, and life wasn't fair.

Bobby left the room on tiptoe with the poster still in his hand, mincing away from her in big soft steps, freezing when a board creaked under his feet, then moving on. Behind him his mom's muttering talk had subsided into low snores again. Bobby made it into the living room and closed her door behind him, holding the knob at full cock until the door was shut tight, not wanting the latch to click. Then he hurried across to the phone, aware only now that he was away from her that his heart was racing and his throat was lined with a taste like old pennies. Any vestige of hunger had vanished.

He picked up the telephone's handset, looked around quickly and narrowly to make sure his mom's door was still shut, then dialed without referring to the poster. The number was burned into his mind: HOusitonic 5–8337.

There was only silence when he finished dialing. That wasn't surprising, either, because there was no HOusitonic exchange in Harwich. And if he felt cold all over (except for his balls and the soles of his feet, which were strangely hot), that was just because he was afraid for Ted. That was all. Just—

There was a stonelike click as Bobby was about to put the handset down. And then a voice said, 'Yeah?'

It's Biderman! Bobby thought wildly. *Cripes, it's Biderman!*
'Yeah?' the voice said again. No, not Biderman's. Too low for Biderman's. But it was a nimrod voice, no doubt about that, and as his skin temperature continued to plummet toward absolute zero, Bobby knew that the man on the other end of the line had some sort of yellow coat in his wardrobe.

Suddenly his eyes grew hot and the backs of them began itching. *Is this the Sagamore Family?* was what he'd meant to ask, and if whoever answered the phone said yes, he'd meant to beg them to leave Ted alone. To tell them he, Bobby Garfield, would do something for them if they'd just leave Ted be – he'd do anything they asked. But now that his chance had arrived he could say nothing. Until this moment he still hadn't completely believed in the low men. Now something was on the other end of the line, something that had nothing in common with life as Bobby Garfield understood it.

'Bobby?' the voice said, and there was a kind of insinuating pleasure in the voice, a sensuous recognition. 'Bobby,' it said again, this time without the question-mark. The flecks began to stream across Bobby's vision; the living room of the apartment suddenly filled with black snow.

'Please . . .' Bobby whispered. He gathered all of his will and forced himself to finish. 'Please let him go.'

'No can do,' the voice from the void told him. 'He belongs to the King. Stay away, Bobby. Don't interfere. Ted's our dog. If you don't want to be our dog, too, stay away.'

Click.

Bobby held the telephone to his ear a moment longer, needing to tremble and too cold to do it. The itching behind his eyes began to fade, though, and the threads falling across his vision began to merge into the general murk. At last he took the phone away from the side of his head, started to put it down, then paused. There were dozens of little red circles on the handset's perforated earpiece. It was as if the voice of the thing on the other end had caused the telephone to bleed.

Panting in soft and rapid little whimpers, Bobby put it back in its cradle and went into his room. *Don't interfere*, the man at the Sagamore Family number had told him. *Ted's our dog.* But Ted wasn't a dog. He was a man, and he was Bobby's friend.

She could have told them where he'll be tonight, Bobby thought. *I think Carol knew. If she did, and if she told Mom—*

Bobby grabbed the Bike Fund jar. He took all the money out of it and left the apartment. He considered leaving his mother a note but didn't. She might call HOusitonic 5–8337 again if he did, and tell the nimrod with the low voice what her Bobby-O was doing. That was one reason for not leaving a note. The other was that if he could warn Ted in time, he'd go with him. Now Ted would *have* to let him come. And if the low men killed him or kidnapped him? Well, those things were almost the same as running away, weren't they?

Bobby took a final look around the apartment, and as he listened to his mother snore he felt an involuntary tugging at his heart and mind. Ted was right: in spite of everything, he loved her still. If there was *ka*, then loving her was part of his.

Still, he hoped to never see her again.

'Bye, Mom,' Bobby whispered. A minute later he was running down Broad Street Hill into the deepening gloom, one hand wrapped around the wad of money in his pocket so none of it would bounce out.

CHAPTER TEN

DOWN THERE AGAIN. CORNER BOYS. LOW MEN IN YELLOW COATS. THE PAYOUT.

He called a cab from the pay telephone at Spicer's, and while he waited for his ride he took down a BRAUTIGAN lost-pet poster from the outside bulletin board. He also removed an upside-down file-card advertising a '57 Rambler for sale by the owner. He crumpled them up and threw them in the trash barrel by the door, not even bothering to look back over his shoulder to see if Old Man Spicer, whose foul temper was legendary among the kids on the west side of Harwich, had seen him do it.

The Sigsby twins were down here now, their jump-ropes put aside so they could play hopscotch. Bobby walked over to them and observed the shapes—

—drawn beside the grid. He got down on his knees, and Dina Sigsby, who had been about to toss her stone at the 7, stopped to watch him. Dianne put her grimy fingers over her mouth and giggled. Ignoring them, Bobby used both of his hands to sweep the shapes into chalk blurs. When he was done he stood up and dusted his hands off. The pole-light in Spicer's tiny three-car parking lot came on; Bobby and the girls grew sudden shadows much longer than they were.

'Why'd you do that, stupid old Bobby Garfield?' Dina asked. 'They were pretty.'

'They're bad luck,' Bobby said. 'Why aren't you at home?' Not that he didn't have a good idea; it was flashing in their heads like the beer-signs in Spicer's window.

'Mumma-Daddy havin a fight,' Dianne said. 'She says he got a girlfriend.' She laughed and her sister joined in, but their eyes were frightened. They reminded Bobby of the littluns in *Lord of the Flies*.

'Go home before it gets all the way dark,' he said.

'Mumma said stay out,' Dina told him.

'Then she's stupid and so is your father. Go on!'

They exchanged a glance and Bobby understood that he had scared them even more. He didn't care. He watched them grab their jump-ropes and go running up the hill. Five minutes later the cab he'd called pulled into the parking area beside the store, its headlights fanning the gravel.

'Huh,' the cabbie said. 'I dunno about taking any little kid to Bridgeport after dark, even if you do got the fare.'

'It's okay,' Bobby said, getting in back. If the cabbie meant to throw him out now, he better have a crowbar in the trunk to do it with. 'My grandfather will meet me.' But not at The Corner Pocket, Bobby had already decided; he wasn't going to pull up to the place in a Checker. Someone might be watching for him. 'At the Wo Fat Noodle Company. That's on Narragansett Avenue.' The Corner Pocket was also on Narragansett. He hadn't remembered the street-name but had found it easily enough in the Yellow Pages after calling the cab.

The driver had started to back out into the street. Now he paused again. 'Nasty Gansett Street? Christ, that's no part of town for a kid. Not even in broad daylight.'

'My grandfather's meeting me,' Bobby repeated. 'He said to tip you half a rock. You know, fifty cents.'

For a moment the cabbie teetered. Bobby tried to think of some other way to persuade him and couldn't think of a thing. Then the cabbie sighed, dropped his flag, and got rolling. As they passed his building, Bobby looked to see if there were any lights on in their apartment. There weren't, not yet. He sat back and waited for Harwich to drop behind them.

The cabbie's name was Roy DeLois, it was on his taxi-meter. He didn't say a word on the ride to Bridgeport. He was sad because he'd had to take Pete to the vet and have him put down. Pete had been fourteen. That was old for a Collie. He had been Roy DeLois's only real friend. *Go on, big boy, eat up, it's on me*, Roy DeLois would say when he fed Pete. He said the same thing every night. Roy DeLois was divorced. Sometimes he went to a stripper club in Hartford. Bobby could see ghost-images of the dancers, most of whom wore feathers and long white gloves. The image of Pete was sharper. Roy DeLois had been okay coming back from the vet's, but when he saw Pete's empty dish in the pantry at home, he had broken down crying.

They passed the William Penn Grille. Bright light streamed from every window and the street was lined with cars on both sides for three blocks, but Bobby saw no crazy DeSotos or other cars that felt like thinly disguised living creatures. The backs of his eyes didn't itch; there were no black threads.

The cab crossed the canal bridge and then they were down there. Loud Spanish-sounding music played from apartment houses with fire escapes zig-zagging up the sides like iron lightning. Clusters of young men with gleaming combed-back hair stood on some streetcorners; clusters of laughing girls stood on others. When the Checker stopped at a red light, a brown-skinned man sauntered over, hips seeming to roll like oil in gabardine slacks that hung below the waistband of his bright white underwear shorts, and offered to wash the cabbie's windshield with a filthy rag he held. Roy DeLois shook his head curtly and squirted away the instant the light changed.

'Goddam spics,' he said. 'They should be barred from the country. Ain't we got enough niggers of our own?'

Narragansett Street looked different at night – slightly scarier, slightly more fabulous as well. Locksmiths . . . check-cashing services . . . a couple of bars spilling out laughter and jukebox music and guys with beer bottles in their hands . . . ROD'S GUNS . . . and yes, just beyond Rod's and next to the shop selling SPECIAL SOUVENIRS, the WO FAT NOODLE CO. From here it couldn't be more than four blocks to The Corner Pocket. It was only eight o'clock. Bobby was in plenty of time.

When Roy DeLois pulled up to the curb, there was eighty cents on his meter. Add in a fifty-cent tip and you were talking about a big hole in the old Bike Fund, but Bobby didn't care. He was never going to make a big deal out of money the way *she* did. If he could warn Ted before the low men could grab him, Bobby would be content to walk forever.

'I don't like leaving you off here,' Roy DeLois said. 'Where's your grandpa?'

'Oh, he'll be right along,' Bobby said, striving for a cheerful tone and almost making it. It was really amazing what you could do when your back was against the wall.

He held out the money. For a moment Roy DeLois hesitated instead of taking the dough; thought about driving him back to Spicer's, but *if the kid's not telling the truth about his grandpa what's he doing down here?* Roy DeLois thought. *He's too young to want to get laid.*

I'm fine, Bobby sent back . . . and yes, he thought he could do that, too − a little, anyway. *Go on, stop worrying, I'm fine.*

Roy DeLois finally took the crumpled dollar and the trio of dimes. 'This is really too much,' he said.

'My grandpa told me to never be stingy like some people are,' Bobby said, getting out of the cab. 'Maybe you ought to get a new dog. You know, a puppy.'

Roy DeLois was maybe fifty, but surprise made him look much younger. 'How . . .'

Then Bobby heard him decide he didn't care how. Roy DeLois put his cab in gear and drove away, leaving Bobby in front of the Wo Fat Noodle Company.

He stood there until the cab's taillights disappeared, then began walking slowly in the direction of The Corner Pocket, pausing long enough to look through the dusty window of SPECIAL SOUVENIRS. The bamboo blind was up but the only special souvenir on display was a ceramic ashtray in the shape of a toilet. There was a groove for a cigarette in the seat.

PARK YOUR BUTT was written on the tank. Bobby considered this quite witty but not much of a window display; he had sort of been hoping for items of a sexual nature. Especially now that the sun had gone down.

He walked on, past B'PORT PRINTING and SHOES REPAIRED WHILE U WAIT and SNAPPY KARDS FOR ALL OKASIONS. Up ahead was another bar, more young men on the corner, and the sound of The Cadillacs: *Brrrrr, black slacks, make ya cool, Daddy-O, when ya put em on you're a-rarin to go.* Bobby crossed the street, trotting with his shoulders hunched, his head down, and his hands in his pockets.

Across from the bar was an out-of-business restaurant with a tattered awning still overhanging its soaped windows. Bobby slipped into its shadow and kept going, shrinking back once when someone shouted and a bottle shattered. When he reached the next corner he re-crossed Nasty Gansett Street on the diagonal, getting back to the side The Corner Pocket was on.

As he went, he tried to tune his mind outward and pick up some sense of Ted, but there was nothing. Bobby wasn't all that surprised. If *he* had been Ted, he would have gone someplace like the Bridgeport Public Library where he could hang around without being noticed. Maybe after the library closed he'd get a bite to eat, kill a little more time that way. Eventually he'd call another cab and come to collect his money. Bobby didn't think he was anywhere close yet, but he kept listening for him. He was listening so hard that he walked into a guy without even seeing him.

'Hey, *cabrón!*' the guy said – laughing, but not in a nice way. Hands grabbed Bobby's shoulders and held him. 'Where was you think you goin, *putino?*'

Bobby looked up and saw four young guys, what his mom would have called corner boys, standing in front of a place called BODEGA. They were Puerto Ricans, he thought, and all wearing sharp-creased slacks. Black boots with pointed toes poked out from beneath their pants cuffs. They were also wearing blue silk jackets with the word DIABLOS written on the back. The I was a devil's pitchfork. Something seemed familiar about the pitchfork, but Bobby had no time to think about that. He realized with a sinking heart that he had wandered into four members of some gang.

'I'm sorry,' he said in a dry voice. 'Really, I . . . 'scuse me.'

He pulled back from the hands holding his shoulders and started around the guy. He made just a single step before one of the others grabbed him. 'Where you goin, *tío*?' this one asked. 'Where you goin, *tío mío*?'

Bobby pulled free, but the fourth guy pushed him back at the second. The second guy grabbed him again, not so gently this time. It was like being surrounded by Harry and his friends, only worse.

'You got any money, *tío*?' asked the third guy. 'Cause this a toll-road, you know.'

They all laughed and moved in closer. Bobby could smell their spicy aftershaves, their hair tonics, his own fear. He couldn't hear their mind-voices, but did he need to? They were probably going to beat him up and steal his money. If he was lucky that was all they'd do . . . but he might not be lucky.

'Little boy,' the fourth guy almost sang. He reached out a hand, gripped the bristles of Bobby's crewcut, and pulled hard enough to make tears well up in Bobby's eyes. 'Little *muchacho*, what you got for money, huh? How much of the good old *dinero*? You have something and we going to let you go. You have nothing and we going to bust your balls.'

'Leave him alone, Juan.'

They looked around — Bobby too — and here came a fifth guy, also wearing a Diablos jacket, also wearing slacks with a sharp crease; he had on loafers instead of pointy-toed boots, and Bobby recognized him at once. It was the young man who had been playing the Frontier Patrol game in The Corner Pocket when Ted was making his bet. No wonder that pitchfork shape had looked familiar — it was tattooed on the guy's hand. His jacket had been tied inside-out around his waist (*no club jacket in here*, he had told Bobby), but he wore the sign of the Diablos just the same.

Bobby tried to look into the newcomer's mind and saw only dim shapes. His ability was fading again, as it had on the day Mrs Gerber took them to Savin Rock; shortly after they left McQuown's stand at the end of the midway, it had been gone. This time the winkle had lasted longer, but it was going now, all right.

'Hey, Dee,' said the boy who had pulled Bobby's hair. 'We just gonna shake this little guy out a little. Make him pay his way across Diablo turf.'

'Not this one,' Dee said. 'I know him. He's my *compadre*.'

'He look like a pansy uptown boy to me,' said the one who had called Bobby *cabrón* and *putino*. 'I teach im a little respect.'

'He don't need no lesson from you,' Dee said. 'You want one from me, *Moso*?'

Moso stepped back, frowning, and took a cigarette out of his pocket. One of the others snapped him a light, and Dee drew Bobby a little farther down the street.

'What you doing down here, *amigo*?' he asked, gripping Bobby's shoulder with the tattooed hand. 'You stupid to be down here alone and you fuckin *loco* to be down here at *night* alone.'

'I can't help it,' Bobby said. 'I have to find the guy I was with yesterday. His name is Ted. He's old and thin and pretty tall. He walks kinda hunched over, like Boris Karloff – you know, the guy in the scary movies?'

'I know Boris Karloff but I don't know no fuckin Ted,' Dee said. 'I don't ever see him. Man, you ought to get outta here.'

'I have to go to The Corner Pocket,' Bobby said.

'I was just there,' Dee said. 'I didn't see no guy like Boris Karloff.'

'It's still too early. I think he'll be there between nine-thirty and ten. I have to be there when he comes, because there's some men after him. They wear yellow coats and white shoes . . . they drive big flashy cars . . . one of them's a purple DeSoto, and—'

Dee grabbed him and spun him against the door of a pawnshop so hard that for a moment Bobby thought he had decided to go along with his corner-boy friends after all. Inside the pawnshop an old man with a pair of glasses pushed up on his bald head looked around, annoyed, then back down at the newspaper he was reading.

'The *jefes* in the long yellow coats,' Dee breathed. 'I seen those guys. Some of the others seen em, too. You don't want to mess with boys like that, *chico*. Something wrong with those boys. They don't look right. Make the bad boys hang around Mallory's Saloon look like good boys.'

Something in Dee's expression reminded Bobby of Sully-John, and he remembered S-J saying he'd seen a couple of weird guys outside Commonwealth Park. When Bobby asked what was weird about them, Sully said he didn't exactly know. Bobby knew, though. Sully had seen the low men. Even then they had been sniffing around.

'When did you see them?' Bobby asked. 'Today?'

'Cat, give me a break,' Dee said. 'I ain't been up but two hours, and most of that I been in the bathroom, makin myself pretty for the street. I seen em comin out of The Corner Pocket, a pair of em – day before yesterday, I think. And that place funny lately.' He thought for a moment, then called, 'Yo, Juan, get your ass over here.'

The crewcut-puller came trotting over. Dee spoke to him in Spanish. Juan spoke back and Dee responded more briefly, pointing to Bobby. Juan leaned over Bobby, hands on the knees of his sharp pants.

'You seen 'ese guys, huh?'

Bobby nodded.

'One bunch in a big purple DeSoto? One bunch in a Cri'sler? One bunch in an Olds 98?'

Bobby only knew the DeSoto, but he nodded.

'Those cars ain't real cars,' Juan said. He looked sideways at Dee to see if Dee was laughing. Dee wasn't; he only nodded for Juan to keep going. 'They something else.'

'I think they're alive,' Bobby said.

Juan's eyes lit up. 'Yeah! Like alive! And 'ose men—'

'What did they look like? I've seen one of their cars, but not *them*.'

Juan tried but couldn't say, at least not in English. He lapsed into Spanish instead. Dee translated some of it, but in an absent fashion; more and more he was conversing with Juan and ignoring Bobby. The other corner boys – and boys were what they really were, Bobby saw – drew close and added their own contributions. Bobby couldn't understand their talk, but he thought they were scared, all of them. They were tough enough guys – down here you had to be tough just to make it through the day – but the low men had frightened them all the same. Bobby caught one final clear image: a tall striding figure in a calf-length mustard-colored coat, the kind of coat men sometimes wore in movies like *Gunfight at the OK Corral* and *The Magnificent Seven*.

'I see four of em comin out of that barber shop with the horse-parlor in the back,' the one who seemed to be named Filio said. 'That's what they do, those guys, go into places and ask questions. Always leave one of their big cars runnin at the curb. You'd think it'd be crazy to do that down here, leave a car runnin at the curb, but who'd steal one of *those* goddam things?'

No one, Bobby knew. If you tried, the steering wheel might turn into a snake and strangle you; the seat might turn into a quicksand pool and drown you.

'They come out all in a bunch,' Filio went on, 'all wearin 'ose long yellow coats even though the day's so hot you could a fried a egg on the fuckin sidewalk. They was all wearin these nice white shoes – sharp, you know how I always notice what people got on their feet, I get hard for that shit – and I don't think . . . I don't think . . .' He paused, gathered himself, and said something to Dee in Spanish.

Bobby asked what he'd said.

'He sayin their shoes wasn' touchin the ground,' Juan replied. His eyes were big. There was no scorn or disbelief in them. 'He sayin they got this big red Cri'sler, and when they go back to it, their fuckin shoes ain't quite touchin the ground.' Juan forked two fingers in front of his mouth, spat through them, then crossed himself.

No one said anything for a moment or two after that, and then Dee bent gravely over Bobby again. 'These are the guys lookin for your frien'?'

'That's right,' Bobby said. 'I have to warn him.'

He had a mad idea that Dee would offer to go with him to The Corner Pocket, and then the rest of the Diablos would join in; they would walk up the street snapping their fingers in unison like the Jets in *West Side Story*. They would be his friends now, gang guys who happened to have really good hearts.

Of course nothing of the sort happened. What happened was Moso wandered off, back toward the place where Bobby had walked into him. The others followed. Juan paused long enough to say, 'You run into those *caballeros* and you gonna be one dead *putino, tío mío.*' Only Dee was left and Dee said, 'He's right. You ought to go back to your own part of the worl', my frien'. Let your *amigo* take care of himself.'

'I can't,' Bobby said. And then, with genuine curiosity: 'Could you?'

'Not against ordinary guys, maybe, but these ain't ordinary guys. Was you just lissen?'

'Yes,' Bobby said. 'But.'

'You crazy, little boy. *Poco loco.*'

'I guess so.' He *felt* crazy, all right. *Poco loco* and then some. Crazy as a shithouse mouse, his mother would have said.

Dee started away and Bobby felt his heart cramp. The big boy got to the corner – his buddies were waiting for him on the other side of the street – then wheeled back, made his finger into a gun, and pointed it at Bobby. Bobby grinned and pointed his own back.

'*Vaya con Dios, mi amigo loco,*' Dee said, then sauntered across the street with the collar of his gang jacket turned up against the back of his neck.

Bobby turned the other way and started walking again, detouring around the pools of light cast by fizzing neon signs and trying to keep in the shadows as much as he could.

Across the street from The Corner Pocket was a mortuary – DESPEGNI FUNERAL PARLOR, it said on the green awning. Hanging in the window was a clock whose face was outlined in a chilly circle of blue neon. Below the clock was a sign which read TIME AND TIDE WAIT FOR NO MAN. According to the clock it was twenty past eight. He was still in time, in plenty of time, and he could see an alley beyond the Pocket where he might wait in relative safety, but Bobby couldn't just park himself and wait, even though he knew that would be the smart thing to do. If he'd really been smart, he never would have come down here in the first place. He wasn't a wise old owl; he was a scared kid who needed help. He doubted if there was any in The Corner Pocket, but maybe he was wrong.

Bobby walked under the banner reading COME IN IT'S KOOL INSIDE. He had never felt less in need of air conditioning in his life; it was a hot night but he was cold all over.

God, if You're there, please help me now. Help me to be brave . . . and help me to be lucky.

Bobby opened the door and went in.

The smell of beer was much stronger and much fresher, and the room with the pinball machines in it banged and jangled with lights and noise. Where before only Dee had been playing pinball, there now seemed to be at least two dozen guys, all of them smoking, all of them wearing strap-style undershirts and Frank Sinatra hello-young-lovers hats, all of them with bottles of Bud parked on the glass tops of the Gottlieb machines.

The area by Len Files's desk was brighter than before because there were more lights on in the bar (where every stool was taken) as well as in the pinball room. The poolhall itself, which had been mostly dark on Wednesday, was now lit like an operating theater. There were men at every table bending and circling and making shots in a blue fog of cigarette smoke; the chairs along the walls were all taken. Bobby could see Old Gee with his feet up on the shoeshine posts, and—

'What the fuck are *you* doing here?'

Bobby turned, startled by the voice and shocked by the sound of that word coming out of a woman's mouth. It was Alanna Files. The door to the living-room area behind the desk was just swinging shut behind her. Tonight she was wearing a white silk blouse that showed her shoulders – pretty shoulders, creamy-white and as round as breasts – and the top of her prodigious bosom. Below the white blouse were the largest pair of red slacks Bobby had ever seen. Yesterday, Alanna had been kind, smiling . . . almost laughing at him, in fact, although in a way Bobby hadn't minded. Tonight she looked scared to death.

'I'm sorry . . . I know I'm not supposed to be in here, but I need to find my friend Ted and I thought . . . thought that . . .' He heard his voice shrinking like a balloon that's been let loose to fly around the room.

351

Something was horribly wrong. It was like a dream he sometimes had where he was at his desk studying spelling or science or just reading a story and everyone started laughing at him and he realized he had forgotten to put his pants on before coming to school, he was sitting at his desk with everything hanging out for everyone to look at, girls and teachers and just everyone.

The beat of the bells in the gameroom hadn't completely quit, but it had slowed down. The flood of conversation and laughter from the bar had dried up almost entirely. The click of pool and billiard balls had ceased. Bobby looked around, feeling those snakes in his stomach again.

They weren't all looking at him, but most were. Old Gee was staring with eyes that looked like holes burned in dirty paper. And although the window in Bobby's mind was almost opaque now – soaped over – he felt that a lot of the people in here had sort of been expecting him. He doubted if they knew it, and even if they did they wouldn't know why. They were kind of asleep, like the people of Midwich. The low men had been in. The low men had—

'Get out, Randy,' Alanna said in a dry little whisper. In her distress she had called Bobby by his father's name. 'Get out while you still can.'

Old Gee had slid out of the shoeshine chair. His wrinkled seersucker jacket caught on one of the foot-pedestals and tore as he started forward, but he paid no attention as the silk lining floated down beside his knee like a toy parachute. His eyes looked more like burned holes than ever. 'Get him,' Old Gee said in a wavery voice. 'Get that kid.'

Bobby had seen enough. There was no help here. He scrambled for the door and tore it open. Behind him he had the sense of people starting to move, but slowly. Too slowly.

Bobby Garfield ran out into the night.

He ran almost two full blocks before a stitch in his side forced him to first slow down, then stop. No one was following and that was good, but if Ted went into The Corner Pocket to collect his money he was finished, done, *kaput*. It wasn't just the low men he had to worry about; now there was Old Gee and the rest of them to worry about, too, and Ted didn't know it. The question was, what could Bobby do about it?

He looked around and saw the storefronts were gone; he'd come to an area of warehouses. They loomed like giant faces from which most of the features had been erased. There was a smell of fish and sawdust and some vague rotted perfume that might have been old meat.

There was *nothing* he could do about it. He was just a kid and it was out of his hands. Bobby realized that, but he also realized he couldn't let Ted walk into The Corner Pocket without at least trying to warn him. There was nothing Hardy Boys-heroic about this, either; he simply couldn't leave without making the effort. And it was his mother who had put him in this position. *His own mother.*

'I hate you, Mom,' he whispered. He was still cold, but sweat was pouring out of his body; every inch of his skin felt wet. 'I don't care what Don Biderman and those other guys did to you, you're a bitch and I hate you.'

Bobby turned and began to trot back the way he had come, keeping to the shadows. Twice he heard people coming and crouched in doorways, making himself small until they had passed by. Making himself small was easy. He had never felt smaller in his life.

This time he turned into the alley. There were garbage cans on one side and a stack of cartons on the other, full of returnable bottles that smelled of beer. This cardboard column was half a foot taller than Bobby, and when he stepped behind it he was perfectly concealed from the street. Once during his wait something hot and furry brushed against his ankle and Bobby started to scream. He stifled most of it before it could get out, looked down, and saw a scruffy alleycat looking back up at him with green headlamp eyes.

'Scat, Pat,' Bobby whispered, and kicked at it. The cat revealed the needles of its teeth, hissed, then did a slow strut back down the alley, weaving around the clots of refuse and strews of broken glass, its tail lifted in what looked like disdain. Through the brick wall beside him Bobby could hear the dull throb of The Corner Pocket's juke. Mickey and Sylvia were singing 'Love Is Strange.' It was strange, all right. A big strange pain in the ass.

From his place of concealment Bobby could no longer see the mortuary clock and he'd lost any sense of how much or how little time was passing. Beyond the beer-and-garbage reek of the alley a summer streetlife opera was going on. People shouted out to each other, sometimes laughing, sometimes angry, sometimes in English, sometimes in one of a dozen other languages. There was a rattle of explosions that made him stiffen – gunshots was his first idea – and then he recognized the sound as firecrackers, probably ladyfingers, and relaxed a little again. Cars blasted by, many of them brightly painted railjobs and jackjobs with chrome pipes and glasspack mufflers.

Once there was what sounded like a fistfight with people gathered around yelling encouragement to the scufflers. Once a lady who sounded both drunk and sad went by singing 'Where the Boys Are' in a beautiful slurry voice. Once there were police sirens which approached and then faded away again.

Bobby didn't doze, exactly, but fell into a kind of daydream. He and Ted were living on a farm somewhere, maybe in Florida. They worked long hours, but Ted could work pretty hard for an old guy, especially now that he had quit smoking and had some of his wind back. Bobby went to school under another name – Ralph Sullivan – and at night they sat on the porch, eating Ted's cooking and drinking iced tea. Bobby read to him from the newspaper and when they went in to bed they slept deeply and their sleep was peaceful, interrupted by no bad dreams. When they went to the grocery store on Fridays, Bobby would check the bulletin board for lost-pet posters or upside-down file-cards advertising items for sale by owner, but he never found any. The low men had lost Ted's scent. Ted was no longer anyone's dog and they were safe on their farm. Not father and son or grandfather and grandson, but only friends.

Guys like us, Bobby thought drowsily. He was leaning against the brick wall now, his head slipping downward until his chin was almost on his chest. *Guys like us, why shouldn't there be a place for guys like us?*

Lights splashed down the alley. Each time this had happened Bobby had peered around the stack of cartons. This time he almost didn't – he wanted to close his eyes and think about the farm – but he forced himself to look, and what he saw was the stubby yellow tailfin of a Checker cab, just pulling up in front of The Corner Pocket.

Adrenaline flooded Bobby and turned on lights in his head he hadn't even known about. He dodged around the stack of boxes, spilling the top two off. His foot struck an empty garbage can and knocked it against the wall. He almost stepped on a hissing furry something – the cat again. Bobby kicked it aside and ran out of the alley. As he turned toward The Corner Pocket he slipped on some sort of greasy goo and went down on one knee. He saw the mortuary clock in its cool blue ring: 9:45. The cab was idling at the curb in front of The Corner Pocket's door. Ted Brautigan was standing beneath the banner reading COME IN IT'S KOOL INSIDE, paying the driver. Bent down to the driver's open window like that, Ted looked more like Boris Karloff than ever.

Across from the cab, parked in front of the mortuary, was a huge Oldsmobile as red as Alanna's pants. It hadn't been there earlier, Bobby was sure of that. Its shape wasn't quite solid. Looking at it didn't just make your eyes want to water; it made your *mind* want to water.

Ted! Bobby tried to yell, but no yell came out – all he could produce was a strawlike whisper. *Why doesn't he feel them?* Bobby thought. *How come he doesn't know?*

Maybe because the low men could block him out somehow. Or maybe the people inside The Corner Pocket were doing the blocking. Old Gee and all the rest. The low men had perhaps turned them into human sponges that could soak up the warning signals Ted usually felt.

More lights splashed the street. As Ted straightened and the Checker pulled away, the purple DeSoto sprang around the corner. The cab had to swerve to avoid it. Beneath the streetlights the DeSoto looked like a huge blood-clot decorated with chrome and glass. Its headlights were moving and shimmering like lights seen underwater . . . and then they *blinked*. They weren't headlights at all. They were eyes.

Ted! Still nothing but that dry whisper came out, and Bobby couldn't seem to get back on his feet. He was no longer sure he even *wanted* to get back on his feet. A terrible fear, as disorienting as the flu and as debilitating as a cataclysmic case of the squitters, was enveloping him. Passing the blood-clot DeSoto outside the William Penn Grille had been bad; to be caught in its oncoming eyelights was a thousand times worse. No – a *million* times.

He was aware that he had torn his pants and scraped blood out of his knee, he could hear Little Richard howling from someone's upstairs window, and he could still see the blue circle around the mortuary clock like a flashbulb afterimage tattooed on the retina, but none of that seemed real. Nasty Gansett Street suddenly seemed no more than a badly painted backdrop. Behind it was some unsuspected reality, and reality was *dark*.

The DeSoto's grille was moving. Snarling. *Those cars ain't real cars*, Juan had said. *They something else*.

They were something else, all right.

'Ted . . .' A little louder this time . . . and Ted heard. He turned toward Bobby, eyes widening, and then the DeSoto bounced up over the curb behind him, its blazing unsteady headlights pinning Ted and making his shadow grow as Bobby's and the Sigsby girls' shadows had grown when the pole-light came on in Spicer's little parking lot.

Ted wheeled back toward the DeSoto, raising one hand to shield his eyes from the glare. More light swept the street. This time it was a Cadillac coming up from the warehouse district, a snot-green Cadillac that looked at least a mile long, a Cadillac with fins like grins and sides that moved like the lobes of a lung. It thumped up over the curb just behind Bobby, stopping less than a foot from his back. Bobby heard a low panting sound. The Cadillac's motor, he realized, was breathing.

Doors were opening in all three cars. Men were getting out – or things that looked like men at first glance. Bobby counted six, counted eight, stopped counting. Each of them wore a long mustard-colored coat – the kind that was called a duster – and on the right front lapel of each was the staring crimson eye Bobby remembered from his dream. He supposed the red eyes were badges. The creatures wearing them were . . . what? Cops? No. A posse, like in a movie? That was a little closer. Vigilantes? Closer still but still not right. They were—

They're regulators. Like in that movie me and S-J saw at the Empire last year, the one with John Payne and Karen Steele.

That was it – oh yes. The regulators in the movie had turned out to be just a bunch of bad guys, but at first you thought they were ghosts or monsters or something. Bobby thought that these regulators really *were* monsters.

One of them grasped Bobby under the arm. Bobby cried out – the contact was quite the most horrible thing he had ever experienced in his life. It made being thrown against the wall by his mother seem like very small change indeed. The low man's touch was like being grasped by a hot-water bottle that had grown fingers . . . only the feel of them kept shifting. It would feel like fingers in his armpit, then like claws. Fingers . . . claws. Fingers . . . claws. That unspeakable touch buzzed into his flesh, reaching both up and down. *It's Jack's stick*, he thought crazily. *The one sharpened at both ends.*

Bobby was pulled toward Ted, who was surrounded by

the others. He stumbled along on legs that were too weak to walk. Had he thought he would be able to warn Ted? That they would run away together down Narragansett Avenue, perhaps even skipping a little, the way Carol used to? That was quite funny, wasn't it?

Incredibly, Ted didn't seem afraid. He stood in the semi-circle of low men and the only emotion on his face was concern for Bobby. The thing gripping Bobby – now with a hand, now with loathsome pulsing rubber fingers, now with a clutch of talons – suddenly let him go. Bobby staggered, reeled. One of the others uttered a high, barking cry and pushed him in the middle of the back. Bobby flew forward and Ted caught him.

Sobbing with terror, Bobby pressed his face against Ted's shirt. He could smell the comforting aromas of Ted's cigarettes and shaving soap, but they weren't strong enough to cover the stench that was coming from the low men – a meaty, garbagey smell – and a higher smell like burning whiskey that was coming from their cars.

Bobby looked up at Ted. 'It was my mother,' he said. 'It was my mother who told.'

'This isn't her fault, no matter what you may think,' Ted replied. 'I simply stayed too long.'

'But was it a nice vacation, Ted?' one of the low men asked. His voice had a gruesome buzz, as if his vocal cords were packed with bugs – locusts or maybe crickets. He could have been the one Bobby spoke to on the phone, the one who'd said Ted was their dog . . . but maybe they all sounded the same. *If you don't want to be our dog, too, stay away*, the one on the phone had said, but he had come down here anyway, and now . . . oh now . . .

359

'Wasn't bad,' Ted replied.

'I hope you at least got laid,' another said, 'because you probably won't get another chance.'

Bobby looked around. The low men stood shoulder to shoulder, surrounding them, penning them in their smell of sweat and maggoty meat, blocking off any sight of the street with their yellow coats. They were dark-skinned, deep-eyed, red-lipped (as if they had been eating cherries) . . . but they weren't what they looked like. They weren't what they looked like at all. Their faces wouldn't stay in their faces, for one thing; their cheeks and chins and hair kept trying to spread outside the lines (it was the only way Bobby could interpret what he was seeing). Beneath their dark skins were skins as white as their pointed reet-petite shoes. *But their lips are still red*, Bobby thought, *their lips are always red.* As their eyes were always black, not really eyes at all but caves. *And they are so tall*, he realized. *So tall and so thin. There are no thoughts like our thoughts in their brains, no feelings like our feelings in their hearts.*

From across the street there came a thick slobbering grunt. Bobby looked in that direction and saw that one of the Oldsmobile's tires had turned into a blackish-gray tentacle. It reached out, snared a cigarette wrapper, and pulled it back. A moment later the tentacle was a tire again, but the cigarette wrapper was sticking out of it like something half swallowed.

'Ready to come back, hoss?' one of the low men asked Ted. He bent toward him, the folds of his yellow coat rustling stiffly, the red eye on the lapel staring. 'Ready to come back and do your duty?'

'I'll come,' Ted replied, 'but the boy stays here.'

More hands settled on Bobby, and something like a living branch caressed the nape of his neck. It set off that buzzing again, something that was both an alarm and a sickness. It rose into his head and hummed there like a hive. Within that lunatic hum he heard first one bell, tolling rapidly, then many. A world of bells in some terrible black night of hot hurricane winds. He supposed he was sensing wherever the low men had come from, an alien place trillions of miles from Connecticut and his mother. Villages were burning under unknown constellations, people were screaming, and that touch on his neck . . . that awful touch . . .

Bobby moaned and buried his head against Ted's chest again.

'He wants to be with you,' an unspeakable voice crooned. 'I think we'll bring him, Ted. He has no natural ability as a Breaker, but still . . . all things serve the King, you know.' The unspeakable fingers caressed again.

'All things serve the *Beam*,' Ted said in a dry, correcting voice. His teacher's voice.

'Not for much longer,' the low man said, and laughed. The sound of it loosened Bobby's bowels.

'Bring him,' said another voice. It held a note of command. They *did* all sound sort of alike, but this was the one he had spoken to on the phone; Bobby was sure.

'No!' Ted said. His hands tightened on Bobby's back. 'He stays here!'

'Who are you to give us orders?' the low man in charge asked. 'How proud you have grown during your little time of freedom, Ted! How *haughty*! Yet soon you'll be back in the same room where you have spent so many years, with the others, and if I say the boy *comes*, then the boy *comes*.'

'If you bring him, you'll have to go on taking what you need from me,' Ted said. His voice was very quiet but very strong. Bobby hugged him as tight as he could and shut his eyes. He didn't want to look at the low men, not ever again. The worst thing about them was that their touch was like Ted's, in a way: it opened a window. But who would want to look through such a window? Who would want to see the tall, red-lipped scissor-shapes as they really were? Who would want to see the owner of that red Eye?

'You're a Breaker, Ted. You were made for it, born to it. And if we tell you to break, you'll break, by God.'

'You can force me, I'm not so foolish as to think you can't . . . but if you leave him here, I'll give what I have to you freely. And I have more to give than you could . . . well, perhaps you *could* imagine it.'

'I want the boy,' the low man in charge said, but now he sounded thoughtful. Perhaps even doubtful. 'I want him as a pretty, something to give the King.'

'I doubt if the Crimson King will thank you for a meaningless pretty if it interferes with his plans,' Ted said. 'There is a gunslinger—'

'Gunslinger, pah!'

'Yet he and his friends have reached the borderland of End-World,' Ted said, and now he was the one who sounded thoughtful. 'If I give you what you want instead of forcing you to take it, I may be able to speed things up by fifty years or more. As you say, I'm a Breaker, made for it and born to it. There aren't many of us. You need every one, and most of all you need me. Because I'm the best.'

'You flatter yourself . . . and you overestimate your importance to the King.'

'Do I? I wonder. Until the Beams break, the Dark Tower stands – surely I don't need to remind you of that. Is one boy worth the risk?'

Bobby hadn't the slightest idea what Ted was talking about and didn't care. All he knew was that the course of his life was being decided on the sidewalk outside a Bridgeport billiard parlor. He could hear the rustle of the low men's coats; he could smell them; now that Ted had touched him again he could feel them even more clearly. That horrible itching behind his eyes had begun again, too. In a weird way it harmonized with the buzzing in his head. The black specks drifted across his vision and he was suddenly sure what they meant, what they were for. In Clifford Simak's book *Ring Around the Sun*, it was a top that took you off into other worlds; you followed the rising spirals. In truth, Bobby suspected, it was the specks that did it. The black specks. They were alive . . .

And they were hungry.

'Let the boy decide,' the leader of the low men said at last. His living branch of a finger caressed the back of Bobby's neck again. 'He loves you so much, Teddy. You're his *te-ka*. Aren't you? That means destiny's friend, Bobby-O. Isn't that what this old smoky-smelling Teddy-bear is to you? Your destiny's friend?'

Bobby said nothing, only pressed his cold throbbing face against Ted's shirt. He now repented coming here with all his heart – would have stayed home hiding under his bed if he had known the truth of the low men – but yes, he supposed Ted was his *te-ka*. He didn't know about stuff like destiny, he was only a kid, but Ted was his friend. *Guys like us*, Bobby thought miserably. *Guys like us.*

'So how do you feel now that you see us?' the low man asked. 'Would you like to come with us so you can be close to good old Ted? Perhaps see him on the odd weekend? Discuss *literature* with your dear old *te-ka*? Learn to eat what we eat and drink what we drink?' The awful fingers again, caressing. The buzzing in Bobby's head increased. The black specks fattened and now *they* looked like fingers – beckoning fingers. 'We eat it hot, Bobby,' the low man whispered. 'And drink it hot as well. Hot . . . and sweet. Hot . . . and sweet.'

'Stop it,' Ted snapped.

'Or would you rather stay with your mother?' the crooning voice went on, ignoring Ted. 'Surely not. Not a boy of your principles. Not a boy who has discovered the joys of friend-ship and *literature*. Surely you'll come with this wheezy old *ka-mai*, won't you? Or will you? Decide, Bobby. Do it now, and knowing that what you decide is what will bide. Now and forever.'

Bobby had a delirious memory of the lobsterback cards blurring beneath McQuown's long white fingers: *Now they go, now they slow, now they rest, here's the test.*

I fail, Bobby thought. *I fail the test.*

'Let me go, mister,' he said miserably. 'Please don't take me with you.'

'Even if it means your *te-ka* has to go on without your wonderful and revivifying company?' The voice was smiling, but Bobby could almost taste the knowing contempt under its cheery surface, and he shivered. With relief, because he understood he was probably going to be let free after all, with shame because he knew what he was doing – crawling, chintzing, chickening out. All the things the good guys in the movies and books he loved never did. But the good guys in the movies and books never had to face anything like the low men in the yellow coats or the horror of the black specks. And what Bobby saw of those things here, outside The Corner Pocket, was not the worst of it either. What if he saw the rest? What if the black specks drew him into a world where he saw the men in the yellow coats as they really were? What if he saw the shapes inside the ones they wore in this world?

'Yes,' he said, and began to cry.

'Yes what?'

'Even if he has to go without me.'

'Ah. And even if it means going back to your mother?'

'Yes.'

'You perhaps understand your bitch of a mother a little better now, do you?'

'Yes,' Bobby said for the third time. By now he was nearly moaning. 'I guess I do.'

'That's enough,' Ted said. 'Stop it.'

But the voice wouldn't. Not yet. 'You've learned how to be a coward, Bobby . . . haven't you?'

'*Yes!*' he cried, still with his face against Ted's shirt. '*A baby, a little chickenshit baby, yes yes yes! I don't care! Just let me go home!*' He drew in a great long unsteady breath and let it out in a scream. '*I WANT MY MOTHER!*' It was the howl of a terrified littlun who has finally glimpsed the beast from the water, the beast from the air.

'All right,' the low man said. 'Since you put it *that* way. Assuming your Teddy-bear confirms that he'll go to work with a will and not have to be chained to his oar as previously.'

'I promise.' Ted let go of Bobby. Bobby remained as he

was, clutching Ted with panicky tightness and pushing his face against Ted's chest, until Ted pushed him gently away.

'Go inside the poolhall, Bobby. Tell Files to give you a ride home. Tell him if he does that, my friends will leave *him* alone.'

'I'm sorry, Ted. I wanted to come with you. I *meant* to come with you. But I can't. I'm so sorry.'

'You shouldn't be hard on yourself.' But Ted's look was heavy, as if he knew that from tonight on Bobby would be able to be nothing else.

Two of the yellowcoats grasped Ted's arms. Ted looked at the one standing behind Bobby – the one who had been caressing the nape of Bobby's neck with that horrible stick-like finger. 'They don't need to do that, Cam. I'll walk.'

'Let him go,' Cam said. The low men holding Ted released his arms. Then, for the last time, Cam's finger touched the back of Bobby's neck. Bobby uttered a choked wail. He thought, *If he does it again I'll go crazy, I won't be able to help it. I'll start to scream and I won't be able to stop. Even if my head bursts open I'll go on screaming.* 'Get inside there, little boy. Do it before I change my mind and take you anyway.'

Bobby stumbled toward The Corner Pocket. The door stood open but empty. He climbed the single step, then turned back. Three of the low men were clustered around Ted, but Ted was walking toward the blood-clot DeSoto on his own.

'Ted!'

Ted turned, smiled, started to wave. Then the one called Cam leaped forward, seized him, whirled him, and thrust him into the car. As Cam swung the DeSoto's back door shut Bobby saw, for just an instant, an incredibly tall, incredibly scrawny being standing inside a long yellow coat, a thing with flesh as white as new snow and lips as red as fresh blood. Deep in its eyesockets were savage points of light and dancing flecks of darkness in pupils which swelled and contracted as Ted's had done. The red lips peeled back, revealing needly teeth that put the alleycat's to shame. A black tongue lolled out from between those teeth and wagged an obscene goodbye. Then the creature in the yellow coat sprinted around the hood of the purple DeSoto, thin legs gnashing, thin knees pumping, and plunged in behind the wheel. Across the street the Olds started up, its engine sounding like the roar of an awakening dragon. Perhaps it *was* a dragon. From its place skewed halfway across the sidewalk, the Cadillac's engine did the same. Living headlights flooded this part of Narragansett Avenue in a pulsing glare. The DeSoto skidded in a U-turn, one fenderskirt scraping up a brief train of sparks from the street, and for a moment Bobby saw Ted's face in the DeSoto's back window. Bobby raised his hand and waved. He thought Ted raised his own in return but could not be sure. Once more his head filled with a sound like hoofbeats.

He never saw Ted Brautigan again.

'Bug out, kid,' Len Files said. His face was cheesy-white, seeming to hang off his skull the way the flesh hung off his sister's upper arms. Behind him the lights of the Gottlieb machines in the little arcade flashed and flickered with no one to watch them; the cool cats who made an evening specialty of Corner Pocket pinball were clustered behind Len Files like children. To Len's right were the pool and billiard players, many of them clutching cues like clubs. Old Gee stood off to one side by the cigarette machine. He didn't have a pool-cue; from one gnarled old hand there hung a small automatic pistol. It didn't scare Bobby. After Cam and his yellowcoat friends, he didn't think anything would have the power to scare him right now. For the time being he was all scared out.

'Put an egg in your shoe and beat it, kid. Now.'

'Better do it, kiddo.' That was Alanna, standing behind the desk. Bobby glanced at her and thought, *If I was older I bet I'd give you something. I bet I would.* She saw his glance – the quality of his glance – and looked away, flushed and frightened and confused.

Bobby looked back at her brother. 'You want those guys back here?'

Len's hanging face grew even longer. 'You kidding?'

'Okay, then,' Bobby said. 'Give me what I want and I'll go away. You'll never see me again.' He paused. 'Or *them.*'

'Whatchu want, kid?' Old Gee asked in his wavering voice. Bobby was going to get whatever he asked for; it was flashing in Old Gee's mind like a big bright sign. That mind was as clear now as it had been when it had belonged to Young Gee, cold and calculating and unpleasant, but it seemed innocent after Cam and his regulators. Innocent as ice cream.

'A ride home,' Bobby said. 'That's number one.' Then – speaking to Old Gee rather than Len – he gave them number two.

Len's car was a Buick: big, long, and new. Vulgar but not low. Just a car. The two of them rode to the sound of danceband music from the forties. Len spoke only once during the trip to Harwich. 'Don't you go tuning that to no rock and roll. I have to listen to enough of that shit at work.'

They drove past the Asher Empire, and Bobby saw there

was a life-sized cardboard cutout of Brigitte Bardot standing to the left of the ticket booth. He glanced at it without very much interest. He felt too old for B.B. now.

They turned off Asher; the Buick slipped down Broad Street Hill like a whisper behind a cupped hand. Bobby pointed out his building. Now the apartment was lit up, all right; every light was blazing. Bobby looked at the clock on the Buick's dashboard and saw it was almost eleven P.M.

As the Buick pulled to the curb Len Files found his tongue again. 'Who were they, kid? Who were those *gonifs?*'

Bobby almost grinned. It reminded him of how, at the end of almost every *Lone Ranger* episode, someone said *Who was that masked man?*

'Low men,' he told Len. 'Low men in yellow coats.'

'I wouldn't want to be your pal right now.'

'No,' Bobby said. A shudder shook through him like a gust of wind. 'Me neither. Thanks for the ride.'

'Don't mention it. Just stay the fuck clear of my felts and greens from now on. You're banned for life.'

The Buick – a boat, a Detroit cabin-cruiser, but not low – drew away. Bobby watched as it turned in a driveway across the street and then headed back up the hill past Carol's building. When it had disappeared around the corner, Bobby looked up at the stars – stacked billions, a spilled bridge of light. Stars and more stars beyond them, spinning in the black.

There is a Tower, he thought. *It holds everything together. There are Beams that protect it somehow. There is a Crimson King, and Breakers working to destroy the Beams . . . not because the Breakers want to but because it wants them to. The Crimson King.*

Was Ted back among the rest of the Breakers yet? Bobby wondered. Back and pulling his oar?

369

I'm sorry, he thought, starting up the walk to the porch. He remembered sitting there with Ted, reading to him from the newspaper. Just a couple of guys. *I wanted to go with you but I couldn't. In the end I couldn't.*

He stopped at the bottom of the porch steps, listening for Bowser around on Colony Street. There was nothing. Bowser had gone to sleep. It was a miracle. Smiling wanly, Bobby got moving again. His mother must have heard the creak of the second porch step – it was pretty loud – because she cried out his name and then there was the sound of her running footsteps. He was on the porch when the door flew open and she ran out, still dressed in the clothes she had been wearing when she came home from Providence. Her hair hung around her face in wild curls and tangles.

'Bobby!' she cried. 'Bobby, oh Bobby! Thank God! Thank God!'

She swept him up, turning him around and around in a kind of dance, her tears wetting one side of his face.

'I wouldn't take their money,' she babbled. 'They called me back and asked for the address so they could send a check and I said never mind, it was a mistake, I was hurt and upset, I said no, Bobby, I said no, I said I didn't want their money.'

Bobby saw she was lying. Someone had pushed an envelope with her name on it under the foyer door. Not a check, three hundred dollars in cash. Three hundred dollars for the return of their best Breaker; three hundred lousy rocks. They were even bigger cheapskates than she was.

'I said I didn't want it, did you hear me?'

Carrying him into the apartment now. He weighed almost a hundred pounds and was too heavy for her but she carried him anyway. As she babbled on, Bobby realized they wouldn't have the police to contend with, at least; she hadn't called them. Mostly she had just been sitting here, plucking at her wrinkled skirt and praying incoherently that he would come home. She loved him. That beat in her mind like the wings of a bird trapped in a barn. She loved him. It didn't help much . . . but it helped a little. Even if it was a trap, it helped a little.

'I said I didn't want it, we didn't need it, they could keep their money. I said . . . I told them . . .'

'That's good, Mom,' he said. 'That's good. Put me down.'

'Where have you been? Are you all right? Are you hungry?'

He answered her questions back to front. 'I'm hungry, yeah, but I'm fine. I went to Bridgeport. I got this.'

He reached into his pants pocket and brought out the remains of the Bike Fund money. His ones and change were mixed into a messy green wad of tens and twenties and fifties. His mother stared at the money as it rained down on the endtable by the sofa, her good eye growing bigger and bigger until Bobby was afraid it might tumble right out of her face. The other eye remained squinched down in its thundercloud of blue-black flesh. She looked like a battered old pirate gloating over freshly unburied treasure, an image Bobby could have done without . . . and one which never entirely left him during the fifteen years between that night and the night of her death. Yet some new and not particularly pleasant part of him *enjoyed* that look – how it rendered her old and ugly and comic, a person who was stupid as well as avaricious. *That's my ma*, he thought in a Jimmy Durante voice. *That's my ma. We both gave him up, but I got paid better than you did, Ma, didn't I? Yeah! Hotcha!*

'Bobby,' she whispered in a trembly voice. She looked like a pirate and sounded like a winning contestant on that Bill Cullen show, *The Price is Right*. 'Oh Bobby, so much *money*! Where did it come from?'

'Ted's bet,' Bobby said. 'This is the payout.'

'But Ted . . . won't he—'

'He won't need it anymore.'

Liz winced as if one of her bruises had suddenly twinged. Then she began sweeping the money together, sorting the bills even as she did so. 'I'm going to get you that bike,' she said. Her fingers moved with the speed of an experienced three-card monte dealer. *No one beats that shuffle*, Bobby thought. *No one has* ever *beaten that shuffle*. 'First thing in the morning. Soon as the Western Auto opens. Then we'll—'

'I don't want a bike,' he said. 'Not from that. And not from you.'

She froze with her hands full of money and he felt her rage bloom at once, something red and electrical. 'No thanks from you, are there? I was a fool to ever expect any. God damn you if you're not the spitting image of your father!' She drew back her hand again with the fingers open. The difference this time was that he knew it was coming. She had blindsided him for the last time.

'How would you know?' Bobby asked. 'You've told so many lies about him you don't remember the truth.'

And this was so. He had looked into her and there was almost no Randall Garfield there, only a box with his name on it . . . his name and a faded image that could have been almost anyone. This was the box where she kept the things that hurt her. She didn't remember about how he liked that Jo Stafford song; didn't remember (if she had ever known) that Randy Garfield had been a real sweetie who'd give you the shirt right off his back. There was no room for things like that in the box she kept. Bobby thought it must be awful to need a box like that.

'He wouldn't buy a drunk a drink,' he said. 'Did you know that?'

'What are you *talking* about?'

'You can't make me hate him . . . and you can't make me into him.' He turned his right hand into a fist and cocked it by the side of his head. 'I won't be his ghost. Tell yourself as many lies as you want to about the bills he didn't pay and the insurance policy he lost out on and all the inside straights he tried to fill, but don't tell them to me. Not anymore.'

'Don't raise your hand to me, Bobby-O. Don't you ever raise your hand to me.'

In answer he held up his other hand, also fisted. 'Come on. You want to hit me? I'll hit you back. You can have some more. Only this time you'll deserve it. Come on.'

She faltered. He could feel her rage dissipating as fast as it had come, and what replaced it was a terrible blackness. In it, he saw, was fear. Fear of her son, fear that he might hurt her. Not tonight, no – not with those grimy little-boy fists. But little boys grew up.

And was he so much better than her that he could look down his nose and give her the old la-de-dah? Was he *any* better? In his mind he heard the unspeakable crooning voice asking if he wanted to go back home even though it meant Ted would have to go on without him. *Yes*, Bobby had said. Even if it meant going back to his bitch of a mother? *Yes*, Bobby had said. You understand her a little bit better now, do you? Cam had asked, and once again Bobby had said yes.

And when she recognized his step on the porch, there had at first been nothing in her mind but love and relief. Those things had been real.

Bobby unmade his fists. He reached up and took her hand, which was still held back to slap . . . although now without much conviction. It resisted at first, but Bobby at last soothed the tension from it. He kissed it. He looked at his mother's battered face and kissed her hand again. He knew her so well and he didn't want to. He longed for the window in his mind to close, longed for the opacity that made love not just possible but necessary. The less you knew, the more you could believe.

'It's just a bike I don't want,' he said. 'Okay? Just a bike.'

'What *do* you want?' she asked. Her voice was uncertain, dreary. 'What *do* you want from me, Bobby?'

'Pancakes,' he said. 'Lots.' He tried a smile. 'I am *so-ooo* hungry.'

She made enough pancakes for both of them and they ate breakfast at midnight, sitting across from each other at the kitchen table. He insisted on helping her with the dishes even though it was going on toward one by then. Why not? he asked her. There was no school the next day, he could sleep as late as he wanted.

As she was letting the water out of the sink and Bobby was putting the last of their silverware away, Bowser began barking over on Colony Street: *roop-roop-roop* into the dark of a new day. Bobby's eyes met his mother's, they laughed, and for a moment knowing was all right.

At first he lay in bed the old way, on his back with his heels spread to the lower corners of the mattress, but the old way no longer felt right. It felt exposed, as if anything that wanted to bag a boy could simply burst out of his closet and unzip his upturned belly with one claw. He rolled over on his side and wondered where Ted was now. He reached out, feeling for something that might be Ted, and there was nothing. Just as there had been nothing earlier, on Nasty Gansett Street. Bobby wished he could cry for Ted, but he couldn't. Not yet.

Outside, crossing the dark like a dream, came the sound of the clock in the town square: one single *bong*. Bobby looked at the luminous hands of the Big Ben on his desk and saw they were standing at one o'clock. That was good.

'They're gone,' Bobby said. 'The low men are gone.'

But he slept on his side with his knees drawn up to his chest. His nights of sleeping wide open on his back were over.

CHAPTER ELEVEN

WOLVES AND LIONS. BOBBY AT BAT. OFFICER RAYMER. BOBBY AND CAROL. BAD TIMES. AN ENVELOPE.

Sully-John returned from camp with a tan, ten thousand healing mosquito bites, and a million tales to tell . . . only Bobby didn't hear many of them. That was the summer the old easy friendship among Bobby and Sully and Carol broke up. The three of them sometimes walked down to Sterling House together, but once they got there they went to different activities. Carol and her girlfriends were signed up for crafts and softball and badminton, Bobby and Sully for Junior Safaris and baseball.

Sully, whose skills were already maturing, moved up from the Wolves to the Lions. And while all the boys went on the swimming and hiking safaris together, sitting in the back of the battered old Sterling House panel truck with their bathing suits and their lunches in paper sacks, S-J more and more often sat with Ronnie Olmquist and Duke Wendell, boys with whom he had been at camp. They told the same old stories about short-sheeting beds and sending the little kids on snipe

376

hunts until Bobby was bored with them. You'd think Sully had been at camp for . . ., fifty years.

On the Fourth of July the Wolves and Lions played their annual head-to-head game. In the decade and a half going back to the end of World War II the Wolves had never won one of these matches, but in the 1960 contest they at least made a game of it – mostly because of Bobby Garfield. He went three-for-three and even without his Alvin Dark glove made a spectacular diving catch in center field. (Getting up and hearing the applause, he wished only briefly for his mother, who hadn't come to the annual holiday outing at Lake Canton.)

Bobby's last hit came during the Wolves' final turn at bat. They were down by two with a runner at second. Bobby drove the ball deep to left field, and as he took off toward first he heard S-J grunt 'Good hit, Bob!' from his catcher's position behind the plate. It *was* a good hit, but he was the potential tying run and should have stopped at second base. Instead he tried to stretch it. Kids under the age of thirteen were almost never able to get the ball back into the infield accurately, but this time Sully's Camp Winnie friend Duke Wendell threw a bullet from left field to Sully's *other* Camp Winnie friend, Ronnie Olmquist. Bobby slid but felt Ronnie's glove slap his ankle a split second before his sneaker touched the bag.

'*Yerrrrr-ROUT!*' cried the umpire, who had raced up from home plate to be on top of the play. On the sidelines, the friends and relatives of the Lions cheered hysterically.

Bobby got up glaring at the ump, a Sterling House counsellor of about twenty with a whistle and a white smear of zinc oxide on his nose. 'I was safe!'

'Sorry, Bob,' the kid said, dropping his ump impersonation

and becoming a counsellor again. 'It was a good hit and a great slide but you were out.'

'Was not! You cheater! Why do you want to cheat?'

'Throw im out!' someone's dad called. 'There's no call for guff like that!'

'Go sit down, Bobby,' the counsellor said.

'I was *safe*!' Bobby shouted. 'Safe by a mile!' He pointed at the man who had advised he be tossed from the game. 'Did he pay you to make sure we lost? That fatso there?'

'Quit it, Bobby,' the counsellor said. How stupid he looked with his little beanie hat from some nimrod college fraternity and his whistle! 'I'm warning you.'

Ronnie Olmquist turned away as if disgusted by the argument. Bobby hated him, too.

'You're nothing but a cheater,' Bobby said. He could hold back the tears pricking the corners of his eyes but not the waver in his voice.

'That's the last I'll take,' the counsellor said. 'Go sit down and cool off. You—'

'Cheating *cocksucker*. That's what *you* are.'

A woman close to third gasped and turned away.

'That's it,' the counsellor said in a toneless voice. 'Get off the field. Right now.'

Bobby walked halfway down the baseline between third and home, his sneakers scuffling, then turned back. 'By the way, a bird shit on your nose. I guess you're too dumb to figure that out. Better go wipe it off.'

It sounded funny in his head but stupid when it came out and nobody laughed. Sully was straddling home plate, big as a house and serious as a heart attack in his ragtags of catching gear. His mask, mended all over with black tape,

378

dangled from one hand. He looked flushed and angry. He also looked like a kid who would never be a Wolf again. S-J had been to Camp Winnie, had short-sheeted beds, had stayed up late telling ghost stories around a campfire. He would be a Lion forever and Bobby hated him.

'What's wrong with you?' Sully asked as Bobby plodded by. Both benches had fallen silent. All the kids were looking at him. All the parents were looking at him, too. Looking at him as though he was something disgusting. Bobby guessed he probably was. Just not for the reasons they thought.

Guess what, S-J, maybe you been to Camp Winnie, but I been down there. Way down there.

'Bobby?'

'Nothing's wrong with me,' he said without looking up. 'Who cares? I'm moving to Massachusetts. Maybe there's less twinkydink cheaters there.'

'Listen, man—'

'Oh, shut up,' Bobby said without looking at him. He looked at his sneakers instead. Just looked at his sneakers and kept on walking.

Liz Garfield didn't make friends ('I'm a plain brown moth, not a social butterfly,' she sometimes told Bobby), but during her first couple of years at Home Town Real Estate she had been on good terms with a woman named Myra Calhoun. (In Liz-ese she and Myra saw eye to eye, marched to the same drummer, were tuned to the same wavelength, etc., etc.) In those days Myra had been Don Biderman's secretary and Liz had been the entire office pool, shuttling between agents, making their appointments and their coffee, typing their correspondence. Myra had left the agency abruptly, without much explanation, in 1955. Liz had moved up to her job as Mr Biderman's secretary in early 1956.

Liz and Myra had remained in touch, exchanging holiday cards and the occasional letter. Myra – who was what Liz called 'a maiden lady' – had moved to Massachusetts and opened her own little real-estate firm. In late June of 1960 Liz wrote her and asked if she could become a partner – a junior one to start with, of course – in Calhoun Real Estate Solutions. She had some capital she could bring with her; it wasn't a lot, but neither was thirty-five hundred dollars a spit in the ocean.

Maybe Miss Calhoun had been through the same wringer his mom had been through, maybe not. What mattered was that she said yes – she even sent his mom a bouquet of flowers, and Liz was happy for the first time in weeks. Perhaps truly happy for the first time in years. What mattered was they were moving from Harwich to Danvers, Massachusetts. They were going in August, so Liz would have plenty of time to get her Bobby-O, her newly quiet and often glum Bobby-O, enrolled in a new school.

What also mattered was that Liz Garfield's Bobby-O had a piece of business to take care of before leaving Harwich.

He was too young and small to do what needed doing in a straightforward way. He would have to be careful, and he'd have to be sneaky. Sneaky was all right with Bobby; he no longer had much interest in acting like Audie Murphy or Randolph Scott in the Saturday-matinee movies, and besides, some people needed ambushing, if only to find out what it felt like. The hiding-place he picked was the little copse of trees where Carol had taken him on the day he went all ushy-gushy and started crying; a fitting spot in which to wait for Harry Doolin, old Mr Robin Hood, Robin Hood, riding through the glen.

Harry had gotten a part-time stockboy job at Total Grocery. Bobby had known that for weeks, had seen him there when he went shopping with his mom. Bobby had also seen Harry walking home after his shift ended at three o'clock. Harry was usually with one or more of his friends. Richie O'Meara was his most common sidekick; Willie Shearman seemed to have dropped out of old Robin Hood's life just as Sully had pretty much dropped out of Bobby's. But whether alone or in company, Harry Doolin always cut across Commonwealth Park on his way home.

Bobby started to drift down there in the afternoons. There was only morning baseball now that it was really hot and by three o'clock Fields A, B, and C were deserted. Sooner or later Harry would walk back from work and past those deserted fields without Richie or any of his other Merrie Men to keep him company. Meanwhile, Bobby spent the hour between three and four P.M. each day in the copse of trees where he had cried with his head in Carol's lap. Sometimes he read a book. The one about George and Lennie made him cry again. *Guys like us, that work on ranches, are the loneliest guys in the world.* That was how George saw it. *Guys like us got nothing to look ahead to.* Lennie thought the two of them were going to get a farm and raise rabbits, but long before Bobby got to the end of the story he knew there would be no farms and no rabbits for George and Lennie. Why? Because people needed a beast to hunt. They found a Ralph or a Piggy or a big stupid hulk of a Lennie and then they turned into low men. They put on their yellow coats, they sharpened a stick at both ends, and then they went hunting.

But guys like us sometimes get a little of our own back, Bobby thought as he waited for the day when Harry would show up alone. *Sometimes we do.*

August sixth turned out to be the day. Harry strolled through the park toward the corner of Broad and Commonwealth still wearing his red Total Grocery apron – what a fucking nimrod – and singing 'Mack the Knife' in a voice that could have melted screws. Careful not to rustle the branches of the close-growing trees, Bobby stepped out behind him and closed in, walking softly on the path and not cocking back his baseball bat until he was close enough to be sure. As he raised it he thought of Ted saying *Three boys against one little girl. They must have thought you were a lion.* But of course Carol wasn't a lion; neither was he. It was Sully who was the Lion and Sully hadn't been there, wasn't here now. The one creeping up behind Harry Doolin wasn't even a Wolf. He was just a hyena, but so what? Did Harry Doolin deserve any better?

Nope, Bobby thought, and swung the bat. It connected with the same satisfying thud he'd felt at Lake Canton when he'd gotten his third and best hit, the one to deep left. Connecting with the small of Harry Doolin's back was even better.

Harry screamed with pain and surprise and went sprawling. When he rolled over, Bobby brought the bat down on his leg at once, the blow this time landing just below the left knee. '*Owwwuuuu!*' Harry screamed. It was most satisfying to hear Harry Doolin scream; close to bliss, in fact. '*Owwwuuu, that hurts! That hurrrts!*'

Can't let him get up, Bobby thought, picking his next spot with a cold eye. *He's twice as big as me, if I miss once and let him get up, he'll tear me limb from limb. He'll fucking kill me.*

Harry was trying to retreat, digging at the gravel path with his sneakers, dragging a groove with his butt, paddling with his elbows. Bobby swung the bat and hit him in the stomach. Harry lost his air and his elbows and sprawled on his back. His eyes were dazed, filled with sunbright tears. His pimples stood out in big purple and red dots. His mouth – thin and mean on the day Rionda Hewson had rescued them – was now a big loose quiver. '*Owwwuuu, stop, I give, I give, oh Jeezis!*'

He doesn't recognize me, Bobby realized. *The sun's in his eyes and he doesn't even know who it is.*

That wasn't good enough. 'Not satisfactory, boys!' was what the Camp Winnie counsellors said after a bad cabin inspection – Sully had told him that, not that Bobby cared; who gave a shit about cabin inspections and making bead wallets?

But he gave a shit about *this*, yes indeed, and he leaned close to Harry's agonized face. 'Remember me, Robin Hood?' he asked. 'You remember me, don't you? I'm the Maltex Baby.'

Harry stopped screaming. He stared up at Bobby, finally recognizing him. 'Get . . . you . . .' he managed.

'You won't get shit,' Bobby said, and when Harry tried to grab his ankle Bobby kicked him in the ribs.

'*Ouuuuuu!*' Harry Doolin cried, reverting to his former scripture. What a creep! Nimrod Infants on Parade! *That probably hurt me more than it hurt you* Bobby thought. *Kicking people when you're wearing sneakers is for dumbbells.*

Harry rolled over. As he scrambled for his feet Bobby uncoiled a home-run swing and drove the bat squarely across Harry's buttocks. The sound was like a carpet-beater hitting a heavy rug – a *wonderful* sound! The only thing that could have improved this moment would have been Mr Biderman also sprawled on the path. Bobby knew exactly where he'd like to hit *him*.

Half a loaf was better than none, though. Or so his mother always said.

'That was for the Gerber Baby,' Bobby said. Harry was lying flat on the path again, sobbing. Snot was running from his nose in thick green streams. With one hand he was feebly trying to rub some feeling back into his numb ass.

Bobby's hands tightened on the taped handle of the bat again. He wanted to lift it and bring it down one final time, not on Harry's shin or Harry's backside but on Harry's head. He wanted to hear the crunch of Harry's skull, and really, wouldn't the world be a better place without him? Little Irish shit. Low little—

Steady on, Bobby, Ted's voice spoke up. *Enough is enough, so just steady on. Control yourself.*

'Touch her again and I'll kill you,' Bobby said. 'Touch *me* again and I'll burn your house down. Fucking nimrod.'

He had squatted by Harry to say this last. Now he got up, looked around, and walked away. By the time he met the Sigsby twins halfway up Broad Street Hill, he was whistling.

In the years which followed, Liz Garfield almost got used to seeing policemen at her door. The first to show up was Officer Raymer, the fat local cop who would sometimes buy the kids peanuts from the guy in the park. When he rang the doorbell of the ground-floor apartment at 149 Broad Street on the evening of August sixth, Officer Raymer didn't look happy. With him was Harry Doolin, who would not be able to sit in an uncushioned seat for a week or more, and his mother, Mary Doolin. Harry mounted the porch steps like an old man, with his hands planted in the small of his back.

When Liz opened the front door, Bobby was by her side. Mary Doolin pointed at him and cried: 'That's him, that's the boy who beat up my Harry! Arrest him! Do your duty!'

'What's this about, George?' Liz asked.

For a moment Officer Raymer didn't reply. He looked from Bobby (five feet four inches tall, ninety-seven pounds) to Harry (six feet one inch tall, one hundred and seventy-five pounds), instead. His large moist eyes were doubtful.

Harry Doolin was stupid, but not so stupid he couldn't read that look. 'He snuck up on me. Got me from behind.'

Raymer bent down to Bobby with his chapped, red-knuckled hands on the shiny knees of his uniform pants. 'Harry Doolin here claims you beat im up in the park whilst he was on his way home from work.' Raymer pronounced *work* as *rurrk*. Bobby never forgot that. 'Says you hid and then lumped im up widda ballbat before he could even turn around. What do you say, laddie? Is he telling the truth?'

Bobby, not stupid at all, had already considered this scene. He wished he could have told Harry in the park that paid was paid and done was done, that if Harry tattled to anyone about Bobby beating him up, then Bobby would tattle right back – would tell about Harry and his friends hurting Carol, which would look much worse. The trouble with that was that Harry's friends would deny it; it would be Carol's word against Harry's, Richie's, and Willie's. So Bobby had walked away without saying anything, hoping that Harry's humiliation – beat up by a little kid half his size – would keep his mouth shut. It hadn't, and looking at Mrs Doolin's narrow face, pinched paintless lips, and furious eyes, Bobby knew why. She had gotten it out of him, that was all. Nagged it out of him, more than likely.

'I never touched him,' Bobby told Raymer, and met Raymer's gaze firmly with his own as he said it.

Mary Doolin gasped, shocked. Even Harry, to whom lying must have been a way of life by the age of sixteen, looked surprised.

'Oh, the straight-out bare-facedness of it!' Mrs Doolin cried. 'You let me talk to him, Officer! I'll get the truth out of him, see if I don't!'

She started forward. Raymer swept her back with one hand, not rising or even taking his eyes from Bobby.

'Now, lad – why would a galoot the size of Harry Doolin say such a thing about a shrimp the size of you if it wasn't true?'

'Don't you be calling my boy a galoot!' Mrs Doolin shrilled. 'Ain't it enough he's been beat within an inch of his life by this coward? Why—'

'Shut up,' Bobby's mom said. It was the first time she'd spoken since asking Officer Raymer what this was about, and her voice was deadly quiet. 'Let him answer the question.'

'He's still mad at me from last winter, that's why,' Bobby told Raymer. 'He and some other big kids from St Gabe's chased me down the hill. Harry slipped on the ice and fell down and got all wet. He said he'd get me. I guess he thinks this is a good way to do it.'

'You liar!' Harry shouted. 'That wasn't me who chased you, that was Billy Donahue! That—'

He stopped, looked around. He'd put his foot in it somehow; a dim appreciation of the fact was dawning on his face.

'It wasn't me,' Bobby said. He spoke quietly, holding Raymer's eyes. 'If I tried to beat up a kid his size, he'd total me.'

'Liars go to hell!' Mary Doolin shouted.

'Where were you around three-thirty this afternoon, Bobby?' Raymer asked. 'Can you answer me that?'

'Here,' Bobby said.

'Miz Garfield?'

'Oh yes,' she said calmly. 'Right here with me all afternoon. I washed the kitchen floor and Bobby cleaned the baseboards. We're getting ready to move, and I want the place to look nice when we do. Bobby complained a little – as boys will do – but he did his chore. And afterward we had iced tea.'

'Liar!' Mrs Doolin cried. Harry only looked stunned. '*Shocking* liar!' She lunged forward again, hands reaching in the general direction of Liz Garfield's neck. Once more Officer Raymer pushed her back without looking at her. A bit more roughly this time.

'You tell me on your oath that he was with you?' Officer Raymer asked Liz.

'On my oath.'

'Bobby, you never touched him? On your oath?'

'On my oath.'

'On your oath before God?'

'On my oath before God.'

'I'm gonna get you, Garfield,' Harry said. 'I'm gonna fix your little red w—'

Raymer swung around so suddenly that if his mother hadn't seized him by one elbow, Harry might have tumbled down the porch steps, reinjuring himself in old places and opening fresh wounds in new ones.

'Shut your ugly stupid pot,' Raymer said, and when Mrs Doolin started to speak, Raymer pointed at her. 'Shut yours as well, Mary Doolin. Maybe if you want to bring beatin charges against someone, you ought to start with yer own damned husband. There'd be more witnesses.'

She gawped at him, furious and ashamed.

Raymer dropped the hand he'd been pointing with, as if it had suddenly gained weight. He gazed from Harry and Mary (neither full of grace) on the porch to Bobby and Liz in the foyer. Then he stepped back from all four, took off his uniform cap, scratched his sweaty head, and put his cap back on. 'Something's rotten in the state of Denmark,' he said at last. 'Someone here's lyin faster'n a hoss can trot.'

'He—' 'You—' Harry and Bobby spoke together, but Officer George Raymer was interested in hearing from neither.

'*Shut up!*' he roared, loud enough to make an old couple strolling past on the other side of the street turn and look. 'I'm declarin the case closed. But if there's any more trouble between the two of you' – pointing at the boys – 'or *you*' – pointing at the mothers – 'there's going to be woe for someone. A word to the wise is sufficient, they say. Harry, will you shake young Robert's hand and say all's well? Do the manly thing? . . . Ah, I thought not. The world's a sad goddamned place. Come on, Doolins. I'll see you home.'

Bobby and his mother watched the three of them go down the steps, Harry's limp now exaggerated to the point of a sailor's stagger. At the foot of the walk Mrs Doolin suddenly cuffed him on the back of the neck. 'Don't make it worse'n it is, you little shite!' she said. Harry did better after that, but he still rolled from starboard to port. To Bobby the boy's residual limp looked like the goods. Probably *was* the goods. That last lick, the one across Harry's ass, had been a grand slam.

Back in the apartment, speaking in that same calm voice, Liz asked: 'Was he one of the boys that hurt Carol?'

'Yes.'

'Can you stay out of his way until we move?'

'I think so.'

'Good,' she said, and then kissed him. She hardly ever kissed him, and it was wonderful when she did.

Less than a week before they moved – the apartment had by then begun to fill up with cardboard boxes and to take on a strange denuded look – Bobby caught up to Carol Gerber in the park. She was walking along by herself for a change. He had seen her out walking with her girlfriends plenty of times, but that wasn't good enough, wasn't what he wanted. Now she was finally alone, and it wasn't until she looked over her shoulder at him and he saw the fear in her eyes that he knew she had been avoiding him.

'Bobby,' she said. 'How are you?'

'I don't know,' he said. 'Okay, I guess. I haven't seen you around.'

'You haven't come up my house.'

'No,' he said. 'No, I—' What? How was he supposed to finish? 'I been pretty busy,' he said lamely.

'Oh. Uh-huh.' He could have handled her being cool to

him. What he couldn't handle was the fear she was trying to hide. The fear of him. As if he was a dog that might bite her. Bobby had a crazy image of himself dropping down on all fours and starting to go *roop-roop-roop*.

'I'm moving away.'

'Sully told me. But he didn't know exactly where. I guess you guys don't chum like you used to.'

'No,' Bobby said. 'Not like we used to. But here.' He reached into his back pocket and brought out a piece of folded-over paper from a school notebook. Carol looked at it doubtfully, reached for it, then pulled her hand back.

'It's just my address,' he said. 'We're going to Massachusetts. A town named Danvers.'

Bobby held out the folded paper but she still wasn't taking it and he felt like crying. He remembered being at the top of the Ferris wheel with her and how it was like being at the top of the whole lighted world. He remembered a towel opening like wings, feet with tiny painted toes pivoting, and the smell of perfume. 'She's dancin to the drag, the cha-cha rag-a-mop,' Freddy Cannon sang from the radio in the other room, and it was Carol, it was Carol, it was Carol.

'I thought you might write,' he said. 'I'll probably be homesick, a new town and all.'

Carol took the paper at last and put it into the pocket of her shorts without looking at it. *Probably throw it away when she gets home*, Bobby thought, but he didn't care. She had taken it, at least. That would be enough springboard for those times when he needed to take his mind away . . . and there didn't have to be any low men in the vicinity for you to need to do that, he had discovered.

'Sully says you're different now.'

Bobby didn't reply.

'*Lots* of people say that, actually.'

Bobby didn't reply.

'Did you beat Harry Doolin up?' she asked, and gripped Bobby's wrist with a cold hand. 'Did you?'

Bobby slowly nodded his head.

Carol threw her arms around his neck and kissed him so hard their teeth clashed. Their mouths parted with an audible smack. Bobby didn't kiss another girl on the mouth for three years . . . and never in his life did he have one kiss *him* like that.

'Good!' she said in a low fierce voice. It was almost a growl. '*Good!*'

Then she ran toward Broad Street, her legs – browned with summer and scabbed by many games and many sidewalks – flashing.

'Carol!' he called after her. 'Carol, wait!'

She ran.

'Carol, I love you!'

She stopped at that . . . or maybe it was just that she'd reached Commonwealth Avenue and had to look for traffic. In any case she paused a moment, head lowered, and then looked back. Her eyes were wide and her lips were parted.

'Carol!'

'I have to go home, I have to make the salad,' she said, and ran away from him. She ran across the street and out of his life without looking back a second time. Perhaps that was just as well.

He and his mom moved to Danvers. Bobby went to Danvers Elementary, made some friends, made even more enemies. The fights started, and not long after, so did the truancies. On the **Comments** section of his first report card, Mrs Rivers wrote: '*Robert is an extremely bright boy. He is also extremely troubled. Will you come and see me about him, Mrs Garfield?*'

Mrs Garfield went, and Mrs Garfield helped as much as she could, but there were too many things about which she could not speak: Providence, a certain lost-pet poster, and how she'd come by the money she'd used to buy into a new business and a new life. The two women agreed that Bobby was suffering from growing pains; that he was missing his old town and old friends as well. He would eventually outlast his troubles. He was too bright and too full of potential not to.

Liz prospered in her new career as a real-estate agent. Bobby did well enough in English (he got an A-Plus on a paper in which he compared Steinbeck's *Of Mice and Men* to Golding's *Lord of the Flies*) and did poorly in the rest of his classes. He began to smoke cigarettes.

Carol *did* write from time to time – hesitant, almost tentative notes in which she talked about school and friends and a weekend trip to New York City with Rionda. Appended to one that arrived in March of 1961 (her letters always came on deckle-edged paper with teddy bears dancing down the sides) was a stark P.S.: *I think my mom & dad are going to get a divorce. He signed up for another 'hitch' and all she does is cry*. Mostly, however, she stuck to brighter things: she was learning to twirl, she had gotten new ice skates on her birthday, she still thought Fabian was cute even if Yvonne and Tina didn't, she had been to a twist party and danced every dance.

As he opened each of her letters and pulled it out Bobby would think, *This is the last. I won't hear from her again. Kids don't write letters for long even if they promise they will. There are too many new things coming along. Time goes by so fast. Too fast. She'll forget me.*

But he would not help her to do so. After each of her letters came he would sit down and write a response. He told her about the house in Brookline his mother sold for twenty-five thousand dollars – six months' salary at her old job in a single commission. He told her about the A-Plus on his English theme. He told her about his friend Morrie, who was teaching him to play chess. He didn't tell her that sometimes he and Morrie went on window-breaking expeditions, riding their bikes (Bobby had finally saved up enough to buy one) as fast as they could past the scuzzy old apartment houses on Plymouth Street and throwing rocks out of their baskets as they went. He skipped the story of how he had told Mr Hurley, the assistant principal at Danvers Elementary, to kiss his rosy red ass and how Mr Hurley had responded by slapping him across the face and calling him an insolent, wearisome little boy. He didn't confide that he had begun shoplifting or that he had been drunk four or five times (once with Morrie, the other times by himself) or that sometimes he walked over to the train tracks and wondered if getting run over by the South Shore Express would be the quickest way to finish the job. Just a whiff of diesel fuel, a shadow falling over your face, and then blooey. Or maybe not that quick.

Each letter he wrote to Carol ended the same way:

> ***You are sadly missed by***
> ***Your friend,***
> ***Bobby***

Weeks would pass with no mail – not for him – and then there would be another envelope with hearts and teddy bears stuck to the back, another sheet of deckle-edged paper, more stuff about skating and baton twirling and new shoes and how she was still stuck on fractions. Each letter was like one more labored breath from a loved one whose death now seems inevitable. One more breath.

Even Sully-John wrote him a few letters. They stopped early in 1961, but Bobby was amazed and touched that Sully would try at all. In S-J's childishly big handwriting and painful misspellings Bobby could make out the approach of a good-hearted teenage boy who would play sports and lay cheer-leaders with equal joy, a boy who would become lost in the thickets of punctuation as easily as he would weave through the defensive lines of opposing football teams. Bobby thought he could even see the man who was waiting for Sully up ahead in the seventies and eighties, waiting for him the way you'd wait for a taxi to arrive: a car salesman who'd eventually own his own dealership. Honest John's, of course; Honest John's Harwich Chevrolet. He'd have a big stomach hanging over his belt and lots of plaques on the wall of his office and he'd coach youth sports and start every peptalk with *Listen up, guys* and go to church and march in parades and be on the city council and all that. It would be a good life, Bobby reckoned – the farm and the rabbits instead of the stick sharpened at both ends. Although for Sully the stick turned out to be waiting after all; it was waiting in Dong Ha Province along with the old *mamasan*, the one who would never completely go away.

Bobby was fourteen when the cop caught him coming out of the convenience store with two sixpacks of beer

(Narragansett) and three cartons of cigarettes (Chesterfields, naturally; twenty-one great tobaccos make twenty wonderful smokes). This was the blond *Village of the Damned* cop.

Bobby told the cop he hadn't broken in, that the back door was open and he'd just *walked* in, but when the cop shone his flashlight on the lock it hung askew in the old wood, half gouged out. *What about this?* the cop asked, and Bobby shrugged. Sitting in the car (the cop let Bobby sit in the front seat with him but wouldn't let him have a butt when Bobby asked), the cop began filling out a form on a clipboard. He asked the sullen, skinny kid beside him what his name was. Ralph, Bobby said. Ralph Garfield. But when they pulled up in front of the house where he now lived with his mom – a whole house, upstairs and downstairs both, times were good – he told the cop he had lied.

'My name's really Jack,' he said.

'Oh yeah?' the blond *Village of the Damned* cop said.

'Yes,' Bobby said, nodding. 'Jack Merridew Garfield. That's me.'

Carol Gerber's letters stopped coming in 1963, which happened to be the year of Bobby's first school expulsion and also the year of his first visit to Massachusetts Youth Correctional in Bedford. The cause of this visit was possession of five marijuana cigarettes, which Bobby and his friends called joysticks. Bobby was sentenced to ninety days, the last thirty forgiven for good behavior. He read a lot of books. Some of the other kids called him Professor. Bobby didn't mind.

When he got out of Bedbug Correctional, Officer

Grandelle – the Danvers Juvenile Officer – came by and asked if Bobby was ready to straighten up and fly right. Bobby said he was, he had learned his lesson, and for awhile that seemed to be true. Then in the fall of 1964 he beat a boy so badly that the boy had to go to the hospital and there was some question of whether or not he would completely recover. The kid wouldn't give Bobby his guitar, so Bobby beat him up and took it. Bobby was playing the guitar (not very well) in his room when he was arrested. He had told Liz he'd bought the guitar, a Silvertone acoustic, in a pawnshop.

Liz stood weeping in the doorway as Officer Grandelle led Bobby to the police car parked at the curb. 'I'm going to wash my hands of you if you don't stop!' she cried after him. 'I mean it! I do!'

'Wash em,' he said, getting in the back. 'Go ahead, Ma, wash em now and save time.'

Driving downtown, Officer Grandelle said, 'I thought you was gonna straighten up and fly right, Bobby.'

'Me too,' Bobby said. That time he was in Bedbug for six months.

When he got out he cashed in his Trailways ticket and hitched home. When he let himself into the house, his mother didn't come out to greet him. 'You got a letter,' she said from her darkened bedroom. 'It's on your desk.'

Bobby's heart began to bang hard against his ribs as soon as he saw the envelope. The hearts and teddy bears were gone – she was too old for them now – but he recognized Carol's handwriting at once. He picked up the letter and tore it open. Inside was a single sheet of paper – deckle-edged –

and another, smaller, envelope. Bobby read Carol's note, the last he ever received from her, quickly.

Dear Bobby,
   How are you. I am fine. You got something from
your old friend, the one who fixed my arm that time.
It came to me because I guess he didn't know where
you were. He put a note in asking me to send it
along. So I am. Say hi to your mom.
Carol

No news of her adventures in twirling. No news of how she was doing with math. No news of boyfriends, either, but Bobby guessed she probably had had a few.

He picked up the sealed envelope with hands that were shaky and numb. His heart was pounding harder than ever. On the front, written in soft pencil, was a single word: his name. It was Ted's handwriting. He knew it at once. Dry-mouthed, unaware that his eyes had filled with tears, Bobby tore open the envelope, which was no bigger than the ones in which children send their first-grade valentines.

What came out first was the sweetest smell Bobby had ever experienced. It made him think of hugging his mother when he was small, the smell of her perfume and deodorant and the stuff she put on her hair; it made him think of how Commonwealth Park smelled in the summer; it made him think of how the Harwich Library stacks had smelled, spicy and dim and somehow explosive. The tears in his eyes over-spilled and began to run down his cheeks. He'd gotten used to feeling old; feeling young again – knowing he *could* feel young again – was a terrible disorienting shock.

There was no letter, no note, no writing of any kind. When Bobby tilted the envelope, what showered down on the surface of his desk were rose petals of the deepest, darkest red he had ever seen.

Heart's blood, he thought, exalted without knowing why. All at once, and for the first time in years, he remembered how you could take your mind away, how you could just put it on parole. And even as he thought of it he felt his thoughts lifting. The rose petals gleamed on the scarred surface of his desk like rubies, like secret light spilled from the world's secret heart.

Not just one world, Bobby thought. *Not just one. There are other worlds than this, millions of worlds, all turning on the spindle of the Tower.*

And then he thought: *He got away from them again. He's free again.*

The petals left no room for doubt. They were all the yes anyone could ever need; all the you-may, all the you-can, all the it's-true.

Now they go, now they slow, Bobby thought, knowing he had heard those words before, not remembering where or knowing why they had recurred to him now. Not caring, either.

Ted was free. Not in this world and time, this time he had run in the other direction . . . but in *some* world.

Bobby scooped up the petals, each one like a tiny silk coin. He cupped them like palmfuls of blood, then raised them to his face. He could have drowned in their sweet reek. Ted was in them, Ted clear as day with his funny stooped way of walking, his baby-fine white hair, and the yellow nicotine spots tattooed on the first two fingers of his right hand. Ted with his carryhandle shopping bags.

As on the day when he had punished Harry Doolin for hurting Carol, he heard Ted's voice. Then it had been mostly imagination. This time Bobby thought it was real, something which had been embedded in the rose petals and left for him.

Steady on, Bobby. Enough is enough, so just steady on. Control yourself.

He sat at his desk for a long time with the rose petals pressed to his face. At last, careful not to lose a single one, he put them back into the little envelope and folded down the torn top.

He's free. He's . . . somewhere. And he remembered.

'He remembered me,' Bobby said. 'He remembered *me.*'

He got up, went into the kitchen, and put on the tea kettle. Then he went into his mother's room. She was on her bed, lying there in her slip with her feet up, and he could see she had started to look old. She turned her face away from him when he sat down next to her, a boy now almost as big as a man, but she let him take her hand. He held it and stroked it and waited for the kettle to whistle. After awhile she turned to look at him. 'Oh Bobby,' she said. 'We've made such a mess of things, you and me. What are we going to do?'

'The best we can,' he said, still stroking her hand. He raised it to his lips and kissed the palm where her lifeline and heart-line tangled briefly before wandering away from each other again. 'The best we can.'

THE SHAWSHANK REDEMPTION

('Rita Hayworth and Shawshank Redemption')

Word fiction and movie fiction differ in one fundamental way: the former is almost always the creation of a solitary mind, the latter a collaborative effort forged by many, from director to costume designer to set decorator. Even the Foley guys (sound men who add everything from footfalls to barking dogs and creaking crickets) play their part. It's a wonder any film adaptations work at all. When they do, it's often because a single creative mind has confidently bound all the other minds together to achieve a clear goal. And it doesn't hurt if the primary work is a relatively short one, where the plot elements are compressed.

The creative mind in the case of *The Shawshank Redemption* was Frank Darabont's. I optioned the rights to him; it was just us guys, with no producer-types in the way, handing out dollars with strings attached. When Frank sent me his original screenplay, it was over a hundred and thirty pages long – an epic length – and incredibly faithful to my story. I finished it with a sad laugh, thinking 'It's wonderful . . . but nobody's going to make it. Why, nothing even blows up.'

But thanks to Castle Rock (which had had success with

Stand By Me; in fact, Rob Reiner's production company is named after my make-believe town in western Maine), it *was* made, and the final cut is a faithful realization of Frank's original screenplay, almost page for page.

It was not — at first — much of a success at the box office. Part of the reason may have been the title, which conveyed no information and called up no image in the potential moviegoer's mind. Unfortunately, nobody could think of a better one, and that included me; I never liked the title of my own story, and don't to this day. The Rita Hayworth part helps a little, but it's still clunky . . . and I flatter myself that I'm ordinarily pretty good with titles (and never mind the wiseass critic who pointed out that '*It* rhymes with *shit* for a reason').

Nevertheless, the movie eventually found its audience. Did it ever! It now commonly appears on lists of the best-loved movies of all time. Do I love it, too? Yes. The story had heart; the movie has more. Frank Darabont, who kept the reins firmly in his own hands by insisting that he direct his own script, is one of the universe's better human beings. That goodness shines through here. I never liked the 'Marriage of Figaro' sequence in the film (it's not in the story), but everything else just shines. The story is hard when it has to be, full of sentiment without being sentimental. This is as good as films get on the subject of how men love each other, and how they survive.

Hope Springs Eternal

RITA HAYWORTH
AND
SHAWSHANK
REDEMPTION

For Russ and Florence Dorr

There's a guy like me in every state and federal prison in America, I guess – I'm the guy who can get it for you. Tailormade cigarettes, a bag of reefer, if you're partial to that, a bottle of brandy to celebrate your son or daughter's high school graduation, or almost anything else . . . within reason, that is. It wasn't always that way.

I came to Shawshank when I was just twenty, and I am one of the few people in our happy little family who is willing to own up to what he did. I committed murder. I put a large insurance policy on my wife, who was three years older than I was, and then I fixed the brakes of the Chevrolet coupé her father had given us as a wedding present. It worked out exactly as I had planned, except I hadn't planned on her stopping to pick up the neighbor woman and the neighbor woman's infant son on the way down Castle Hill and into town. The brakes let go and the car crashed through the bushes at the edge of the town common, gathering speed. Bystanders said it must have been doing fifty or better when it hit the base of the Civil War statue and burst into flames.

I also hadn't planned on getting caught, but caught I was. I got a season's pass into this place. Maine has no death-penalty, but the District Attorney saw to it that I was tried for all three deaths and given three life sentences, to run one after the other. That fixed up any chance of parole I might have, for a long, long time. The judge called what I had done 'a hideous, heinous crime', and it was, but it is also in the past now. You can look it up in the yellowing files of the Castle Rock *Call*, where the big headlines announcing my conviction look sort of funny and antique next to the news of Hitler and Mussolini and FDR's alphabet soup agencies.

Have I rehabilitated myself, you ask? I don't know what that word means, at least as far as prisons and corrections go. I think it's a politician's word. It may have some other meaning, and it may be that I will have a chance to find out, but that is the future . . . something cons teach themselves not to think about. I was young, good-looking, and from the poor side of town. I knocked up a pretty, sulky, headstrong girl who lived in one of the fine old houses on Carbine Street. Her father was agreeable to the marriage if I would take a job in the optical company he owned and 'work my way up'. I found out that what he really had in mind was keeping me in his house and under his thumb, like a disagreeable pet that has not quite been housebroken and which may bite. Enough hate eventually piled up to cause me to do what I did. Given a second chance I would not do it again, but I'm not sure that means I am rehabilitated.

Anyway, it's not me I want to tell you about; I want to tell you about a guy named Andy Dufresne. But before I can tell you about Andy, I have to explain a few other things about myself. It won't take long.

As I said, I've been the guy who can get it for you here at Shawshank for damn near forty years. And that doesn't just mean contraband items like extra cigarettes or booze, although those items always top the list. But I've gotten thousands of other items for men doing time here, some of them perfectly legal yet hard to come by in a place where you've supposedly been brought to be punished. There was one fellow who was in for raping a little girl and exposing himself to dozens of others; I got him three pieces of pink Vermont marble and he did three lovely sculptures out of them – a baby, a boy of about twelve, and a bearded young man. He called them The Three Ages of Jesus, and those pieces of sculpture are now in the parlor of a man who used to be governor of this state.

Or here's a name you may remember if you grew up north of Massachusetts – Robert Alan Cote. In 1951 he tried to rob the First Mercantile Bank of Mechanic Falls, and the hold-up turned into a bloodbath – six dead in the end, two of them members of the gang, three of them hostages, one of them a young state cop who put his head up at the wrong time and got a bullet in the eye. Cote had a penny collection. Naturally they weren't going to let him have it in here, but with a little help from his mother and a middleman who used to drive a laundry truck, I was able to get it for him. I told him, Bobby, you must be crazy, wanting to have a coin collection in a stone hotel full of thieves. He looked at me and smiled and said, I know where to keep them. They'll be safe enough. Don't you worry. And he was right. Bobby Cote died of a brain tumor in 1967, but that coin collection has never turned up.

I've gotten men chocolates on Valentine's Day; I got three of those green milkshakes they serve at McDonald's around St Paddy's Day for a crazy Irishman named O'Malley; I even arranged for a midnight showing of *Deep Throat* and *The Devil in Miss Jones* for a party of twenty men who had pooled their resources to rent the films . . . although I ended up doing a week in solitary for that little escapade. It's the risk you run when you're the guy who can get it.

I've gotten reference books and fuck-books, joke novelties like handbuzzers and itching powder, and on more than one occasion I've seen that a long-timer has gotten a pair of panties from his wife or his girlfriend . . . and I guess you'll know what guys in here do with such items during the long nights when time draws out like a blade. I don't get all those things gratis, and for some items the price comes high. But I don't do it *just* for the money; what good is money to me? I'm never going to own a Cadillac car or fly off to Jamaica for two weeks in February. I do it for the same reason that a good butcher will only sell you fresh meat: I got a reputation and I want to keep it. The only two things I refuse to handle are guns and heavy drugs. I won't help anyone kill himself or anyone else. I have enough killing on my mind to last me a lifetime.

Yeah, I'm a regular Neiman-Marcus. And so when Andy Dufresne came to me in 1949 and asked if I could smuggle Rita Hayworth into the prison for him, I said it would be no problem at all. And it wasn't.

When Andy came to Shawshank in 1948, he was thirty years old. He was a short neat little man with sandy hair and small, clever hands. He wore gold-rimmed spectacles. His fingernails were always clipped, and they were always clean. That's a funny thing to remember about a man, I suppose, but it seems to sum Andy up for me. He always looked as if he should have been wearing a tie. On the outside he had been a vice-president in the trust department of a large Portland bank. Good work for a man as young as he was, especially when you consider how conservative most banks are . . . and you have to multiply that conservatism by ten when you get up into New England, where folks don't like to trust a man with their money unless he's bald, limping, and constantly plucking at his pants to get his truss around straight. Andy was in for murdering his wife and her lover.

As I believe I have said, everyone in prison is an innocent man. Oh, they read that scripture the way those holy rollers on TV read the Book of Revelation. They were the victims of judges with hearts of stone and balls to match, or incompetent lawyers, or police frame-ups, or bad luck. They read the scripture, but you can see a different scripture in their faces. Most cons are a low sort, no good to themselves or anyone else, and their worst luck was that their mothers carried them to term.

In all my years at Shawshank, there have been less than ten men whom I believed when they told me they were innocent. Andy Dufresne was one of them, although I only became convinced of his innocence over a period of years. If I had been on the jury that heard his case in Portland Superior Court over six stormy weeks in 1947–48, I would have voted to convict, too.

It was one hell of a case, all right; one of those juicy ones with all the right elements. There was a beautiful girl with society connections (dead), a local sports figure (also dead), and a prominent young businessman in the dock. There was this, plus all the scandal the newspapers could hint at. The prosecution had an open-and-shut case. The trial only lasted as long as it did because the DA was planning to run for the US House of Representatives and he wanted John Q Public to get a good long look at his phiz. It was a crackerjack legal circus, with spectators getting in line at four in the morning, despite the subzero temperatures, to assure themselves of a seat.

The facts of the prosecution's case that Andy never contested were these: That he had a wife, Linda Collins Dufresne; that in June of 1947 she had expressed an interest in learning the game of golf at the Falmouth Hills Country Club; that she did indeed take lessons for four months; that her instructor was the Falmouth Hills golf pro, Glenn Quentin; that in late August of 1947 Andy learned that Quentin and his wife had become lovers; that Andy and Linda Dufresne argued bitterly on the afternoon of 10 September 1947; that the subject of their argument was her infidelity.

He testified that Linda professed to be glad he knew; the sneaking around, she said, was distressing. She told Andy that she planned to obtain a Reno divorce. Andy told her he would see her in hell before he would see her in Reno. She went off to spend the night with Quentin in Quentin's rented bungalow not far from the golf course. The next morning his cleaning woman found both of them dead in bed. Each had been shot four times.

It was that last fact that militated more against Andy than any of the others. The DA with the political aspirations made a great deal of it in his opening statement and his closing summation. Andrew Dufresne, he said, was not a wronged husband seeking a hot-blooded revenge against his cheating wife; that, the DA said, could be understood, if not condoned. But this revenge had been of a much colder type. Consider! the DA thundered at the jury. Four and four! Not six shots, but eight! *He had fired the gun empty . . . and then stopped to reload so he could shoot each of them again!* FOUR FOR HIM

AND FOUR FOR HER, the Portland *Sun* blared. The Boston *Register* dubbed him The Even-Steven Killer.

A clerk from the Wise Pawnshop in Lewiston testified that he had sold a six-shot .38 Police Special to Andrew Dufresne just two days before the double murder. A bartender from the country club bar testified that Andy had come in around seven o'clock on the evening of 10 September, had tossed off three straight whiskeys in a twenty-minute period – when he got up from the bar-stool he told the bartender that he was going up to Glenn Quentin's house and he, the bartender, could 'read about the rest of it in the papers'. Another clerk, this one from the Handy-Pik store a mile or so from Quentin's house, told the court that Dufresne had come in around quarter to nine on the same night. He purchased cigarettes, three quarts of beer, and some dish-towels. The county medical examiner testified that Quentin and the Dufresne woman had been killed between eleven p.m. and two a.m. on the night of September 10th–11th. The detective from the Attorney General's office who had been in charge of the case testified that there was a turnout less than seventy yards from the bungalow, and that on the afternoon of September 11th, three pieces of evidence had been removed from that turnout: first item, two empty quart bottles of Narragansett Beer (with the defendant's finger-prints on them); the second item, twelve cigarette ends (all Kools, the defendant's brand); third item, a plaster moulage of a set of tire tracks (exactly matching the tread-and-wear pattern of the tires on the defendant's 1947 Plymouth).

In the living room of Quentin's bungalow, four dishtowels had been found lying on the sofa. There were bullet-holes through them and powder-burns on them. The detective theorized (over the agonized objections of Andy's lawyer) that the murderer had wrapped the towels around the muzzle of the murder-weapon to muffle the sound of the gunshots.

Andy Dufresne took the stand in his own defense and told his story calmly, coolly, and dispassionately. He said he had begun to hear distressing rumors about his wife and Glenn Quentin as early as the last week in July. In August he had become distressed enough to investigate a bit. On an evening when Linda was supposed to have gone shopping in Portland after her tennis lesson, Andy had followed her and Quentin to Quentin's one-story rented house (inevitably dubbed 'the love-nest' by the papers). He had parked in the turnout until Quentin drove her back to the country club where her car was parked, about three hours later.

'Do you mean to tell this court that your wife did not recognize your brand-new Plymouth sedan behind Quentin's car?' the DA asked him on cross-examination.

'I swapped cars for the evening with a friend,' Andy said, and this cool admission of how well-planned his investigation had been did him no good at all in the eyes of the jury.

After returning the friend's car and picking up his own, he had gone home. Linda had been in bed, reading a book. He asked her how her trip to Portland had been. She replied that it had been fun, but she hadn't seen anything she liked well enough to buy. 'That's when I knew for sure,' Andy told the breathless spectators. He spoke in the same calm, remote voice in which he delivered almost all of his testimony.

'What was your frame of mind in the seventeen days between then and the night your wife was murdered?' Andy's lawyer asked him.

'I was in great distress,' Andy said calmly, coldly. Like a man reciting a shopping list he said that he had considered suicide, and had even gone so far as to purchase a gun in Lewiston on September 8th.

His lawyer then invited him to tell the jury what had happened after his wife left to meet Glenn Quentin on the night of the murders. Andy told them . . . and the impression he made was the worst possible.

I knew him for close to thirty years, and I can tell you he was the most self-possessed man I've ever known. What was right with him he'd only give you a little at a time. What was wrong with him he kept bottled up inside. If he ever had a dark night of the soul, as some writer or other has called it, you would never know. He was the type of man who, if he had decided to commit suicide, would do it without leaving a note but not until his affairs had been put neatly in order. If he had cried on the witness stand, or if his voice had thickened and grown hesitant, even if he had started yelling at that Washington-bound District Attorney, I don't believe he would have gotten the life sentence he wound up with. Even if he had've he would have been out on parole by 1954. But he told his story like a recording machine, seeming to say to the jury: this is it. Take it or leave it. They left it.

He said he was drunk that night, that he'd been more or less drunk since August 24th, and that he was a man who didn't handle his liquor very well. Of course that by itself would have been hard for any jury to swallow. They just couldn't see this coldly self-possessed young man in the neat double-breasted three-piece woollen suit ever getting falling-down drunk over his wife's sleazy little affair with some small-town golf pro. I believed it because I had a chance to watch Andy that those six men and six women didn't have.

Andy Dufresne took just four drinks a year all the time I knew him. He would meet me in the exercise yard every year about a week before his birthday and then again about two weeks before Christmas. On each occasion he would arrange for a bottle of Jack Daniels. He bought it the way most cons arrange to buy their stuff – the slave's wages they pay in here, plus a little of his own. Up until 1965 what you got for your time was a dime an hour. In '65 they raised it all the way up to a quarter. My commission on liquor was and is ten per cent, and when you add on that surcharge to the price of a fine sippin' whiskey like the Black Jack, you get an idea of how many hours of Andy Dufresne's sweat in the prison laundry was going to buy his four drinks a year.

On the morning of his birthday, September 20th, he would have himself a big knock, and then he'd have another that night after light out. The following day he'd give the rest of the bottle back to me, and I would share it around. As for the other bottle, he dealt himself one drink Christmas night and another on New Year's Eve. Then that bottle would also come to me with instructions to pass it on. Four drinks a year – and that is the behavior of a man who has been bitten hard by the bottle. Hard enough to draw blood.

He told the jury that on the night of the tenth he had been so drunk he could only remember what had happened in little isolated snatches. He had gotten drunk that afternoon – 'I took on a double helping of Dutch courage' is how he put it – before taking on Linda.

After she left to meet Quentin, he remembered deciding

to confront them. On the way to Quentin's bungalow, he swung into the country club for a couple of quick ones. He could not, he said, remember telling the bartender he could 'read about the rest of it in the papers', or saying anything to him at all. He remembered buying beer in the Handy-Pik, but not the dishtowels. 'Why would I want dishtowels?' he asked, and one of the papers reported that three of the lady jurors shuddered.

Later, much later, he speculated to me about the clerk who had testified on the subject of those dishtowels, and I think it's worth jotting down what he said. 'Suppose that, during their canvass for witnesses,' Andy said one day in the exercise yard, 'they stumble on this fellow who sold me the beer that night. By then three days have gone by. The facts of the case have been broadsided in all the papers. Maybe they ganged up on the guy, five or six cops, plus the dick from the Attorney General's office, plus the DA's assistant. Memory is a pretty subjective thing, Red. They could have started out with "Isn't it possible that he purchased four or five dishtowels?" and worked their way up from there. If enough people *want* you to remember something, that can be a pretty powerful persuader.'

I agreed that it could.

'But there's one even more powerful,' Andy went on in that musing way of his. 'I think it's at least possible that he convinced himself. It was the limelight. Reporters asking him questions, his picture in the papers . . . all topped, of course, by his star turn in court. I'm not saying that he deliberately falsified his story, or perjured himself. I think it's possible that he could have passed a lie detector test with flying colours, or sworn on his mother's sacred name that I bought those dishtowels. But still . . . memory is such a *goddam* subjective thing.

'I know this much: even though my own lawyer thought I had to be lying about half my story, he never bought that business about the dishtowels. It's crazy on the face of it. I was pig-drunk, too drunk to have been thinking about muffling the gunshots. If I'd done it, I just would have let them rip.'

He went up to the turnout and parked there. He drank beer and smoked cigarettes. He watched the lights downstairs in Quentin's place go out. He watched a single light go on upstairs . . . and fifteen minutes later he watched that one go out. He said he could guess the rest.

'Mr Dufresne, did you then go up to Glenn Quentin's house and kill the two of them?' his lawyer thundered.

'No, I did not,' Andy answered. By midnight, he said, he was sobering up. He was also feeling the first signs of a bad hangover. He decided to go home and sleep it off and think about the whole thing in a more adult fashion the next day. 'At that time, as I drove home, I was beginning to think that the wisest course would be to simply let her go to Reno and get her divorce.'

'Thank you, Mr Dufresne.'

The DA popped up.

'You divorced her in the quickest way you could think of, didn't you? You divorced her with a .38 revolver wrapped in dishtowels, didn't you?'

'No sir, I did not,' Andy said calmly.

'And then you shot her lover.'

'No, sir.'

'You mean you shot Quentin first?'

'I mean I didn't shoot either one of them. I drank two quarts of beer and smoked however many cigarettes that the police found at the turnout. Then I drove home and went to bed.'

'You told the jury that between August twenty-fourth and September tenth, you were feeling suicidal.'

'Yes, sir.'

'Suicidal enough to buy a revolver.'

'Yes.'

'Would it bother you overmuch, Mr Dufresne, if I told you that you do not seem to me to be the suicidal type?'

'No,' Andy said, 'but you don't impress me as being terribly sensitive, and I doubt very much that, if I *were* feeling suicidal, I would take my problem to you.'

There was a slight tense titter in the courtroom at this, but it won him no points with the jury.

'Did you take your thirty-eight with you on the night of September tenth?'

'No; as I've already testified—'

'Oh, yes!' The DA smiled sarcastically. 'You threw it into the river, didn't you? The Royal River. On the afternoon of September ninth.'

'Yes, sir.'

'One day before the murders.'

'Yes, sir.'

'That's convenient, isn't it?'

'It's neither convenient nor inconvenient. Only the truth.'

'I believe you heard Lieutenant Mincher's testimony?' Mincher had been in charge of the party which had dragged the stretch of the Royal near Pond Bridge, from which Andy had testified he had thrown the gun. The police had not found it.

'Yes, sir. You know I heard it.'

'Then you heard him tell the court that they found no gun, although they dragged for three days. That was rather convenient, too, wasn't it?'

'Convenience aside, it's a fact that they didn't find the gun,' Andy responded calmly. 'But I should like to point out to both you and the jury that the Pond Road Bridge is very close to where the Royal River empties into the Bay of Yarmouth. The current is strong. The gun may have been carried out into the bay itself.'

'And so no comparison can be made between the riflings on the bullets taken from the bloodstained corpses of your wife and Mr Glenn Quentin and the riflings on the barrel of your gun. That's correct, isn't it, Mr Dufresne?'

'Yes.'

'That's also rather convenient, isn't it?'

At that, according to the papers, Andy displayed one of the few slight emotional reactions he allowed himself during the entire six-week period of the trial. A slight, bitter smile crossed his face.

'Since I am innocent of this crime, sir, and since I am telling the truth about throwing my gun into the river the day before the crime took place, then it seems to me decidedly inconvenient that the gun was never found.'

The DA hammered at him for two days. He re-read the Handy-Pik clerk's testimony about the dishtowels to Andy. Andy repeated that he could not recall buying them, but admitted that he also couldn't remember *not* buying them.

Was it true that Andy and Linda Dufresne had taken out a

joint insurance policy in early 1947? Yes, that was true. And if acquitted, wasn't it true that Andy stood to gain fifty thousand dollars in benefits? True. And wasn't it true that he had gone up to Glenn Quentin's house with murder in his heart, and wasn't it *also* true that he had indeed committed murder twice over? No, it was not true. Then what did he think had happened, since there had been no signs of robbery?

'I have no way of knowing that, sir,' Andy said quietly.

The case went to the jury at 1:00 P.M. on a snowy Wednesday afternoon. The twelve jurymen and women came back at 3:30. The bailiff said they would have been back earlier, but they had held off in order to enjoy a nice chicken dinner from Bentley's Restaurant at the county's expense. They found him guilty, and brother, if Maine had the death penalty, he would have done the airdance before that spring's crocuses poked their heads out of the dirt.

The DA had asked him what he thought had happened, and Andy slipped the question – but he did have an idea, and I got it out of him late one evening in 1955. It had taken those seven years for us to progress from nodding acquaintances to fairly close friends – but I never felt really close to Andy until 1960 or so, and I believe I was the only one who ever did get really close to him. Both being long-timers, we were in the same cellblock from beginning to end, although I was halfway down the corridor from him.

'What do I think?' He laughed – but there was no humor in the sound. 'I think there was a lot of bad luck floating around that night. More than could ever get together in the same short span of time again. I think it must have been some stranger, just passing through. Maybe someone who had a flat tire on that road after I went home. Maybe a burglar. Maybe a psychopath. He killed them, that's all. And I'm here.'

As simple as that. And he was condemned to spend the rest of his life in Shawshank – or the part of it that mattered. Five years later he began to have parole hearings, and he was turned down just as regular as clockwork in spite of being a model prisoner. Getting a pass out of Shawshank when you've got *murder* stamped on your admittance-slip is slow work, as slow as a river eroding a rock. Seven men sit on the board, two more than at most state prisons, and every one of those seven has an ass as hard as the water drawn up from a mineral-spring well. You can't buy those guys, you can't sweet-talk them, you can't cry for them. As far as the board in here is concerned, money don't talk, and *nobody* walks. There were other reasons in Andy's case as well . . . but that belongs a little further along in my story.

There was a trusty, name of Kendricks, who was into me for some pretty heavy money back in the fifties, and it was four years before he got it all paid off. Most of the interest he paid me was information – in my line of work, you're dead if you can't find ways of keeping your ear to the ground. This Kendricks, for instance, had access to records I was never going to see running a stamper down in the goddam plate-shop.

Kendricks told me that the parole board vote was 7–0 against Andy Dufresne through 1957, 6–1 in '58, 7–0 again in '59, and 5–2 in '60. After that I don't know, but I do know that sixteen years later he was still in Cell 14 of Cellblock 5. By then, 1976, he was fifty-seven. They probably would have gotten big-hearted and let him out around 1983.

They give you life, and that's what they take – all of it that counts, anyway. Maybe they set you loose someday, but . . . well, listen: I knew this guy, Sherwood Bolton, his name was, and he had this pigeon in his cell. From 1945 until 1953, when they let him out, he had that pigeon. He wasn't any Birdman of Alcatraz; he just had this pigeon. Jake, he called him. He set Jake free a day before he, Sherwood, that is, was to walk, and Jake flew away just as pretty as you could want. But about a week after Sherwood Bolton left our happy little family, a friend of mine called me over to the west corner of the exercise yard, where Sherwood used to hang out, and my friend said: 'Isn't that Jake, Red?' It was. That pigeon was just as dead as a turd.

I remember the first time Andy Dufresne got in touch with me for something; I remember like it was yesterday. That wasn't the time he wanted Rita Hayworth, though. That came later. In that summer of 1948 he came around for something else.

Most of my deals are done right there in the exercise yard, and that's where this one went down. Our yard is big, much bigger than most. It's a perfect square, ninety yards on a side. The north side is the outer wall, with a guard-tower at either end. The guards up there are armed with binoculars and riot guns. The main gate is in that north side. The truck loading-bays are on the south side of the yard. There are five of them. Shawshank is a busy place during the work-week – deliveries in, deliveries out. We have the licence-plate factory, and a big industrial laundry that does all the prison wetwash, plus that of Kittery Receiving Hospital and the Eliot Sanatorium. There's also a big automotive garage where mechanic inmates fix prison, state, and municipal vehicles – not to mention the private cars of the screws, the administration officers . . . and, on more than one occasion, those of the parole board.

The east side is a thick stone wall full of tiny slit windows. Cellblock 5 is on the other side of that wall. The west side is Administration and the infirmary. Shawshank has never been as overcrowded as most prisons, and back in '48 it was only filled to something like two-thirds capacity, but at any given time there might be eighty to a hundred and twenty cons on the yard – playing toss with a football or a baseball, shooting craps, jawing at each other, making deals. On Sunday the place was even more crowded; on Sunday the place would have looked like a country holiday . . . if there had been any women.

It was on a Sunday that Andy first came to me. I had just finished talking to Elmore Armitage, a fellow who often came in handy to me, about a radio when Andy walked up. I knew who he was, of course; he had a reputation for being a snob and a cold fish. People were saying he was marked for trouble already. One of the people saying so was Bogs Diamond, a bad man to have on your case. Andy had no cellmate, and I'd heard that was just the way he wanted it, although people were already saying he thought his shit smelled sweeter than the ordinary. But I don't have to listen to rumors about a man when I can judge him for myself.

'Hello,' he said. 'I'm Andy Dufresne.' He offered his hand and I shook it. He wasn't a man to waste time being social; he got right to the point. 'I understand that you're a man who knows how to get things.'

I agreed that I was able to locate certain items from time to time.

'How do you do that?' Andy asked.

'Sometimes,' I said, 'things just seem to come into my hand. I can't explain it. Unless it's because I'm Irish.'

He smiled a little at that. 'I wonder if you could get me a rock-hammer.'

'What would that be, and why would you want it?'

Andy looked surprised. 'Do you make motivations a part of your business?' With words like those I could understand how he had gotten a reputation for being the snobby sort, the kind of guy who likes to put on airs – but I sensed a tiny thread of humor in his question.

'I'll tell you,' I said. 'If you wanted a toothbrush, I wouldn't ask questions. I'd just quote you a price. Because a toothbrush, you see, is a non-lethal sort of a weapon.'

'You have strong feelings about lethal weapons?'

'I do.'

An old friction-taped baseball flew toward us and he turned, cat-quick, and picked it out of the air. It was a move Frank Malzone would have been proud of. Andy flicked the ball back to where it had come from – just a quick and easy-looking flick of the wrist, but that throw had some mustard on it, just the same. I could see a lot of people were watching us with one eye as they went about their business. Probably the guards in the tower were watching, too. I won't gild the lily; there are cons that swing weight in any prison, maybe four or five in a small one, maybe two or three dozen in a big one. At Shawshank I was one of those with some weight, and what I thought of Andy Dufresne would have a lot to do with how his time went. He probably knew it too, but he wasn't kowtowing or sucking up to me, and I respected him for that.

'Fair enough. I'll tell you what it is and why I want it. A rock-hammer looks like a miniature pickaxe – about so long.' He held his hands about a foot apart, and that was when I first noticed how neatly kept his nails were. 'It's got a small sharp pick on one end and a flat, blunt hammerhead on the other. I want it because I like rocks.'

'Rocks,' I said.

'Squat down here a minute,' he said.

I humored him. We hunkered down on our haunches like Indians.

Andy took a handful of exercise yard dirt and began to sift it between his neat hands, so it emerged in a fine cloud. Small pebbles were left over, one or two sparkly, the rest dull and plain. One of the dull ones was quartz, but it was only dull until you'd rubbed it clean. Then it had a nice milky glow. Andy did the cleaning and then tossed it to me. I caught it and named it.

'Quartz, sure,' he said. 'And look. Mica. Shale, silted granite. Here's a piece of graded limestone, from when they cut this place out of the side of the hill.' He tossed them away and dusted his hands. 'I'm a rockhound. At least . . . I *was* a rockhound. In my old life. I'd like to be one again, on a limited scale.'

'Sunday expeditions in the exercise yard?' I asked, standing up. It was a silly idea, and yet . . . seeing that little piece of quartz had given my heart a funny tweak. I don't know exactly why; just an association with the outside world, I suppose. You didn't think of such things in terms of the yard. Quartz was something you picked out of a small, quick-running stream.

'Better to have Sunday expeditions here than no Sunday expeditions at all,' he said.

'You could plant an item like that rock-hammer in some-body's skull,' I remarked.

'I have no enemies here,' he said quietly.

'No?' I smiled. 'Wait awhile.'

'If there's trouble, I can handle it without using a rock-hammer.'

'Maybe you want to try an escape? Going under the wall? Because if you do –'

He laughed politely. When I saw the rock-hammer three weeks later, I understood why.

'You know,' I said, 'if anyone sees you with it, they'll take it away. If they saw you with a spoon, they'd take it away. What are you going to do, just sit down here in the yard and start bangin' away?'

'Oh, I believe I can do a lot better than that.'

I nodded. That part of it really wasn't my business, anyway. A man engages my services to get him something. Whether he can keep it or not after I get it is his business.

'How much would an item like that go for?' I asked. I was beginning to enjoy his quiet, low-key style. When you've spent ten years in stir, as I had then, you can get awfully tired of the bellowers and the braggarts and the loud-mouths. Yes, I think it would be fair to say I liked Andy from the first.

'Eight dollars in any rock-and-gem shop,' he said, 'but I realize that in a business like yours you work on a cost-plus basis—'

'Cost plus ten per cent is my going rate, but I have to go up some on a dangerous item. For something like the gadget you're talking about, it takes a little more goose-grease to get the wheels turning. Let's say ten dollars.'

'Ten it is.'

I looked at him, smiling a little. 'Have you *got* ten dollars?'

'I do,' he said quietly.

A long time after, I discovered that he had better than five hundred. He had brought it in with him. When they check you in at this hotel, one of the bellhops is obliged to bend you over and take a look up your works – but there are a lot of works, and, not to put too fine a point on it, a man who is really determined can get a fairly large item quite a ways up them – far enough to be out of sight, unless the bellhop you happen to draw is in the mood to pull on a rubber glove and go prospecting.

'That's fine,' I said. 'You ought to know what I expect if you get caught with what I get you.'

'I suppose I should,' he said, and I could tell by the slight change in his gray eyes that he knew exactly what I was going to say. It was a slight lightening, a gleam of his special ironic humor.

'If you get caught, you'll say you found it. That's about the long and short of it. They'll put you in solitary for three or four weeks . . . plus, of course, you'll lose your toy and you'll get a black mark on your record. If you give them my name, you and I will never do business again. Not for so much as a pair of shoelaces or a bag of Bugler. And I'll send some fellows around to lump you up. I don't like violence, but you'll understand my position. I can't allow it to get around that I can't handle myself. That would surely finish me.'

'Yes. I suppose it would, I understand, and you don't need to worry.'

'I never worry,' I said. 'In a place like this there's no percentage in it.'

He nodded and walked away. Three days later he walked

up beside me in the exercise yard during the laundry's morning break. He didn't speak or even look my way, but pressed a picture of the Hon. Alexander Hamilton into my hand as neatly as a good magician does a card-trick. He was a man who adapted fast. I got him his rock-hammer. I had it in my cell for one night, and it was just as he described it. It was no tool for escape (it would have taken a man just about six hundred years to tunnel under the wall using that rock-hammer, I figured), but I still felt some misgivings. If you planted that pickaxe end in a man's head, he would surely never listen to *Fibber McGee and Molly* on the radio again. And Andy had already begun having trouble with the sisters. I hoped it wasn't them he was wanting the rock-hammer for.

In the end, I trusted my judgment. Early the next morning, twenty minutes before the wake-up horn went off, I slipped the rock-hammer and a package of Camels to Ernie, the old trusty who swept the Cellblock 5 corridors until he was let free in 1956. He slipped it into his tunic without a word, and I didn't see the rock-hammer again for nineteen years.

The following Sunday Andy walked over to me in the exercise yard again. He was nothing to look at that day, I can tell you. His lower lip was swelled up so big it looked like a summer sausage, his right eye was swollen half-shut, and there was an ugly washboard scrape across one cheek. He was having his troubles with the sisters, all right, but he never mentioned them. 'Thanks for the tool,' he said, and walked away.

I watched him curiously. He walked a few steps, saw something in the dirt, bent over, and picked it up. It was a small rock. Prison fatigues, except for those worn by mechanics when they're on the job, have no pockets. But there are ways to get around that. The little pebble disap-peared up Andy's sleeve and didn't come down. I admired that . . . and I admired him. In spite of the problems he was having, he was going on with his life. There are thousands who don't or won't or can't, and plenty of them aren't in prison, either. And I noticed that, although his face still looked as if a twister had happened to it, his hands were still neat and clean, the nails well-kept.

I didn't see much of him over the next six months; Andy spent a lot of that time in solitary.

A few words about the sisters.

In a lot of pens they are known as bull queers or jailhouse susies – just lately the term in fashion is 'killer queens'. But in Shawshank they were always the sisters. I don't know why, but other than the name I guess there was no difference.

It comes as no surprise to most these days that there's a lot of buggery going on inside the walls – except to some of the new fish, maybe, who have the misfortune to be young, slim, good-looking, and unwary – but homosexuality, like straight sex, comes in a hundred different shapes and forms. There are men who can't stand to be without sex of some kind and turn to another man to keep from going crazy. Usually what follows is an arrangement between two funda-mentally heterosexual men, although I've sometimes wondered if they are quite as heterosexual as they thought they were going to be when they get back to their wives or their girlfriends.

There are also men who get 'turned' in prison. In the current parlance they 'go gay', or 'come out of the closet'.

Mostly (but not always) they play the female, and their favors are competed for fiercely.

And then there are the sisters.

They are to prison society what the rapist is to the society outside the walls. They're usually long-timers, doing hard bullets for brutal crimes. Their prey is the young, the weak, and the inexperienced . . . or, as in the case of Andy Dufresne, the weak-looking. Their hunting grounds are the showers, the cramped, tunnel-like area way behind the industrial washers in the laundry, sometimes the infirmary. On more than one occasion rape has occurred in the closet-sized projection booth behind the auditorium. Most often what the sisters take by force they could have had for free, if they wanted it; those who have been turned always seem to have 'crushes' on one sister or another, like teenage girls with their Sinatras, Presleys, or Redfords. But for the sisters, the joy has always been in taking it by force . . . and I guess it always will be.

Because of his small size and fair good looks (and maybe also because of that very quality of self-possession I had admired), the sisters were after Andy from the day he walked in. If this was some kind of fairy story, I'd tell you that Andy fought the good fight until they left him alone. I wish I could say that, but I can't. Prison is no fairy-tale world.

The first time for him was in the shower less than three days after he joined our happy Shawshank family. Just a lot of slap and tickle that time, I understand. They like to size you up before they make their real move, like jackals finding out if the prey is as weak and hamstrung as it looks.

Andy punched back and bloodied the lip of a big, hulking sister named Bogs Diamond – gone these many years since to who knows where. A guard broke it up before it could go any further, but Bogs promised to get him – and Bogs did.

The second time was behind the washers in the laundry. A lot has gone on in that long, dusty, and narrow space over the years; the guards know about it and just let it be. It's dim and littered with bags of washing and bleaching compound, drums of Hexlite catalyst, as harmless as salt if your hands are dry, murderous as battery acid if they're wet. The guards don't like to go back there. There's no room to maneuver, and one of the first things they teach them when they come to work in a place like this is to never let the cons get you in a place where you can't back up.

Bogs wasn't there that day, but Henley Backus, who had been washroom foreman down there since 1922, told me that four of his friends were. Andy held them at bay for a while with a scoop of Hexlite, threatening to throw it in their eyes if they came any closer, but he tripped trying to back around one of the big Washex four-pockets. That was all it took. They were on him.

I guess the phrase gang-rape is one that doesn't change much from one generation to the next. That's what they did to him, those four sisters. They bent him over a gearbox and one of them held a Phillips screwdriver to his temple while they gave him the business. It rips you up some, but not bad – am I speaking from personal experience, you ask? – I only wish I weren't. You bleed for a while. If you don't want some clown asking you if you just started your period, you wad up a bunch of toilet paper and keep it down the back of your underwear until it stops. The bleeding really is like a menstrual flow; it keeps up for two, maybe three days, a slow trickle. Then it stops. No harm done, unless they've done something even more unnatural to you. No *physical* harm done – but rape is rape, and eventually you have to look at your face in the mirror again and decide what to make of yourself.

Andy went through that alone, the way he went through everything alone in those days. He must have come to the conclusion that others before him had come to, namely, that there are only two ways to deal with the sisters: fight them and get taken, or just get taken.

He decided to fight. When Bogs and two of his buddies came after him a week or so after the laundry incident ('I heard ya got broke in,' Bogs said, according to Ernie, who was around at the time), Andy slugged it out with them. He broke the nose of a fellow named Rooster MacBride, a heavy-gutted farmer who was in for beating his stepdaughter to death. Rooster died in here, I'm happy to add.

They took him, all three of them. When it was done, Rooster and the other egg – it might have been Pete Verness, but I'm not completely sure – forced Andy down to his knees. Bogs Diamond stepped in front of him. He had a pearl-handled razor in those days with the words *Diamond Pearl* engraved on both sides of the grip. He opened it and said, 'I'm gonna open my fly now, mister man, and you're going to swallow what I give you to swallow. And when you done swallowed mine, you're gonna swallow Rooster's. I guess you done broke his nose and I think he ought to have something to pay for it.'

Andy said, 'Anything of yours that you stick in my mouth, you're going to lose it.'

Bogs looked at Andy like he was crazy, Ernie said.

'No,' he told Andy, talking to him slowly, like Andy was a stupid kid. 'You didn't understand what I said. You do anything like that and I'll put all eight inches of this steel into your ear. Get it?'

'I understand what you said. I don't think you understand *me*. I'm going to bite whatever you stick into my mouth. You can put that razor in my brain, I guess, but you should know that a sudden serious brain injury causes the victim to simultaneously urinate, defecate . . . and bite down.'

He looked up at Bogs, smiling that little smile of his, old Ernie said, as if the three of them had been discussing stocks and bonds with him instead of throwing it to him just as hard as they could. Just as if he was wearing one of his three-piece bankers' suits instead of kneeling on a dirty broom-closet floor with his pants around his ankles and blood trickling down the insides of his thighs.

'In fact,' he went on, 'I understand that the bite-reflex is sometimes so strong that the victim's jaws have to be pried open with a crowbar or a jackhandle.'

Bogs didn't put anything in Andy's mouth that night in late February of 1948, and neither did Rooster MacBride, and so far as I know, no one else ever did, either. What the three of them did was to beat Andy within an inch of his life, and all four of them ended up doing a jolt in solitary. Andy and Rooster MacBride went by way of the infirmary.

How many times did that particular crew have at him? I don't know. I think Rooster lost his taste fairly early on – being in nose-splints for a month can do that to a fellow – and Bogs Diamond left off that summer, all at once.

That was a strange thing. Bogs was found in his cell, badly beaten, one morning in early June, when he didn't show up in the breakfast nose-count. He wouldn't say who had done it, or how they had gotten to him, but being in my business, I know that a screw can be bribed to do almost anything except get a gun for an inmate. They didn't make big salaries then, and they don't now. And in those days there was no electronic locking system, no closed-circuit TV, no master-switches which controlled whole areas of the prison. Back in 1948, each cellblock had its own turnkey. A guard could have been bribed real easy to let someone – maybe two or three someones – into the block, and, yes, even into Diamond's cell.

Of course a job like that would have cost a lot of money. Not by outside standards, no. Prison economics are on a smaller scale. When you've been in here a while, a dollar bill in your hand looks like a twenty did outside. My guess is, that if Bogs was done, it cost someone a serious piece of change – fifteen bucks, we'll say, for the turnkey, and two or three apiece for each of the lump-up guys.

I'm not saying it was Andy Dufresne, but I do know that he brought in five hundred dollars when he came, and he was a banker in the straight world – a man who understands better than the rest of us the ways in which money can become power.

And I know this: After the beating – the three broken ribs, the hemorrhaged eye, the sprained back and the dislocated hip – Bogs Diamond left Andy alone. In fact, after that he left everyone pretty much alone. He got to be like a high wind in the summertime, all bluster and no bite. You could say, in fact, that he turned into a 'weak sister'.

That was the end of Bogs Diamond, a man who might eventually have killed Andy if Andy hadn't taken steps to prevent it (if it *was* him who took the steps). But it wasn't the end of Andy's trouble with the sisters. There was a little hiatus, and then it began again, although not so hard nor so often. Jackals like easy prey, and there were easier pickings around than Andy Dufresne.

He always fought them, that's what I remember. He knew, I guess, that if you let them have at you even once, without fighting it, it got that much easier to let them have their way without fighting next time. So Andy would turn up with bruises on his face every once in a while, and there was the matter of the two broken fingers six or eight months after Diamond's beating. Oh yes – and sometime in late 1949, the man landed in the infirmary with a broken cheekbone that was probably the result of someone swinging a nice chunk of pipe with the business-end wrapped in flannel. He always fought back, and as a result, he did his time in solitary. But I don't think solitary was the hardship for Andy that it was for some men. He got along with himself.

The sisters was something he adjusted himself to – and then, in 1950, it stopped almost completely. That is a part of my story that I'll get to in due time.

In the fall of 1948, Andy met me one morning in the exercise yard and asked me if I could get him half a dozen rock-blankets.

'What the hell are those?' I asked.

He told me that was just what rockhounds called them; they were polishing cloths about the size of dishtowels. They were heavily padded, with a smooth side and a rough side – the smooth side like fine-grained sandpaper, the rough side almost as abrasive as industrial steel wool (Andy also kept a box of that in his cell, although he didn't get it from me – I imagine he kited it from the prison laundry).

I told him I thought we could do business on those, and I ended up getting them from the very same rock-and-gem shop where I'd arranged to get the rock-hammer. This time I charged Andy my usual ten per cent and not a penny more. I didn't see anything lethal or even dangerous in a dozen 7″ x 7″ squares of padded cloth. Rock-blankets, indeed.

It was about five months later that Andy asked if I could get him Rita Hayworth. That conversation took place in the auditorium, during a movie-show. Nowadays we get the movie-shows once or twice a week, but back then the shows were a monthly event. Usually the movies we got had a morally uplifting message to them, and this one, *The Lost Weekend*, was no different. The moral was that it's dangerous to drink. It was a moral we could take some comfort in.

Andy maneuvred to get next to me, and about halfway through the show he leaned a little closer and asked if I could get him Rita Hayworth. I'll tell you the truth, it kind of tickled me. He was usually cool, calm, and collected, but that night he was jumpy as hell, almost embarrassed, as if he was asking me to get him a load of Trojans or one of those sheepskin-lined gadgets that are supposed to 'enhance your solitary pleasure,' as the magazines put it. He seemed over-charged, a man on the verge of blowing his radiator.

'I can get her,' I said. 'No sweat, calm down. You want the big one or the little one?' At that time Rita was my best girl (a few years before it had been Betty Grable) and she came in two sizes. For a buck you could get the little Rita. For two-fifty you could have the big Rita, four feet high and all woman.

'The big one,' he said, not looking at me. I tell you, he was a hot sketch that night. He was blushing just like a kid trying to get into a kootch show with his big brother's draft-card. 'Can you do it?'

'Take it easy, sure I can. Does a bear shit in the woods?' The audience was applauding and catcalling as the bugs came out of the walls to get Ray Milland, who was having a bad case of the DT's.

'How soon?'

'A week. Maybe less.'

'Okay.' But he sounded disappointed, as if he had been hoping I had one stuffed down my pants right then. 'How much?'

I quoted him the wholesale price. I could afford to give him this one at cost; he'd been a good customer, what with his rock-hammer and his rock-blankets. Furthermore, he'd been a good boy – on more than one night when he was having his problems with Bogs, Rooster, and the rest, I wondered how long it would be before he used the rock-hammer to crack someone's head open.

Posters are a big part of my business, just behind the booze and cigarettes, usually half a step ahead of the reefer. In the 60s the business exploded in every direction, with a lot of people wanting funky hang-ups like Jimi Hendrix, Bob Dylan, that Easy Rider poster. But mostly it's girls; one pinup queen after another.

A few days after I spoke to Ernie, a laundry driver I did business with back then brought in better than sixty posters, most of them Rita Hayworths. You may even remember the picture; I sure do. Rita is dressed – sort of – in a bathing suit, one hand behind her head, her eyes half closed, those full, sulky red lips parted. They called it Rita Hayworth, but they might as well have called it Woman in Heat.

The prison administration knows about the black market, in case you were wondering. Sure they do. They probably know as much about my business as I do myself. They live with it because they know that a prison is like a big pressure cooker, and there have to be vents somewhere to let off steam. They make the occasional bust, and I've done time in solitary a time or three over the years, but when it's something like posters, they wink. Live and let live. And when a big Rita Hayworth went up in some fishie's cell, the assumption was that it came in the mail from a friend or a relative. Of course all the care-packages from friends and relatives are opened and the contents inventoried, but who goes back and re-checks the inventory sheets for something as harmless as a Rita Hayworth or an Ava Gardner pin-up? When you're in a pressure-cooker you learn to live and let live or somebody will carve you a brand-new mouth just above the Adam's apple. You learn to make allowances.

It was Ernie again who took the poster up to Andy's cell, 14, from my own, 6. And it was Ernie who brought back the note, written in Andy's careful hand, just one word: 'Thanks.'

A little while later, as they filed us out for morning chow, I glanced into his cell and saw Rita over his bunk in all her swimsuited glory, one hand behind her head, her eyes half-closed, those soft, satiny lips parted. It was over his bunk where he could look at her nights, after lights out, in the glow of the arc sodiums in the exercise yard.

But in the bright morning sunlight, there were dark slashes

across her face – the shadow of the bars on his single slit-window.

Now I'm going to tell you what happened in mid-May of 1950 that finally ended Andy's three-year series of skirmishes with the sisters. It was also the incident which eventually got him out of the laundry and into the library, where he filled out his work-time until he left our happy little family earlier this year.

You may have noticed how much of what I've told you already is hearsay – someone saw something and told me and I told you. Well, in some cases I've simplified it even more than it really was, and have actually repeated (or will repeat) fourth- or fifth-hand information. That's the way it is here. The grapevine is very real, and you have to use it if you're going to stay ahead. Also, of course, you have to know how to pick out the grains of truth from the chaff of lies, rumors, and wish-it-had-beens.

You may also have gotten the idea that I'm describing someone who's more legend than man, and I would have to agree that there's some truth to that. To us long-timers who knew Andy over a space of years, there was an element of fantasy to him, a sense, almost, of myth-magic, if you get what I mean. That story I passed on about Andy refusing to give Bogs Diamond a head-job is part of that myth, and how he kept on fighting the sisters is part of it, and how he got the library job is part of it, too . . . but with one important difference: I was there and I saw what happened, and I swear on my mother's name that it's all true. The oath of a convicted murderer may not be worth much, but believe this: I don't lie.

Andy and I were on fair speaking terms by then. The guy fascinated me. Looking back to the poster episode, I see there's one thing I neglected to tell you, and maybe I should. Five weeks after he hung Rita up (I'd forgotten all about it by then, and had gone on to other deals), Ernie passed a small white box through the bars of my cell.

'From Dufresne,' he said, low, and never missed a stroke with his push-broom.

'Thanks, Ernie,' I said, and slipped him half a pack of Camels.

Now what the hell was this, I was wondering as I slipped the cover from the box. There was a lot of white cotton inside, and below that . . .

I looked for a long time. For a few minutes it was like I didn't even dare touch them, they were so pretty. There's a crying shortage of pretty things in the slam, and the real pity of it is that a lot of men don't even seem to miss them.

There were two pieces of quartz in that box, both of them carefully polished. They had been chipped into driftwood shapes. There were little sparkles of iron pyrities in them like flecks of gold. If they hadn't been so heavy, they would have served as a fine pair of men's cufflinks – they were that close to being a matched set.

How much work went into creating those two pieces? Hours and hours after lights out, I knew that. First the chipping and shaping, and then the almost endless polishing and finishing with those rock-blankets. Looking at them, I felt the warmth that any man or woman feels when he or she is looking at something pretty, something that has been *worked* and *made* – that's the thing that really separates us from the animals, I think – and I felt something else, too. A sense of awe for the man's brute persistence. But I never knew just how persistent Andy Dufresne could be until much later.

In May of 1950, the powers that be decided that the roof of the license-plate factory ought to be resurfaced with roofing tar. They wanted it done before it got too hot up there, and they asked for volunteers for the work, which was planned to take about a week. More than seventy men spoke up, because it was outside work and May is one damn fine month for outside work. Nine or ten names were drawn out of a hat, and two of them happened to be Andy's and my own.

For the next week we'd be marched out to the exercise yard after breakfast, with two guards up front and two more behind . . . plus all the guards in the towers keeping a weather eye on the proceedings through their field-glasses for good measure.

Four of us would be carrying a big extension ladder on those morning marches – I always got a kick out of the way Dickie Betts, who was on that job, called that sort of ladder an extensible – and we'd put it up against the side of that low, flat building. Then we'd start bucket-brigading hot buckets of tar up to the roof. Spill that shit on you and you'd jitterbug all the way to the infirmary.

There were six guards on the project, all of them picked on the basis of seniority. It was almost as good as a week's vacation, because instead of sweating it out in the laundry or the plate-shop or standing over a bunch of cons cutting pulp or brush somewhere out in the willywags, they were having a regular May holiday in the sun, just sitting there with their backs up against the low parapet, shooting the bull back and forth.

They didn't even have to keep more than half an eye on us, because the south wall sentry post was close enough so that the fellows up there could have spit their chews on us, if they'd wanted to. If anyone on the roof-sealing party had made one funny move, it would take four seconds to cut him smack in two with .45 caliber machine-gun bullets. So those screws just sat there and took their ease. All they needed was a couple of six-packs buried in crushed ice, and they would have been the lords of all creation.

One of them was a fellow named Byron Hadley, and in that year of 1950, he'd been at Shawshank longer than I had. Longer than the last two wardens put together, as a matter of fact. The fellow running the show in 1950 was a prissy-looking downeast Yankee named George Dunahy. He had a degree in penal administration. No one liked him, as far as I could tell, except the people who had gotten him his appointment. I heard that he wasn't interested in anything but compiling statistics for a book (which was later published by a small New England outfit called Light Side Press, where he probably had to pay to have it done), which team won the intramural baseball championship each September, and getting a death-penalty law passed in Maine. A regular bear for the death-penalty was George Dunahy. He was fired off the job in 1953, when it came out he was running a discount auto repair service down in the prison garage and splitting the profits with Byron Hadley and Greg Stammas. Hadley and Stammas came out of that one okay – they were old hands at keeping their asses covered – but Dunahy took a walk. No one was sorry to see him go, but nobody was exactly pleased to see Greg Stammas step into his shoes, either. He was a short man with a tight, hard gut and the coldest brown eyes you ever saw. He always had a painful, pursed little grin on his face, as if he had to go to the bathroom and couldn't quite manage it. During Stammas's tenure as warden there was a lot of brutality at Shawshank, and although I have no proof, I believe there were maybe half a dozen moonlight burials in the stand of scrub forest that lies east of the prison. Dunahy was bad, but Greg Stammas was a cruel, wretched, cold-hearted man.

He and Byron Hadley were good friends. As warden, George Dunahy was nothing but a posturing figurehead; it was Stammas, and through him, Hadley, who actually administered the prison.

Hadley was a tall, shambling man with thinning red hair. He sunburned easily and he talked loud and if you didn't move fast enough to suit him, he'd clout you with his stick. On that day, our third on the roof, he was talking to another guard named Mert Entwhistle.

Hadley had gotten some amazingly good news, so he was griping about it. That was his style – he was a thankless man with not a good word for anyone, a man who was convinced that the whole world was against him. The world had cheated him out of the best years of his life, and the world would be more than happy to cheat him out of the rest. I have seen some screws that I thought were almost saintly, and I think I know why that happens – they are able to see the difference between their own lives, poor and struggling as they might be, and the lives of the men they are paid by the state to watch over. These guards are able to formulate a comparison concerning pain. Others can't, or won't.

For Byron Hadley there was no basis of comparison. He could sit there, cool and at his ease under the warm May sun and find the gall to mourn his own good luck while less than ten feet away a bunch of men were working and sweating and burning their hands on great big buckets filled with bubbling tar, men who had to work so hard in their ordinary round of days that this looked like a *respite*. You may remember the old question, the one that's supposed to define your outlook on life when you answer it. For Byron Hadley the answer would always be *half empty, the glass is half empty*. Forever and ever, amen. If you gave him a cool drink of apple cider, he'd think about vinegar. If you told him his wife had always been faithful to him, he'd tell you it was because she was so damn ugly.

So there he sat, talking to Mert Entwhistle loud enough for all of us to hear, his broad white forehead already starting to redden with the sun. He had one hand thrown back over the low parapet surrounding the roof. The other was on the butt of his .38.

We all got the story along with Mert. It seemed that Hadley's older brother had gone off to Texas some fourteen years ago and the rest of the family hadn't heard from the son of a bitch since. They had all assumed he was dead, and good riddance. Then, a week and a half ago, a lawyer had called them long-distance from Austin. It seemed that Hadley's brother had died four months ago, and a rich man at that ('It's frigging incredible how lucky some assholes can get,' this paragon of gratitude on the plate-shop roof said). The money had come as a result of oil and oil-leases, and there was close to a million dollars.

No, Hadley wasn't a millionaire – that might have made

even him happy, at least for a while – but the brother had left a pretty damned decent bequest of thirty-five thousand dollars to each surviving member of his family back in Maine, if they could be found. Not bad. Like getting lucky and winning a sweepstakes.

But to Byron Hadley the glass was always half-empty. He spent most of the morning bitching to Mert about the bite that the goddam government was going to take out of his windfall. 'They'll leave me about enough to buy a new car with,' he allowed, 'and then what happens? You have to pay the damn taxes on the car, and the repairs and maintenance, you get your goddam kids pestering you to take 'em for a ride with the top down –'

'And to *drive* it, if they're old enough,' Mert said. Old Mert Entwhistle knew which side his bread was buttered on, and he didn't say what must have been as obvious to him as to the rest of us: If that money's worrying you so bad, Byron old kid old sock, I'll just take it off your hands. After all, what are friends for?

'That's right, wanting to drive it, wanting to *learn* to drive on it, for Chrissake,' Byron said with a shudder. 'Then what happens at the end of the year? If you figured the tax wrong and you don't have enough left over to pay the overdraft, you got to pay out of your own pocket, or maybe even borrow it from one of those kikey loan agencies. And they audit you anyway, you know. It don't matter. And when the government audits you, they always take more. Who can fight Uncle Sam? He puts his hand inside your shirt and squeezes your tit until it's purple, and you end up getting the short end. Christ.'

He lapsed into a morose silence, thinking of what terrible

bad luck he'd had to inherit that $35,000. Andy Dufresne had been spreading tar with a big Padd brush less than fifteen feet away and now he tossed it into his pail and walked over to where Mert and Hadley were sitting.

We all tightened up, and I saw one of the other screws, Tim Youngblood, drag his hand down to where his pistol was holstered. One of the fellows in the sentry tower struck his partner on the arm and they both turned, too. For one moment I thought Andy was going to get shot, or clubbed, or both.

Then he said, very softly, to Hadley: 'Do you trust your wife?'

Hadley just stared at him. He was starting to get red in the face, and I knew that was a bad sign. In about three seconds he was going to pull his billy and give Andy the butt end of it right in the solar plexus, where that big bundle of nerves is. A hard enough hit there can kill you, but they always go for it. If it doesn't kill you it will paralyze you long enough to forget whatever cute move it was that you had planned.

'Boy,' Hadley said, 'I'll give you just one chance to pick up that Padd. And then you're goin' off this roof on your head.'

Andy just looked at him, very calm and still. His eyes were like ice. It was as if he hadn't heard. And I found myself wanting to tell him how it was, to give him the crash course. The crash course is you *never* let on that you hear the guards talking, you *never* try to horn in on their conversation unless you're asked (and then you always tell them just what they want to hear and shut up again). Black man, white man, red man, yellow man, in prison it doesn't matter because we've got our own brand of equality. In prison every con's a nigger

445

and you have to get used to the idea if you intend to survive men like Hadley and Greg Stammas, who really would kill you just as soon as look at you. When you're in stir you belong to the state and if you forget it, woe is you. I've known men who've lost eyes, men who've lost toes and fingers; I knew one man who lost the tip of his penis and counted himself lucky that was all he lost. I wanted to tell Andy that it was already too late. He could go back and pick up his brush and there would still be some big lug waiting for him in the showers that night, ready to charlie-horse both of his legs and leave him writhing on the cement. You could buy a lug like that for a pack of cigarettes or three Baby Ruths. Most of all, I wanted to tell him not to make it any worse than it already was.

What I did was to keep on running tar onto the roof as if nothing at all was happening. Like everyone else, I look after my own ass first. I have to. It's cracked already, and in Shawshank there have always been Hadleys willing to finish the job of breaking it.

Andy said, 'Maybe I put it wrong. Whether you trust her or not is immaterial. The problem is whether or not you believe she would ever go behind your back, try to hamstring you.'

Hadley got up. Mert got up. Tim Youngblood got up. Hadley's face was as red as the side of a firebarn. 'Your only problem,' he said, 'is going to be how many bones you still get unbroken. You can count them in the infirmary. Come on, Mert. We're throwing this sucker over the side.'

Tim Youngblood drew his gun. The rest of us kept tarring like mad. The sun beat down. They were going to do it; Hadley and Mert were simply going to pitch him over the side. Terrible accident. Dufresne, prisoner 81433-SHNK, was taking a couple of empties down and slipped on the ladder. Too bad.

They laid hold of him, Mert on the right arm, Hadley on the left. Andy didn't resist. His eyes never left Hadley's red, horsey face.

'If you've got your thumb on her, Mr Hadley,' he said in that same calm, composed voice, 'there's not a reason why you shouldn't have every cent of that money. Final score, Mr Byron Hadley thirty-five thousand, Uncle Sam zip.'

Mert started to drag him toward the edge. Hadley just stood still. For a moment Andy was like a rope between them in a tug-of-war game. Then Hadley said, 'Hold on one second, Mert. What do you mean, boy?'

'I mean, if you've got your thumb on your wife, you can give it to her,' Andy said.

'You better start making sense, boy, or you're going over.'

'The IRS allows you a one-time-only gift to your spouse,' Andy said. 'It's good up to sixty thousand dollars.'

Hadley was now looking at Andy as if he had been poleaxed. 'Naw, that ain't right,' he said. 'Tax *free*?'

'Tax free,' Andy said. 'IRS can't touch one cent.'

'How would you know a thing like that?'

Tim Youngblood said: 'He used to be a banker, Byron. I s'pose he might—'

'Shut ya head, Trout,' Hadley said without looking at him. Tim Youngblood flushed and shut up. Some of the guards called him Trout because of his thick lips and buggy eyes. Hadley kept looking at Andy. 'You're the smart banker who shot his wife. Why should I believe a smart banker like you? So I can wind up in here breaking rocks right alongside you? You'd like that, wouldn't you?'

Andy said quietly, 'If you went to jail for tax evasion, you'd go to a federal penitentiary, not Shawshank. But you won't. The tax-free gift to the spouse is a perfectly legal loophole. I've done dozens . . . no, hundreds of them. It's meant primarily for people with small businesses to pass on, or for people who come into one-time-only windfalls. Like yourself.'

'I think you're lying,' Hadley said, but he didn't – you could see he didn't. There was an emotion dawning on his face, something that was grotesque overlying that long, ugly countenance and that receding, sunburned brow. An almost obscene emotion when seen on the features of Byron Hadley. It was hope.

'No, I'm not lying. There's no reason why you should take my word for it, either. Engage a lawyer—'

'Ambulance-chasing highway-robbing cocksuckers!' Hadley cried.

Andy shrugged. 'Then go to the IRS. They'll tell you the same thing for free. Actually, you don't need me to tell you at all. You would have investigated the matter for yourself.'

'You fucking-A. I don't need any smart wife-killing banker to show me where the bear shit in the buckwheat.'

'You'll need a tax lawyer or a banker to set up the gift for you and that will cost you something,' Andy said. 'Or . . . if you were interested, I'd be glad to set it up for you nearly free of charge. The price would be three beers apiece for my co-workers—'

'Co-workers,' Mert said, and let out a rusty guffaw. He slapped his knee. A real knee-slapper was old Mert, and I hope he died of intestinal cancer in a part of the world where morphine is as of yet undiscovered. 'Co-workers, ain't that cute? Co-workers! You ain't got any—'

'Shut your friggin' trap,' Hadley growled, and Mert shut. Hadley looked at Andy again. 'What was you saying?'

'I was saying that I'd only ask three beers apiece for my co-workers, if that seems fair,' Andy said. 'I think a man feels more like a man when he's working out of doors in the springtime if he can have a bottle of suds. That's only my opinion. It would go down smooth, and I'm sure you'd have their gratitude.'

I have talked to some of the other men who were up there that day – Rennie Martin, Logan St Pierre, and Paul Bonsaint were three of them – and we all saw the same thing then . . . *felt* the same thing. Suddenly it was Andy who had the upper hand. It was Hadley who had the gun on his hip and the billy in his hand, Hadley who had his friend Greg Stammas behind him and the whole prison administration behind Stammas, the whole power of the state behind *that*, but all at once in that golden sunshine it didn't matter, and I felt my heart leap up in my chest as it never had since the truck drove me and four others through the gate back in 1938 and I stepped out into the exercise yard.

Andy was looking at Hadley with those cold, clear, calm eyes, and it wasn't just the thirty-five thousand then, we all agreed on that. I've played it over and over in my mind and I *know*. It was man against man, and Andy simply *forced* him, the way a strong man can force a weaker man's wrist to the table in a game of Indian wrestling. There was no reason, you see, why Hadley couldn't've given Mert the nod at that very minute, pitched Andy overside onto his head, and still taken Andy's advice.

No reason. *But he didn't.*

'I could get you all a couple of beers if I wanted to,'

Hadley said. 'A beer does taste good while you're workin'.' The colossal prick even managed to sound magnanimous.

'I'd just give you one piece of advice the IRS wouldn't bother with,' Andy said. His eyes were fixed unwinkingly on Hadley's. 'Make the gift to your wife if you're *sure*. If you think there's even a chance she might double-cross you or backshoot you, we could work out something else—'

'Double-cross me?' Hadley asked harshly. 'Double-cross *me*? Mr Hotshot Banker, if she ate her way through a boxcar of Ex-Lax, she wouldn't dare fart unless I gave her the nod.'

Mert, Youngblood, and the other screws yucked it up dutifully. Andy never cracked a smile.

'I'll write down the forms you need,' he said. 'You can get them at the post office, and I'll fill them out for your signature.'

That sounded suitably important, and Hadley's chest swelled. Then he glared around at the rest of us and hollered, 'What are you jimmies starin' at? Move your asses, goddammit!' He looked back at Andy. 'You come over here with me, hotshot. And listen to me well: if you're Jewing me somehow, you're gonna find yourself chasing your head around Shower C before the week's out.'

'Yes, I understand that,' Andy said softly.

And he did understand it. The way it turned out, he understood a lot more than I did – more than any of us did.

That's how, on the second-to-last day of the job, the convict crew that tarred the plate-factory roof in 1950 ended up sitting in a row at ten o'clock on a spring morning, drinking Black Label beer supplied by the hardest screw that ever walked a turn at Shawshank Prison. That beer was piss-warm, but it was still the best I ever had in my life. We sat and drank it and felt the sun on our shoulders, and not even the expression of half-amusement, half-contempt on Hadley's face – as if he was watching apes drink beer instead of men – could spoil it. It lasted twenty minutes, that beer-break, and for those twenty minutes we felt like free men. We could have been drinking beer and tarring the roof of one of our own houses.

Only Andy didn't drink. I already told you about his drinking habits. He sat hunkered down in the shade, hands dangling between his knees, watching us and smiling a little. It's amazing how many men remember him that way, and amazing how many men were on that work-crew when Andy Dufresne faced down Byron Hadley. I thought there were nine or ten of us, but by 1955 there must have been two hundred of us, maybe more . . . if you believed what you heard.

So, yeah – if you asked me to give you a flat-out answer to the question of whether I'm trying to tell you about a man or a legend that got made up around the man, like a pearl around a little piece of grit – I'd have to say that the answer lies somewhere in between. All I know for sure is that Andy Dufresne wasn't much like me or anyone else I ever knew since I came inside. He brought in five hundred dollars jammed up his back porch, but somehow that graymeat son of a bitch managed to bring in something else as well. A sense of his own worth, maybe, or a feeling that he would be the winner in the end . . . or maybe it was only a sense of freedom, even inside these goddamned grey walls. It was a kind of inner light he carried around with him. I only knew him to lose that light once, and that is also a part of this story.

By World Series time of 1950 – this was the year the Philadelphia Whiz Kids dropped four straight, you will remember – Andy was having no more trouble from the sisters. Stammas and Hadley had passed the word. If Andy Dufresne came to either of them or any of the other screws that formed a part of their coterie, and showed so much as a single drop of blood in his underpants, every sister in Shawshank would go to bed that night with a headache. They didn't fight it. As I have pointed out, there was always an eighteen-year-old car thief or a firebug or some guy who'd gotten his kicks handling little children. After the day on the plate-shop roof, Andy went his way and the sisters went theirs.

He was working in the library then, under a tough old con named Brooks Hatlen. Hatlen had gotten the job back in the late 20s because he had a college education. Brooksie's degree was in animal husbandry, true enough, but college educations in institutes of lower learning like The Shank are so rare that it's a case of beggars not being able to be choosers.

In 1952 Brooksie, who had killed his wife and daughter after a losing streak at poker back when Coolidge was President, was paroled. As usual, the state in all its wisdom had let him go long after any chance he might have had to become a useful part of society was gone. He was sixty-eight and arthritic when he tottered out of the main gate in his Polish suit and his French shoes, his parole papers in one hand and a Greyhound bus ticket in the other. He was crying when he left. Shawshank was his world. What lay beyond its walls was as terrible to Brooks as the Western Seas had been to superstitious 13th-century sailors. In prison, Brooksie had been a person of some importance. He was the head librarian, an educated man. If he went to the Kittery library and asked for a job, they wouldn't give him a library card. I heard he died in a home for indigent old folks up Freeport way in 1952, and at that he lasted about six months longer than I thought he would. Yeah, I guess the state got its own back on Brooksie, all right. They trained him to like it inside the shithouse and then they threw him out.

Andy succeeded to Brooksie's job, and he was head librarian for twenty-three years. He used the same force of will I'd seen him use on Byron Hadley to get what he wanted for the library, and I saw him gradually turn one small room (which still smelled of turpentine because it had been a paint closet until 1922 and had never been properly aired) lined with *Reader's Digest Condensed Books* and *National Geographics* into the best prison library in New England.

He did it a step at a time. He put a suggestion box by the door and patiently weeded out such attempts at humour as *More Fuk-Boox Pleeze* and *Escape in 10 EZ Lesions*. He got hold of the things the prisoners seemed serious about. He wrote to three major book clubs in New York and got two of them, The Literary Guild and The Book of the Month Club, to send editions of all their major selections to us at a special cheap rate. He discovered a hunger for information on such small hobbies as soap-carving, woodworking, sleight of hand, and card solitaire. He got all the books he could on such subjects. And those two jailhouse staples, Erle Stanley Gardner and Louis L'Amour. Cons never seem to get enough of the courtroom or the open range. And yes, he did keep a box of fairly spicy paperbacks under the checkout desk, loaning them out carefully and making sure they always got back. Even so, each new acquisition of that type was quickly read to tatters.

He began to write to the State Senate in Augusta in 1954. Stammas was warden by then, and he used to pretend Andy was some sort of mascot. He was always in the library, shooting the bull with Andy, and sometimes he'd even throw a paternal arm around Andy's shoulders or give him a goose. He didn't fool anybody. Andy Dufresne was no one's mascot.

He told Andy that maybe he'd been a banker on the outside, but that part of his life was receding rapidly into his past and he had better get a hold on the facts of prison life. As far as that bunch of jumped-up Republican Rotarians in Augusta was concerned, there were only three viable expenditures of the taxpayers' money in the field of prisons and corrections. Number one was more walls, number two was more bars, and number three was more guards. As far as the State Senate was concerned, Stammas explained, the folks in Thomaston and Shawshank and Pittsfield and South Portland were the scum of the earth. They were there to do hard time, and by God and Sonny Jesus, it was hard time they were going to do. And if there were a few weevils in the bread, wasn't that just too fucking bad?

Andy smiled his small, composed smile and asked Stammas what would happen to a block of concrete if a drop of water fell on it once every year for a million years. Stammas laughed and clapped Andy on the back. 'You got no million years, old horse, but if you did, I believe you'd do it with that same little grin on your face. You go on and write your letters. I'll even mail them for you if you pay for the stamps.'

Which Andy did. And he had the last laugh, although Stammas and Hadley weren't around to see it. Andy's requests for library funds were routinely turned down until 1960, when he received a check for two hundred dollars – the Senate probably appropriated it in hopes that he would shut up and go away. Vain hope. Andy felt that he had finally gotten one foot in the door and he simply redoubled his efforts; two letters a week instead of one. In 1962 he got four hundred dollars, and for the rest of the decade the library received seven hundred dollars a year like clockwork. By 1971 that had risen to an even thousand. Not much stacked up against what your average small-town library receives, I guess, but a thousand bucks can buy a lot of recycled Perry Mason stories and Jake Logan Westerns. By the time Andy left, you could go into the library (expanded from its original paint-locker to three rooms), and find just about anything you'd want. And if you couldn't find it, chances were good that Andy could get it for you.

Now you're asking yourself if all this came about just because Andy told Byron Hadley how to save the taxes on his wind-fall inheritance. The answer is yes . . . and no. You can probably figure out what happened for yourself.

Word got around that Shawshank was housing its very own pet financial wizard. In the late spring and the summer of 1950, Andy set up two trust funds for guards who wanted to assure a college education for their kids, he advised a couple of others who wanted to take small fliers in common stock (and they did pretty damn well, as things turned out;

one of them did so well he was able to take an early retirement two years later), and I'll be damned if he didn't advise the warden himself, old Lemon Lips George Dunahy, on how to go about setting up a tax-shelter for himself. That was just before Dunahy got the bum's rush, and I believe he must have been dreaming about all the millions his book was going to make him. By April of 1951, Andy was doing the tax returns for half the screws at Shawshank, and by 1952, he was doing almost all of them. He was paid in what may be a prison's most valuable coin: simple good will.

Later on, after Greg Stammas took over the warden's office, Andy became even more important — but if I tried to tell you the specifics of just how, I'd be guessing. There are some things I know about and others I can only guess at. I know that there were some prisoners who received all sorts of special considerations — radios in their cells, extraordinary visiting privileges, things like that — and there were people on the outside who were paying for them to have those privileges. Such people are known as 'angels' by the prisoners. All at once some fellow would be excused from working in the plate-shop on Saturday forenoons, and you'd know that fellow had an angel out there who'd coughed up a chunk of dough to make sure it happened. The way it usually works is that the angel will pay the bribe to some middle-level screw, and the screw will spread the grease both up and down the administrative ladder.

Then there was the discount auto repair service that laid Warden Dunahy low. It went underground for a while and then emerged stronger than ever in the late fifties. And some of the contractors that worked at the prison from time to time were paying kickbacks to the top administration officials, I'm pretty sure, and the same was almost certainly true of the companies whose equipment was bought and installed in the laundry and the license-plate shop and the stamping-mill that was built in 1963.

By the late sixties there was also a booming trade in pills, and the same administrative crowd was involved in turning a buck on that. All of it added up to a pretty good-sized river of illicit income. Not like the pile of clandestine bucks that must fly around a really big prison like Attica or San Quentin, but not peanuts, either. And money itself becomes a problem after a while. You can't just stuff it into your wallet and then shell out a bunch of crumpled twenties and dog-eared tens when you want a pool built in your back yard or an addition put on your house. Once you get past a certain point, you have to explain where that money came from . . . and if your explanations aren't convincing enough, you're apt to wind up wearing a number yourself.

So there was a need for Andy's services. They took him out of the laundry and installed him in the library, but if you wanted to look at it another way, they never took him out of the laundry at all. They just set him to work washing dirty money instead of dirty sheets. He funnelled it into stocks, bonds, tax-free municipals, you name it.

He told me once about ten years after that day on the plate-shop roof that his feelings about what he was doing were pretty clear, and that his conscience was relatively un-troubled. The rackets would have gone on with him or without him. He had not asked to be sent to Shawshank, he went on; he was an innocent man who had been victimized by colossal bad luck, not a missionary or a do-gooder.

'Besides, Red,' he told me with that same half-grin, 'what

457

I'm doing in here isn't all *that* different from what I was doing outside. I'll hand you a pretty cynical axiom: the amount of expert financial help an individual or company needs rises in direct proportion to how many people that person or business is screwing.

'The people who run this place are stupid, brutal monsters for the most part. The people who run the straight world are brutal and monstrous, but they happen not to be quite as stupid, because the standard of competence out there is a little higher. Not much, but a little.'

'But the pills,' I said. 'I don't want to tell you your business, but they make me nervous. Reds, uppers, downers, nembutals − now they've got these things they call Phase Fours. I won't get anything like that. Never have.'

'No,' Andy said. 'I don't like the pills either. Never have. But I'm not much of a one for cigarettes or booze, either. But I don't push the pills. I don't bring them in, and I don't sell them once they are in. Mostly it's the screws who do that.'

'But—'

'Yeah, I know. There's a fine line there. What it comes down to, Red, is some people refuse to get their hands dirty at all. That's called sainthood, and the pigeons land on your shoulders and crap all over your shirt. The other extreme is to take a bath in the dirt and deal any goddamned thing that will turn a dollar − guns, switchblades, big H, what the hell. You ever have a con come up to you and offer you a contract?'

I nodded. It's happened a lot of times over the years. You are, after all, the man who can get it. And they figure if you can get them a nine-bolt battery for their transistor radio or a carton of Luckies or a lid of reefer, you can put them in touch with a guy who'll use a knife.

'Sure you have,' Andy agreed. 'But you don't do it. Because guys like us, Red, we know there's a third choice. An alternative to staying simon-pure or bathing in the filth and the slime. It's the alternative that grown-ups all over the world pick. You balance off your walk through the hog-wallow against what it gains you. You choose the lesser of two evils and try to keep your good intentions in front of you. And I guess you judge how well you're doing by how well you sleep at night . . . and what your dreams are like.'

'Good intentions,' I said, and laughed. 'I know all about that, Andy. A fellow can toddle right off to hell on that road.'

'Don't you believe it,' he said, growing somber. 'This is hell right here. Right here in The Shank. They sell pills and I tell them what to do with the money. But I've also got the library, and I know of over two dozen guys who have used the books in here to help them pass their high school equivalency tests. Maybe when they get out of here they'll be able to crawl off the shitheap. When we needed that second room back in 1957, I got it. Because they want to keep me happy. I work cheap. That's the trade-off.'

'And you've got your own private quarters.'

'Sure. That's the way I like it.'

The prison population had risen slowly all through the fifties, and it damn near exploded in the sixties, what with every college-age kid in America wanting to try dope and the perfectly ridiculous penalties for the use of a little reefer. But in all that time Andy never had a cellmate, except for a big, silent Indian named Normaden (like all Indians in The Shank, he was called Chief), and Normaden didn't last long. A lot of the other long-timers thought Andy was crazy, but Andy just smiled. He lived alone and he liked it that way . . . and as he'd said, they liked to keep him happy. He worked cheap.

Prison time is slow time, sometimes you'd swear it's stop-time, but it passes. It passes. George Dunahy departed the scene in a welter of newspaper headlines shouting SCANDAL and NEST-FEATHERING. Stammas succeeded him, and for the next six years Shawshank was a kind of living hell. During the reign of Greg Stammas, the beds in the infirmary and the cells in the solitary wing were always full.

One day in 1958 I looked at myself in a small shaving mirror I kept in my cell and saw a forty-year-old man looking back at me. A kid had come in back in 1938, a kid with a big mop of carrotty red hair, half-crazy with remorse, thinking about suicide. That kid was gone. The red hair was half grey and starting to recede. There were crow's tracks around the eyes. On that day I could see an old man inside, waiting his time to come out. It scared me. Nobody wants to grow old in stir.

Stammas went early in 1959. There had been several investigative reporters sniffing around, and one of them even did four months under an assumed name, for a crime made up out of whole cloth. They were getting ready to drag out SCANDAL and NEST-FEATHERING again, but before they could bring the hammer down on him, Stammas ran. I can understand that; boy, can I ever. If he had been tried and convicted, he could have ended up right in here. If so, he might have lasted all of five hours. Byron Hadley had gone two years earlier. The sucker had a heart attack and took an early retirement.

Andy never got touched by the Stammas affair. In early

1959 a new warden was appointed, and a new assistant warden, and a new chief of guards. For the next eight months or so, Andy was just another con again. It was during that period that Normaden, the big half-breed Passamaquoddy, shared Andy's cell with him. Then everything just started up again. Normaden was moved out, and Andy was living in solitary splendour again. The names at the top change, but the rackets never do.

I talked to Normaden once about Andy. 'Nice fella,' Normaden said. It was hard to make out anything he said because he had a harelip and a cleft palate; his words all came out in a slush. 'I liked it there. He never made fun. But he didn't want me there. I could tell.' Big shrug. 'I was glad to go, me. Bad draft in that cell. All the time cold. He don't let nobody touch his things. That's okay. Nice man, never made fun. But big draft.'

Rita Hayworth hung in Andy's cell until 1955, if I remember right. Then it was Marilyn Monroe, that picture from *The Seven Year Itch* where she's standing over a subway grating and the warm air is flipping her skirt up. Marilyn lasted until 1960, and she was considerably tattered about the edges when Andy replaced her with Jayne Mansfield. Jayne was, you should pardon the expression, a bust. After only a year or so she was replaced with an English actress – might have been Hazel Court, but I'm not sure. In 1966 that one came down and Raquel Welch went up for a record-breaking six-year engagement in Andy's cell. The last poster to hang there was a pretty country-rock singer whose name was Linda Ronstadt.

I asked him once what the posters meant to him, and he gave me a peculiar, surprised sort of look. 'Why, they mean the same thing to me as they do to most cons, I guess,' he said. 'Freedom. You look at those pretty women and you feel like you could almost . . . not quite but *almost* step right through and be beside them. Be free. I guess that's why I always liked Raquel Welch the best. It wasn't just her; it was that beach she was standing on. Looked like she was down in Mexico somewhere. Someplace quiet, where a man would be able to hear himself think. Didn't you ever feel that way about a picture, Red? That you could almost step right through it?'

I said I'd never really thought of it that way.

'Maybe someday you'll see what I mean,' he said, and he was right. Years later I saw exactly what he meant . . . and when I did, the first thing I thought of was Normaden, and about how he'd said it was always cold in Andy's cell.

A terrible thing happened to Andy in late March or early April of 1963. I have told you that he had something that most of the other prisoners, myself included, seemed to lack. Call it a sense of equanimity, or a feeling of inner peace, maybe even a constant and unwavering faith that someday the long nightmare would end. Whatever you want to call it, Andy Dufresne always seemed to have his act together. There was none of that sullen desperation about him that seems to afflict most lifers after a while; you could never smell hopelessness on him. Until that late winter of '63.

We had another warden by then, a man named Samuel Norton. The Mather brothers, Cotton and Increase, would have felt right at home with Sam Norton. So far as I know, no one had ever seen him so much as crack a smile. He had a thirty-year pin from the Baptist Advent Church of Eliot.

His major innovation as the head of our happy family was to make sure that each incoming prisoner had a New Testament. He had a small plaque on his desk, gold letters inlaid in teakwood, which said CHRIST IS MY SAVIOR. A sampler on the wall, made by his wife, read: HIS JUDGMENT COMETH AND THAT RIGHT EARLY. This latter sentiment cut zero ice with most of us. We felt that the judgment had already occurred, and we would be willing to testify with the best of them that the rock would not hide us nor the dead tree give us shelter. He had a Bible quote for every occasion, did Mr Sam Norton, and whenever you meet a man like that, my best advice to you would be to grin big and cover up your balls with both hands.

There were less infirmary cases than in the days of Greg Stammas, and so far as I know the moonlight burials ceased altogether, but this is not to say that Norton was not a believer in punishment. Solitary was always well populated. Men lost their teeth not from beatings but from bread and water diets. It began to be called grain and drain, as in 'I'm on the Sam Norton grain and drain train, boys.'

The man was the foulest hypocrite that I ever saw in a high position. The rackets I told you about earlier continued to flourish, but Sam Norton added his own new wrinkles. Andy knew about them all, and because we had gotten to be pretty good friends by that time, he let me in on some of them. When Andy talked about them, an expression of amused, disgusted wonder would come over his face, as if he was telling me about some ugly, predatory species of bug that was, by its very ugliness and greed, somehow more comic than terrible.

It was Warden Norton who instituted the 'Inside-Out'

program you may have read about some sixteen or seventeen years back; it was even written up in *Newsweek*. In the press it sounded like a real advance in practical corrections and rehabilitation. There were prisoners out cutting pulpwood, prisoners repairing bridges and causeways, prisoners constructing potato cellars. Norton called it 'Inside-Out' and was invited to explain it to damn near every Rotary and Kiwanis club in New England, especially after he got his picture in *Newsweek*. The prisoners called it 'road-ganging', but so far as I know, none of them were ever invited to express their views to the Kiwanians or the Loyal Order of the Moose.

Norton was right in there on every operation, thirty-year church-pin and all, from cutting pulp to digging storm-drains to laying new culverts on state highways, there was Norton, skimming off the top. There were a hundred ways to do it – men, materials, you name it. But he had it coming another way, as well. The construction businesses in the area were deathly afraid of Norton's Inside-Out program, because prison labor is slave labor, and you can't compete with that. So Sam Norton, he of the Testaments and the thirty-year church-pin, was passed a good many thick envelopes under the table during his fifteen-year tenure as Shawshank's warden. And when an envelope was passed, he would either overbid the project, not bid at all, or claim that all his Inside-Outers were committed elsewhere. It has always been something of a wonder to me that Norton was never found in the trunk of a Thunderbird parked off a highway somewhere down in Massachusetts with his hands tied behind his back and half a dozen bullets in his head.

Anyway, as the old barrelhouse song says, My God, how

the money rolled in. Norton must have subscribed to the old Puritan notion that the best way to figure out which folks God favors is by checking their bank accounts.

Andy Dufresne was his right hand in all of this, his silent partner. The prison library was Andy's hostage to fortune. Norton knew it, and Norton used it. Andy told me that one of Norton's favorite aphorisms was *One hand washes the other.* So Andy gave good advice and made useful suggestions. I can't say for sure that he hand-tooled Norton's Inside-Out program, but I'm damned sure he processed the money for the Jesus-shouting son of a whore. He gave good advice, made useful suggestions, the money got spread around, and . . . son of a bitch! The library would get a new set of automotive repair manuals, a fresh set of Grolier Encyclo-pedias, books on how to prepare for the Scholastic Achieve-ment Tests. And, of course, more Erle Stanley Gardners and more Louis L'Amours.

And I'm convinced that what happened happened because Norton just didn't want to lose his good right hand. I'll go further: it happened because he was scared of what might happen — what Andy might say against him — if Andy ever got clear of Shawshank State Prison.

I got the story a chunk here and a chunk there over a space of seven years, some of it from Andy — but not all. He never wanted to talk about that part of his life, and I don't blame him. I got parts of it from maybe half a dozen different sources. I've said once that prisoners are nothing but slaves, but they have that slave habit of looking dumb and keeping their ears open. I got it backwards and forwards and in the middle, but I'll give it to you from point A to point Z, and maybe you'll understand why the man spent about ten months in a bleak, depressed daze. See, I don't think he knew the truth until 1963, fifteen years after he came into this sweet little hell-hole. Until he met Tommy Williams, I don't think he knew how bad it could get.

Tommy Williams joined our happy little Shawshank family in November of 1962. Tommy thought of himself as a native of Massachusetts, but he wasn't proud; in his twenty-seven years he'd done time all over New England. He was a professional thief, and as you may have guessed, my own feeling was that he should have picked another profession.

He was a married man, and his wife came to visit each and every week. She had an idea that things might go better with Tommy – and consequently better with their three-year-old son and herself – if he got his high school degree. She talked him into it, and so Tommy Williams started visiting the library on a regular basis.

For Andy, this was an old routine by then. He saw that Tommy got a series of high school equivalency tests. Tommy would brush up on the subjects he had passed in high-school – there weren't many – and then take the test. Andy also saw that he was enrolled in a number of correspondence courses covering the subjects he had failed in school or just missed by dropping out.

He probably wasn't the best student Andy ever took over the jumps, and I don't know if he ever did get his high school diploma, but that forms no part of my story. The important thing was that he came to like Andy Dufresne very much, as most people did after a while.

On a couple of occasions he asked Andy 'what a smart guy like you is doing in the joint' – a question which is the rough equivalent of that one that goes 'What's a nice girl like you doing in a place like this?' But Andy wasn't the type to tell him; he would only smile and turn the conversation into some other channel. Quite normally, Tommy asked someone else, and when he finally got the story, I guess he also got the shock of his young life.

The person he asked was his partner on the laundry's steam ironer and folder. The inmates call this device the mangler, because that's exactly what it will do to you if you aren't paying attention and get your bad self caught in it. His partner was Charlie Lathrop, who had been in for about twelve years on a murder charge. He was more than glad to reheat the details of the Dufresne murder trial for Tommy; it broke the monotony of pulling freshly pressed bedsheets out of the machine and tucking them into the basket. He was just getting to the jury waiting until after lunch to bring in their guilty verdict when the trouble whistle went off and the mangle grated to a stop. They had been feeding in freshly washed sheets from the Eliot Nursing Home at the far end; these were spat out dry and neatly pressed at Tommy's and Charlie's end at the rate of one every five seconds. Their job was to grab them, fold them, and slap them into the cart, which had already been lined with brown paper.

But Tommy Williams was just standing there, staring at Charlie Lathrop, his mouth unhinged all the way to his chest. He was standing in a drift of sheets that had come through clean and which were now sopping up all the wet muck on the floor – and in a laundry wetwash, there's plenty of muck.

So the head bull that day, Homer Jessup, comes rushing over, bellowing his head off and on the prod for trouble. Tommy took no notice of him. He spoke to Charlie as if

467

old Homer, who had busted more heads than he could probably count, hadn't been there.

'What did you say that golf pro's name was?'

'Quentin,' Charlie answered back, all confused and upset by now. He later said that the kid was as white as a truce flag. 'Glenn Quentin, I think. Something like that, anyway—'

'Here now, here now,' Homer Jessup roared, his neck as red as a rooster's comb. 'Get them sheets in cold water! Get quick! Get quick, by Jesus, you—'

'Glenn Quentin, oh my God,' Tommy Williams said, and that was all he got to say because Homer Jessup, that least peaceable of men, brought his billy down behind his ear. Tommy hit the floor so hard he broke off three of his front teeth. When he woke up he was in solitary, and confined to same for a week, riding a boxcar on Sam Norton's famous grain and drain train. Plus a black mark on his report card.

That was in early February in 1963, and Tommy Williams went around to six or seven other long-timers after he got out of solitary and got pretty much the same story. I know; I was one of them. But when I asked him why he wanted it, he just clammed up.

Then one day he went to the library and spilled one helluva big budget of information to Andy Dufresne. And for the first and last time, at least since he had approached me about the Rita Hayworth poster like a kid buying his first pack of Trojans, Andy lost his cool . . . only this time he blew it entirely.

I saw him later that day, and he looked like a man who has stepped on the business end of a rake and given himself a good one, whap between the eyes. His hands were trembling, and when I spoke to him, he didn't answer. Before that afternoon was out he had caught up with Billy Hanlon, who was the head screw, and set up an appointment with Warden Norton for the following day. He told me later that he didn't sleep a wink all that night; he just listened to a cold winter wind howling outside, watched the searchlights go around and around, putting long, moving shadows on the cement walls of the cage he had called home since Harry Truman was President, and tried to think it all out. He said it was as if Tommy had produced a key which fitted a cage in the back of his mind, a cage like his own cell. Only instead of holding a man, that cage held a tiger, and that tiger's name was Hope. Williams had produced the key that unlocked the cage and the tiger was out, willy-nilly, to roam his brain.

Four years before, Tommy Williams had been arrested in Rhode Island, driving a stolen car that was full of stolen merchandise. Tommy turned in his accomplice, the DA played ball, and he got a lighter sentence . . . two to four, with time served. Eleven months after beginning his term, his old cell-mate got a ticket out and Tommy got a new one, a man named Elwood Blatch. Blatch had been busted for burglary with a weapon and was serving six to twelve.

'I never seen such a high-strung guy,' Tommy said. 'A man like that should never want to be a burglar, specially not with a gun. The slightest little noise, he'd go three feet into the air . . . and come down shooting, more likely than not. One night he almost strangled me because some guy down the hall was whopping on his cell bars with a tin cup.

'I did seven months with him, until they let me walk free. I got time served and time off, you understand. I can't say we talked because you didn't, you know, exactly hold a conversation with El Blatch. *He* held a conversation with *you*. He talked all the time. Never shut up. If you tried to get a word in, he'd shake his fist at you and roll his eyes. It gave me the cold chills whenever he done that. Big tall guy he was, mostly bald, with these green eyes set way down deep in the sockets. Jeez, I hope I never see him again.

'It was like a talkin' jag every night. Where he grew up, the orphanages he run away from, the jobs he done, the women he fucked, the crap games he cleaned out. I just let him run on. My face ain't much, but I didn't want it, you know, rearranged for me.

'According to him, he'd burgled over two hundred joints. It was hard for me to believe, a guy like him who went off like a firecracker every time someone cut a loud fart, but he swore it was true. Now . . . listen to me, Red. I know guys sometimes make things up after they know a thing, but even before I knew about this golf pro guy, Quentin, I remember thinking that if El Blatch ever burgled *my* house, and I found out about it later, I'd have to count myself just about the luckiest motherfucker going still to be alive. Can you imagine him in some lady's bedroom, sifting through her jool'ry box, and she coughs in her sleep or turns over quick? It gives me the cold chills just to think of something like that, I swear on my mother's name it does.

'He said he'd killed people, too. People that gave him shit. At least that's what he said. And I believed him. He sure looked like a man that could do some killing. He was just so fucking high-strung! Like a pistol with a sawed-off firing pin. I knew a guy who had a Smith & Wesson Police Special with a sawed-off firing pin. It wasn't no good for nothing, except maybe for something to jaw about. The pull on that gun was so light that it would fire if this guy, Johnny Callahan, his name was, if he turned his record-player on full volume and put it on top of one of the speakers. That's how El Blatch was. I can't explain it any better. I just never doubted that he had greased some people.

'So one night, just for something to say, I go: "Who'd you kill?" Like a joke, you know. So he laughs and says, "There's one guy doing time up-Maine for these two people I killed. It was this guy and the wife of the slob who's doing time. I was creeping their place and the guy started to give me some shit."

'I can't remember if he ever told me the woman's name or not,' Tommy went on. 'Maybe he did. But in New England, Dufresne's like Smith or Jones in the rest of the country, because there's so many Frogs up here. Dufresne, Lavesque, Ouelette, Poulin, who can remember Frog names? But he told me the guy's name. He said the guy was Glenn Quentin and he was a prick, a big rich prick, a golf pro. El said he thought the guy might have cash in the house, maybe as much as five thousand dollars. That was a lot of money back then, he says to me. So I go, "When was that?" And he goes, "After the war. Just after the war."

'So he went in and he did the joint and they woke up and the guy gave him some trouble. That's what *El* said. Maybe the guy just started to snore, that's what *I* say. Anyway, El said Quentin was in the sack with some hotshot lawyer's wife and they sent the lawyer up to Shawshank State Prison. Then he laughs this big laugh. Holy Christ, I was never so glad of anything as I was when I got my walking papers from that place.'

★   ★   ★

I guess you can see why Andy went a little wonky when Tommy told him that story, and why he wanted to see the warden right away. Elwood Blatch had been serving a six-to-twelve rap when Tommy knew him four years before. By the time Andy heard all of this, in 1963, he might be on the verge of getting out . . . or already out. So those were the two prongs of the spit Andy was roasting on – the idea that Blatch might still be in on one hand, and the very real possibility that he might be gone like the wind on the other.

There were inconsistencies in Tommy's story, but aren't there always in real life? Blatch told Tommy the man who got sent up was a hotshot lawyer, and Andy was a banker, but those are two professions that people who aren't very educated could easily get mixed up. And don't forget that twelve years had gone by between the time Blatch was reading the clippings about the trial and the time he told the tale to Tommy Williams. He also told Tommy he got better than a thousand dollars from a footlocker Quentin had in his closet, but the police said at Andy's trial that there had been no sign of burglary. I have a few ideas about that. First, if you take the cash and the man it belonged to is dead, how are you going to know anything was stolen, unless someone else can tell you it was there to start with? Second, who's to say Blatch wasn't lying about that part of it? Maybe he didn't want to admit killing two people for nothing. Third, maybe there were signs of burglary and the cops either overlooked them – cops can be pretty dumb – or deliberately covered them up so they wouldn't screw the DA's case. The guy was running for public office, remember, and he needed a con-viction to run on. An unsolved burglary-murder would have done him no good at all.

But of the three, I like the middle one best. I've known a few Elwood Blatches in my time at Shawshank – the trigger-pullers with the crazy eyes. Such fellows want you to think they got away with the equivalent of the Hope Diamond on every caper, even if they got caught with a two-dollar Timex and nine bucks on the one they're doing time for.

And there was one thing in Tommy's story that convinced Andy beyond a shadow of a doubt. Blatch hadn't hit Quentin at random. He had called Quentin 'a big rich prick', and he had *known* Quentin was a golf pro. Well, Andy and his wife had been going out to that country club for drinks and dinner once or twice a week for a couple of years, and Andy had done a considerable amount of drinking there once he found out about his wife's affair. There was a marina with the country club, and for a while in 1947 there had been a part-time grease-and-gas jockey working there who matched Tommy's description of Elwood Blatch. A big tall man, mostly bald, with deep-set green eyes. A man who had an unpleasant way of looking at you, as though he was sizing you up. He wasn't there long, Andy said. Either he quit or Briggs, the fellow in charge of the marina, fired him. But he wasn't a man you forgot. He was too striking for that.

So Andy went to see Warden Norton on a rainy, windy day with big gray clouds scudding across the sky above the gray walls, a day when the last of the snow was starting to melt away and show lifeless patches of last year's grass in the fields beyond the prison.

The warden has a good-sized office in the administration wing, and behind the warden's desk there's a door which connects with the assistant warden's office. The assistant warden was out that day, but a trustee was there. He was a half-lame fellow whose real name I have forgotten; all the inmates, me included, called him Chester, after Marshal Dillon's sidekick. Chester was supposed to be watering the plants and dusting and waxing the floor. My guess is that the plants went thirsty that day and the only waxing that was done happened because of Chester's dirty ear polishing the keyhole plate of that connecting door.

He heard the warden's main door open and close and then Norton saying, 'Good morning, Dufresne, how can I help you?'

'Warden,' Andy began, and old Chester told us that he could hardly recognize Andy's voice it was so changed. 'Warden . . . there's something . . . something's happened to me that's . . . that's so . . . so . . . I hardly know where to begin.'

'Well, why don't you just begin at the beginning?' the warden said, probably in his sweetest let's-all-turn-to-the-23rd-psalm-and-read-in-unison voice. 'That usually works the best.'

And so Andy did. He began by refreshing Norton of the details of the crime he had been imprisoned for. Then he told the warden exactly what Tommy Williams had told him. He also gave out Tommy's name, which you may think wasn't so wise in light of later developments, but I'd just ask you what else he could have done, if his story was to have any credibility at all.

When he had finished, Norton was completely silent for some time. I can just see him, probably tipped back in his office chair under the picture of Governor Reed hanging on the wall, his fingers steepled, his liver lips pursed, his brow wrinkled into ladder rungs halfway to the crown of his head, his thirty-year pin gleaming mellowly.

'Yes,' he said finally. 'That's the damnedest story I ever heard. But I'll tell you what surprises me most about it, Dufresne.'

'What's that, sir?'

'That you were taken in by it.'

'Sir? I don't understand what you mean.' And Chester said that Andy Dufresne, who had faced down Byron Hadley on the plate-shop roof thirteen years before, was almost floundering for words.

'Well now,' Norton said. 'It's pretty obvious to me that this young fellow Williams is impressed with you. Quite taken with you, as a matter of fact. He hears your tale of woe, and it's quite natural of him to want to . . . cheer you up, let's say. Quite natural. He's a young man, not terribly bright. Not surprising he didn't realize what a state it would put you into. Now what I suggest is—'

'Don't you think I thought of that?' Andy asked. 'But I'd never told Tommy about the man working down at the marina. I never told *anyone* that – it never even crossed my mind! But Tommy's description of his cellmate and that man . . . they're *identical*!'

'Well now, you may be indulging in a little selective perception there,' Norton said with a chuckle. Phrases like that, selective perception, are required learning for people in the penology and corrections business, and they use them all they can.

'That's not it at all. Sir.'

'That's your slant on it,' Norton said, 'but mine differs. And let's remember that I have only your word that there *was* such a man working at the Falmouth Hills Country Club back then.'

'No, sir,' Andy broke in again. 'No, that isn't true. Because—'

'Anyway,' Norton overrode him, expansive and loud, 'let's just look at it from the other end of the telescope, shall we? Suppose – just suppose, now – that there really *was* a fellow named Elwood Blotch.'

'Blatch,' Andy said tightly.

'Blatch, by all means. And let's say he *was* Thomas Williams's cellmate in Rhode Island. The chances are excellent that he has been released by now. *Excellent.* Why, we don't even know how much time he might have done there before he ended up with Williams, do we? Only that he was doing a six-to-twelve.'

'No. We don't know how much time he'd done. But Tommy said he was a bad actor, a cut-up. I think there's a fair chance that he may still be in. Even if he's been released, the prison will have a record of his last known address, the names of his relatives—'

'And both would almost certainly be dead ends.'

Andy was silent for a moment, and then he burst out: 'Well, it's a *chance*, isn't it?'

'Yes, of course it is. So just for a moment, Dufresne, let's assume that Blatch exists and that he is still safely ensconced in the Rhode Island State Penitentiary. Now what is he going to say if we bring this kettle of fish to him in a bucket? Is he going to fall down on his knees, roll his eyes, and say "I did it! I did it! By all means add a life term onto my burglary charge!"?'

'How can you be so obtuse?' Andy said, so low that Chester could barely hear. But he heard the warden just fine.

'What? What did you call me?'

'*Obtuse!*' Andy cried. 'Is it deliberate?'

'Dufresne, you've taken five minutes of my time – no, seven – and I have a very busy schedule today. So I believe we'll just declare this little meeting closed and—'

'The country club will have all the old time-cards, don't you realize that?' Andy shouted. 'They'll have tax-forms and W-2s and unemployment compensation forms, all with his name on them! There will be employees there now that were there then, maybe Briggs himself! It's been fifteen years, not forever! They'll remember him! *They will remember Blatch!* If I've got Tommy to testify to what Blatch told him, and Briggs to testify that Blatch was there, actually *working* at the country club, I can get a new trial! I can—'

'Guard! *Guard!* Take this man away!'

'What's the *matter* with you?' Andy said, and Chester told me he was very nearly screaming by then. 'It's my life, my chance to get out, don't you see that? And you won't make a single long-distance call to at least verify Tommy's story? Listen, I'll pay for the call! I'll pay for—'

Then there was a sound of thrashing as the guards grabbed him and started to drag him out.

'Solitary,' Warden Norton said dryly. He was probably fingering his thirty-year pin as he said it. 'Bread and water.'

And so they dragged Andy away, totally out of control now, still screaming at the warden; Chester said you could hear him even after the door was shut: '*It's my life! It's my life, don't you understand it's my life?*'

Twenty days on the grain and drain train for Andy down there in solitary. It was his second jolt in solitary, and his dust-up with Norton was his first real black mark since he had joined our happy little family.

I'll tell you a little bit about Shawshank's solitary while we're on the subject. It's something of a throwback to those hardy pioneer days of the early-to-mid-1700s in Maine. In those days no one wasted much time with such things as 'penology' and 'rehabilitation' and 'selective perception'. In those days, you were taken care of in terms of absolute black and white. You were either guilty or innocent. If you were guilty, you were either hung or put in gaol. And if you were sentenced to gaol, you did not go to an institution. No, you dug your own gaol with a spade provided to you by the Province of Maine. You dug it as wide and as deep as you could during the period between sunup and sundown. Then they gave you a couple of skins and a bucket, and down you went. Once down, the gaoler would bar the top of your hole, throw down some grain or maybe a piece of maggoty meat once or twice a week, and maybe there would be a dipperful of barley soup on Sunday night. You pissed in the bucket, and you held up the same bucket for water when the gaoler came around at six in the morning. When it rained, you used the bucket to bail out your gaol-cell . . . unless, that is, you wanted to drown like a rat in a rainbarrel.

No one spent a long time 'in the hole', as it was called; thirty months was an unusually long term, and so far as I've been able to tell, the longest term ever spent from which an inmate actually emerged alive was served by the so-called 'Durham Boy', a fourteen-year-old psychopath who castrated a schoolmate with a piece of rusty metal. He did seven years, but of course he went in young and strong.

You have to remember that for a crime that was more serious than petty theft or blasphemy or forgetting to put a snotrag in your pocket when out of doors on the Sabbath, you were hung. For low crimes such as those just mentioned and for others like them, you'd do your three or six or nine months in the hole and come out fishbelly white, cringing from the wide-open spaces, your eyes half-blind, your teeth more than likely rocking and rolling in their sockets from the scurvy, your feet crawling with fungus. Jolly old Province of Maine. Yo-ho-ho and a bottle of rum.

Shawshank's Solitary Wing was nowhere as bad as that . . . I guess. Things come in three major degrees in the human experience, I think. There's good, bad, and terrible. And as you go down into progressive darkness toward terrible, it gets harder and harder to make subdivisions.

To get to Solitary Wing you were led down twenty-three steps to a basement level where the only sound was the drip of water. The only light was supplied by a series of dangling sixty-watt bulbs. The cells were keg-shaped, like those wall-safes rich people sometimes hide behind a picture. Like a safe, the round doorways were hinged, and solid instead of barred. You get ventilation from above, but no light except for your own sixty-watt bulb, which was turned off from a master-switch promptly at 8:00 P.M., an hour before lights-out in the rest of the prison. The wire wasn't in a wire mesh cage or anything like that. The feeling was that if you wanted to exist down there in the dark, you were welcome to it. Not many did . . . but after eight, of course, you had no choice. You had a bunk bolted to the wall and a can with no toilet seat. You had three ways to spend your time: sitting, shitting, or sleeping. Big choice. Twenty days could get to seem like a year. Thirty days could seem like two, and forty days like ten. Sometimes you could hear rats in the ventilation system. In a situation like that, subdivisions of terrible tend to get lost.

If anything at all can be said in favor of solitary, it's just that you get time to think. Andy had twenty days in which to think while he enjoyed his grain and drain, and when he got out he requested another meeting with the warden. Request denied. Such a meeting, the warden told him, would be 'counter-productive'. That's another of those phrases you have to master before you can go to work in the prisons and corrections field.

Patiently, Andy renewed his request. And renewed it. And renewed it. He had changed, had Andy Dufresne. Suddenly, as that spring of 1963 bloomed around us, there were lines in his face and sprigs of gray showing in his hair. He had lost that little trace of a smile that always seemed to linger around his mouth. His eyes stared out into space more often, and you get to know that when a man stares that way, he is counting up the years served, the months, the weeks, the days.

He renewed his request and renewed it. He was patient. He had nothing but time. It got to be summer. In Washington, President Kennedy was promising a fresh assault on poverty and on civil rights inequalities, not knowing he had only half a year to live. In Liverpool, a musical group called The Beatles was emerging as a force to be reckoned with in British music, but I guess that no one Stateside had yet heard of them. The Boston Red Sox, still four years away from what New England folks call The Miracle of '67, were languishing in the cellar of the American League. All of those things were going on out in a larger world where people walked free.

Norton saw him near the end of June, and this conversation I heard about from Andy himself some seven years later.

'If it's the squeeze, you don't have to worry,' Andy told Norton in a low voice. 'Do you think I'd talk that up? I'd be cutting my own throat. I'd be just as indictable as—'

'That's enough,' Norton interrupted. His face was as long and cold as a slate gravestone. He leaned back in his office chair until the back of his head almost touched the sampler reading HIS JUDGMENT COMETH AND THAT RIGHT EARLY.

'But—'

'Don't you ever mention money to me again,' Norton said. 'Not in this office, not anywhere. Not unless you want to see that library turned back into a storage room and paint-locker again. Do you understand?'

'I was trying to set your mind at ease, that's all.'

'Well now, when I need a sorry son of a bitch like you to set my mind at ease, I'll retire. I agreed to this appointment because I got tired of being pestered, Dufresne. I want it to stop. If you want to buy this particular Brooklyn Bridge, that's your affair. Don't make it mine. I could hear crazy stories like yours twice a week if I wanted to lay myself open to them. Every sinner in this place would be using me for a crying towel. I had more respect for you. But this is the end. The end. Have we got an understanding?'

'Yes,' Andy said. 'But I'll be hiring a lawyer, you know.'

'What in God's name for?'

'I think we can put it together,' Andy said. 'With Tommy Williams and with my testimony and corroborative testimony from records and employees at the country club, I think we can put it together.'

481

'Tommy Williams is no longer an inmate of this facility.'

'What?'

'He's been transferred.'

'Transferred *where*?'

'Cashman.'

At that, Andy fell silent. He was an intelligent man, but it would have taken an extraordinarily stupid man not to smell *deal* all over that. Cashman was a minimum-security prison far up north in Aroostook County. The inmates pick a lot of potatoes, and that's hard work, but they are paid a decent wage for their labor and they can attend classes at CVI, a pretty decent vocational-technical institute, if they so desire. More important to a fellow like Tommy, a fellow with a young wife and a child, Cashman had a furlough program . . . which meant a chance to live like a normal man, at least on the weekends. A chance to build a model plane with his kid, have sex with his wife, maybe go on a picnic.

Norton had almost surely dangled all of that under Tommy's nose with only one string attached: not one more word about Elwood Blatch, not now, not ever. Or you'll end up doing hard time in Thomaston down there on scenic Route 1 with the real hard guys, and instead of having sex with your wife you'll be having it with some old bull queer.

'But why?' Andy said. 'Why would—'

'As a favour to you,' Norton said calmly, 'I checked with Rhode Island. They did have an inmate named Elwood Blatch. He was given what they call a PP – provisional parole, another one of these crazy liberal programs to put criminals out on the streets. He's since disappeared.'

Andy said: 'The warden down there . . . is he a friend of yours?'

Sam Norton gave Andy a smile as cold as a deacon's watchchain. 'We are acquainted,' he said.

'*Why?*' Andy repeated. 'Can't you tell me why you did it? You knew I wasn't going to talk about . . . about anything you might have had going. You *knew* that. So *why?*'

'Because people like you make me sick,' Norton said deliberately. 'I like you right where you are, Mr Dufresne, and as long as I am warden here at Shawshank, you are going to be right here. You see, you used to think that you were better than anyone else. I have gotten pretty good at seeing that on a man's face. I marked it on yours the first time I walked into the library. It might as well have been written on your forehead in capital letters. That look is gone now, and I like that just fine. It is not just that you are a useful vessel, never think that. It is simply that men like you need to learn humility. Why, you used to walk around that exercise yard as if it was a living room and you were at one of those cocktail parties where the hellbound walk around coveting each others' wives and husbands and getting swinishly drunk. But you don't walk around that way anymore. And I'll be watching to see if you should start to walk that way again. Over a period of years, I'll be watching you with great pleasure. Now get the hell out of here.'

'Okay. But all the extracurricular activities stop now, Norton. The investment counseling, the scams, the free tax advice. It all stops. Get H & R Block to tell you how to declare your income.'

Warden Norton's face first went brick-red . . . and then all the color fell out of it. 'You're going back into solitary for that. Thirty days. Bread and water. Another black mark. And while you're in, think about this: if *anything* that's been going on should stop, the library goes. I will make it my personal business to see that it goes back to what it was before you came here. And I will make your life . . . very hard. Very difficult. You'll do the hardest time it's possible to do. You'll lose that one-bunk Hilton down in Cellblock 5, for starters, and you'll lose those rocks on the windowsill, and you'll lose any protection the guards have given you against the sodomites. You will . . . lose everything. Clear?'

I guess it was clear enough.

Time continued to pass – the oldest trick in the world, and maybe the only one that really is magic. But Andy Dufresne had changed. He had grown harder. That's the only way I can think of to put it. He went on doing Warden Norton's dirty work and he held onto the library, so outwardly things were about the same. He continued to have his birthday drinks and his year-end holiday drinks; he continued to share out the rest of each bottle. I got him fresh rock-polishing cloths from time to time, and in 1967 I got him a new rock-hammer – the one I'd gotten him nineteen years ago had plumb worn out. *Nineteen years!* When you say it sudden like that, those three syllables sound like the thud and double-locking of a tomb door. The rock-hammer, which had been a ten-dollar item back then, went for twenty-two by '67. He and I had a sad little grin over that.

Andy continued to shape and polish the rocks he found in the exercise yard, but the yard was smaller by then; half of what had been there in 1950 had been asphalted over in 1962. Nonetheless, he found enough to keep him occupied, I guess. When he had finished with each rock he would put it carefully on his window ledge, which faced east. He told me he liked to look at them in the sun, the pieces of the planet he had taken up from the dirt and shaped. Schists, quartzes, granites. Funny little mica sculptures that were held together with airplane glue. Various sedimentary conglomerates that were polished and cut in such a way that you could see why Andy called them 'millennium sandwiches' – the layers of different material that had built up over a period of decades and centuries.

Andy would give his stones and his rock-sculptures away from time to time in order to make room for new ones. He gave me the greatest number, I think – counting the stones that looked like matched cufflinks, I had five. There was one of the mica sculptures I told you about, carefully crafted to look like a man throwing a javelin, and two of the sedimentary conglomerates, all the levels showing in smoothly polished cross-section. I've still got them, and I take them down every so often and think about what a man can do, if he has time enough and the will to use it, a drop at a time.

So, on the outside, at least, things were about the same. If Norton had wanted to break Andy as badly as he had said, he would have had to look below the surface to see the change. But if he *had* seen how different Andy had become, I think Norton would have been well-satisfied with the four years following his clash with Andy.

He had told Andy that Andy walked around the exercise yard as if he were at a cocktail party. That isn't the way I would have put it, but I know what he meant. It goes back to what I said about Andy wearing his freedom like an invisible coat, about how he never really developed a prison mentality. His eyes never got that dull look. He never developed the walk that men get when the day is over and

they are going back to their cells for another endless night
– that flat-footed, hump-shouldered walk. Andy walked with
his shoulders squared and his step was always light, as if he
were heading home to a good home-cooked meal and a
good woman instead of to a tasteless mess of soggy vegeta-
bles, lumpy mashed potato, and a slice or two of that fatty,
gristly stuff most of the cons called mystery meat . . . that,
and a picture of Raquel Welch on the wall.

But for those four years, although he never became *exactly*
like the others, he did become silent, introspective, and
brooding. Who could blame him? So maybe it was Warden
Norton who was pleased . . . at least, for a while.

His dark mood broke around the time of the 1967 World
Series. That was the dream year, the year the Red Sox won
the pennant instead of placing ninth, as the Las Vegas bookies
had predicted. When it happened – when they won the
American League pennant – a kind of ebullience engulfed
the whole prison. There was a goofy sort of feeling that if
the Dead Sox could come to life, then maybe *anybody* could
do it. I can't explain that feeling now, any more than an ex-
Beatlemaniac could explain *that* madness, I suppose. But it
was real. Every radio in the place was tuned to the games
as the Red Sox pounded down the stretch. There was gloom
when the Sox dropped a pair in Cleveland near the end, and
a nearly riotous joy when Rico Petrocelli put away the pop
fly that clinched it. And then there was the gloom that came
when Lonborg was beaten in the seventh game of the Series
to end the dream just short of complete fruition. It probably
pleased Norton to no end, the son of a bitch. He liked his
prison wearing sackcloth and ashes.

But for Andy, there was no tumble back down into gloom. He wasn't much of a baseball fan anyway, and maybe that was why. Nevertheless, he seemed to have caught the current of good feeling, and for him it didn't peter out again after the last game of the Series. He had taken that invisible coat out of the closet and put it on again.

I remember one bright-gold fall day in very late October, a couple of weeks after the World Series had ended. It must have been a Sunday, because the exercise yard was full of men 'walking off the week' – tossing a Frisbee or two, passing around a football, bartering what they had to barter. Others would be at the long table in the Visitors' Hall, under the watchful eyes of the screws, talking with their relatives, smoking cigarettes, telling sincere lies, receiving their picked-over care packages.

Andy was squatting Indian-fashion against the wall, chunking two small rocks together in his hands, his face turned up into the sunlight. It was surprisingly warm, that sun, for a day so late in the year.

'Hello, Red,' he called. 'Come on and sit a spell.'

I did.

'You want this?' he asked, and handed me one of the two carefully polished 'millennium sandwiches' I just told you about.

'I sure do,' I said. 'It's very pretty. Thank you.'

He shrugged and changed the subject. 'Big anniversary coming up for you next year.'

I nodded. Next year would make me a thirty-year man. Sixty per cent of my life spent in Shawshank Prison.

'Think you'll ever get out?'

'Sure. When I have a long white beard and just about three marbles left rolling around upstairs.'

He smiled a little and then turned his face up into the sun again, his eyes closed. 'Feels good.'

'I think it always does when you know the damn winter's almost right on top of you.'

He nodded, and we were silent for a while.

'When I get out of here,' Andy said finally, 'I'm going where it's warm all the time.' He spoke with such calm assurance you would have thought he had only a month or so left to serve. 'You know where I'm goin', Red?'

'Nope.'

'Zihuatanejo,' he said, rolling the word softly from his tongue like music. 'Down in Mexico. It's a little place maybe twenty miles from Playa Azul and Mexico Highway 37. It's a hundred miles north-west of Acapulco on the Pacific Ocean. You know what the Mexicans say about the Pacific?'

I told him I didn't.

'They say it has no memory. And that's where I want to finish out my life, Red. In a warm place that has no memory.'

He had picked up a handful of pebbles as he spoke; now he tossed them, one by one, and watched them bounce and roll across the baseball diamond's dirt infield, which would be under a foot of snow before long.

'Zihuatanejo. I'm going to have a little hotel down there. Six cabanas along the beach, and six more set further back, for the highway trade. I'll have a guy who'll take my guests out charter fishing. There'll be a trophy for the guy who catches the biggest marlin of the season, and I'll put his picture up in the lobby. It won't be a family place. It'll be a place for people on their honeymoons . . . first or second varieties.'

'And where are you going to get the money to buy this fabulous place?' I asked. 'Your stock account?'

He looked at me and smiled. 'That's not so far wrong,' he said. 'Sometimes you startle me, Red.'

'What are you talking about?'

'There are really only two types of men in the world when it comes to bad trouble,' Andy said, cupping a match between his hands and lighting a cigarette. 'Suppose there was a house full of rare paintings and sculptures and fine old antiques, Red? And suppose the guy who owned the house heard that there was a monster of a hurricane headed right at it. One of those two kinds of men just hopes for the best. The hurricane will change course, he says to himself. No right-thinking hurricane would ever dare wipe out all these Rembrandts, my two Degas horses, my Jackson Pollocks and my Paul Klees. Furthermore, God wouldn't allow it. And if worse comes to worst, they're insured. That's one sort of man. The other sort just assumes that hurricane is going to tear right through the middle of his house. If the weather bureau says the hurricane just changed course, this guy assumes it'll change back in order to put his house on ground zero again. This second type of guy knows there's no harm in hoping for the best as long as you're prepared for the worst.'

I lit a cigarette of my own. 'Are you saying you prepared for the eventuality?'

'Yes. I prepared for the *hurricane*. I knew how bad it looked. I didn't have much time, but in the time I had, I operated. I had a friend – just about the only person who stood by me – who worked for an investment company in Portland. He died about six years ago.'

'Sorry.'

'Yeah.' Andy tossed his butt away. 'Linda and I had about fourteen thousand dollars. Not a big bundle, but hell, we were young. We had our whole lives ahead of us.' He grimaced a little, then laughed. 'When the shit hit the fan, I started lugging my Rembrandts out of the path of the hurricane. I sold my stocks and paid the capital gains tax just like a good little boy. Declared everything. Didn't cut any corners.'

'Didn't they freeze your estate?'

'I was charged with murder, Red, not dead! You can't freeze the assets of an innocent man – thank God. And it was a while before they even got brave enough to charge me with the crime. Jim – my friend – and I, we had some time. I got hit pretty good, just dumping everything like that. Got my nose skinned. But at the time I had worse things to worry about than a small skinning on the stock market.'

'Yeah, I'd say you did.'

'But when I came to Shawshank it was all safe. It's still safe. Outside these walls, Red, there's a man that no living soul has ever seen face to face. He has a Social Security card and a Maine driver's license. He's got a birth certificate. Name of Peter Stevens. Nice, anonymous name, huh?'

'Who is he?' I asked. I thought I knew what he was going to say, but I couldn't believe it.

'Me.'

'You're not going to tell me that you had time to set up a false identity while the bulls were sweating you,' I said, 'or that you finished the job while you were on trial for—'

'No, I'm not going to tell you that. My friend Jim was the one who set up the false identity. He started after my appeal was turned down, and the major pieces of identification were in his hands by the spring of 1950.'

'He must have been a pretty close friend,' I said. I was not sure how much of this I believed – a little, a lot, or none.

But the day was warm and the sun was out, and it was one hell of a good story. 'All of that's one hundred per cent illegal, setting up a false ID like that.'

'He was a close friend,' Andy said. 'We were in the war together. France, Germany, the occupation. He was a good friend. He knew it was illegal, but he also knew that setting up a false identity in this country is very easy and very safe. He took my money – my money with all the taxes on it paid so the IRS wouldn't get too interested – and invested it for Peter Stevens. He did that in 1950 and 1951. Today it amounts to three hundred and seventy thousand dollars, plus change.'

I guess my jaw made a thump when it dropped against my chest, because he smiled.

'Think of all the things people wish they'd invested in since 1950 or so, and two or three of them will be things Peter Stevens was into. If I hadn't ended up in here, I'd probably be worth seven or eight million bucks by now. I'd have a Rolls . . . and probably an ulcer as big as a portable radio.'

His hands went to the dirt and began sifting out more pebbles. They moved gracefully, restlessly.

'I was hoping for the best and expecting the worst – nothing but that. The false name was just to keep what little capital I had untainted. It was lugging the paintings out of the path of the hurricane. But I had no idea that the hurricane . . . that it could go on as long as it has.'

I didn't say anything for a while. I guess I was trying to absorb the idea that this small, spare man in prison gray next to me could be worth more money than Warden Norton would make in the rest of his miserable life, even with the scams thrown in.

'When you said you could get a lawyer, you sure weren't kidding,' I said at last. 'For that kind of dough you could have hired Clarence Darrow, or whoever's passing for him these days. Why didn't you, Andy? Christ! You could have been out of here like a rocket.'

He smiled. It was the same smile that had been on his face when he'd told me he and his wife had had their whole lives ahead of them. 'No,' he said.

'A good lawyer would have sprung the Williams kid from Cashman whether he wanted to go or not,' I said. I was getting carried away now. 'You could have gotten your new trial, hired private detectives to look for that guy Blatch, and blown Norton out of the water to boot. Why not, Andy?'

'Because I outsmarted myself. If I ever try to put my hands on Peter Stevens's money from inside here, I'd lose every cent of it. My friend Jim could have arranged it, but Jim's dead. You see the problem?'

I saw it. For all the good the money could do Andy, it might as well have really belonged to another person. In a way, it did. And if the stuff it was invested in suddenly turned bad, all Andy could do would be to watch the plunge, to trace it day after day on the stocks-and-bonds page of the *Press-Herald*. It's a tough life if you don't weaken, I guess.

'I'll tell you how it is, Red. There's a big hayfield in the town of Buxton. You know where Buxton is at, don't you?'

I said I did. It lies right next door to Scarborough.

'That's right. And at the north end of this particular hayfield there's a rock wall, right out of a Robert Frost poem. And somewhere along the base of that wall is a rock that has no business in a Maine hayfield. It's a piece of volcanic glass, and until 1947 it was a paperweight on my office desk. My friend Jim put it in that wall. There's a key underneath it. The key opens a safe deposit box in the Portland branch of the Casco Bank.'

'I guess you're in a pack of trouble,' I said. 'When your friend Jim died, the IRS must have opened all of his safety deposit boxes. Along with the executor of his will, of course.'

Andy smiled and tapped the side of my head. 'Not bad. There's more up there than marshmallows, I guess. But we took care of the possibility that Jim might die while I was in the slam. The box is in the Peter Stevens name, and once a year the firm of lawyers that served as Jim's executors sends a check to the Casco to cover the rental of the Stevens box.

'Peter Stevens is inside that box, just waiting to get out. His birth certificate, his S.S. card, and his driver's license. The license is six years out of date because Jim died six years ago, true, but it's still perfectly renewable for a five-dollar fee. His stock certificates are there, the tax-free municipals, and about eighteen bearer bonds in the amount of ten thousand dollars each.'

I whistled.

'Peter Stevens is locked in a safe deposit box at the Casco Bank in Portland and Andy Dufresne is locked in a safe deposit box at Shawshank,' he said. 'Tit for tat. And the key that unlocks the box and the money and the new life is under a hunk of black glass in a Buxton hayfield. Told you this much, so I'll tell you something else, Red — for the last twenty years, give or take, I have been watching the papers with a more than usual interest for news of any construction projects in Buxton. I keep thinking that someday soon I'm going to read that they're putting a highway through there, or erecting a new community hospital, or building a shopping

STEPHEN KING

center. Burying my new life under ten feet of concrete, or spitting it into a swamp somewhere with a big load of fill.'

I blurted, 'Jesus Christ, Andy, if all of this is true, how do you keep from going crazy?'

He smiled. 'So far, all quiet on the Western front.'

'But it could be years—'

'It will be. But maybe not as many as the state and Warden Norton think it's going to be. I just can't afford to wait that long. I keep thinking about Zihuatanejo and that small hotel. That's all I want from my life now, Red, and I don't think that's too much to want. I didn't kill Glenn Quentin and I didn't kill my wife, and that hotel . . . it's not too much to want. To swim and get a tan and sleep in a room with open windows and *space* . . . that's not too much to want.'

He slung the stones away.

'You know, Red,' he said in an offhand voice, 'a place like that . . . I'd have to have a man who knows how to get things.'

I thought about it for a long time. And the biggest draw-back in my mind wasn't even that we were talking pipedreams in a shitty little prison exercise yard with armed guards looking down at us from their sentry posts. 'I couldn't do it,' I said. 'I couldn't get along on the outside. I'm what they call an institutional man now. In here I'm the man who can get it for you, yeah. But out there, anyone can get it for you. Out there, if you want posters or rock-hammers or one particular record or a boat-in-a-bottle model kit, you can use the fucking Yellow Pages. In here, *I'm* the fucking Yellow Pages. I wouldn't know how to begin. Or where.'

'You underestimate yourself,' he said. 'You're a self-educated man, a self-made man. A rather remarkable man, I think.'

'Hell, I don't even have a high school diploma.'

'I know that,' he said. 'But it isn't just a piece of paper that makes a man. And it isn't just prison that breaks one, either.'

'I couldn't hack it outside, Andy. I know that.'

He got up. 'You think it over,' he said casually, just as the inside whistle blew. And he strolled off, as if he was a free man who had just made another free man a proposition. And for a while just that was enough to make me *feel* free. Andy could do that. He could make me forget for a time that we were both lifers, at the mercy of a hard-ass parole board and a psalm-singing warden who liked Andy Dufresne right where he was. After all, Andy was a lap-dog who could do tax-returns. What a wonderful animal!

But by that night in my cell I felt like a prisoner again. The whole idea seemed absurd, and that mental image of blue water and white beaches seemed more cruel than foolish – it dragged at my brain like a fishhook. I just couldn't wear that invisible coat the way Andy did. I fell asleep that night and dreamed of a great glassy black stone in the middle of a hayfield; a stone shaped like a giant blacksmith's anvil. I was trying to rock the stone up so I could get the key that was underneath. It wouldn't budge; it was just too damned big.

And in the background, but getting closer, I could hear the baying of bloodhounds.

Which leads us, I guess, to the subject of jailbreaks.

Sure, they happen from time to time in our happy little family. You don't go over the wall, though, not at Shawshank, not if you're smart. The searchlight beams go all night, probing long white fingers across the open fields that surround the prison on three sides and the stinking marshland on the fourth.

Cons do go over the wall from time to time, and the search-lights almost always catch them. If not, they get picked up trying to thumb a ride on Highway 6 or Highway 99. If they try to cut across country, some farmer sees them and just phones the location in to the prison. Cons who go over the wall are stupid cons. Shawshank is no Canon City, but in a rural area a man humping his ass across country in a grey pyjama suit sticks out like a cockroach on a wedding cake.

Over the years, the guys who have done the best – maybe oddly, maybe not so oddly – are the guys who did it on the spur of the moment. Some of them have gone out in the middle of a cartful of sheets; a convict sandwich on white, you could say. There was a lot of that when I first came in here, but over the years they have more or less closed that loophole.

Warden Norton's famous 'Inside-Out' program produced its share of escapees, too. They were the guys who decided they liked what lay to the right of the hyphen better than what lay to the left. And again, in most cases it was a very casual kind of thing. Drop your blueberry rake and stroll into the bushes while one of the screws is having a glass of water at the truck or when a couple of them get too involved in arguing over yards passing or rushing on the old Boston Patriots.

In 1969, the Inside-Outers were picking potatoes in Sabbatus. It was the third of November and the work was almost done. There was a guard named Henry Pugh – and he is no longer a member of our happy little family, believe me – sitting on the back bumper of one of the potato trucks and having his lunch with his carbine across his knees when a beautiful (or so it was told to me, but sometimes these things get exaggerated) ten-point buck strolled out of the cold early afternoon mist. Pugh went after it with visions of just how that trophy would look mounted in his rec room, and while he was doing it, three of his charges just walked away. Two were recaptured in a Lisbon Falls pinball parlor. The third has not been found to this day.

I suppose the most famous case of all was that of Sid Nedeau. This goes back to 1958, and I guess it will never be topped. Sid was out lining the ball-field for a Saturday intramural baseball game when the three o'clock inside whistle blew, signalling the shift-change for the guards. The parking lot is just beyond the exercise yard, on the other side of the electrically-operated main gate. At three the gate opens and the guards coming on duty and those going off mingle. There's a lot of back-slapping and bullyragging, comparison of league bowling scores and the usual number of tired old ethnic jokes.

Sid just trundled his lining machine right out through the gate, leaving a three-inch baseline all the way from third base in the exercise yard to the ditch on the far side of Route 6, where they found the machine overturned in a pile of lime. Don't ask me how he did it. He was dressed in his prison uniform, he stood six-feet-two, and he was billowing clouds of lime-dust behind him. All I can figure is that, it being Friday afternoon and all, the guards going off were so happy to be going off, and the guards coming on were so down-hearted to be coming on, that the members of the former group never got their heads out of the clouds and those in the latter never got their noses off their shoetops . . . and old Sid Nedeau just sort of slipped out between the two.

So far as I know, Sid is still at large. Over the years, Andy

Dufresne and I had a good many laughs over Sid Nedeau's great escape, and when we heard about that airline hijacking for ransom, the one where the guy parachuted from the back door of the airplane, Andy swore up and down that D B Cooper's real name was Sid Nedeau.

'And he probably had a pocketful of baseline lime in his pocket for good luck,' Andy said. 'That lucky son of a bitch.'

But you should understand that a case like Sid Nedeau, or the fellow who got away clean from the Sabbatus potato-field crew, guys like that are winning the prison version of the Irish Sweepstakes. Purely a case of six different kinds of luck somehow jelling together all at the same moment. A stiff like Andy could wait ninety years and not get a similar break.

Maybe you remember, a ways back, I mentioned a guy named Henley Backus, the washroom foreman in the laundry. He came to Shawshank in 1922 and died in the prison infirmary thirty-one years later. Escapes and escape attempts were a hobby of his, maybe because he never quite dared to take the plunge himself. He could tell you a hundred different schemes, all of them crackpot, and all of them had been tried in the Shank at one time or another. My favourite was the tale of Beaver Morrison, a b & e convict who tried to build a glider from scratch in the plate-factory basement. The plans he was working from were in a circa-1900 book called *The Modern Boy's Guide to Fun and Adventure*. Beaver got it built without being discovered, or so the story goes, only to discover there was no door from the basement big enough to get the damned thing out. When Henley told that story, you could bust a gut laughing, and he knew a dozen – no, two dozen – just as funny.

When it came to detailing Shawshank bust-outs, Henley had it down chapter and verse. He told me once that during his time there had been better than four hundred escape attempts *that he knew of.* Really think about that for a moment before you just nod your head and read on. Four *hundred* escape attempts! That comes out to 12.9 escape attempts for every year Henley Backus was in Shawshank and keeping track of them. The Escape Attempt of the Month Club. Of course most of them were pretty slipshod affairs, the sort of thing that ends up with a guard grabbing some poor, sidling slob's arm and growling, 'Where do you think *you're* going, you happy asshole?'

Henley said he'd class maybe sixty of them as more serious attempts, and he included the 'prison break' of 1937, the year before I arrived at the Shank. The new administration wing was under construction then and fourteen cons got out, using construction equipment in a poorly locked shed. The whole of southern Maine got into a panic over those fourteen 'hardened criminals', most of whom were scared to death and had no more idea of where they should go than a jackrabbit does when it's headlight-pinned to the highway with a big truck bearing down on it. Not one of those fourteen got away. Two of them were shot dead – by civilians, not police officers or prison personnel – but none got away.

How many *had* gotten away between 1938, when I came here, and that day in October when Andy first mentioned Zihuatanejo to me? Putting my information and Henley's together, I'd say ten. Ten that got away clean. And although it isn't the kind of thing you can know for sure, I'd guess that at least half of those ten are doing time in other institutions

of lower learning like the Shank. Because you *do* get institu-
tionalized. When you take away a man's freedom and teach
him to live in a cell, he seems to lose his ability to think in
dimensions. He's like that jackrabbit I mentioned, frozen in
the oncoming lights of the truck that is bound to kill it. More
often than not a con who's just out will pull some dumb job
that hasn't a chance in hell of succeeding . . . and why? Because
it'll get him back inside. Back where he understands how
things work.

Andy wasn't that way, but I was. The idea of seeing the
Pacific *sounded* good, but I was afraid that actually being there
would scare me to death − the bigness of it.

Anyhow, the day of that conversation about Mexico, and
about Mr Peter Stevens . . . that was the day I began to believe
that Andy had some idea of doing a disappearing act. I hoped
to God he would be careful if he did, and still, I wouldn't
have bet money on his chances of succeeding. Warden Norton,
you see, was watching Andy with a special close eye. Andy
wasn't just another deadhead with a number to Norton; they
had a working relationship, you might say. Also, he had brains
and he had heart. Norton was determined to use the one
and crush the other.

As there are honest politicians on the outside − ones who
stay bought − there are honest prison guards, and if you are
a good judge of character and if you have some loot to spread
around, I suppose it's possible that you could buy enough
look-the-other-way to make a break. I'm not the man to
tell you such a thing has never been done, but Andy Dufresne
wasn't the man who could do it. Because, as I've said, Norton
was watching. Andy knew it, and the screws knew it, too.

Nobody was going to nominate Andy for the Inside-Out

program, not as long as Warden Norton was evaluating the nominations. And Andy was not the kind of man to try a casual Sid Nedeau type of escape.

If I had been him, the thought of that key would have tormented me endlessly. I would have been lucky to get two hours' worth of honest shut-eye a night. Buxton was less than thirty miles from Shawshank. So near and yet so far.

I still thought his best chance was to engage a lawyer and try for the retrial. Anything to get out from under Norton's thumb. Maybe Tommy Williams could be shut up by nothing more than a cushy furlough program, but I wasn't entirely sure. Maybe a good old Mississippi hardass lawyer could crack him . . . and maybe that lawyer wouldn't even have to work that hard. Williams had honestly liked Andy. Every now and then I'd bring these points up to Andy, who would only smile, his eyes far away, and say he was thinking about it.

Apparently he'd been thinking about a lot of other things, as well.

In 1975, Andy Dufresne escaped from Shawshank. He hasn't been recaptured, and I don't think he ever will be. In fact, I don't think Andy Dufresne even exists anymore. But I think there's a man down in Zihuatanejo, Mexico named Peter Stevens. Probably running a very new small hotel in this year of our Lord 1976.

I'll tell you what I know and what I think; that's about all I can do, isn't it?

On 12 March 1975, the cell doors in Cellblock 5 opened at 6.30 A.M., as they do every morning around here except

Sunday. And as they do every day except Sunday, the inmates of those cells stepped forward into the corridor and formed two lines as the cell doors slammed shut behind them. They walked up to the main cellblock gate, where they were counted off by two guards before being sent on down to the cafeteria for a breakfast of oatmeal, scrambled eggs, and fatty bacon.

All of this went according to routine until the count at the cellblock gate. There should have been twenty-seven. Instead, there were twenty-six. After a call to the Captain of the Guards, Cellblock 5 was allowed to go to breakfast.

The Captain of the Guards, a not half-bad fellow named Richard Gonyar, and his assistant, a jolly prick named Dave Burkes, came down to Cellblock 5 right away. Gonyar reopened the cell doors and he and Burkes went down the corridor together, dragging their sticks over the bars, their guns out. In a case like that what you usually have is someone who has been taken sick in the night, so sick he can't even step out of his cell in the morning. More rarely, someone had died . . . or committed suicide.

But this time, they found a mystery instead of a sick man or a dead man. They found no man at all. There were fourteen cells in Cellblock 5, seven to a side, all fairly neat – restriction of visiting privileges is the penalty for a sloppy cell at Shawshank – and all very empty.

Gonyar's first assumption was that there had been a miscount or a practical joke. So instead of going off to work after breakfast, the inmates of Cellblock 5 were sent back to their cells, joking and happy. Any break in the routine was always welcome.

Cell doors opened; prisoners stepped in; cell doors closed.

Some clown shouting, 'I want my lawyer, I want my lawyer, you guys run this place just like a frigging prison.'

Burkes: 'Shut up in there, or I'll rank you.'

The clown: 'I ranked your wife, Burkie.'

Gonyar: 'Shut up, all of you, or you'll spend the day in there.'

He and Burkes went up the line again, counting noses. They didn't have to go far.

'Who belongs in this cell?' Gonyar asked the rightside night guard.

'Andrew Dufresne,' the rightside answered, and that was all it took. Everything stopped being routine right then. The balloon went up.

In all the prison movies I've seen, this wailing horn goes off when there's been a break. That never happens at Shawshank. The first thing Gonyar did was to get in touch with the warden. The second thing was to get a search of the prison going. The third was to alert the State Police in Scarborough to the possibility of a breakout.

That was the routine. It didn't call for them to search the suspected escapee's cell, and so no one did. Not then. Why would they? It was a case of what you see is what you get. It was a small square room, bars on the window and bars on the sliding door. There was a toilet and an empty cot. Some pretty rocks on the windowsill.

And the poster, of course. It was Linda Ronstadt by then. The poster was right over his bunk. There had been a poster there, in that exact same place, for twenty-six years. And when someone – it was Warden Norton himself, as it turned out, poetic justice if there ever was any – looked behind it, they got one hell of a shock.

But that didn't happen until six-thirty that night, almost

twelve hours after Andy had been reported missing, prob-ably twenty hours after he had actually made his escape.

Norton hit the roof.

I have it on good authority – Chester, the trusty, who was waxing the hall floor in the Admin Wing that day. He didn't have to polish any keyplates with his ear that day; he said you could hear the warden clear down to Records & Files as he chewed on Rich Gonyar's ass.

'What do you mean, you're "satisfied he's not on the prison grounds"? What does that mean? It means you didn't find him! You better find him! You better! Because I want him! Do you hear me? I want him!'

Gonyar said something.

'Didn't happen on your shift? That's what *you* say. So far as *I* can tell, no one knows *when* it happened. Or how. Or if it really did. Now, I want him in my office by three o'clock this afternoon, or some heads are going to roll. I can promise you that, and I *always* keep my promises.'

Something else from Gonyar, something that seemed to provoke Norton to even greater rage.

'No? Then look at this! *Look at this!* You recognize it? Last night's tally for Cellblock 5. Every prisoner accounted for! Dufresne was locked up last night at nine and it is impossible for him to be gone now! *It is impossible! Now you find him!*'

But at three that afternoon Andy was still among the missing. Norton himself stormed down to Cellblock 5, where the rest of us had been locked up all of that day. Had we been questioned? We had spent most of that long day being questioned by harried screws who were feeling the breath of the dragon on the backs of their necks. We all said the same thing: we had seen nothing, heard nothing. And so far as I know, we were all telling the truth. I know that I was. All we could say was that Andy had indeed been in his cell at the time of the lock-in, and at lights-out an hour later.

One wit suggested that Andy had poured himself out through the keyhole. The suggestion earned the guy four days in solitary. They were uptight.

So Norton came down – stalked down – glaring at us with blue eyes nearly hot enough to strike sparks from the tempered steel bars of our cages. He looked at us as if he believed we were all in on it. Probably he did believe it.

He went into Andy's cell and looked around. It was just as Andy had left it, the sheets of his bunk turned back but without looking slept-in. Rocks on the windowsill . . . but not all of them. The ones he liked best he took with him.

'Rocks,' Norton hissed, and swept them off the window-ledge with a clatter. Gonyar, who was now on overtime, winced but said nothing.

Norton's eyes fell on the Linda Ronstadt poster. Linda was looking back over her shoulder, her hands tucked into the back pockets of a very tight pair of fawn-coloured slacks. She was wearing a halter and she had a deep California tan. It must have offended the hell out of Norton's Baptist sensibilities, that poster. Watching him glare at it, I remembered what Andy had once said about feeling he could almost step through the picture and be with the girl.

In a very real way, that was exactly what he did – as Norton was only seconds from discovering.

'Wretched thing!' he grunted, and ripped the poster from the wall with a single swipe of his hand.

And revealed the gaping, crumbled hole in the concrete behind it.

Gonyar wouldn't go in.

Norton ordered him – God, they must have heard Norton ordering Rich Gonyar to go in there all over the prison – and Gonyar just refused him, point-blank.

'I'll have your job for this!' Norton screamed. He was as hysterical as a woman having a hot-flash. He had utterly blown his cool. His neck had turned a rich, dark red, and two veins stood out, throbbing, on his forehead. 'You can count on it, you . . . you Frenchman! I'll have your job and I'll see to it that you never get another one in any prison system in New England!'

Gonyar silently held out his service pistol to Norton, butt first. He'd had enough. He was then two hours overtime, going on three, and he'd just had enough. It was as if Andy's defection from our happy little family had driven Norton right over the edge of some private irrationality that had been there for a long time . . . certainly he was crazy that night.

I don't know what that private irrationality might have been, of course. But I do know that there were twenty-eight cons listening to Norton's little dust-up with Rich Gonyar that evening as the last of the light faded from a dull late-winter sky, all of us hard-timers and long-line riders who had seen the administrators come and go, the hard-asses and the candy-asses alike, and we all knew that Warden Samuel Norton had just passed what the engineers like to call 'the breaking strain'.

And by God, it almost seemed to me that somewhere I could hear Andy Dufresne laughing.

Norton finally got a skinny drink of water on the night shift to go into that hole that had been behind Andy's poster of Linda Ronstadt. The skinny guard's name was Rory Tremont, and he was not exactly a ball of fire in the brains department. Maybe he thought he was going to win a Bronze Star or something. As it turned out, it was fortunate that Norton got someone of Andy's approximate height and build to go in there; if they had sent a big-assed fellow – as most prison guards seem to be – the guy would have stuck in there as sure as God made green grass . . . and he might be there still.

Tremont went in with a nylon filament rope, which someone had found in the trunk of his car, tied around his waist and a big six-battery flashlight in one hand. By then Gonyar, who had changed his mind about quitting and who seemed to be the only one there still able to think clearly, had dug out a set of blueprints. I knew well enough what they showed him – a wall which looked, in cross-section, like a sandwich. The entire wall was ten feet thick. The inner and outer sections were each about four feet thick. In the center was two feet of pipe-space, and you want to believe that was the meat of the thing . . . in more ways than one.

Tremont's voice came out of the hole, sounding hollow and dead. 'Something smells awful in here, Warden.'

'Never mind that! Keep going.'

Tremont's lower legs disappeared into the hole. A moment later his feet were gone, too. His light flashed dimly back and forth.

'Warden, it smells pretty damn bad.'

'Never *mind*, I said!' Norton cried.

Dolorously, Tremont's voice floated back: 'Smells like shit. Oh God, that's what it is, it's *shit*, oh my God lemme outta here I'm gonna blow my groceries oh shit it's shit oh my *Gawwwwwd*—' And then came the unmistakable sound of Rory Tremont losing his last couple of meals.

Well, that was it for me. I couldn't help myself. The whole day – hell no, the last thirty *years* – all came up on me at once and I started laughing fit to split, a laugh such as I'd never had since I was a free man, the kind of laugh I never expected to have inside these gray walls. And oh dear *God* didn't it feel good!

'Get that man out of here!' Warden Norton was screaming, and I was laughing so hard I didn't know if he meant me or Tremont. I just went on laughing and kicking my feet and holding onto my belly. I couldn't have stopped if Norton had threatened to shoot me dead-bang on the spot. '*Get him OUT!*'

Well, friends and neighbors, I was the one who went. Straight down to solitary, and there I stayed for fifteen days. A long shot. But every now and then I'd think about poor old not-too-bright Rory Tremont bellowing *oh shit it's shit*, and then I'd think about Andy Dufresne heading south in his own car, dressed in a nice suit, and I'd just have to laugh. I did that fifteen days in solitary practically standing on my head. Maybe because half of me was with Andy Dufresne, Andy Dufresne who had waded in shit and came out clean on the other side, Andy Dufresne, headed for the Pacific.

I heard the rest of what went on that night from half a dozen sources. There wasn't all that much, anyway. I guess that Rory

Tremont decided he didn't have much left to lose after he'd lost his lunch and dinner, because he did go on. There was no danger of falling down the pipe-shaft between the inner and outer segments of the cellblock wall; it was so narrow that Tremont actually had to wedge himself down. He said later that he could only take half-breaths and that he knew what it would be like to be buried alive.

What he found at the bottom of the shaft was a master sewer-pipe which served the fourteen toilets in Cellblock 5, a porcelain pipe that had been laid thirty-three years before. It had been broken into. Beside the jagged hole in the pipe, Tremont found Andy's rock-hammer.

Andy had gotten free, but it hadn't been easy.

The pipe was even narrower than the shaft Tremont had just descended. Rory Tremont didn't go in, and so far as I know, no one else did, either. It must have been damn near unspeakable. A rat jumped out of the pipe as Tremont was examining the hole and the rock-hammer, and he swore later that it was nearly as big as a cocker spaniel pup. He went back up the crawlspace to Andy's cell like a monkey on a stick.

Andy had gone into that pipe. Maybe he knew that it emptied into a stream five hundred yards beyond the prison on the marshy western side. I think he did. The prison blue-prints were around, and Andy would have found a way to look at them. He was a methodical cuss. He would have known or found out that the sewer-pipe running out of Cellblock 5 was the last one in Shawshank not hooked into the new waste-treatment plant, and he would have known it was do it by mid-1975 or do it never, because in August they were going to switch us over to the new waste-treatment plant, too.

Five hundred yards. The length of five football fields. Just shy of a mile. He crawled that distance, maybe with one of those small Penlites in his hand, maybe with nothing but a couple of books of matches. He crawled through foulness that I either can't imagine or don't want to imagine. Maybe the rats scattered in front of him, or maybe they went for him the way such animals sometimes will when they've had a chance to grow bold in the dark. He must have had just enough clearance at the shoulders to keep moving, and he probably had to shove himself through the places where the lengths of pipe were joined. If it had been me, the claustrophobia would have driven me mad a dozen times over. But he did it.

At the far end of the pipe they found a set of muddy footprints leading out of the sluggish, polluted creek the pipe fed into. Two miles from there a search party found his prison uniform – that was a day later.

The story broke big in the papers, as you might guess, but no one within a fifteen-mile radius of the prison stepped forward to report a stolen car, stolen clothes, or a naked man in the moonlight. There was not so much as a barking dog in a farmyard. He came out of the sewer-pipe and he disappeared like smoke.

But I am betting he disappeared in the direction of Buxton.

Three months after that memorable day, Warden Norton resigned. He was a broken man, it gives me great pleasure to report. The spring was gone from his step. On his last day he shuffled out with his head down like an old con shuffling down to the infirmary for his codeine pills. It was Gonyar who took over, and to Norton that must have seemed like the unkindest cut of all. For all I know, Sam Norton is down there in Eliot now, attending services at the Baptist church every Sunday, and wondering how the hell Andy Dufresne ever could have gotten the better of him.

I could have told him; the answer to the question is simplicity itself. Some have got it, Sam. And some don't, and never will.

That's what I know; now I'm going to tell you what I think. I may have it wrong on some of the specifics, but I'd be willing to bet my watch and chain that I've got the general outline down pretty well. Because, with Andy being the sort of man that he was, there's only one or two ways that it could have been. And every now and then, when I think it out, I think of Normaden, that half-crazy Indian. 'Nice fella,' Normaden had said after celling with Andy for six or eight months. 'I was glad to go, me. Bad draft in that cell. All the time cold. He don't let nobody touch his things. That's okay. Nice man, never make fun. But big draft.' Poor crazy Normaden. He knew more than all the rest of us, and he knew it sooner. And it was eight long months before Andy could get him out of there and have the cell to himself again. If it hadn't been for the eight months Normaden had spent with him after Warden Norton first came in, I do believe that Andy would have been free before Nixon resigned.

I believe now that it began in 1949, way back then – not with the rock-hammer, but with the Rita Hayworth poster. I told you how nervous he seemed when he asked for that, nervous and filled with suppressed excitement. At the time I thought it was just embarrassment, that Andy was the sort of guy who'd never want someone else to know that he had feet of clay and wanted a woman . . . even if it was only a fantasy-woman. But I think now that I was wrong. I think now that Andy's excitement came from something else altogether.

What was responsible for the hole that Warden Norton eventually found behind the poster of a girl that hadn't even been born when that photo of Rita Hayworth was taken? Andy Dufresne's perseverance and hard work, yeah – I don't take any of that away from him. But there were two other elements in the equation: a lot of luck, and WPA concrete.

You don't need me to explain the luck, I guess. The WPA concrete I checked out for myself. I invested some time and a couple of stamps and wrote first to the University of Maine History Department and then to a fellow whose address they were able to give me. This fellow had been foreman of the WPA project that built the Shawshank Max Security Wing.

The wing, which contains Cellblocks 3, 4, and 5, was built in the years 1934–37. Now, most people don't think of cement and concrete as 'technological developments', the way we think of cars and oil furnaces and rocket-ships, but they really are. There was no modern cement until 1870 or so, and no modern concrete until after the turn of the century. Mixing concrete is as delicate a business as making bread. You can get it too watery or not watery enough. You can get the sand-mix too thick or too thin, and the same is true of the gravel-mix. And back in 1934, the science of mixing the stuff was a lot less sophisticated than it is today.

The walls of Cellblock 5 were solid enough, but they weren't exactly dry and toasty. As a matter of fact, they were and are pretty damned dank. After a long wet spell they would sweat and sometimes even drip. Cracks had a way of appearing, some an inch deep, and were routinely mortared over.

Now here comes Andy Dufresne into Cellblock 5. He's a man who graduated from the University of Maine's school of business, but he's also a man who took two or three geology courses along the way. Geology had, in fact, become his chief hobby. I imagine it appealed to his patient, meticulous nature. A ten-thousand-year ice age here. A million years of mountain-building there. Tectonic plates grinding against each other deep under the earth's skin over the millennia. *Pressure.* Andy told me once that all of geology is the study of pressure.

And time, of course.

He had time to study those walls. Plenty of time. When the cell door slams and the lights go out, there's nothing else to look at.

First-timers usually had a hard time adjusting to the confinement of prison life. They get screw-fever. Sometimes they have to be hauled down to the infirmary and sedated a couple of times before they get on the beam. It's not unusual to hear some new member of our happy little family banging on the bars of his cell and screaming to be let out . . . and before the cries have gone on for long, the chant starts up along the cellblock: 'Fresh *fish*, hey little fishie, fresh *fish*, fresh *fish*, got fresh *fish* today!'

Andy didn't flip out like that when he came to the Shank in 1948, but that's not to say that he didn't feel many of the same things. He may have come close to madness; some do, and some go sailing right over the edge. Old life blown away in the wink of an eye, indeterminate nightmare stretching out ahead, a long season in hell.

So what did he do, I ask you? He searched almost desperately for something to divert his restless mind. Oh, there are all sorts of ways to divert yourself, even in prison; it seems like the human mind is full of an infinite number of possibilities when it comes to diversion. I told you about the sculptor and his *Three Ages of Jesus*. There were coin collectors who were always losing their collections to thieves, stamp collectors, one fellow who had postcards from thirty-five different countries – and let me tell you, he would have turned out your lights if he'd caught you diddling with his postcards.

Andy got interested in rocks. And the walls of his cell.

I think that his initial intention might have been to do no more than to carve his initials into the wall where the poster of Rita Hayworth would soon be hanging. His initials, or maybe a few lines from some poem. Instead, what he found was that interestingly weak concrete. Maybe he started to carve his initials and a big chunk of the wall fell out. I can see him, lying there on his bunk, looking at that broken chunk of concrete, turning it over in his hands. Never mind the wreck of your whole life, never mind that you got railroaded into this place by a whole trainload of bad luck. Let's forget all that and look at this piece of concrete.

Some months further along he might have decided it would be fun to see how much of that wall he could take out. But you can't just start digging into your wall and then, when the weekly inspection (or one of the surprise inspections that are always turning up interesting caches of booze, drugs, dirty pictures, and weapons) comes around, say to the guard: 'This? Just excavating a little hole in my cell wall. Not to worry, my good man.'

No, he couldn't have that. So he came to me and asked if I could get him a Rita Hayworth poster. Not a little one but a big one.

And, of course, he had the rock-hammer. I remember thinking when I got him that gadget back in '48 that it would take a man six hundred years to burrow through the wall with it. True enough. But Andy only had to go through *half* the wall – and even with the soft concrete, it took him two rock-hammers and twenty-seven years to do it.

Of course he lost most of one of those years to Normaden, and he could only work at night, preferably late at night, when almost everybody is asleep – including the guards who work the night shift. But I suspect the thing which slowed him down the most was getting rid of the wall as he took it out. He could muffle the sound of his work by wrapping the head of his hammer in rock-polishing cloths, but what to do with the pulverized concrete and the occasional chunks that came out whole?

I think he must have broken up the chunks into pebbles and . . .

I remembered the Sunday after I had gotten him the rock-hammer. I remember watching him walk across the exercise yard, his face puffy from his latest go-round with the sisters. I saw him stoop, pick up a pebble . . . and it disappeared up his sleeve. That inside sleeve-pocket is an old prison trick. Up your sleeve or just inside the cuff of your pants. And I have another memory, very strong but unfocused, maybe something I saw more than once. This memory is of Andy Dufresne walking across the exercise yard on a hot summer day when the air was utterly still. Still, yeah . . . except for the little breeze that seemed to be blowing sand around Andy Dufresne's feet.

So maybe he had a couple of cheaters in his pants below the knees. You loaded the cheaters up with fill and then just strolled around, your hands in your pockets, and when you feel safe and unobserved, you gave the pockets a little twitch. The pockets, of course, are attached by string or strong thread to the cheaters. The fill goes cascading out of your pantslegs as you walk. The World War II POWs who were trying to tunnel out used the dodge.

The years went past and Andy brought his wall out to the exercise yard cupful by cupful. He played the game with administrator after administrator, and they thought it was because he wanted to keep the library growing. I have no doubt that was part of it, but the main thing Andy wanted was to keep Cell 14 in Cellblock 5 a single occupancy.

I doubt if he had any real plans or hopes of breaking out, at least not at first. He probably assumed the wall was ten feet of solid concrete, and that if he succeeded in boring all the way through it, he'd come out thirty feet over the exercise yard. But like I say, I don't think he was worried overmuch about breaking through. His assumption could have run this way: I'm only making a foot of progress every seven years or so; therefore, it would take me seventy years to break through; that would make me one hundred and one years old.

Here's a second assumption I would have made, had I been Andy: that eventually I would be caught and get a lot of solitary time, not to mention a very large black mark on my record. After all, there was the regular weekly inspection and a surprise toss – which usually came at night – every second week or so. He must have decided that things couldn't go on for long. Sooner or later, some screw was going to peek behind Rita Hayworth just to make sure Andy didn't have a sharpened spoon-handle or some marijuana reefers Scotch-taped to the wall.

And his response to that second assumption must have been *to hell with it*. Maybe he even made a game out of it. How far in can I get before they find out? Prison is a goddam boring place, and the chance of being surprised by an unscheduled inspection in the middle of the night while he had his poster unstuck probably added some spice to his life during the early years.

And I do believe it would have been impossible for him to get away just on dumb luck. Not for twenty-seven years. Nevertheless, I have to believe that for the first two years – until mid-May of 1950, when he helped Byron Hadley get around the tax on his windfall inheritance – that's exactly what he did get by on.

Or maybe he had something more than dumb luck going for him even back then. He had money, and he might have been slipping someone a little squeeze every week to take it easy on him. Most guards will go along with that if the price is right; it's money in their pockets and the prisoner gets to keep his whack-off pictures or his tailormade cigarettes. Also, Andy was a model prisoner – quiet, well-spoken, respectful, non-violent. It's the crazies and the stampeders that get their cells turned upside-down at least once every six months, their mattresses unzipped, their pillows taken away and cut open, the outflow pipe from their toilets carefully probed.

Then, in 1950, Andy became something more than a model prisoner. In 1950, he became a valuable commodity, a murderer who did tax returns better than H & R Block.

He gave gratis estate-planning advice, set up tax-shelters, filled out loan applications (sometimes creatively). I can remember him sitting behind his desk in the library, patiently going over a car-loan agreement paragraph by paragraph with a screwhead who wanted to buy a used DeSoto, telling the guy what was good about the agreement and what was bad about it, explaining to him that it was possible to shop for a loan and not get hit quite so bad, steering him away from the finance companies which in those days were sometimes little better than legal loan-sharks. When he'd finished, the screwhead started to put out his hand . . . and then drew it back to himself quickly. He'd forgotten for a moment, you see, that he was dealing with a mascot, not a man.

Andy kept up on the tax laws and the changes in the stock market, and so his usefulness didn't end after he'd been in cold storage for a while, as it might have done. He began to get his library money, his running war with the sisters had ended, and nobody tossed his cell very hard. He was a good nigger.

Then one day, very late in the going – perhaps around October of 1967 – the long-time hobby suddenly turned into something else. One night while he was in the hole up to his waist with Raquel Welch hanging down over his ass, the pick end of his rock-hammer must have suddenly sunk into concrete past the hilt.

He would have dragged some chunks of concrete back, but maybe he heard others falling down into that shaft, bouncing back and forth, clinking off that standpipe. Did he know by then that he was going to come upon that shaft, or was he totally surprised? I don't know. He might have seen the prison blueprints by then or he might not have. If not, you can be damned sure he found a way to look at them not long after.

All at once he must have realized that, instead of just playing a game, he was playing for high stakes . . . in terms of his own life and his own future, the highest. Even then he couldn't have known for sure, but he must have had a pretty good idea because it was right around then that he talked to me about Zihuatanejo for the first time. All of a sudden, instead of just being a toy, that stupid hole in the wall became his master – if he knew about the sewer-pipe at the bottom, and that it led under the outer wall, it did, anyway.

He'd had the key under the rock in Buxton to worry about for years. Now he had to worry that some eager-beaver new guard would look behind his poster and expose the whole thing, or that he would get another cellmate, or that he would, after all those years, suddenly be transferred. He had all those things on his mind for the next eight years. All I can say is that he must have been one of the coolest men who ever lived. I would have gone completely nuts after a while, living with all that uncertainty. But Andy just went on playing the game.

He had to carry the possibility of discovery for another eight years – the *probability* of it, you might say, because no matter how carefully he stacked the cards in his favour, as an inmate of a state prison, he just didn't have that many to stack . . . and the gods had been kind to him for a very long time; some nineteen years.

The most ghastly irony I can think of would have been if he had been offered a parole. Can you imagine it? Three days before the parolee is actually released, he is transferred into the light security wing to undergo a complete physical and a battery of vocational tests. While he's there, his old cell is completely cleaned out. Instead of getting his parole, Andy would have gotten a long turn downstairs in solitary, followed by some more time upstairs . . . but in a different cell.

If he broke into the shaft in 1967, how come he didn't escape until 1975?

I don't know for sure – but I can advance some pretty good guesses.

First, he would have become more careful than ever. He was too smart to just push ahead at flank speed and try to get out in eight months, or even in eighteen. He must have gone on widening the opening on the crawlspace a little at a time. A hole as big as a teacup by the time he took his New Year's Eve drink that year. A hole as big as a dinner-plate by the time he took his birthday drink in 1968. As big as a serving-tray by the time the 1969 baseball season opened.

For a time I thought it should have gone much faster than it apparently did – after he broke through, I mean. It seemed to me that, instead of having to pulverize the crap and take it out of his cell in the cheater gadgets I have described, he could simply let it drop down the shaft. The length of time he took makes me believe that he didn't dare do that. He might have decided that the noise would arouse someone's suspicions. Or, if he knew about the sewer-pipe, as I believe he must have, he would have been afraid that a falling chunk of concrete would break it before he was ready, screwing up the cellblock sewage system and leading to an investigation. And an investigation, needless to say, would lead to ruin.

Still and all, I'd guess that, by the time Nixon was sworn in for his second term, the hole would have been wide enough for him to wriggle through . . . and probably sooner than that. Andy was a small guy.

Why didn't he go then?

That's where my educated guesses run out, folks; from this point they become progressively wilder. One possibility is that the crawlspace itself was clogged with crap and he had to clear it out. But that wouldn't account for all the time. So what was it?

I think that maybe Andy got scared.

I've told you as well as I can how it is to be an institutional man. At first you can't stand those four walls, then you get so you can abide them, then you get so you accept them . . . and then, as your body and your mind and your spirit adjust to life on an HO scale, you get to love them. You are told when to eat, when you can write letters, when you can smoke. If you're at work in the laundry or the plate-shop, you're assigned five minutes of each hour when you can go to the bathroom. For thirty-five years, my time was twenty-five minutes after the hour, and after thirty-five years, that's the only time I ever felt the need to take a piss or have a crap: twenty-five minutes past the hour. And if for some reason I couldn't go, the need would pass at thirty after, and come back at twenty-five past the next hour.

I think Andy may have been wrestling with that tiger – that institutional syndrome – and also with the bulking fears that all of it might have been for nothing.

How many nights must he have lain awake under his poster, thinking about that sewer line, knowing that the one chance was all he'd ever get? The blueprints might have told him

521

how big the pipe's bore was, but a blueprint couldn't tell him what it would be like inside that pipe – if he would be able to breathe without choking, if the rats were big enough and mean enough to fight instead of retreating . . . and a blueprint couldn't've told him what he'd find at the end of the pipe, when and if he got there. Here's a joke even funnier than the parole would have been: Andy breaks into the sewer line, crawls through five hundred yards of choking, shit-smelling darkness, and comes up against a heavy-gauge mesh screen at the end of it all. Ha, ha, very funny.

That would have been on his mind. And if the long shot actually came in and he was able to get out, would he be able to get some civilian clothes and get away from the vicinity of the prison undetected? Last of all, suppose he got out of the pipe, got away from Shawshank before the alarm was raised, got to Buxton, overturned the right rock . . . and found nothing beneath? Not necessarily something so dramatic as arriving at the right field and discovering that a high-rise apartment building had been erected on the spot, or that it had turned into a supermarket parking lot. It could have been that some little kid who liked rocks noticed that piece of volcanic glass, turned it over, saw the deposit-box key, and took both it and the rock back to his room as souvenirs. Maybe a November hunter kicked the rock, left the key exposed, and a squirrel or a crow with a liking for bright shiny things had taken it away. Maybe there had been spring floods one year, breeching the wall, washing the key away. Maybe anything.

So I think – wild guess or not – that Andy just froze in place for a while. After all, you can't lose if you don't bet. What did he have to lose, you ask? His library, for one thing.

The poison peace of institutional life, for another. Any future chance to grab his safe identity.

But he finally did it, just as I have told you. He tried . . . and, my! Didn't he succeed in spectacular fashion? You tell me!

But *did* he get away, you ask? What happened after? What happened when he got to that meadow and turned over the rock . . . always assuming the rock was still there?

I can't describe that scene for you, because this institutional man is still in this institution, and expects to be for years to come.

But I'll tell you this. Very late in the summer of 1975, on 15 September to be exact, I got a postcard which had been mailed from the tiny town of McNary, Texas. That town is on the American side of the border, directly across from El Porvenir. The message side of the card was totally blank. But I know. I know it in my heart as surely as I know that we're all going to die someday.

McNary was where he crossed. McNary, Texas.

So that's my story, Jack. I never believed how long it would take to write it all down, or how many pages it would take. I started writing just after I got that postcard, and here I am finishing up on 14 January 1976. I've used three pencils right down to knuckle-stubs, and a whole tablet of paper. I've kept the pages carefully hidden . . . not that many could read my hen-tracks, anyway.

It stirred up more memories than I ever would have believed. Writing about yourself seems to be a lot like sticking a branch into clear river-water and roiling up the muddy bottom.

Well, you weren't writing about yourself, I hear someone in the peanut-gallery saying. *You were writing about Andy Dufresne. You're nothing but a minor character in your own story.* But you know, that's just not so. It's *all* about me, every damned word of it. Andy was the part of me they could never lock up, the part of me that will rejoice when the gates finally open for me and I walk out in my cheap suit with my twenty dollars of mad-money in my pocket. That part of me will rejoice no matter how old and broken and scared the rest of me is. I guess it's just that Andy had more of that part than me, and used it better.

There are others here like me, others who remember Andy. We're glad he's gone, but a little sad, too. Some birds are not meant to be caged, that's all. Their feathers are too bright, their songs too sweet and wild. So you let them go, or when you open the cage to feed them they somehow fly out past you. And the part of you that knows it was wrong to imprison them in the first place rejoices, but still, the place where you live is that much more drab and empty for their departure.

That's the story and I'm glad I told it, even if it is a bit inconclusive and even though some of the memories the pencil prodded up (like that branch poking up the river-mud) made me feel a little sad and even older than I am. Thank you for listening. And Andy: If you're really down there, as I believe you are, look at the stars for me just after sunset, and touch the sand, and wade in the water, and feel free.

I never expected to take up this narrative again, but here I am with the dog-eared, folded pages open on the desk in front of me. Here I am adding another three or four pages, writing in a brand-new tablet. A tablet I bought in a store — I just walked into a store on Portland's Congress Street and bought it.

I thought I had put finish to my story in a Shawshank prison cell on a bleak January day in 1976. Now it's late June of 1977 and I am sitting in a small, cheap room of the Brewster Hotel in Portland, adding to it.

The window is open, and the sound of the traffic floating in seems huge, exciting, and intimidating. I have to look constantly over at the window and reassure myself that there are no bars on it. I sleep poorly at night because the bed in this room, as cheap as the room is, seems much too big and luxurious. I snap awake every morning promptly at six-thirty, feeling disorientated and frightened. My dreams are bad. I have a crazy feeling of free fall. The sensation is as terrifying as it is exhilarating.

What has happened in my life? Can't you guess? I was paroled. After thirty-eight years of routine hearings and routine details (in the course of those thirty-eight years, three lawyers died on me), my parole was granted. I suppose they decided that, at the age of fifty-eight, I was finally used up enough to be deemed safe.

I came very close to burning the document you have just read. They search outgoing parolees just as carefully as they search incoming 'new fish'. And beyond containing enough dynamite to assure me of a quick turnaround and another six or eight years inside, my 'memoirs' contained something else: the name of the town where I believe Andy Dufresne to be. Mexican police gladly cooperate with the American police, and I didn't want my freedom — or my unwillingness

525

to give up the story I'd worked so long and hard to write – to cost Andy his.

Then I remembered how Andy had brought in his five hundred dollars back in 1948, and I took out my story of him the same way. Just to be on the safe side, I carefully rewrote each page which mentioned Zihuatanejo. If the papers had been found during my 'outside search', as they call it at the Shank, I would have gone back in on turn-around . . . but the cops would have been looking for Andy in a Peruvian seacoast town named Las Intrudres.

The Parole Committee got me a job as a 'stock-room assistant' at the big FoodWay Market at the Spruce Mall in South Portland – which means I became just one more ageing bag-boy. There's only two kinds of bag-boys, you know; the old ones and the young ones. No one ever looks at either kind. If you shop at the Spruce Mall FoodWay, I may have even taken your groceries out to your car . . . but you'd have had to have shopped there between March and April of 1977, because that's as long as I worked there.

At first I didn't think I was going to be able to make it on the outside at all. I've described prison society as a scaled-down model of your outside world, but I had no idea of how *fast* things moved on the outside; the *raw speed* people move at. They even talk faster. And louder.

It was the toughest adjustment I've ever had to make, and I haven't finished making it yet . . . not by a long way. Women, for instance. After hardly knowing that they were half of the human race for forty years, I was suddenly working in a store filled with them. Old women, pregnant women wearing T-shirt with arrows pointing downward and the printed motto reading BABY HERE, skinny women with their nipples poking out of their shirts – a woman wearing something like that when I went in would have gotten arrested and then had a sanity hearing – women of every shape and size. I found myself going around with a semi-hard almost all the time and cursing myself for being a dirty old man.

Going to the bathroom, that was another thing. When I had to go (and the urge always came on me at twenty-five past the hour), I had to fight the almost overwhelming need to check it with my boss. Knowing that was something I could just go and do in this too-bright outside world was one thing; adjusting my inner self to that knowledge after all those years of checking it with the nearest screwhead or facing two days in solitary for the oversight . . . that was something else.

My boss didn't like me. He was a young guy, twenty-six or -seven, and I could see that I sort of disgusted him, the way a cringing, servile old dog that crawls up to you on its belly to be petted will disgust a man. Christ, I disgusted myself. But . . . I couldn't make myself stop. I wanted to tell him: *That's what a whole life in prison does for you, young man. It turns everyone in a position of authority into a master, and you into every master's dog. Maybe you know you've become a dog, even in prison, but since everyone else in gray is a dog, too, it doesn't seem to matter so much. Outside, it does.* But I couldn't tell a young guy like him. He would never understand. Neither would my P.O., a big, bluff ex-Navy man with a huge red beard and a large stock of Polish jokes. He saw me for about five minutes every week. 'Are you staying out of the bars, Red?' he'd ask when he'd run out of Polish jokes. I'd say yeah, and that would be the end of it until next week.

Music on the radio. When I went in, the big bands were

just getting up a good head of steam. Now every song sounds like it's about fucking. So many cars. At first I felt like I was taking my life into my hands every time I crossed the street.

There was more – *everything* was strange and frightening – but maybe you get the idea, or can at least grasp a corner of it. I began to think about doing something to get back in. When you're on parole, almost anything will serve. I'm ashamed to say it, but I began to think about stealing some money or shoplifting stuff from the FoodWay, anything, to get back in where it was quiet and you knew everything that was going to come up in the course of the day.

If I had never known Andy, I probably would have done that. But I kept thinking of him, spending all those years chipping patiently away at the cement with his rock-hammer so he could be free. I thought of that and it made me ashamed and I'd drop the idea again. Oh, you can say he had more reason to be free than I did – he had a new identity and a lot of money. But that's not really true, you know. Because he didn't know for sure that the new identity was still there, and without the new identity, the money would always be out of reach. No, what he needed was just to be free, and if I kicked away what I had, it would be like spitting in the face of everything he had worked so hard to win back.

So what I started to do on my time off was to hitchhike a ride down to the little town of Buxton. This was in the early April of 1977, the snow just starting to melt off the fields, the air just beginning to be warm, the baseball teams coming north to start a new season playing the only game I'm sure God approves of. When I went on these trips, I carried a Silva compass in my pocket.

There's a big hayfield in Buxton, Andy had said, *and at the north end of that hayfield there's a rock wall, right out of a Robert Frost poem. And somewhere along the base of that wall is a rock that has no earthly business in a Maine hayfield.*

A fool's errand, you say. How many hayfields are there in a small rural town like Buxton? Fifty? A hundred? Speaking from personal experience, I'd put it at even higher than that, if you add in the fields now cultivated which might have been haygrass when Andy went in. And if I did find the right one, I might never know it. Because I might overlook that black piece of volcanic glass, or, much more likely, Andy put it into his pocket and took it with him.

So I'd agree with you. A fool's errand, no doubt about it. Worse, a dangerous one for a man on parole, because some of those fields were clearly marked with NO TRESPASSING signs. And, as I've said, they're more than happy to slam your ass back inside if you get out of line. A fool's errand . . . but so is chipping at a blank concrete wall for twenty-eight years. And when you're no longer the man who can get it for you and just an old bag-boy, it's nice to have a hobby to take your mind off your new life. My hobby was looking for Andy's rock.

So I'd hitchhike to Buxton and walk the roads. I'd listen to the birds, to the spring runoff in the culverts, examine the bottles the retreating snows had revealed – all useless non-returnables, I am sorry to say; the world seems to have gotten awfully spendthrift since I went into the slam – and looking for hayfields.

Most of them could be eliminated right off. No rock walls. Others had rock walls, but my compass told me they were facing the wrong direction. I walked these wrong ones anyway. It was a comfortable thing to be doing, and on those outings I really *felt* free, at peace. An old dog walked with me one Saturday. And one day I saw a winter-skinny deer.

Then came 23 April, a day I'll not forget even if I live another fifty-eight years. It was a balmy Saturday afternoon, and I was walking up what a little boy fishing from a bridge told me was called The Old Smith Road. I had taken a lunch in a brown FoodWay bag, and had eaten it sitting on a rock by the road. When I was done I carefully buried my leavings, as my dad had taught me before he died, when I was a sprat no older than the fisherman who had named the road for me.

Around two o'clock I came to a big field on my left. There was a stone wall at the far end of it, running roughly north-west. I walked back to it, squelching over the wet ground, and began to walk the wall. A squirrel scolded me from an oak tree.

Three-quarters of the way to the end, I saw the rock. No mistake. Black glass and as smooth as silk. A rock with no earthly business in a Maine hayfield. For a long time I just looked at it, feeling that I might cry, for whatever reason. The squirrel had followed me, and it was still chattering away. My heart was beating madly.

When I felt I had myself under control, I went to the rock, squatted beside it – the joints in my knees went off like a double-barrelled shotgun – and let my hand touch it. It was real. I didn't pick it up because I thought there would be anything under it; I could just as easily have walked away without finding what was beneath. I certainly had no plans to take it away with me, because I didn't feel it was mine to take – I had a feeling that taking that rock from the field would have been the worst kind of theft. No, I only picked it up to feel it better, to get the heft of the thing, and, I suppose, to prove its reality by feeling its satiny texture against my skin.

I had to look at what was underneath for a long time. My eyes saw it, but it took a while for my mind to catch up. It was an envelope, carefully wrapped in a plastic bag to keep away the damp. My name was written across the front in Andy's clear script.

I took the envelope and left the rock where Andy had left it, and Andy's friend before him.

> *Dear Red,*
>
> *If you're reading this, then you're out. One way or another, you're out. And if you've followed along this far, you might be willing to come a little further. I think you remember the name of the town, don't you? I could use a good man to help me get my project on wheels.*
>
> *Meantime, have a drink on me – and do think it over. I will be keeping an eye out for you. Remember that hope is a good thing, Red, maybe the best of things, and no good thing ever dies. I will be hoping that this letter finds you, and finds you well.*
>
> *Your friend,*
> *Peter Stevens*

I didn't read that letter in the field. A kind of terror had come over me, a need to get away from there before I was seen. To make what may be an appropriate pun, I was in terror of being apprehended.

I went back to my room and read it there, with the smell

of old men's dinners drifting up the stairwell to me – Beefaroni, Rice-a-Roni, Noodle Roni. You can bet that whatever the old folks of America, the ones on fixed incomes, are eating tonight, it almost certainly ends in *roni*.

I opened the envelope and read the letter and then I put my head in my arms and cried. With the letter there were twenty new fifty-dollar bills.

And here I am in the Brewster Hotel, technically a fugitive from justice again – parole violation is my crime. No one's going to throw up any roadblocks to catch a criminal wanted on that charge, I guess – wondering what I should do now.

I have this manuscript. I have a small piece of luggage about the size of a doctor's bag that holds everything I own. I have nineteen fifties, four tens, a five, three ones, and assorted change. I broke one of the fifties to buy this tablet of paper and a deck of smokes.

Wondering what I should do.

But there's really no question. It always comes down to just two choices. Get busy living or get busy dying.

First I'm going to put this manuscript back in my bag. Then I'm going to buckle it up, grab my coat, go downstairs, and check out of this fleabag. Then I'm going to walk uptown to a bar and put that five dollar bill down in front of the bartender and ask him to bring me two straight shots of Jack Daniels – one for me and one for Andy Dufresne. Other than a beer or two, they'll be the first drinks I've taken as a free man since 1938. Then I am going to tip the bartender a dollar and thank him kindly. I will leave the bar and walk up Spring Street to the Greyhound terminal there and buy a bus ticket to El Paso by way of New York City. When I get to El Paso, I'm going to buy a ticket to McNary. And when I get to McNary, I guess I'll have a chance to find out if an old crook like me can find a way to float across the border and into Mexico.

Sure I remember the name. Zihuatanejo. A name like that is just too pretty to forget.

I find I am excited, so excited I can hardly hold the pencil in my trembling hand. I think it is the excitement that only a free man can feel, a free man starting a long journey whose conclusion is uncertain.

I hope Andy is down there.

I hope I can make it across the border.

I hope to see my friend and shake his hand.

I hope the Pacific is as blue as it has been in my dreams.

I *hope*.

CHILDREN OF
THE CORN

The movie version is a kind of avatar of '70s horror movies – even the spilled blood looks ready to snort coke and disco at the drop of a BeeGees tune – and it has a line in it (not in the story, you will notice) that my kids still giggle over: 'Outlander, we have your woman!' But awww, c'mon . . . it's not s'bad. To me, it had a *Wicker Man*-ish feel (the first *Wicker Man*, the good one), and Linda Hamilton, who would go on to *Terminator* glory, certainly gives it her all.

Yet sometimes giving one's all is not enough. Sometimes the story is better simply because one's imagination is never on a budget. I think the written version is spookier, because the *corn* is spookier. On film, it just looks like . . . *corn*. On film, corn is never going to give Dracula a run for his money.

One other note: *Children of the Corn* has generated more awful sequels than any other story in my *oeuvre*. There's *Children of the Corn II, III,* and *IV*, at least. Possibly more (I eventually lost count). If my Internet connection weren't down as I write this, I'd check and see if there wasn't even a *Children of the Corn in Space*. I almost think there was. The only one I was really rooting for was *Children of the Corn Meet Leprechaun*. I wanted to hear that little leprechaun guy shouting 'Give me back me corn!' in his cute little Irish accent.

CHILDREN OF
THE CORN

CHILDREN OF
THE CORN

Burt turned the radio on too loud and didn't turn it down because they were on the verge of another argument and he didn't want it to happen. He was desperate for it not to happen.

Vicky said something.

'What?' he shouted.

'Turn it down! Do you want to break my eardrums?'

He bit down hard on what might have come through his mouth and turned it down.

Vicky was fanning herself with her scarf even though the T-Bird was air-conditioned. 'Where are we, anyway?'

'Nebraska.'

She gave him a cold, neutral look. 'Yes, Burt. I know we're in Nebraska, Burt. But where the hell *are* we?'

'You've got the road atlas. Look it up. Or can't you read?'

'Such wit. This is why we got off the turnpike. So we could look at three hundred miles of corn. And enjoy the wit and wisdom of Burt Robeson.'

He was gripping the steering wheel so hard his knuckles were white. He decided he was holding it that tightly because if he loosened up, why, one of those hands might just fly off and hit the ex-Prom Queen beside him right in the chops. We're saving our marriage, he told himself. Yes. We're doing it the same way us grunts went about saving villages in the war.

'Vicky,' he said carefully. 'I have driven fifteen hundred miles on turnpikes since we left Boston. I did all that driving myself because you refused to drive. Then—'

'I did not refuse!' Vicky said hotly. 'Just because I get migraines when I drive for a long time—'

'Then when I asked you if you'd navigate for me on some of the secondary roads, you said sure, Burt. Those were your exact words. Sure, Burt. Then—'

'Sometimes I wonder how I ever wound up married to you.'

'By saying two little words.'

She stared at him for a moment, white-lipped, and then picked up the road atlas. She turned the pages savagely.

It *had* been a mistake leaving the turnpike, Burt thought morosely. It was a shame, too, because up until then they had been doing pretty well, treating each other almost like human beings. It had sometimes seemed that this trip to the coast, ostensibly to see Vicky's brother and his wife but actually a last-ditch attempt to patch up their own marriage, was going to work.

But since they left the pike, it had been bad again. How bad? Well, terrible, actually.

'We left the turnpike at Hamburg, right?'

'Right.'

'There's nothing more until Gatlin,' she said. 'Twenty miles. Wide place in the road. Do you suppose we could stop there and get something to eat? Or does your almighty schedule say we have to go until two o'clock like we did yesterday?'

He took his eyes off the road to look at her. 'I've about had it, Vicky. As far as I'm concerned, we can turn right here and go home and see that lawyer you wanted to talk to. Because this isn't working at—'

She had faced forward again, her expression stonily set. It suddenly turned to surprise and fear. '*Burt look out you're going to*—'

He turned his attention back to the road just in time to see something vanish under the T-Bird's bumper. A moment later, while he was only beginning to switch from gas to brake, he felt something thump sickeningly under the front and then the back wheels. They were thrown forward as the car braked along the center line, decelerating from fifty to zero along black skidmarks.

'A dog,' he said. 'Tell me it was a dog, Vicky.'

Her face was a pallid, cottage-cheese color. 'A boy. A little boy. He just ran out of the corn and . . . congratulations, tiger.'

She fumbled the car door open, leaned out, threw up.

Burt sat straight behind the T-Bird's wheel, hands still gripping it loosely. He was aware of nothing for a long time but the rich, dark smell of fertilizer.

Then he saw that Vicky was gone and when he looked in the outside mirror he saw her stumbling clumsily back toward a heaped bundle that looked like a pile of rags. She was ordinarily a graceful woman but now her grace was gone, robbed.

It's manslaughter. That's what they call it. I took my eyes off the road.

He turned the ignition off and got out. The wind rustled

softly through the growing man-high corn, making a weird sound like respiration. Vicky was standing over the bundle of rags now, and he could hear her sobbing.

He was halfway between the car and where she stood and something caught his eye on the left, a gaudy splash of red amid all the green, as bright as barn paint.

He stopped, looking directly into the corn. He found himself thinking (anything to untrack from those rags that were not rags) that it must have been a fantastically good growing season for corn. It grew close together, almost ready to bear. You could plunge into those neat, shaded rows and spend a day trying to find your way out again. But the neatness was broken here. Several tall cornstalks had been broken and leaned askew. And what was that further back in the shadows?

'Burt!' Vicky screamed at him. 'Don't you want to come see? So you can tell all your poker buddies what you bagged in Nebraska? Don't you—' But the rest was lost in fresh sobs. Her shadow was puddled starkly around her feet. It was almost noon.

Shade closed over him as he entered the corn. The red barn paint was blood. There was a low, somnolent buzz as flies lit, tasted, and buzzed off again . . . maybe to tell others. There was more blood on the leaves further in. Surely it couldn't have splattered this far? And then he was standing over the object he had seen from the road. He picked it up.

The neatness of the rows was disturbed here. Several stalks were canted drunkenly, two of them had been broken clean off. The earth had been gouged. There was blood. The corn rustled. With a little shiver, he walked back to the road.

Vicky was having hysterics, screaming unintelligible words

at him, crying, laughing. Who would have thought it could end in such a melodramatic way? He looked at her and saw he wasn't having an identity crisis or a difficult life transition or any of those trendy things. He hated her. He gave her a hard slap across the face.

She stopped short and put a hand against the reddening impression of his fingers. 'You'll go to jail, Burt,' she said solemnly.

'I don't think so,' he said, and put the suitcase he had found in the corn at her feet.

'What—?'

'I don't know. I guess it belonged to him.' He pointed to the sprawled, face-down body that lay in the road. No more than thirteen, from the look of him.

The suitcase was old. The brown leather was battered and scuffed. Two hanks of clothesline had been wrapped around it and tied in large, clownish grannies. Vicky bent to undo one of them, saw the blood greased into the knot, and withdrew.

Burt knelt and turned the body over gently.

'I don't want to look,' Vicky said, staring down helplessly anyway. And when the staring, sightless face flopped up to regard them, she screamed again. The boy's face was dirty, his expression a grimace of terror. His throat had been cut.

Burt got up and put his arms around Vicky as she began to sway. 'Don't faint,' he said very quietly. 'Do you hear me, Vicky? Don't faint.'

He repeated it over and over and at last she began to recover and held him tight. They might have been dancing, there on the noon-struck road with the boy's corpse at their feet.

'Vicky?'

'What?' Muffled against his shirt.

'Go back to the car and put the keys in your pocket. Get the blanket out of the back seat, and my rifle. Bring them here.'

'The rifle?'

'Someone cut his throat. Maybe whoever is watching us.'

Her head jerked up and her wide eyes considered the corn. It marched away as far as the eye could see, undulating up and down small dips and rises of land.

'I imagine he's gone. But why take chances? Go on. Do it.'

She walked stiltedly back to the car, her shadow following, a dark mascot who stuck close at this hour of the day. When she leaned into the back seat, Burt squatted beside the boy. White male, no distinguishing marks. Run over, yes, but the T-Bird hadn't cut the kid's throat. It had been cut raggedly and inefficiently – no army sergeant had shown the killer the finer points of hand-to-hand assassination – but the final effect had been deadly. He had either run or been pushed through the last thirty feet of corn, dead or mortally wounded. And Burt Robeson had run him down. If the boy had still been alive when the car hit him, his life had been cut short by thirty seconds at most.

Vicky tapped him on the shoulder and he jumped.

She was standing with the brown army blanket over her left arm, the cased pump shotgun in her right hand, her face averted. He took the blanket and spread it on the road. He rolled the body on to it. Vicky uttered a desperate little moan.

'You okay?' He looked up at her. 'Vicky?'

'Okay,' she said in a strangled voice.

He flipped the sides of the blanket over the body and scooped it up, hating the thick, dead weight of it. It tried to make a U in his arms and slither through his grasp. He clutched it tighter and they walked back to the T-Bird.

'Open the trunk,' he grunted.

The trunk was full of travel stuff, suitcases and souvenirs. Vicky shifted most of it into the back seat and Burt slipped the body into the made space and slammed the trunk lid down. A sigh of relief escaped him.

Vicky was standing by the driver's side door, still holding the cased rifle.

'Just put it in the back and get in.'

He looked at his watch and saw only fifteen minutes had passed. It seemed like hours.

'What about the suitcase?' she asked.

He trotted back down the road to where it stood on the white line, like the focal point in an Impressionist painting. He picked it up by its tattered handle and paused for a moment. He had a strong sensation of being watched. It was a feeling he had read about in books, mostly cheap fiction, and he had always doubted its reality. Now he didn't. It was as if there were people in the corn, maybe a lot of them, coldly estimating whether the woman could get the gun out of the case and use it before they could grab him, drag him into the shady rows, cut his throat—

Heart beating thickly, he ran back to the car, pulled the keys out of the trunk lock, and got in.

Vicky was crying again. Burt got them moving, and before a minute had passed, he could no longer pick out the spot where it had happened in the rear-view mirror.

'What did you say the next town was?' he asked.

'Oh.' She bent over the road atlas again. 'Gatlin. We should be there in ten minutes.'

'Does it look big enough to have a police station?'

'No. It's just a dot.'

'Maybe there's a constable.'

They drove in silence for a while. They passed a silo on the left. Nothing else but corn. Nothing passed them going the other way, not even a farm truck.

'Have we passed anything since we got off the turnpike, Vicky?'

She thought about it. 'A car and a tractor. At that intersection.'

'No, since we got on this road. Route 17.'

'No. I don't think we have.' Earlier this might have been the preface to some cutting remark. Now she only stared out of her half of the windshield at the unrolling road and the endless dotted line.

'Vicky? Could you open the suitcase?'

'Do you think it might matter?'

'Don't know. It might.'

While she picked at the knots (her face was set in a peculiar way – expressionless but tight-mouthed – that Burt remembered his mother wearing when she pulled the innards out of the Sunday chicken), Burt turned on the radio again.

The pop station they had been listening to was almost obliterated in static and Burt switched, running the red marker slowly down the dial. Farm reports. Buck Owens. Tammy Wynette. All distant, nearly distorted into babble. Then, near the end of the dial, one single word blared out of the speaker, so loud and clear that the lips which uttered it might have been directly beneath the grill of the dashboard speaker.

'*ATONEMENT!*' this voice bellowed.

Burt made a surprised grunting sound. Vicky jumped.

'*ONLY BY THE BLOOD OF THE LAMB ARE WE SAVED!*' the voice roared, and Burt hurriedly turned the sound down. This station was close, all right. So close that . . . yes, there it was. Poking out of the corn at the horizon, a spidery red tripod against the blue. The radio tower.

'Atonement is the word, brothers 'n' sisters,' the voice told them, dropping to a more conversational pitch. In the background, off-mike, voices murmured amen. 'There's some that thinks it's okay to get out in the world, as if you could work and walk in the world without being smirched by the world. Now is that what the word of God teaches us?'

Off-mike but still loud: 'No!'

'*HOLY JESUS!*' the evangelist shouted, and now the words came in a powerful, pumping cadence, almost as compelling as a driving rock-and-roll beat: 'When they gonna know that way is death? When they gonna know that the wages of the world are paid on the other side? Huh? Huh? The Lord has said there's many mansions in His house. But there's no room for the fornicator. No room for the coveter. No room for the defiler of the corn. No room for the hommasexshul. No room—'

Vicky snapped it off. 'That drivel makes me sick.'

'What did he say?' Burt asked her. 'What did he say about corn?'

'I didn't hear it.' She was picking at the second clothesline knot.

'He said something about corn. I know he did.'

'I got it!' Vicky said, and the suitcase fell open in her lap. They were passing a sign that said: GATLIN 5 MI. DRIVE CAREFULLY PROTECT OUR CHILDREN. The sign had been put up by the Elks. There were .22 bullet holes in it.

'Socks,' Vicky said. 'Two pairs of pants . . . a shirt . . . a belt . . . a string tie with a—' She held it up, showing him the peeling gilt neck clasp. 'Who's that?'

Burt glanced at it. 'Hopalong Cassidy, I think.'

'Oh.' She put it back. She was crying again.

After a moment, Burt said: 'Did anything strike you funny about that radio sermon?'

'No. I heard enough of that stuff as a kid to last me for ever. I told you about it.'

'Didn't you think he sounded kind of young? That preacher?'

She uttered a mirthless laugh. 'A teenager, maybe, so what? That's what's so monstrous about that whole trip. They like to get hold of them when their minds are still rubber. They know how to put all the emotional checks and balances in. You should have been at some of the tent meetings my mother and father dragged me to . . . some of the ones I was "saved" at.

'Let's see. There was Baby Hortense, the Singing Marvel. She was eight. She'd come on and sing "Leaning on the Everlasting Arms" while her daddy passed the plate, telling everybody to "dig deep, now, let's not let this little child of God down." Then there was Norman Staunton. He used to preach hellfire and brimstone in this Little Lord Fauntleroy suit with short pants. He was only seven.'

She nodded at his look of unbelief.

'They weren't the only two, either. There were plenty of

them on the circuit. They were good *draws*.' She spat the word. 'Ruby Stampnell. She was a ten-year-old faith healer. The Grace Sisters. They used to come out with little tin-foil haloes over their heads and – *oh!*'

'What is it?' He jerked around to look at her, and what she was holding in her hands. Vicky was staring at it raptly. Her slowly seining hands had snagged it on the bottom of the suitcase and had brought it up as she talked. Burt pulled over to take a better look. She gave it to him wordlessly.

It was a crucifix that had been made from twists of corn husk, once green, now dry. Attached to this by woven corn-silk was a dwarf corncob. Most of the kernels had been care-fully removed, probably dug out one at a time with a pocket-knife. Those kernels remaining formed a crude cruci-form figure in yellowish bas-relief. Corn-kernel eyes, each slit longways to suggest pupils. Outstretched kernel arms, the legs together, terminating in a rough indication of bare feet. Above, four letters also raised from the bone-white cob: I N R I.

'That's a fantastic piece of workmanship,' he said.

'It's hideous,' she said in a flat, strained voice. 'Throw it out.'

'Vicky, the police might want to see it.'

'Why?'

'Well, I don't know why. Maybe—'

'Throw it out. Will you please do that for me? I don't want it in the car.'

'I'll put it in back. And as soon as we see the cops, we'll get rid of it one way or the other. I promise. Okay?'

'Oh, do whatever you want with it!' she shouted at him. 'You will anyway!'

Troubled, he threw the thing in back, where it landed

on a pile of clothes. Its corn-kernel eyes stared raptly at the T-Bird's dome light. He pulled out again, gravel splurting from beneath the tyres.

'We'll give the body and everything that was in the suitcase to the cops,' he promised. 'Then we'll be shut of it.'

Vicky didn't answer. She was looking at her hands.

A mile further on, the endless cornfields drew away from the road, showing farmhouses and outbuildings. In one yard they saw dirty chickens pecking listlessly at the soil. There were faded cola and chewing-gum ads on the roofs of barns. They passed a tall billboard that said: ONLY JESUS SAVES. They passed a café with a Conoco gas island, but Burt decided to go on into the center of town, if there was one. If not, they could come back to the café. It only occurred to him after they had passed it that the parking lot had been empty except for a dirty old pickup that had looked like it was sitting on two flat tires.

Vicky suddenly began to laugh, a high, giggling sound that struck Burt as being dangerously close to hysteria.

'What's so funny?'

'The signs,' she said, gasping and hiccupping. 'Haven't you been reading them? When they called this the Bible Belt, they sure weren't kidding. Oh Lordy, there's another bunch.' Another burst of hysterical laughter escaped her, and she clapped both hands over her mouth.

Each sign had only one word. They were leaning on whitewashed sticks that had been implanted in the sandy shoulder, long ago by the looks; the whitewash was flaked and faded. They were coming up at eighty-foot intervals and Burt read:

A . . . CLOUD . . . BY . . . DAY . . . A . . . PILLAR . . . OF . . .
FIRE . . . BY . . . NIGHT

'They only forgot one thing,' Vicky said, still giggling helplessly.

'What?' Burt asked, frowning.

'Burma Shave.' She held a knuckled fist against her open mouth to keep in the laughter, but her semi-hysterical giggles flowed around it like effervescent ginger-ale bubbles.

'Vicky, are you all right?'

'I will be. Just as soon as we're a thousand miles away from here, in sunny sinful California with the Rockies between us and Nebraska.'

Another group of signs came up and they read them silently.

TAKE . . . THIS . . . AND . . . EAT . . . SAITH . . . THE . . .
LORD . . . GOD

Now why, Burt thought, should I immediately associate that indefinite pronoun with corn? Isn't that what they say when they give you communion? It had been so long since he had been to church that he really couldn't remember. He wouldn't be surprised if they used cornbread for holy wafer around these parts. He opened his mouth to tell Vicky that, and then thought better of it.

They breasted a gentle rise and there was Gatlin below them, all three blocks of it, looking like a set from a movie about the Depression.

'There'll be a constable,' Burt said, and wondered why the sight of that hick one-timetable town dozing in the sun should have brought a lump of dread into his throat.

They passed a speed sign proclaiming that no more than thirty was now in order, and another sign, rust-flecked, which said: YOU ARE NOW ENTERING GATLIN, NICEST LITTLE TOWN IN NEBRASKA — OR ANYWHERE ELSE! POP. 5431.

Dusty elms stood on both sides of the road, most of them diseased. They passed the Gatlin Lumberyard and a 76 gas station, where the price signs swung slowly in a hot noon breeze: REG 35.9 HI-TEST 38.9, and another which said: HI TRUCKERS DIESEL FUEL AROUND BACK.

They crossed Elm Street, then Birch Street, and came up on the town square. The houses lining the streets were plain wood with screened porches. Angular and functional. The lawns were yellow and dispirited. Up ahead a mongrel dog walked slowly out into the middle of Maple Street, stood looking at them for a moment, then lay down in the road with its nose on its paws.

'Stop,' Vicky said. 'Stop right here.'

Burt pulled obediently to the curb.

'Turn around. Let's take the body to Grand Island. That's not too far, is it? Let's do that.'

'Vicky, what's wrong?'

'What do you mean, what's wrong?' she asked, her voice rising thinly. 'This town is empty, Burt. There's nobody here but us. Can't you feel that?'

He had felt something, and still felt it. But—

'It just seems that way,' he said. 'But it sure is a one-hydrant town. Probably all up in the square, having a bake sale or a bingo game.'

'*There's no one here.*' She said the words with a queer, strained emphasis. 'Didn't you see that 76 station back there?'

'Sure, by the lumberyard, so what?' His mind was else-where, listening to the dull buzz of a cicada burrowing into one of the nearby elms. He could smell corn, dusty roses, and fertilizer – of course. For the first time they were off the turnpike and in a town. A town in a state he had never been in before (although he had flown over it from time to time in United Airlines 747s) and somehow it felt all wrong but all right. Somewhere up ahead there would be a drugstore with a soda fountain, a movie house named the Bijou, a school named after JFK.

'Burt, the prices said thirty-five-nine for regular and thirty-eight-nine for high octane. Now how long has it been since anyone in this country paid those prices?'

'At least four years,' he admitted. 'But, Vicky—'

'We're right in town, Burt, and there's not a car! *Not one car!*'

'Grand Island is seventy miles away. It would look funny if we took him there.'

'I don't care.'

'Look, let's just drive up to the courthouse and—'

'*No!*'

There, damn it, there. Why our marriage is falling apart, in a nutshell. No I won't. No sir. And furthermore, I'll hold my breath till I turn blue if you don't let me have my way.

'Vicky,' he said.

'I want to get out of here, Burt.'

'Vicky, listen to me.'

'Turn around. Let's go.'

'Vicky, will you stop a minute?'

'I'll stop when we're driving the other way. Now let's go.'

'*We have a dead child in the trunk of our car!*' he roared at her, and took a distinct pleasure at the way she flinched, the way her face crumbled. In a slightly lower voice he went on: 'His throat was cut and he was shoved out into the road and I ran him over. Now I'm going to drive up to the court-house or whatever they have here, and I'm going to report it. If you want to start walking toward the pike, go to it. I'll pick you up. But don't you tell me to turn around and drive seventy miles to Grand Island like we had nothing in the trunk but a bag of garbage. He happens to be some mother's son, and I'm going to report it before whoever killed him gets over the hills and far away.'

'You bastard,' she said, crying. 'What am I doing with you?'

'I don't know,' he said. 'I don't know any more. But the situation can be remedied, Vicky.'

He pulled away from the curb. The dog lifted its head at the brief squeal of the tires and then lowered it to its paws again.

They drove the remaining block to the square. At the corner of Main and Pleasant, Main Street split in two. There actually was a town square, a grassy park with a bandstand in the middle. On the other end, where Main Street became one again, there were two official-looking buildings. Burt could make out the lettering on one: GATLIN MUNICIPAL CENTER.

'That's it,' he said. Vicky said nothing.

Halfway up the square, Burt pulled over again. They were beside a lunch room, the Gatlin Bar and Grill.

'Where are you going?' Vicky asked with alarm as he opened his door.

'To find out where everyone is. Sign in the window there says "open".'

'You're not going to leave me here alone.'

'So come. Who's stopping you?'

She unlocked her door and stepped out as he crossed in front of the car. He saw how pale her face was and felt an instant of pity. Hopeless pity.

'Do you hear it?' she asked as he joined her.

'Hear what?'

'The nothing. No cars. No people. No tractors. Nothing.'

And then, from a block over, they heard the high and joyous laughter of children.

'I hear kids,' he said. 'Don't you?'

She looked at him, troubled.

He opened the lunchroom door and stepped into dry, antiseptic heat. The floor was dusty. The sheen on the chrome was dull. The wooden blades of the ceiling fans stood still. Empty tables. Empty counter stools. But the mirror behind the counter had been shattered and there was something else . . . in a moment he had it. All the beer taps had been broken off. They lay along the counter like bizarre party favors.

Vicky's voice was gay and near to breaking. 'Sure. Ask anybody. Pardon me, sir, but could you tell me—'

'Oh, shut up.' But his voice was dull and without force. They were standing in a bar of dusty sunlight that fell through the lunchroom's big plate-glass window and again he had that feeling of being watched and he thought of the boy they had in their trunk, and of the high laughter of children. A phrase came to him for no reason, a legal-sounding phrase, and it began to repeat mystically in his mind: *Sight unseen. Sight unseen. Sight unseen.*

His eyes traveled over the age-yellowed cards thumb-tacked up behind the counter: CHEESEBURG. 35¢ WORLD'S BEST JOE 10¢ STRAWBERRY RHUBARB PIE 25¢ TODAY'S SPECIAL HAM & RED EYE GRAVY W/MASHED POT 80¢.

How long since he had seen lunchroom prices like that?

Vicky had the answer. 'Look at this,' she said shrilly. She was pointing at the calendar on the wall. 'They've been at that bean supper for twelve years, I guess.' She uttered a grinding laugh.

He walked over. The picture showed two boys swimming in a pond while a cute little dog carried off their clothes. Below the picture was the legend: COMPLIMENTS OF GATLIN LUMBER & HARDWARE. *You Breakum, We Fixum.* The month on view was August 1964.

'I don't understand,' he faltered, 'but I'm sure—'

'You're sure!' she cried hysterically. 'Sure, you're sure! That's part of your trouble, Burt, you've spent your whole life being *sure*!'

He turned back to the door and she came after him.

'Where are you going?'

'To the Municipal Center.'

'Burt, why do you have to be so stubborn? You know something's wrong here. Can't you just admit it?'

'I'm not being stubborn. I just want to get shut of what's in that trunk.'

They stepped out on to the sidewalk, and Burt was struck afresh with the town's silence, and with the smell of fertilizer. Somehow you never thought of that smell when you buttered an ear and salted it and bit in. Compliments of sun, rain, all sorts of man-made phosphates, and a good healthy dose of cow shit. But somehow this smell was different from the one he had grown up with in rural upstate New York. You could say whatever you wanted to about organic fertilizer, but there was something almost fragrant about it when the spreader was laying it down in the fields. Not one of your great perfumes, God no, but when the late-afternoon spring breeze would pick up and waft it over the freshly turned fields, it *was* a smell with good associations. It meant winter was over for good. It meant that school doors were going to bang closed in six weeks or so and spill everyone out into summer. It was a smell tied irrevocably in his mind with other aromas that *were* perfume: timothy grass, clover, fresh earth, hollyhocks, dogwood.

But they must do something different out here, he thought. The smell was close but not the same. There was a sickish-sweet undertone. Almost a death smell. As a medical orderly in Vietnam, he had become well versed in that smell.

Vicky was sitting quietly in the car, holding the corn crucifix in her lap and staring at it in a rapt way Burt didn't like.

'Put that thing down,' he said.

'No,' she said without looking up. 'You play your games and I'll play mine.'

He put the car in gear and drove up to the corner. A dead stoplight hung overhead, swinging in a faint breeze. To the left was a neat white church. The grass was cut. Neatly kept flowers grew beside the flagged path up to the door. Burt pulled over.

'What are you doing?'

'I'm going to go in and take a look,' Burt said. 'It's the only place in town that looks as if there isn't ten years' dust on it. And look at the sermon board.'

She looked. Neatly pegged white letters under glass read: THE POWER AND GRACE OF HE WHO WALKS BEHIND THE ROWS. The date was 27 July 1976 – the Sunday before.

'He Who Walks Behind the Rows,' Burt said, turning off

557

the ignition. 'One of the nine thousand names of God only used in Nebraska, I guess. Coming?'

She didn't smile. 'I'm not going in with you.'

'Fine. Whatever you want.'

'I haven't been in a church since I left home and I don't want to be in *this* church and I don't want to be in *this town*, Burt. I'm scared out of my mind, can't we just *go*?'

'I'll only be a minute.'

'I've got my keys, Burt. If you're not back in five minutes, I'll just drive away and leave you here.'

'Now just wait a minute, lady.'

'That's what I'm going to do. Unless you want to assault me like a common mugger and take my keys. I suppose you could do that.'

'But you don't think I will.'

'No.'

Her purse was on the seat between them. He snatched it up. She screamed and grabbed for the shoulder strap. He pulled it out of her reach. Not bothering to dig, he simply turned the bag upside down and let everything fall out. Her key-ring glittered amid tissues, cosmetics, change, old shopping lists. She lunged for it but he beat her again and put the keys in his own pocket.

'You didn't have to do that,' she said, crying. 'Give them to me.'

'No,' he said, and gave her a hard, meaningless grin. 'No way.'

'*Please, Burt! I'm scared!*' She held her hand out, pleading now.

'You'd wait two minutes and decide that was long enough.'

'I wouldn't—'

'And then you'd drive off laughing and saying to yourself, "That'll teach Burt to cross me when I want something." Hasn't that pretty much been your motto during our married life? That'll teach Burt to cross me?'

He got out of the car.

'Please, Burt?' she screamed, sliding across the seat. 'Listen . . . I know . . . we'll drive out of town and call from a phone booth, okay? I've got all kinds of change. I just . . . we can . . . *don't leave me alone, Burt, don't leave me out here alone!*'

He slammed the door on her cry and then leaned against the side of the T-Bird for a moment, thumbs against his closed eyes. She was pounding on the driver's side window and calling his name. She was going to make a wonderful impression when he finally found someone in authority to take charge of the kid's body. Oh yes.

He turned and walked up the flagstone path to the church doors. Two or three minutes, just a look around, and he would be back out. Probably the door wasn't even unlocked.

But it pushed in easily on silent, well-oiled hinges (reverently oiled, he thought, and that seemed funny for no really good reason) and he stepped into a vestibule so cool it was almost chilly. It took his eyes a moment to adjust to the dimness.

The first thing he noticed was a pile of wooden letters in the far corner, dusty and jumbled indifferently together. He went to them, curious. They looked as old and forgotten as the calendar in the bar and grill, unlike the rest of the vestibule, which was dust-free and tidy. The letters were about two feet high, obviously part of a set. He spread them out on the carpet – there were eighteen of them – and shifted them around like anagrams. HURT BITE CRAG CHAP CS. Nope. CRAP TARGET CHIBS HUC. That wasn't much good either. Except for the CH in CHIBS. He quickly assembled the word CHURCH and was left looking at RAP TAGET CIBS. Foolish. He was squatting here playing idiot games with a bunch of letters while Vicky was going nuts out in the car. He started to get up, and then saw it. He formed BAPTIST, leaving RAG EC – and by changing two letters he had GRACE. GRACE BAPTIST CHURCH. The letters must have been out front. They had taken them down and had thrown them indifferently in the corner, and the church had been painted since then so that you couldn't even see where the letters had been.

Why?

It wasn't the Grace Baptist Church any more, that was why. So what kind of church was it? For some reason that question caused a trickle of fear and he stood up quickly, dusting his fingers. So they had taken down a bunch of letters, so what? Maybe they had changed the place into Flip Wilson's Church of What's Happening Now.

But what had happened then?

He shook it off impatiently and went through the inner doors. Now he was standing at the back of the church itself, and as he looked toward the nave, he felt fear close around his heart and squeeze tightly. His breath drew in, loud in the pregnant silence of this place.

The space behind the pulpit was dominated by a gigantic portrait of Christ, and Burt thought: If nothing else in this town gave Vicky the screaming meemies, this would.

The Christ was grinning, vulpine. His eyes were wide and staring, reminding Burt uneasily of Lon Chaney in *The Phantom of the Opera*. In each of the wide black pupils someone (a sinner, presumably) was drowning in a lake of fire. But the oddest thing was that this Christ had green hair . . . hair which on closer examination revealed itself to be a twining mass of early-summer corn. The picture was crudely done but effective. It looked like a comic-strip mural done by a gifted child – an Old Testament Christ, or a pagan Christ that might slaughter his sheep for sacrifice instead of leading them.

At the foot of the left-hand ranks of pews was a pipe organ, and Burt could not at first tell what was wrong with it. He walked down the left-hand aisle and saw with slowly dawning horror that the keys had been ripped up, the stops had been pulled out . . . and the pipes themselves filled with dry cornhusks. Over the organ was a carefully lettered plaque which read: MAKE NO MUSIC EXCEPT WITH HUMAN TONGUE SAITH THE LORD GOD.

Vicky was right. Something was terribly wrong here. He debated going back to Vicky without exploring any further, just getting into the car and leaving town as quickly as possible, never mind the Municipal Building. But it grated on him. Tell the truth, he thought. You want to give her Ban 5000 a workout before going back and admitting she was right to start with.

He would go back in a minute or so.

He walked toward the pulpit, thinking: People must go through Gatlin all the time. There must be people in the neighboring towns who have friends and relatives here. The Nebraska SP must cruise through from time to time. And what about the power company? The stoplight had been dead. Surely they'd know if the power had been off for twelve long years. Conclusion: What seemed to have happened in Gatlin was impossible.

Still, he had the creeps.

He climbed the four carpeted steps to the pulpit and looked out over the deserted pews, glimmering in the half-shadows. He seemed to feel the weight of those eldritch and decidedly unchristian eyes boring into his back.

There was a large Bible on the lectern, opened to the thirty-eighth chapter of Job. Burt glanced down at it and read: 'Then the Lord answered Job out of the whirlwind, and said, Who is this that darkeneth counsel by words without knowledge? . . . Where wast thou when I laid the foundations of the earth? Declare, if thou hast understanding.' The Lord. He Who Walks Behind the Rows. Declare if thou hast understanding. And please pass the corn.

He fluttered the pages of the Bible, and they made a dry whispering sound in the quiet – the sound that ghosts might make if there really were such things. And in a place like this you could almost believe it. Sections of the Bible had been chopped out. Mostly from the New Testament, he saw. Someone had decided to take on the job of amending Good King James with a pair of scissors.

But the Old Testament was intact.

He was about to leave the pulpit when he saw another book on a lower shelf and took it out, thinking it might be a church record of weddings and confirmations and burials.

He grimaced at the words stamped on the cover, done inexpertly in gold leaf: THUS LET THE INIQUITOUS BE CUT DOWN SO THAT THE GROUND MAY BE FERTILE AGAIN SAITH THE LORD GOD OF HOSTS.

There seemed to be one train of thought around here, and Burt didn't care much for the track it seemed to ride on.

He opened the book to the first wide, lined sheet. A child had done the lettering, he saw immediately. In places an ink eraser had been carefully used, and while there were no misspellings, the letters were large and childishly made, drawn rather than written. The first column read:

Amos Deigan (Richard), b. Sept. 4, 1945   Sept. 4, 1964

Isaac Renfrew (William), b. Sept. 19, 1945   Sept. 19, 1964

Zepeniah Kirk (George), b. Oct. 14, 1945   Oct. 14, 1964

Mary Wells (Roberta), b. Nov. 12, 1945   Nov. 12, 1964

Yemen Hollis (Edward), b. Jan. 5, 1946   Jan. 5, 1965

Frowning, Burt continued to turn through the pages. Three-quarters of the way through, the double columns ended abruptly:

Rachel Stigman (Donna), b. June 21, 1957   June 21, 1976

Moses Richardson (Henry), b. July 29, 1957

Malachi Boardman (Craig), b. August 15, 1957

The last entry in the book was for Ruth Clawson (Sandra), b. April 30, 1961. Burt looked at the shelf where he had found this book and came up with two more. The first had the same INIQUITOUS BE CUT DOWN logo, and it continued the same record, the single column tracing birth dates and names. In early September of 1964 he found Job Gilman (Clayton), b. September 6, and the next entry was Eve Tobin, b. June 16, 1965. No second name in parentheses.

The third book was blank.

Standing behind the pulpit, Burt thought about it.

Something had happened in 1964. Something to do with religion, and corn . . . and children.

Dear God we beg thy blessing on the crop. For Jesus' sake, amen.

And the knife raised high to sacrifice the lamb – but had it been a lamb? Perhaps a religious mania had swept them.

Alone, all alone, cut off from the outside world by hundreds of square miles of the rustling secret corn. Alone under seventy million acres of blue sky. Alone under the watchful eye of God, now a strange green God, a God of corn, grown old and strange and hungry. He Who Walks Behind the Rows.

Burt felt a chill creep into his flesh.

Vicky, let me tell you a story. It's about Amos Deigan, who was born Richard Deigan on 4 September 1945. He took the name Amos in 1964, fine Old Testament name, Amos, one of the minor prophets. Well, Vicky, what happened – don't laugh – is that Dick Deigan and his friends – Billy Renfrew, George Kirk, Roberta Wells, and Eddie Hollis among others – they got religion and they killed off their parents. All of them. Isn't that a scream? Shot them in their beds, knifed them in their bathtubs, poisoned their suppers, hung them, or disembowelled them, for all I know.

Why? The corn. Maybe it was dying. Maybe they got the idea somehow that it was dying because there was too much sinning. Not enough sacrifice. They would have done it in the corn, in the rows.

And somehow, Vicky, I'm quite sure of this, somehow they decided that nineteen was as old as any of them could live. Richard 'Amos' Deigan, the hero of our little story, had his nineteenth birthday on 4 September 1964 – the date in the book. I think maybe they killed him. Sacrificed him in the corn. Isn't that a silly story?

But let's look at Rachel Stigman, who was Donna Stigman until 1964. She turned nineteen on 21 June, just about a month ago. Moses Richardson was born on 29 July – just three days from today he'll be nineteen. Any idea what's going to happen to ole Mose on the twenty-ninth?

I can guess.

Burt licked his lips, which felt dry.

One other thing, Vicky. Look at this. We have Job Gilman (Clayton) born on 6 September 1964. No other births until 16 June 1965. A gap of ten months. Know what I think? They killed all the parents, even the pregnant ones, that's what I think. And one of *them* got pregnant in October of 1964 and gave birth to Eve. Some sixteen- or seventeen-year-old girl. *Eve. The first woman.*

He thumbed back through the book feverishly and found the Eve Tobin entry. Below it: 'Adam Greenlaw, b. July 11, 1965'.

They'd be just eleven now, he thought, and his flesh began to crawl. And maybe they're out there. Someplace.

But how could such a thing be kept secret? How could it go on?

How unless the God in question approved?

'Oh Jesus,' Burt said into the silence, and that was when the T-Bird's horn began to blare into the afternoon, one long continuous blast.

Burt jumped from the pulpit and ran down the center aisle. He threw open the outer vestibule door, letting in hot sunshine, dazzling. Vicky was bolt upright behind the steering wheel, both hands plastered on the horn ring, her head swivelling wildly. From all around the children were coming. Some of them were laughing gaily. They held knives, hatchets, pipes, rocks, hammers. One girl, maybe eight, with beautiful long blond hair, held a jackhandle. Rural weapons. Not a gun among them. Burt felt a wild urge to scream out: *Which of you is Adam and Eve? Who are the mothers? Who are the daughters? Fathers? Sons?*

Declare, if thou hast understanding.

They came from the side streets, from the town green, through the gate in the chain-link fence around the school playground a block further east. Some of them glanced indifferently at Burt, standing frozen on the church steps, and some nudged each other and pointed and smiled . . . the sweet smiles of children.

The girls were dressed in long brown wool and faded sun-bonnets. The boys, like Quaker parsons, were all in black and wore round-crowned flat-brimmed hats. They streamed across the town square toward the car, across lawns, a few came across the front yard of what had been the Grace Baptist Church until 1964. One or two of them almost close enough to touch.

'The shotgun!' Burt yelled. 'Vicky, get the shotgun!'

But she was frozen in her panic, he could see that from the steps. He doubted if she could even hear him through the closed windows.

They converged on the Thunderbird. The axes and hatchets and chunks of pipe began to rise and fall. My God, am I seeing this? he thought frozenly. An arrow of chrome fell off the side of the car. The hood ornament went flying. Knives crawled spirals through the sidewalls of the tires and the car settled. The horn blared on and on. The windshield and side windows went opaque and cracked under the onslaught . . . and then the safety glass sprayed inwards and he could see again. Vicky was crouched back, only one hand on the horn ring now, the other thrown up to protect her face. Eager young hands reached in, fumbling for the lock/unlock button. She beat them away wildly. The horn became intermittent and then stopped altogether.

The beaten and dented driver's side door was hauled open. They were trying to drag her out but her hands were wrapped around the steering wheel. Then one of them leaned in, knife in hand, and—

His paralysis broke and he plunged down the steps, almost falling, and ran down the flagstone walk, toward them. One of them, a boy about sixteen with long red hair spilling out from beneath his hat, turned toward him, almost casually, and something flicked through the air. Burt's left arm jerked backward, and for a moment he had the absurd thought that he had been punched at long distance. Then the pain came, so sharp and sudden that the world went gray.

He examined his arm with a stupid sort of wonder. A buck and a half Pensy jack-knife was growing out of it like a strange tumor. The sleeve of his J. C. Penney sports shirt was turning red. He looked at it for what seemed like forever, trying to understand how he could have grown a jack-knife . . . was it possible?

When he looked up, the boy with red hair was almost on top of him. He was grinning, confident.

'Hey, you bastard,' Burt said. His voice was creaking, shocked.

'Remand your soul to God, for you will stand before His throne momentarily,' the boy with the red hair said, and clawed for Burt's eyes.

Burt stepped back, pulled the Pensy out of his arm, and stuck it into the red-haired boy's throat. The gush of blood was immediate, gigantic. Burt was splashed with it. The red-haired boy began to gobble and walk in a large circle. He clawed at the knife, trying to pull it free, and was unable. Burt watched him, jaw hanging agape. None of this was happening. It was a dream. The red-haired boy gobbled and walked. Now his sound was the only one in the hot early afternoon. The others watched, stunned.

This part of it wasn't in the script, Burt thought numbly. Vicky and I, we were in the script. And the boy in the corn, who was trying to run away. But not one of their own. He stared at them savagely, wanting to scream, *How do you like it?*

The red-haired boy gave one last weak gobble, and sank to his knees. He stared up at Burt for a moment, and then his hands dropped away from the shaft of the knife, and he fell forward.

A soft sighing sound from the children gathered around the Thunderbird. They stared at Burt. Burt stared back at them, fascinated . . . and that was when he noticed that Vicky was gone.

'Where is she?' he asked. 'Where did you take her?'

One of the boys raised a blood-streaked hunting knife toward his throat and made a sawing motion there. He grinned. That was the only answer.

From somewhere in back, an older boy's voice, soft: 'Get him.'

The boys began to walk toward him. Burt backed up. They began to walk faster. Burt backed up faster. The shotgun, the goddamned shotgun! Out of reach. The sun cut their shadows darkly on the green church lawn . . . and then he was on the sidewalk. He turned and ran.

'*Kill him!*' someone roared, and they came after him.

He ran, but not quite blindly. He skirted the Municipal Building – no help there, they would corner him like a rat – and ran on up Main Street, which opened out and became the highway again two blocks further up. He and Vicky would have been on that road now and away, if he had only listened.

His loafers slapped against the sidewalk. Ahead of him he could see a few more business buildings, including the Gatlin Ice Cream Shoppe and – sure enough – the Bijou Theater. The dust-clotted marquee letters read NOW HOWING L MITED EN AGEMEN ELI A TH TAYLOR CLEOPA RA. Beyond the next cross street was a gas station that marked the edge of town. And beyond that the corn, closing back in to the sides of the road. A green tide of corn.

Burt ran. He was already out of breath and the knife wound in his upper arm was beginning to hurt. And he was leaving a trail of blood. As he ran he yanked his handkerchief from his back pocket and stuck it inside his shirt.

He ran. His loafers pounded the cracked cement of the sidewalk, his breath rasped in his throat with more and more heat. His arm began to throb in earnest. Some mordant part of his brain tried to ask if he thought he could run all the way to the next town, if he could run twenty miles of two-lane blacktop.

He ran. Behind him he could hear them, fifteen years younger and faster than he was, gaining. Their feet slapped on the pavement. They whooped and shouted back and forth to each other. They're having more fun than a five-alarm fire, Burt thought disjointedly. They'll talk about it for years.

Burt ran.

He ran past the gas station marking the edge of town. His breath gasped and roared in his chest. The sidewalk ran out under his feet. And now there was only one thing to do, only one chance to beat them and escape with his life. The houses were gone, the town was gone. The corn had surged in a soft green wave back to the edges of the road. The green, swordlike leaves rustled softly. It would be deep in there, deep and cool, shady in the rows of man-high corn.

He ran past a sign that said: YOU ARE NOW LEAVING GATLIN, NICEST LITTLE TOWN IN NEBRASKA — OR ANYWHERE ELSE! DROP IN ANYTIME!

I'll be sure to do that, Burt thought dimly.

He ran past the sign like a sprinter closing on the tape and then swerved left, crossing the road, and kicked his loafers away. Then he was in the corn and it closed behind him and over him like the waves of a green sea, taking him in. Hiding him. He felt a sudden and wholly unexpected relief sweep him, and at the same moment he got his second wind. His lungs, which had been shallowing up, seemed to unlock and give him more breath.

He ran straight down the first row he had entered, head ducked, his broad shoulders swiping the leaves and making them tremble. Twenty yards in he turned right, parallel to the road again, and ran on, keeping low so they wouldn't see his dark head of hair bobbing amid the yellow corn tassels. He doubled back toward the road for a few moments, crossed more rows, and then put his back to the road and hopped randomly from row to row, always delving deeper and deeper into the corn.

At last, he collapsed on to his knees and put his forehead against the ground. He could only hear his own taxed breathing, and the thought that played over and over in his mind was: *Thank God I gave up smoking, thank God I gave up smoking, thank God—*

Then he could hear them, yelling back and forth to each other, in some cases bumping into each other ('Hey, this is my row!'), and the sound heartened him. They were well away to his left and they sounded very poorly organized.

He took his handkerchief out of his shirt, folded it, and stuck it back in after looking at the wound. The bleeding seemed to have stopped in spite of the workout he had given it.

He rested a moment longer, and was suddenly aware that he felt *good*, physically better than he had in years . . . excepting the throb of his arm. He felt well exercised, and suddenly grappling with a clearcut (no matter how insane) problem after two years of trying to cope with the incubotic gremlins that were sucking his marriage dry.

It wasn't right that he should feel this way, he told himself. He was in deadly peril of his life, and his wife had been carried off. She might be dead now. He tried to summon up Vicky's face and dispel some of the odd good feeling by doing so, but her face wouldn't come. What came was the red-haired boy with the knife in his throat.

He became aware of the corn fragrance in his nose now, all around him. The wind through the tops of the plants made a sound like voices. Soothing. Whatever had been done in the name of this corn, it was now his protector.

But they were getting closer.

Running hunched over, he hurried up the row he was in, crossed over, doubled back, and crossed over more rows. He tried to keep the voices always on his left, but as the afternoon progressed, that became harder to do. The voices had grown faint, and often the rustling sound of the corn obscured them altogether. He would run, listen, run again. The earth was hard-packed, and his stockinged feet left little or no trace.

When he stopped much later the sun was hanging over the fields to his right, red and inflamed, and when he looked at his watch he saw that it was quarter past seven. The sun had stained the corntops a reddish gold, but here the shadows were dark and deep. He cocked his head, listening. With the coming of sunset the wind had died entirely and the corn stood still, exhaling its aroma of growth into the warm air. If they were still in the corn they were either far away or just hunkered down and listening. But Burt didn't think a bunch of kids, even crazy ones, could be quiet for that long. He suspected they had done the most kidlike thing, regardless of the consequences for them; they had given up and gone home.

He turned toward the setting sun, which had sunk between the raftered clouds on the horizon, and began to walk. If he cut on a diagonal through the rows, always keeping the setting sun ahead of him, he would be bound to strike Route 17 sooner or later.

The ache in his arm had settled into a dull throb that was nearly pleasant, and the good feeling was still with him. He decided that as long as he was here, he would let the good feeling exist in him without guilt. The guilt would return when he had to face the authorities and account for what had happened in Gatlin. But that could wait.

He pressed through the corn, thinking he had never felt so keenly aware. Fifteen minutes later the sun was only a hemisphere poking over the horizon and he stopped again, his new awareness clicking into a pattern he didn't like. It was vaguely . . . well, vaguely frightening.

He cocked his head. The corn was rustling.

Burt had been aware of that for some time, but he had

just put it together with something else. The wind was still. How could that be?

He looked around warily, half expecting to see the smiling boys in their Quaker coats creeping out of the corn, their knives clutched in their hands. Nothing of the sort. There was still that rustling noise. Off to the left.

He began to walk in that direction, not having to bull through the corn any more. The row was taking him in the direction he wanted to go, naturally. The row ended up ahead. Ended? No, emptied out into some sort of clearing. The rustling was there.

He stopped, suddenly afraid.

The scent of the corn was strong enough to be cloying. The rows held on to the sun's heat and he became aware that he was plastered with sweat and chaff and thin spider strands of cornsilk. The bugs ought to be crawling all over him . . . but they weren't.

He stood still, staring toward that place where the corn opened out on to what looked like a large circle of bare earth.

There were no minges or mosquitoes in here, no black-flies or chiggers – what he and Vicky had called 'drive-in bugs' when they had been courting, he thought with sudden and unexpectedly sad nostalgia. And he hadn't seen a single crow. How was that for weird, a cornpatch with no crows?

In the last of the daylight he swept his eyes closely over the row of corn to his left. And saw that every leaf and stalk was perfect, which was just not possible. No yellow blight. No tattered leaves, no caterpillar eggs, no burrows, no—

His eyes widened.

My God, there aren't any weeds!

Not a single one. Every foot and a half the corn plants rose from the earth. There was no witchgrass, jimson, pike-weed, whore's hair, or poke salad. Nothing.

Burt stared up, eyes wide. The light in the west was fading. The raftered clouds had drawn back together. Below them the golden light had faded to pink and ocher. It would be dark soon enough.

It was time to go down to the clearing in the corn and see what was there – hadn't that been the plan all along? All the time he had thought he was cutting back to the highway, hadn't he been being led to this place?

Dread in his belly, he went on down to the row and stood at the edge of the clearing. There was enough light for him to see what was here. He couldn't scream. There didn't seem to be enough air left in his lungs. He tottered in on legs like slats of splintery wood. His eyes bulged from his sweaty face.

'Vicky,' he whispered. 'Oh, Vicky, my God—'

She had been mounted on a crossbar like a hideous trophy, her arms held at the wrists and her legs at the ankles with twists of common barbed wire, seventy cents a yard at any hardware store in Nebraska. Her eyes had been ripped out. The sockets were filled with the moonflax of cornsilk. Her jaws were wrenched open in a silent scream, her mouth filled with cornhusks.

On her left was a skeleton in a moldering surplice. The nude jawbone grinned. The eye sockets seemed to stare at Burt jocularly, as if the one-time minister of the Grace Baptist Church was saying: *It's not so bad, being sacrificed by pagan devil-children in the corn is not so bad, having your eyes ripped out of your skull according to the Laws of Moses is not so bad—*

To the left of the skeleton in the surplice was a second

skeleton, this one dressed in a rotting blue uniform. A hat hung over the skull, shading the eyes, and on the peak of the cap was a greenish-tinged badge reading POLICE CHIEF.

That was when Burt heard it coming: not the children but something much larger, moving through the corn and toward the clearing. Not the children, no. The children wouldn't venture into the corn at night. This was the holy place, the place of He Who Walks Behind the Rows.

Jerkily Burt turned to flee. The row he had entered the clearing by was gone. Closed up. All the rows had closed up. It was coming closer now and he could hear it, pushing through the corn. He could hear it breathing. An ecstasy of superstitious terror seized him. It was coming. The corn on the far side of the clearing had suddenly darkened, as if a gigantic shadow had blotted it out.

Coming.

He Who Walks Behind the Rows.

It began to come into the clearing. Burt saw something huge, bulking up to the sky . . . something green with terrible red eyes the size of footballs.

Something that smelled like dried cornhusks years in some dark barn.

He began to scream. But he did not scream long.

Some time later, a bloated orange harvest moon came up.

The children of the corn stood in the clearing at midday, looking at the two crucified skeletons and the two bodies . . . the bodies were not skeletons yet, but they would be. In time. And here, in the heartlands of Nebraska, in the corn, there was nothing but time.

'Behold, a dream came to me in the night, and the Lord did shew all this to me.'

They all turned to look at Isaac with dread and wonder, even Malachi. Isaac was only nine, but he had been the Seer since the corn had taken David a year ago. David had been nineteen and he had walked into the corn on his birthday, just as dusk had come drifting down the summer rows.

Now, small face grave under his round-crowned hat, Isaac continued:

'And in my dream the Lord was a shadow that walked behind the rows, and he spoke to me in the words he used to our older brothers years ago. He is much displeased with this sacrifice.'

They made a sighing, sobbing noise and looked at the surrounding walls of green.

'And the Lord did say: Have I not given you a place of killing, that you might make sacrifice there? And have I not shewn you favor? But this man has made a blasphemy within me, and I have completed this sacrifice myself. Like the Blue Man and the false minister who escaped many years ago.'

'The Blue Man . . . the false minister,' they whispered, and looked at each other uneasily.

'So now is the Age of Favor lowered from nineteen plantings and harvestings to eighteen,' Isaac went on relentlessly. 'Yet be fruitful and multiply as the corn multiplies, that my favor may be shewn you, and be upon you.'

Isaac ceased.

The eyes turned to Malachi and Joseph, the only two among this party who were eighteen. There were others back in town, perhaps twenty in all.

They waited to hear what Malachi would say, Malachi

who had led the hunt for Japheth, who evermore would be known as Ahaz, cursed of God. Malachi had cut the throat of Ahaz and had thrown his body out of the corn so the foul body would not pollute it or blight it.

'I obey the word of God,' Malachi whispered.

The corn seemed to sigh its approval.

In the weeks to come the girls would make many corncob crucifixes to ward off further evil.

And that night all of those now above the Age of Favor walked silently into the corn and went to the clearing, to gain the continued favor of He Who Walks Behind the Rows.

'Goodbye, Malachi,' Ruth called. She waved disconsolately. Her belly was big with Malachi's child and tears coursed silently down her cheeks. Malachi did not turn. His back was straight. The corn swallowed him.

Ruth turned away, still crying. She had conceived a secret hatred for the corn and sometimes dreamed of walking into it with a torch in each hand when dry September came and the stalks were dead and explosively combustible. But she also feared it. Out there, in the night, something walked, and it saw everything . . . even the secrets kept in human hearts.

Dusk deepened into night. Around Gatlin the corn rustled and whispered secretly. It was well pleased.